CAPTIVE OF DESIRE

"What...." Jessica cleared her throat when her voice came out in a croak. "What are you going to do with me now?"

He took a step closer, and Jessica shuddered slightly and closed her eyes. His hands cupped her shoulders, then stroked down her back to her bound wrists. His fingers worked with the knot for a few seconds and her hands fell free.

"Open your eyes. Look at me."

She obeyed the whispered command and found his lips hovering a scant inch from her own, his eyes mesmerizing her.

"What am I going to do with you now?" he growled softly. "Right now, I'm going to show you one of the other dangers a pretty lady like you might run into wandering around alone in the dark. And to satisfy myself, I'm gonna see if that mouth of yours tastes as sweet as it looks."

MONTANA SURRENDER

TRANA MAE SIMMONS

LEISURE BOOKS **NEW YORK CITY**

A LEISURE BOOK®

August 1993

Published by

Dorchester Publishing Co., Inc.
276 Fifth Avenue
New York, NY 10001

Printed in the United States of America.

To my mother and father, Mumaw and Pupaw, with love.
And Martha Behringer, for her faith in me.

Chapter 1

Little Big Horn Valley, Montana—1893

The cooler evening breeze chased away a little of the summer heat, whispering tendrils of sable hair around Jessica Callaghan's face. While the men around her swung down from their mounts, she sat in her saddle for a moment longer, focusing on the westward miles they had yet to travel.

No attempt at estimating could put a scale to the map drawn on the piece of rolled-up hide she found among Uncle Pete's small bundle of possessions. Landmarks stood out clearly, but the past week of travel had proven it might be only an hour, or as much as a day, between each marker. The short explanation accompanying the map, written in Pete's spidery hand, left a host of unanswered questions.

The setting sun transformed the low-hanging clouds on

the western horizon to magenta and crimson, and silver-gray shadows slid down the hillsides, bleaching the colors from the valley where the riders had stopped. Jessica barely noticed the sounds behind her as the men set up camp. Experienced from years of living in the open, they went about their individual tasks with speed and efficiency, glancing now and then at the young woman sitting lost in thought on the huge roan stallion.

It's strange what shapes the clouds take, she mused silently. *The center of that one looks almost like a horseman.*

Staring at the sun sent dots dancing before her gaze and she blinked, then rubbed at her eyes. In that brief instant the last visible inch of sun slipped behind the hilltop, leaving a band of fire in its wake. Jessica searched for the strangely shaped cloud, but it had vanished with the disappearing sun.

"Jes, you better get down and stretch your legs before they grow attached to that there saddle."

Jessica glanced down at the wizened man limping toward her. If anyone needed a break from the saddle, it was Ned. His lame leg had to be paining him after the many days on horseback, though he'd die before complaining.

Jessica smiled at the plucky little man, then slid from the saddle. "We're getting close, Ned. I can feel it."

Glancing around to make sure none of the hands stood within earshot, Ned lowered his voice before he spoke. "I hope you're right, Jes. The boys are gettin' awful uneasy 'bout bein' this close to Indian territory and that old battle site."

"You don't have to remind me of that, Ned, since I've been listening to their mutterings all day, too. But the Indians have been under control for years."

"Maybe so," Ned agreed with a nod. "But there's a

few of us can remember when that weren't the case. And the closer we get to that there Little Big Horn battlefield, the stronger those memories and the thoughts of ghosts prowlin' the valley get. Some folks say the spirits of men killed violently linger around where they died."

Jessica shrugged impatiently and pulled her hat off to shake her hair free. She wasn't about to get into another of their seemingly endless disputes—not with her goal so close. Turning slightly away from Ned, her eyes again fell on the line of hilltops stretching out before her. In the fast fading light, their silhouettes softened into indistinct impressions, while somewhere in the distance a howling coyote made her stallion shift restlessly.

Ned studied the slender woman beside him as he waited to see what effect his words would have. Even in the dim light her sable hair glowed with luster and a full day under the hat hadn't matted the glossy tendrils, but her profile showed him a chin lifted in stubborn defiance under full lips tinged with pink. Behind him, a man put a match to the kindling of the fire, and when Jessica faced him again, Ned could see the flames reflected in the gold specks of her brown eyes.

"That battle took place almost seventeen years ago, Ned," she said with a barely concealed intolerance, forgetting almost at once her vow of a second ago. "The Sioux and Cheyenne are peaceful now."

Ned spat a wad of tobacco juice to the side. "I ain't sayin' they ain't. I was just tryin' to point out that there's a bad atmosphere lingers around places like that. Spooky, it is, knowin' 'bout all those deaths happenin' so near."

"Don't tell me you believe in ghosts, Ned!"

" 'Course not! But you better keep somethin' else in mind, too. Those Indians might think they have some sort of claim on that gold that's supposed to be buried

11

around here. Custer rode into land the Indians had been told was theirs. I'll bet you that one of these days the tribes are gonna demand some sort of satisfaction for all those broken treaties. And I've known an Indian or two in my life. They've got an awful strong belief in the spirits protectin' what they think is theirs."

"Sounds to me like you've got a leaning toward believing in ghosts, whether you admit it or not. But . . ." Jessica held up a hand to thwart Ned's denial. "But I realize that a lot of people might think they have a claim to that gold, Ned, even the government. You know as well as I do, though, that by now that gold belongs to whoever finds it."

"It was an army payroll, Jes."

"We discussed all this before we left Wyoming, Ned. The army ought to have done something about tracing it if they were that interested! That gold's going to help me build the ranch back up to what it was before my father died!"

"You gotta find it first."

Ned almost regretted his flat words when Jessica's eyes filled with the familiar pain as she recalled the reason for their journey. But, Lordy, someone had to at least try to make her understand how much danger she could be placing herself in.

"I'll find it, Ned," Jessica said in a ravaged voice. "I have to. That spring blizzard wiped out almost all of the few cattle we had left."

She took a deep breath and a spurt of temper chased away a little of her distress. "And Mr. Olson already told me he wouldn't risk any of his damned bank's money on a woman running a spread. He made me so blasted mad I almost spit in his face!"

"Knowin' you, it's a wonder you didn't," Ned said with

a chuckle as he decided to drop the argument—at least for now. They both needed their rest this evening and he wouldn't gain a thing by pushing Jessica. He well knew how quickly that stubborn streak of hers could flare into mutinous defiance, though he had to admit the last couple years had tempered it under a slowly growing maturity.

The coyote yipped again and another one joined in. A second later a third animal added his voice to the song. Echoes rebounded from the hillsides around them, the reverberating sounds making it impossible to determine how many animals actually surrounded them.

Jessica looked at Ned to see his head cocked and a frown on his face. "What's wrong, Ned? It's just coyotes."

"Couple of them don't sound right. Could be there's some human coyotes out there."

The picture of the strange cloud flashed in Jessica's mind. "Ned," she said, "I thought I saw someone on a horse just at sunset, but he was gone so fast I decided I'd imagined him."

A rifle bullet spat dirt at Jessica's feet. Ned's shoulder hit her in the side, knocking her to the ground even as the sound of another shot followed a split second later. With a strength she wouldn't have thought him capable of, Ned immediately pulled her up into a crouch and they ran toward the sheltering rocks at the foot of the west hillside.

Behind them, pandemonium reigned among the horses rearing and plunging against the lead ropes tied to the picket line as a barrage of shots followed the first one. Jessica's stallion—still untied—disappeared from the campsite.

As suddenly as they had begun, the shots ceased and a deathlike silence descended. Jessica squirmed out from under Ned's protective body, and huddled beside him as

13

Ned slowly raised his head to peer through a crack in the rock. Her breath drawn and her heart pounding, she steeled herself as they waited for the sounds of a further attack. She clenched her fists and closed her eyes in an unconscious effort to shut out the blood-soaked scene she imagined Ned would see in the camp. They had been completely out in the open. How many of her men would Ned see lying out there?

A long moment later, Ned eased himself down beside Jessica and hawked his wad of tobacco from where it lodged halfway down his throat.

"Guess that was your horseman, Jes," he said quietly after he cleared his voice to speak. "Along with a bunch of his friends."

"Where . . . where are the men?"

"They're all right here with us in these rocks," Ned assured her. "Nobody was hit."

Relief shot through Jessica. "But all those shots!"

"Shhhh, Jes. We haven't heard anyone leave yet."

"What reason would anyone have to attack us, Ned?" Jessica asked in a softer voice. "We're not threatening anyone and we sure as heck aren't packing any valuables."

"Could be they're just tryin' to warn us off."

Jessica watched Ned shift around so he could peer over the rock again. In the dim light, she saw him wince in pain.

"Ned, your leg. You've hurt it again."

"Naw, Jes. It's just a touch stiff. Hush now while I try and figure out what to do next."

"What ya' think, Ned?" Jessica heard a voice call in a hoarse whisper from behind a nearby rock.

"Did any of the boys manage to grab their rifles, Patches?" Ned returned in a low voice.

"Yeah, all of them, I think," Patches replied. "They

ain't been far from their guns all day."

"Wish I'd of grabbed mine," Ned muttered under his breath.

"I've got my derringer, Ned, but it won't do any good at this distance. And we're not going to just sit here and wait for them to come closer." Jessica eased herself around until she could see over the edge of the rock. "Patches," she ordered in a low voice, "send a couple of the men up that slope while the rest of you cover them."

Patches poked his grizzled face around the rock sheltering him, and Jessica drew in an angry gasp when she realized he was looking at Ned to confirm her order. After Ned nodded slightly, Patches ducked back from sight and Jessica heard a murmured conversation. A second later two shadows moved from behind the rocks.

"When this is over, we're going to have a talk with those men about who gives orders around here, Ned," Jessica said in a grim voice.

Ned ignored her, and Jessica concentrated on the slope as she watched the two men slip from cover to cover, seeking to make their way up the embankment and flush out the attackers. Two well-placed shots sent both men scrambling back down the hill again. Jessica's men immediately fired at the flashes from the attacker's rifle, and she ducked back down, flattening herself against the rock as loud reports from the rifles intermingled with ricochets of bullets.

Beside Jessica, Ned determinedly kept watch, his face thrust close to the crack in the rock and his fingers flexing unconsciously for his missing rifle. "Somethin's wrong here," he muttered when no answering fire sounded from the top of the hill.

"Tell the men to stop firin', Patches!" he called. "We're wastin' ammo!"

No sooner did the men comply than a chilling cry

split the air, echoing from hilltop to hilltop. A thunder of hooves followed and a huge paint stallion galloped out onto the top of the ridge above them. Immediately, the men fired at the rider, their shots sounding almost like the report from a single rifle.

The rider vanished behind the ridge top without giving a sign that even one of the men's bullets had made contact. A second later, an eerie, mocking laughter echoed through the silence. The sound of the laughter covered up the returning hoofbeats, and the rider appeared to materialize again out of thin air.

The paint reared defiantly, and the rider on its back shook his rifle over his head, mocking them. Echoes of the laughter faded as another cry left the rider's lips, this one a laughing disparagement of the men's ineffective aims. The stallion's hooves dropped back to the dirt and the horse floated along the gathering mist of the ridge top for a second before disappearing again beneath the horizon. A moment later, the sound of its lone hoofbeats mingled with the rumble of several more sets of hooves joining its flight.

"Shoot, damn it!" Jessica realized Ned was standing above her, screaming the words over and over. "Damn it, why in the hell didn't you keep shootin'?"

"Don't, Ned." Jessica forced herself to shake off her own stunned amazement and stood up to lay a hand on his arm. "It's no use now. They're gone."

Ned grabbed his hat from his head and flung it into the dirt. His angry eyes watched the men creep out timidly from the shelter of their rocks and he turned his furious gaze on Patches.

"Damn it, Patches, what's wrong with you?" he shouted.

"I didn't see you shootin' neither, Ned," Patches returned in a voice laced with fear. "'Sides, we'd've been wastin' our bullets, like you said before. Can't hit a ghost."

"A ghost?" Ned snorted. "That wasn't no ghost. That was a plain flesh-and-blood man on a horse! And I didn't have my damned rifle! If I'd of had it, I'd of shown you that was no ghost!"

"Then why didn't any of *our* bullets hit him, huh?" Patches asked. "Wasn't no way we could have all missed him."

"Stop it, both of you," Jessica said firmly. "Whoever was out there's gone now and it's too dark to try to follow. I want two men up on that ridge on guard tonight, just in case the attackers do try to return. The rest of you finish setting up camp and get something to eat started."

"But, Jes—"

"I mean it, Ned. Arguing won't get us anywhere at this point. We can discuss it as soon as we get something in our stomachs. Oh, no! Ned, where's Cinnabar?"

"Last I seen of him, he was hightailin' it up toward the top of that north ridge, Miss Jes," Patches answered her. "Guess he wasn't tied before the shootin' started."

"That horse of yours will be all right, Jes," Ned soothed.

"You can't be sure of that, Ned. You and Patches saddle back up and I'll take one of the packhorses. We have to find him."

"Hold on a second, Jes." Ned reached for her arm and led her a distance away from the men. "Look," he said, keeping both their backs to the men, "it's foolish to go wanderin' around out there in the dark after what just happened. That stallion won't go far. Hell, you raised him from a wild colt and ain't too many people can even get close to him. He'll probably be standin' right there in the picket line in the mornin'."

"What you're really trying to tell me is that there's probably not a one of those scared, namby-pamby hands standing back there who will leave this camp with us to help search. Isn't that right?"

Ned's deep sigh was Jessica's only answer, and she tried to control the anger stealing through her, losing the battle almost immediately.

"And what about you, Ned?" she asked in a scornful voice. "Is your buried belief in ghosts coming through?"

"Now, Jes. All I'm tryin' to say is that right now ain't the time to go pushin' those hands into any showdown. You're right. They're scared. And whoever was up on that ridge planned it just that way. He made sure we didn't know how many men he had with him, so we wouldn't be stupid enough to come after them."

Someone behind them cleared his voice with a soft harumph. "Uh . . . Ned."

Jessica whirled and faced the cowhand. "What is it, Rusty?" she demanded, her anger giving a sharp edge to the authority in her voice.

Rusty glanced behind him to make sure Patches was still there. "Well, Miss Jes, seems like one of our packhorses run off, too. The one with our food on it."

"That tears it!" Jessica said in exasperation. "If you men think I'm going to bed down here with an empty stomach, you've got another think coming. Who tied that horse and left the knot loose enough so it could get away when the shooting started?"

Patches stepped forward. "I did, Miss Jes. But I tied that rope strong. Only way that horse could've got away would've been to break that picket rope. And it's still tied tight."

Patches's words gave Jessica pause. Though he was older than most of the rest of the men, he still maintained his status as her top hand. If Patches said he tied that rope, that darn rope was tied.

"Then how did the horse get loose?" she asked in exasperation. "Do you have any explanation, Patches?"

"I think someone slipped in here and took it," Patches said with a nervous shrug of his shoulders.

"Or somethin'," Rusty muttered.

"I suppose you mean a *ghost,* Rusty," Jessica flared, ignoring the calming hand Ned laid on her arm.

"Didn't you notice what the rest of us did?" Patches asked, directing his words at Ned. "The other hands are all mutterin' about it. They only saw three bullets ever hit the ground—that one near Miss Jes's feet and the two fired at the men tryin' to climb that hill. Rest of them shots never even kicked up a puff of dirt or nicked a rock."

"Yeah," Ned admitted. "But there's got to be some reason for it. Could be they shot in the air. Just wanted to scare us."

"Then how come we didn't see no more than three flashes from rifles—even though it sounded like at least a dozen men was shootin' at us?" Rusty broke in. "Huh, Ned? How come?"

With an effort, Jessica kept her jaw from dropping open. As Ned shook his head in bewilderment, she briefly played the scene of a few minutes ago over in her mind. Rusty and Patches were right, and try as she might, she couldn't come up with an explanation any more than Ned could.

"The only way we're goin' to get to the bottom of this is to wait until mornin' and go out and read the sign," Ned said reasonably. "Right now, let's get over there and see what we can dig up among us out of our saddlebags for grub. Most of you boys carry a little somethin' to snack on when we're ridin' all day, don't you?"

Rusty and Patches nodded a reluctant agreement and fell in behind Ned as he moved toward the fire. Jessica took a step after them, then hesitated as she glanced around her. The men all had their saddlebags, but hers were on Cinnabar, and Uncle Pete's map was still hidden in the lining. She didn't really suppose it mattered much about losing the map; on the off chance something like that might happen, she had memorized it before she even left Wyoming. And without the note left behind with the other few of her uncle's mementos, she doubted anyone could make sense of the scrawls on the map.

But she had stowed at least two apples in her bags, along with a sandwich made from leftovers of their noon meal, wrapped in her extra bandanna. More than once, Ned's wife, Mattie, had shaken her head at Jessica's hearty appetite, but her active life never allowed so much as an extra ounce to settle on her slender hips.

In the dim light, Jessica thought she could make out a faint path rising along the hillside beside her. If she walked to the top, she could whistle for her stallion. Ringing out across the hilltops, the sound would cover more area.

Hesitating for another second, Jessica looked toward the campfire. The glow from the fire clearly showed the men occupied with digging through their gear. Behind them, the light from a nearly full moon crept over the horizon. The moon would give her enough light to see by, instead of having to call attention to herself by going for a lantern. Ned would probably insist on sending at least half the men with her, and she'd had about all she could stomach of their whining for one day. She'd enjoy a few moments to herself.

Ghosts. Spirits. With a determined effort, Jessica pushed aside the haunting words and walked toward the path. Lord knew what kind of concoction the men would come up with from their various saddlebags.

Probably some meatless son-of-a-gun stew. Her mouth watered at the thought of her sandwich of thick pieces of fried ham she had stuffed between the slices of bread.

Chapter 2

As soon as Jessica's booted foot hit the path, she realized it was a well-traveled indentation, wide enough for a person on horseback. She followed the trail until it began bending around the hillside, where it would take her out of sight of the camp. Pausing, she glanced back to see if anyone had noticed her departure.

The figures below her were smaller now, and the two men who stood up from among the otherwise occupied men headed toward the top of the north ridge. At least they had remembered her order to post a guard.

For just a second she pondered whether it might be safer to join the two guards and try to call Cinnabar from that position. But the mood the men were in would probably have them spooking at every shadow and provoke her to give them the scathing edge of her tongue for their foolishness. No. She would prove her point about their asinine fear of ghosts by showing them that even a woman wasn't afraid of the dark.

"Go back."

Jessica cocked her head. She could swear she heard a whisper carried on the wind, a warning note in the sibilant hiss. Probably just a trick played by the night breeze blowing down the hillside, she rationalized. Squaring her shoulders, she marched up the trail.

A tremulous wail set Jessica's heart thumping until she recognized the voice of a screech owl perched in one of the trees higher on the hill. At least, she thought that's what it was. Somehow it didn't sound exactly like the owls she heard in Wyoming. She pushed the unwelcome thought of the old superstition of the screech owl's cry portending death out of her mind when her stomach growled.

A few tendrils of mist crawled down the hillside in the cooling temperature, but when Jessica glanced up at the top of the hill, she found it clear. The mist would settle into the lower elevations as the night wore on, and she would wake up in the morning with her bedroll covered with dew. She had spent enough nights out in the open at her ranch to know this was a common occurrence.

Jessica rounded a huge boulder beside the trail and stopped abruptly. Several yards in front of her, the trail ended at a cliff face on the side of the hill.

"Now, this doesn't make any sense at all." She spoke aloud, more for the comfort of her own voice than any fear of the darkness, she assured herself. "Why would anyone use this trail if it doesn't go anywhere except to that cliff?"

Setting her hands on her hips, she glared at the offending obstacle in her path, then up again to the top of the hill. Maybe in daylight she might be able to find a way around the cliff, but she sure as heck couldn't see any way to do that now.

"Looks like I'm going to have to go back there and face those stupid scaredy cats," she muttered under her breath.

"Go back!"

Clearly she heard the whisper this time and the hair rose on the back of her neck when a low keening sound followed the words. Her heart lurched with fear as a cloud scuttled across the moon, momentarily dimming the light as she vainly strived to peer through the darkness.

The pain of her nails biting into her palms made Jessica gasp, and she unclenched her hands and shook her head in ridicule at her actions. Someone had to be playing a trick on her—someone human, since she sure as hell didn't believe in ghosts. Her chin lifted in stubborn challenge of the obviousness of the ploy to frighten her, and she took a couple of steps forward, scanning the area again through the thickening mists impeding her vision.

In one of the heaviest portions of mist, an apparition appeared that froze the very marrow in her bones.

The ghostly head of an Indian chief rose through the mists, his eyes red and glowing, the feathered bonnet tumbling down his back outlined in shining phosphorus. The face slowly climbed higher in the mist and the faint outline of the chief's body came into view, transparent enough for her to make out the shadows of the rocks behind it.

"Go back. There is evil here."

The unearthly sound of the voice prickled her scalp in fear and sweat broke out on her forehead. The soft, downy hairs on her arms rose under a spreading onrush of dread and the scream building in her chest struggled to make it past her paralyzed throat muscles. She gulped as her knees trembled and her mind shouted for her to run.

Jessica's legs wilted under her and she threw out a hand to the boulder by her side. An inky blackness swirled at the edge of her vision. She wouldn't faint. She never fainted. She wouldn't.

Her numb hand refused to grasp the boulder and slowly she sank to the ground, her terrified gaze still on the unholy thing before her. Struggling against the threatening unconsciousness, she tore her eyes from the apparition with a mental wrench and wrapped her arms around her knees. Curled in a tight ball, she labored against the paralysis in her chest, her shoulders heaving.

A small cascade of rocks rattled down the hillside, unheard by Jessica over the pounding in her chest. Her first awareness was of a pair of comforting hands gripping the iron-tense muscles in her shoulders and a gravelly voice in her ear.

"Take some deep breaths. Don't hold your breath in like that or you'll faint. Oh, hell."

A sharp thump between Jessica's shoulder blades loosened her muscles and she drew in a draught of oxygen. Blew it out. Then another in.

"There. You've got it now."

And she also had enough breath now to scream. She lifted her head and drew in another immense inhalation. Her throat muscles tensed.

The man behind her guessed her intention. A callused hand covered her mouth, the fingers and heel gripping her cheeks and the palm pressing hard against her lips. His other arm snaked around her waist and pulled her tightly back against his chest, effectively immobilizing her against any effort to escape.

Jessica's eyes flew to the spot on the hillside where the apparition had stood, but she found only empty mist. She knew where it had disappeared to—and Ned had been right. A real, flesh-and-blood body held her, not some ghostly spirit that had decided to rise from its grave and haunt the countryside.

And she had reacted in the same spineless manner as her hands moments before. Her growing humiliation and desire for retaliation chased any lingering cobwebs from her mind, sharpening her senses. She had only herself to depend on to get out of this.

With a conscious effort, Jessica relaxed her muscles and felt the tentative loosening of the hand on her mouth. With a violent wrench, she tore her face free and threw her head back, encountering a hard chin behind her.

"Ouch, you little wildcat."

Jessica took advantage of the man's pain to grip the little finger of the hand he held on her waist. Frantically, she threw all her strength into bending it back until she thought surely it would break. He gave a grunt of pain and pulled his hand away. Jessica scrambled free, another scream building in her throat, though she had little hope of it traveling as far as the camp. She had walked too far.

A hand grabbed her booted foot and her breath left Jessica's chest in a whoosh as she fell again to the hard-packed trail. A hard object pressed into the side of her tender stomach—her derringer. Good Lord. She must have been terrified a moment ago to have forgotten that she had the little gun. Swiftly, she shifted around and pulled the small pistol from her pocket.

The man batted the gun away and it flew from her fingers in an arch, tumbling down the hillside. A cry of dismay left Jessica's lips, cut off abruptly when the man's body covered hers and he thrust his bandanna between her lips and tied it behind her head. Panic-stricken, she struggled under the threatening weight, her body snaking from side to side, her feet scrambling in the dirt and rocks beneath her. She wouldn't let herself be taken!

"No you don't. Not this time," the presence holding her said.

Quicker than she thought possible, she found her hands tied with a rawhide thong he jerked from his leggings and her feet followed a bare second later. A picture of calves bound for branding incongruously flashed in her mind, furthering her embarrassment at her predicament.

The man rose to his knees, his body shadowing the light from the moon. "Look, I'm sorry as hell about this, but it seems like the only way you'll listen to me. Damn it, I'm not going to hurt you."

Her terror-stricken eyes gazing up at him told the man she didn't believe a word he said. He leaned closer to her, his breath feathering her face and his hand unconsciously stroking the silky strands of hair away from it.

"I mean it," he said quietly. "I'll carry you closer to your camp and let you go if you promise me to talk those men with you into leaving in the morning. It's not safe for you around here."

Jessica stared up into the dark countenance above her, her eyes straining as she tried to make out his features in the darkness and forced her muscles into immobility. His body and the rock above them blocked most of the moonlight and she could only see dark, rather longer than usual hair spilling around the man's face.

And lips—lips just full enough to be sensuous. The thought crept into her mind before she could stop it. Lips that came closer again as he whispered in a manner meant to soothe her.

"That's better, pretty lady. Now, if you'll behave yourself, I'll pick you up."

His body straightened and he rose over her, stretching his muscles for a moment before he reached down toward her. His legs spread, he tensed himself to pick up her dead weight.

In a swift movement Jessica pulled her knees toward her chest and brought her feet up with every bit of strength she could muster toward his groin. Mattie had been right. It worked. She heard his muffled grunt, and rolled away from him as he collapsed a few feet from her.

Ignoring the sharp stones digging into her knees, Jessica scrambled to the boulder and turned her back to it. Pushing with her hands tied behind her back and her feet, she managed to stand up. Her bound hands threw her off balance for a second, but she steadied herself and spent a precious, useless second working against the binding. The rawhide knot pulled tighter when she twisted against it.

She couldn't waste any more time. Searching with her fingers, she located a sharp projection on the boulder and sawed the rawhide binding against it. She glanced at the man, expecting to see him still doubled over in misery. Her arms stilled and her eyes flew wide in horror as a completely different sight met her eyes.

He sat watching her and as soon as her eyes fell on him, he slowly rose to his feet. He advanced on her. One step. Two. He towered over her, and Jessica's head met the resistance of the rock behind her as she sought to keep her terrified gaze on his face. Now the moonlight filtered down on them and she could make out eyes even darker than her own, high cheekbones, and a straight nose.

"You didn't really think that little tap would disable me, did you, pretty lady?"

She most certainly had. Indeed, she had noticed his hesitant step as he advanced and the slight limp. But she also recognized the thread of steel mixed with the anger in his voice. She cringed against the rock, the hard surface biting into her tender back.

"You wouldn't listen, would you?" he went on in a softer voice when she continued to stare frantically at him. "I only wanted you to get your fanny back to camp where you'd be safe. A woman's got no damned business wandering around by herself. Hell, these hills are full of panthers and snakes!"

When his hand came out, Jessica tried again without success to shrink back into the unyielding rock. But he only cupped his hand on the side of her face and stood staring down at her, his head shaking from side to side in consternation. His thumb stroked the soft curve of her cheekbone above the bandanna in her mouth.

"So now what, huh, pretty lady? Do I turn you loose and let you run screaming to high heaven back into camp? Or do I take you with me and have a band of angry cowhands swarming around here while they look for you?"

Jessica wrenched her head upright with a start. Why, she'd been leaning into that cupped hand, enjoying the feathering stroke of his thumb on her cheek and the soothing sound of his voice. The bandanna gagged her when she gasped in a startled breath and a fit of coughing overtook her.

Hastily, the man hooked his thumb into the bandanna and pulled it free from her mouth before he untied it. He gathered her close to him, entwining his fingers in the silky mass of curls and drawing her head down onto his chest. As soon as her coughing abated, he scooped her up and sat her on a stone outcropping on the other side of the trail.

For a long second Jessica only stared at him. Her tongue came out and she slowly flicked it around her dry lips, moistening them. Her eyes widened when she heard him give a soft grunt under his breath, and she found herself unable to tear her gaze away from his face, now level with her own.

"What . . ." Jessica cleared her throat when her voice came out in a croak. "What *are* you going to do with me now?"

He moved closer, and Jessica shuddered slightly and closed her eyes. A whiff of mint-tinged breath wafted across her face and his hands cupped her shoulders, then stroked down her back to her bound wrists. His fingers worked the knot for a few seconds and her hands fell free.

"Open your eyes. Look at me."

She obeyed the whispered command and found his lips hovering a scant inch from her own, his eyes mesmerizing her.

"What am I going to do with you now?" he growled softly. "Right now, I'm going to show you one of the other dangers a pretty little lady like you might run into wandering around alone in the dark. And to satisfy myself, I'm gonna see if that mouth of yours tastes as sweet as it looks."

Slowly, deliberately, he closed the distance separating their lips. His lips gently took hers, but not for long. He wrenched his mouth away and drew in a startled breath.

Some tiny thread of reason cried in Jessica's mind, telling her the thing to do now was scream. Instead, her lips almost instinctively followed his and she held her head back, offering them freely again.

For a silent moment he stared down at her before he bent slowly to taste her again. Her lips clung once more to his, and he moaned as he pulled her to gather her closer to him. Wildly, greedily, he answered her longing with a deep, searing kiss.

Her arms went around his neck and she clung to him, glorying in the feelings of warmth and safety washing over her. They chased away any last lingering vestige of the fear she had felt earlier.

Jessica didn't even give a semblance of having heard the shout, but it clearly met the man's ears. Reluctantly this time he drew his mouth away. In answer to the puzzled longing in her eyes, he cupped her chin in his palm.

"Later, pretty lady. Maybe we'll get a chance to finish this later. Right now, I think I hear rescue on the way for you." He continued under his breath, "And not a moment too soon."

Jessica's face flamed as reason returned. She sat frozen in disbelief at her own actions as the man drew a knife from the scabbard on his belt to cut the rawhide binding her feet. But she didn't miss the tenderness in his gesture when he rose and smoothed her disheveled hair back from her face, his fingers lingering for a second in the silkiness.

"You won't scream, will you?" he asked quietly. "I need time to get away."

Scream? Her muddled head couldn't even remember what the word meant. Somehow she found herself shaking her head no.

"Jessica! Jessica, where are you?" The shout sounded from close by—too close.

"I've got to go." He turned away, then stopped abruptly. "Oh, hell!"

He buried his fingers in her hair one last time and kissed her deeply. "Bye, pretty lady," he murmured when he raised his head. "Maybe we'll meet again."

Jessica blinked and he was gone.

"Jes! Jes, answer me!" Ned's voice came from a few scant yards away, just beyond the huge boulder. "God,

Patches. You don't think it could've got Jes?"

A spill of lantern light reached Jessica from down the trail. Just as she drew in a breath to assure Ned she was just around the bend ahead of him, she heard Patches's voice.

"Look, Ned. We're still on the right track. Here's another boot print."

For some reason the anxiety she caught in Patches's voice pleased her. He and Ned deserved to worry after their stupid actions this evening. Telling herself she was only keeping her silence for spite, Jessica still couldn't stop herself from glancing around for the man who had been with her an instant ago.

I need time to get away, pretty lady. She could almost swear the gravelly whisper was real, instead of an echo in her mind.

"Oh!" Jessica's breath escaped from her pursed lips. What the hell was she doing protecting a strange man? A strange man who had. . . .

"N–Ned." She had to draw in her breath again when the word barely whispered past her lips. "Ned! I'm coming!"

Welcome light bathed Jessica after she slid from the outcropping and started forward to meet the men.

"Where the hell have you been?" Ned's voice stopped Jessica in her tracks.

"I've been looking for Cinnabar," she fired back at him. "I didn't figure I'd get any help out of that bunch of scaredy cats back in camp!"

"That stallion of yours went up over the north hill," Ned shot right back. "Why'd you climb this one?"

"Oh, for heaven's sake, Ned. This hill was the closest and I figured I'd climb up here and whistle for him. We don't know which way he went after he bolted."

"You've been gone from camp a lot longer than it would have taken you to climb this far, Jes," Ned said, the anger his worry over her had caused calming somewhat now that he had found her. "Good God, Jes. We've been lookin' for you for over fifteen minutes. Didn't you hear us yellin'?"

Jessica only shrugged in answer to Ned's question. "The trail ends just up there at a cliff," she explained instead. "And it's a lot more peaceful and quiet here than back in camp. I was sick and tired of listening to a bunch of superstitious cowboys, scared in their boots and bandying about their fear of ghosts."

"What if you'd gotten hurt out here, Jes?"

"Then I'd have expected my men to come looking for me. But I'll bet if they had, they'd have paired off like lovers because they were afraid of the dark. I expect more from the men who work under me, Ned—a hell of a lot more."

"Woman's got no business wanderin' around after dark by herself," Patches muttered, reminding Jessica of the stranger's words.

"I'll bet you even check under the bunks in the bunkhouse before you go to bed at night to make sure there aren't any monsters there, don't you, Patches?" Jessica said in a sweetly sarcastic voice.

"Jes," Ned warned.

"Oh, let's go. I hope you've at least managed to dig up something that's halfway palatable to eat for supper."

Jessica grabbed the lantern Ned held and glared at the two men. Patches refused to meet her gaze, and hurriedly turned back down the trail, his own lantern lighting his way. As soon as he disappeared, Jessica swung the lantern around and held it high, peering through the light at the path beyond.

"What are you looking for, Jes?"

"Uh . . . oh, I'm just making sure I didn't miss finding where this trail winds around that cliff face. This seems like an awfully well-traveled path just to come to a dead end."

Jessica swiped absently at the tic in her cheek. Her nerves must still be jumpy from her encounter with the mysterious apparition. She darned sure wasn't going to admit to Ned that her own foolish actions had indeed placed her in a dangerous situation, though.

She held the lantern a fraction higher, but nothing met her eyes except the misted shadows of rocks and the cliff face beyond her. She flushed slightly, glad her back was to Ned. And she damned sure wasn't going to admit to Ned that she had met a man on the trail whose kisses made her head spin. How in the world could she ever explain it to him, when her own mind shied away from admitting her feelings?

Turning around, she caught sight of Ned's puzzled look, and walked past him to lead the way back to camp. She desperately wanted to talk to someone, but she'd had her share of scoldings from Ned over the years. Though she knew in her heart he only spoke out of concern, she couldn't think of any way to tell him that wouldn't end up with a well-deserved chastisement. Shoot. He would probably put her on a leash until he could ship her back to Wyoming!

Later, after she forced down a plate of the concoction the men had devised, Jessica spread her bedroll a ways off from the men. She'd spent enough nights during roundups to know she would never get any sleep if she didn't distance herself from them a little. Most of them snored, and one or two of them even suffered bouts of flatulence now and then.

Jessica shifted on her side and stared through the black night in the direction of the trail she had climbed earlier. Who was he? Definitely not a ghost. Those hands on her had been all too real. And those lips—and that steel-hardened body. She blushed furiously as she recalled her reaction to the stranger's kisses. Oh, why hadn't she overcome her embarrassment and told Ned about him? Why hadn't she ordered her men after his dastardly hide to avenge her honor at the liberties he had taken with her?

Liberties he had taken with her? She shook her head silently in disgust as she recalled her lips following his, almost begging him to kiss her again. Her hand came up unconsciously and she ran a tentative finger around her mouth. Her movement thrust her breasts against her blouse and the friction of the fabric pebbled her nipples to hard points.

Jessica snorted contemptuously and dropped her hand. Determinedly closing her eyes, she ordered her muscles to relax in sleep, but her mind remained crammed with jumbled questions. What *had* happened out there? Who was he? He'd been alone when she met him, but earlier it had sounded like the entire Seventh Cavalry shooting at them. And why hadn't any of their bullets hit him?

And how could remembering the feel of his fingers on her skin and his lips on her own make her think about being curled up in front of a roaring winter fire on a bearskin rug? Not alone either. A shadow lay beside her—a ghostly shadow with dark, silky hair, dark eyes, and broad, muscular shoulders, unhidden by a shirt. Broad, naked shoulders, as naked as her own body.

She woke the next morning tired and achy, after tossing and turning on the hard ground well into the night. She rubbed her eyes briefly and sat up with a shot when she lowered her hands. A large, cloth bag tied with a drawstring lay by her side. Grabbing it, she pulled it to her and loosened the string, breathing in with delight when the smell of smoked ham hit her nose.

Groping in the bag, Jessica drew out a smaller sack from which dust wafted. Flour. For biscuits. She upended the bag and shook out the rest of the contents. Two bumpy bags hit the ground beside an entire smoked ham. One revealed coffee beans and the other soup beans, enough food to at least feed them for a day or so.

Jessica gave a soft crow of satisfaction and started to scramble to her feet. Just then her eyes fell on the pommel of Ned's saddle, which she had used for a pillow the night before. She tentatively reached out and untied the bouquet of wildflowers, already beginning to wilt from lack of water. Hastily glancing over her shoulder to assure herself she was, as usual, the first one up, she stuffed the flowers inside her bedroll to hide them.

From a spot on the side of the hill near the hidden cave, he sat watching them as they broke camp. The frown left his face when he saw the group of riders, a slender woman at the front of them, head in the direction of the nearest town to replenish their supplies, instead of making a search for their nighttime attacker.

As the group passed over the ridge in the trail, he stood and reached for the reins of the paint stallion. For a moment, he remained lost in thought. Luckily, he had been prepared. The idea to scare anyone away from his hiding place had been fueled by the stories about the battlefield. He had seen even grown men's blood run cold at some of the stories told around nighttime campfires. He sure as hell hadn't scared that feisty little filly with those men for very long, though. Was she foolishly brave, or just damned foolish?

He didn't usually act on impulse, but his actions of the night before crept into his mind. It had been an instinctive impulse to go to her when she collapsed—one that could have proven a hell of a lot more dangerous than just revealing his presence to her. He still had a tender ache in his groin this morning. If her kick had landed a couple inches to the right . . . And he was damned lucky she hadn't made her men comb the hills for him this morning instead of just riding off.

But the most dangerous impulse, the one that had kept him sleepless after he had finally bedded down . . . He could still remember the powerful pull when he had started to leave her perched on the rock outcropping. He had just wanted one more taste of those lips. One more second of the strange, sweet fire that had raced through his blood when he had held her close.

Remembering that brought thoughts of a home and future filled with someone who cared about him—even loved him. He could almost imagine being curled up in front of a winter fire on a bearskin rug, his woman in his arms. Maybe a couple of kids tucked away safely in the loft?

He snorted his derision at himself and swung up onto the paint. Hell, he had given up any thoughts of ever finding love in this star-crossed world after even his father had betrayed him. He had closed the doors around his heart and had locked them securely, vowing never again to suffer another battering of a tentative thread of love spun out.

Only one vow kept him going now, and he had to maintain his freedom to carry it out. He didn't have a damned thing to call his own anymore except the paint. Even his name was more or less borrowed—a name stained now with the outlaw brand. One way or another he'd find a way to erase that stain and make those two sons of bitches pay—not only for what they had done to him, but also for ruining the life of the innocent woman he cared for.

He nudged the paint forward. The stallion willingly climbed the rise above him and he pulled him to a halt while still shadowed in a copse of trees. From here, he could see the riders again.

Oh, hell! Not that way, you little fool! But he didn't dare show himself when Jessica led her men down the wrong fork of the trail—the fork not leading to Hardin City, where he had tied the roan stallion and packhorse for them to find. Instead, they were headed toward the town of Baker's Valley. Damn it! Now how in hell would he get the horses back to them?

And that headstrong little idiot was just reckless enough to find herself in a peck of trouble in a place like Baker's Valley—if her actions of the night before were any indication of how she usually acted.

Chapter 3

The town seems prosperous enough, Jessica mused to herself as she pulled her horse to a stop at the hitching rail in front of the general store. Most of the building fronts around her looked like they were actually part of the building, not a false front hiding a ramshackle structure.

She slid from the horse's back and gazed across the street at the bank. Not wood like the majority of the buildings, it had been constructed from bricks and even hewn stones hauled in from somewhere. The front windows gleamed and the gold gilt outlining the letters, Baker's Bank and Casualty, looked freshly painted.

Jessica turned to loop the reins over the railing, and nodded at a woman passing by on the wooden walkway. The woman wore a clean, but faded, gingham dress, with a freshly starched sunbonnet hiding her hair. The woman's mouth tightened briefly, but Jessica received a curt nod in return.

Something just didn't seem right, Jessica caught herself thinking. The town teemed with people, wagons, and buggies, the usual weekday bustle. Maybe it being a weekday, a workday, was the problem. The gaiety that developed when people got together on Saturdays after a long week of work on outlying ranches was missing.

She and Ned had ridden through the section of town where the saloons had been built, but even those establishments held a subdued atmosphere. Only a house, surrounded by bright flower beds, set off by itself at the edge of town had caught her eye as having a cheerful air.

Jessica climbed the two steps from the street up to the walkway, with Ned right behind her. Something was bothering him this morning, too, but so far he hadn't said anything to her. Instead, he kept hovering around her like a cow that had just found its missing calf. She shrugged slightly. Knowing Ned, she would find out sooner or later what he had on his mind.

Two more women passed by, both of them eyeing her suspiciously before they returned the same brief nod as the lone woman had. These two were more stylishly dressed. Perhaps they were two of the town's matrons instead of ranching wives, but the same strain filled their faces.

Jessica shook off the curiosity that Mattie had told her more than once led to her sticking her nose into places it had no business. Her only reasons for being in town were to pick up more supplies and to give the sheriff notice about her two missing horses in case they showed up at one of the ranches. She shouldn't be dwelling on the almost hostile atmosphere she found in Baker's Valley. Baker's Valley. Such a lovely name for a town with an unhappy atmosphere.

Ned held the door of the general store open and Jessica walked past him, unconsciously shaking her head.

The short, stout storekeeper stood behind the counter with his back to Jessica, one of his hands holding a dust rag as he brushed at the shelves. A white fringe ran around the bottom of his mostly bald head and Jessica smiled to herself when she caught sight of him. From the back, he looked like a small, jolly elf. But when he turned at the tinkle of bells over the door announcing a customer, a pair of flat, blue eyes in a lined face watched them as they crossed the room.

Jessica threaded her way past barrels filled with apples, pickles, and various other goods, sniffing appreciatively. The smell of leather saddles stacked nearby and harnesses hanging on the walls mingled with the food odors and a pang of longing for Mr. Georgeton's general store back home briefly shot through her. Then her eyes widened when she noticed a barrel filled with sawdust-packed ice at the end of the counter.

"Oh, good." She grabbed two bottles of sarsaparilla from the barrel and turned to hand one to Ned. "Look, Ned. Are you as thirsty as I am?"

"I'll thank you to pay for those first before you open them, miss," the storekeeper's voice said from behind her.

Jessica gasped and whirled around. "Of course I mean to pay for them," she said in a controlled manner as she stared at the man's outstretched hand. "You don't think I'd just walk in off the street and help myself with no thought of paying for what I took, do you?"

The storekeeper shrugged and kept his hand extended. "Been known to happen."

Jessica set her drink down with a thump and reached into her riding-skirt pocket to fish out her small coin purse. She snapped it open and met the storekeeper's gaze.

"How much?" she asked curtly.

41

"Nickel apiece."

Jessica carefully drew out the exact amount and dropped it into the man's hand. She watched him push the buttons on the huge register on the counter and place the money in the drawer before he looked back at her.

"Anything else I can do for you?" he asked in a more reasonable voice.

"I had thought to buy a few supplies," she fired back at him. "But maybe I should look for another establishment to purchase them from. One with perhaps a more friendly management, who would be more appreciative of the money I spent."

"Suit yourself. Only thing is, this is the only store in town's got the goods you need. Mr. Baker, he don't believe in too much competition."

"Baker?" Jessica questioned. "The same person who runs the bank across the street?"

"Yep. And the hotel and most of the rest of the town 'cept for Miss Idalee's place. And he don't just run them. He owns them."

"It looks like I'll have to deal with this Mr. Baker then," Jessica said with a sigh. "I'll need to have funds transferred from my bank back home to pay for my supplies. I don't suppose you'd like to have my order now, so you can begin getting it ready while I take care of the transfer?"

Something about Jessica's beautiful face above the stained and travel-worn clothing melted a little of the man's arrogance. His face softened and Jessica caught a glimpse of the man she had thought he was when she first entered the store.

"I really can't, miss." He glanced to where Ned stood off to one side, allowing Jessica to handle the transaction, but keeping a comforting nearness to her.

"You understand, don't you, sir?" the storekeeper pleaded with Ned. "I only work here. I have to take orders from the owner, and I need my job. My wife, she ain't well and all our kids are gone. It's just me to take care of her, and doctor bills ain't cheap these days."

"I understand," Ned replied, nodding. "Come on, Jes. We'll get things done at the bank and come back."

Jessica started to turn away, but stopped when she felt the storekeeper's hand on her arm.

"You forgot your sarsaparilla, miss," he said when she looked back at him. Picking up a clean rag from under the counter, he wiped the sawdust from the bottle before he opened it and handed it to her.

"Enjoy it, miss," he said. "It's truly a hot day out there."

Jessica nodded her thanks and turned to follow Ned. Once outside, Ned paused beside a wooden bench at the front of the store.

"Let's sit a moment and have our drinks before we go over to the bank, Jes."

Uh-oh, Jessica thought silently. But she settled herself beside him, sipping at her cool drink and unbuttoning the top button of her blouse.

The storekeeper was right. It really was hot and she fanned herself with one hand and took another long drink of sarsaparilla. Her eyes scanned the passing parade of people and vehicles while she rested and waited for Ned to speak. She only hoped he would come to the point at once, and not spin out one of his long-winded tales like he usually did. There wasn't much expectation of that, though. Ned took his own sweet time making a point after he finally got started.

The town nestled in a beautiful setting. She had looked out at the surrounding countryside from the top of each foothill they had passed over on their way here. South of them, the Bighorn Mountains, still snowcapped, stretched their blue peaks into the distance and the rolling foothills they had traveled through were green and fertile.

Jessica heard a train whistle from the other end of town, and a cloud of smoke accompanied a screech of brakes when the train pulled into the station. Earlier, after spending some time searching out a suitable campsite where the men could wait for them, she and Ned had ridden across the tracks leaving town.

Jessica glanced to where the gelding she had borrowed from Patches stood tied to the railing, but his roan color reminded her too much of Cinnabar. Her eyes strayed to the street beyond the horse.

The street didn't lack for traffic, nor did the boardwalk where they sat. Wagons passed each other, and now and then a buggy with a couple in it went slowly by. On both sides of the walkway, people hurried along, some with their arms filled with purchases.

Only one lone old man Jessica took for a prospector didn't seem in a hurry to go anywhere. He stood leaning against a post on the other side of the street, his ragged hat brim tipped down.

Tired of the long silence between them, Jessica nudged Ned's arm. "Do you notice anything unusual about all the people here, Ned?"

"Not many young folks 'mong them," Ned answered.

"Why, you're right, Ned," Jessica agreed. "I hadn't even noticed that. What I'd been thinking of was how tired and unhappy everyone looks."

"That, too," Ned said with a nod. "I don't think I'd like to live in this town."

"Me neither. Well, as soon as we get some supplies and see the sheriff, we can get out of here. But you know what else I think? I think maybe we better get a couple of rooms at the hotel first and clean up before we go to the bank. The men don't expect us back until tomorrow anyway, and I'd sure feel better if I met this Mr. Baker looking a little cleaner than I do now."

Jessica started to rise to her feet, but stopped when Ned reached for her arm.

"In a minute, Jes. First, I want to talk to you about somethin'."

Jessica sighed deeply and settled back on the bench when Ned turned to face her. "Spit it out, Ned. I've known all morning something was on your mind."

"Guess we both know each other pretty well, Jes. Hell, there was times I—"

"Changed my nappies when Mattie was too busy after my mother died," Jessica interrupted. "Yes, Ned. You've told me that before. How could we not know each other well, when just about every memory I have includes you and Mattie?"

"Then I guess you remember that little coyote pup you brought home?" Ned went on.

"What about it, Ned?"

"You remember what you told your daddy and me first about how you came to have that pup? How it had followed you home? Hell, that little pup wasn't hardly old enough to eat, let alone walk down out of the hills by itself."

Jessica's face took on a defiant look. "I didn't think Daddy would let me keep it! He said coyotes ate chickens and were a nuisance. And someone had shot its mother. I couldn't leave it out there to die, too. Besides, for heaven's sake, Ned, I was only six years old."

"But he did let you keep it, Jes. Until you had to set it free to go back to the wild."

"I remember," Jessica said with a sigh. "Daddy penned the chickens up after that so one of the men wouldn't shoot the pup by mistake if it came back."

"Yeah," Ned drawled. "You were only six years old then. I guess at one time or another, every little kid growin' up thinks they can slip somethin' over on their mommy or daddy. You never tried anythin' like that from then on."

"Are you trying to tell me I've lied to you about something, Ned? I don't appreciate that insinuation one damned bit!"

"Don't reckon you do," Ned said mildly. "And, no, I'm not sayin' you lied. You're old enough to have a right to your privacy about some things. After all, you're twenty years old—almost a woman grown."

"I am grown, Ned. I've had to be these last two years since Daddy died."

"Maybe so. Maybe that little tic on your face last night didn't mean nothin'. Only thing is, the last time I saw that happen to you was fourteen years ago."

Ned kept his gaze steadily on her, noticing the flush staining her cheeks and the way she dropped her brown eyes from his.

"You know, Jes, I never heard of nothin' like what happened to us ever happenin' before. Whoever would have thought someone would steal our food, then slip back into our camp and leave us some more?"

"Perhaps your *ghost* had a tender heart!"

"Maybe so. Sure are a lot of unanswered questions about the whole mess. Why didn't you call out to us when we were huntin' you, Jes? We were close enough for you to hear us for a long time before you let us know where you were. Why'd you let us worry about you so long?"

"You're correct about one thing, Ned. I'm definitely old enough to have a right to my privacy." Jessica rose to her feet. "Now, are you ready to go to the hotel? I'm also old enough to enjoy the thought of a good long soak in a hot bath."

Ned chuckled as he rose beside her. "Didn't used to, Jes. Why, I remember when we had to chase you down on Saturday night to scrub you in the tin tub before church the next day."

Jessica groaned under her breath and turned her back on him to stride down the walkway, but Ned quickly caught up to her and took her arm.

"Guess you'll tell me what happened out there when you get ready," he said quietly. "I just hope it's not somethin' you should've let me know right away. Baker's Hotel is just a couple doors down," he said with a quick change of subject when Jessica flashed him a belligerent glare. "I saw it when we rode in. We might as well go there. Reckon from what I've seen of this town it'll be the only place rentin' rooms."

The moment they stopped at the hotel door, two men who surged through a set of batwing doors just down the street caught Jessica's attention. The men laughingly stumbled to a pair of horses tied at the hitching rail and fumbled with their stirrups. One man managed to climb aboard, then sat hooting at his companion's attempts to mount his own horse.

The horse shied sideways, tangling the man's foot in the stirrup momentarily before knocking him off balance. The man sat down, his rear kicking up puffs of dust from the street.

"Why, you stupid son of a—"

"Watch it, Red," the man on his horse said. "There's ladies around here."

Red jumped to his feet and grabbed the trailing reins of his horse. "I don't give a damn!" he snarled. "This mangy cayuse has throwed me for the last time."

"Ain't the horse's fault, Red," the other man said with a guffaw. "It's all that red-eye you drank inside." Throwing back his head, he laughed loudly.

Red snarled an oath and jerked on his horse's reins. The animal neighed loudly and tossed his head, protesting the bite of the spade bit in its tender mouth. When it danced away again as Red tried to mount, he brought the reins viciously down across the animal's soft nose.

"Stop it!"

"Oh Lord, Jessica. Don't."

Chapter 4

Ned's words fell on deaf ears. Jessica ran down the walkway and jumped into the street. She caught Red's arm as he lifted it for the third time to punish his horse.

"Get out of here, you little—"

Red shook Jessica off as easily as a fly on his arm and she landed in the dusty street, dangerously near the prancing hooves of the horse. She lay stunned for an instant, choking on the dust around her, and heard the man called Red land yet another whip of the reins on the horse. Managing to roll to the side a bit, she struggled to get her feet under her and crouched in the street.

Jessica glanced up just in time to see the horse rear over her. The terrified animal's shoulder knocked Red aside, but the deadly hooves poised directly over Jessica.

A scream of panic left Jessica's mouth at the same instant a pair of strong hands grabbed her under the arms to drag her out of harm's way. When the horse fell back to earth, its hooves hit the exact spot where she had crouched.

Before Jessica could thank her rescuer, she felt herself lifted up and seated on the edge of the walkway with a thump.

"Stay there, you fool," the man growled in her ear.

Jessica's mouth dropped open as she watched the old prospector stride back out into the street and approach Red. Surely that old man wasn't going to take on a drunken cowboy!

"You all right, Jes?" Ned questioned as he knelt beside her.

"Fine, Ned. But we can't let that old man get into a fight."

"Looks to me like he can handle himself. These old mountain men are tougher than they look."

Mountain men? Ned's words stirred a flicker of recognition in Jessica's mind as she watched the old man jerk Red to his feet. He did remind her of Uncle Pete, especially dressed in his tattered buckskins with his hair and beard matted. Pete had usually arrived for his visits looking much like the man out there. But Uncle Pete always smelled a lot worse, Jessica caught herself thinking.

Red's companion urged his horse around and jumped from its back just as the old man's arm came back to retaliate for a blow Red had landed in the old man's stomach. The two men rolled into the dirt street, and Red pulled his pistol, aiming it determinedly at the two combatants, waiting for an opening where he wouldn't hit his friend.

Jessica screamed a warning just as a shot split the air, drowning out her voice. The scene in front of her froze for a second; then Red slowly held his pistol out to his side and the two men in the street separated and rose to their feet.

"What the hell's going on here?"

"Aw, Sheriff," Red whined. "This old buzzard attacked us for no reason."

Jessica gasped in astonishment and scrambled upright. She turned to see the man behind her keeping his pistol trained on the street. A silver badge on his chest proclaimed his status in the town.

"He's lying, Sheriff," she exclaimed. "He was beating his horse and we were trying to stop him. No animal deserves to be treated that way by a drunk who can't even get in his saddle."

"That true, Waco?"

"Weren't me, Sheriff," Waco denied. "It was Red here."

"Thanks a lot," Red grumbled.

"Hey, I ain't takin' no fall for you. Kept you from gettin' the sh . . ." He glanced at Jessica. "Kept you from gettin' beat up, didn't I?"

"That old buzzard couldn't've—"

"All right, that's enough," the sheriff said. "Both of you get on those nags and hightail it back out to the Lazy B. I don't want to see your ugly faces in here again until the end of the month when you get paid. Else I might just have to tell Mr. Baker how his fine livestock's being treated."

"What about him, Sheriff?" Red's nod indicated the old mountain man who had been standing by silently. "Thought we had a law in this town against vagrants. Bet he don't have a dime in his pockets."

"That true, old man?" the sheriff asked.

The old man bent down and rescued his hat from the dust before he answered. He slapped the dirt from the ragged headgear and plopped it into place.

"Well," he drawled in a cracked voice, "I ain't so sure I wanta answer that."

"You can answer it here or we can go over to the jail where I can search you," the sheriff returned flatly. He moved the barrel of his pistol slightly to emphasize his words.

"Oh, put that gun away, Sheriff," Jessica demanded. "That man works for me. I've hired him as a guide."

"What the hell—"

"Shush, Ned," Jessica interrupted. "He's the man I told you about a while ago. Remember?"

Ned immediately caught on to Jessica's ploy. "Oh, he's the one, huh?"

"And just what is the name of your *guide*, miss?"

"Carson," Ned said.

"Jedidiah," Jessica said.

"Well, which is it?" the sheriff demanded with an exasperated sigh.

"Carson," Jessica said.

"Jedidiah," Ned said.

The old man shuffled over and climbed the steps. "It's Jedidiah Carson, Sheriff," he said as he extended his hand.

Jessica looked at the old man skeptically as he shook hands with the sheriff. Did this old reprobate really have the strength to pull her out from under a rearing horse and set her down on the steps? Even Ned, a good head shorter but at least twenty years younger than this man had to be, would have had trouble doing that.

He looked large enough under those tattered buckskins, but Jessica noticed his hand, covered with age spots, tremble when he pulled it back to his side. The brim of the slouch hat hid what little of his features escaped the straggly hair and beard on his face, except for the dark eyes with wrinkles in the corners.

Whatever. She couldn't bring herself to let him go to jail after he rescued her. She could release him from his supposed job later.

"You any kin to Kit?" she heard the sheriff say.

"Naw, don't think so," Jedidiah replied. "Say, anybody got a chaw?"

Ned chuckled and dug into his shirt pocket. He watched the old man take a hefty bite from the plug of tobacco, then shook his head when Jedidiah held it out to him.

"I got plenty," Ned said. "And we better get on over to the hotel now. Wouldn't want all them rooms to be full and us have to sleep in the livery."

"I assume your *guide* is going to be staying at the hotel with you, miss . . ."

"Callaghan," Jessica replied when the sheriff raised a questioning eyebrow. "And of course he is."

"Now just a minute," Jedidiah said around the cud in his mouth. "I . . ."

Jessica firmly placed a hand on each man's arm and started to lead them toward the hotel before the sheriff could question her further. After a few steps, she glanced up in surprise at Jedidiah. An unexpectedly muscular arm lay under the buckskin sleeve. No wonder he had been able to lift her so easily. Why, she even felt a stir of pleasure. . . .

Jessica flushed and dropped the arms of both men. But when she slowed her steps and glanced curiously at Jedidiah, he wrapped his arm around her waist and urged her forward.

Jessica pulled at the fingers digging into her side. "I can walk perfectly well by myself. Let go of me," she insisted.

The fingers refused to loosen. "Got spunk, don't she?" Jedidiah tossed across her at Ned. "Too bad she don't know when to use it and when to keep it bottled up."

Instantly, Jessica recalled his words when he had seated her on the walkway. He had called her a fool! She dug at the fingers on her waist, but they only shifted and caught her just below her breast. Astonishing her, her nipples pebbled. Sputtering ineffectively around the confusion clouding her mind, Jessica's feet barely touched the sidewalk as Jedidiah resolutely marched her toward the hotel door.

At the entrance, Jedidiah released her and Jessica turned her furious gaze on him. "If you ever . . ."

Ned dropped a hand on Jessica's shoulder and gave her a little shake. "Now we wouldn't want our new friend to think we don't appreciate his help, would we? You know, we really oughta find out your true name before we register here," he continued smoothly when Jessica drew in a startled breath at Ned's defense of the mountain man.

The old man hawked the chaw from his mouth and spit it into the street before he answered. "Jedidiah Carson will do just fine. Fact is." He scratched his bushy beard for a moment. "Fact is, I been in the mountains so long, I cain't rightly remember my name. Maybe I never had one."

Jessica watched in amazement as Ned nodded his agreement and held the door open for her. She gritted her teeth and walked stiffly through the door, but not before she tossed one last, gold-flecked glance of anger at Jedidiah.

At the hotel desk, an elderly clerk curtly pushed the register across at them. Jessica wasn't a bit surprised that he withheld the pen for her to sign her name with until she dug into her pocket with a sigh.

"One night's eight bits each," the clerk informed her when Jessica raised a questioning brow at him. "Figure on stayin' again tomorrow, I'll need another eight bits each by nine tomorrow mornin'."

"By nine?" Jessica asked in astonishment. "Why, the bank probably doesn't even open until nine. I have business there that may extend into tomorrow."

"Then perhaps you'll want three rooms for two days?"

"No," Jessica denied. "We'll manage. But we will each want a bath, and I'll need a maid to press the wrinkles from the dress I have in my bag."

"That'll be an extra four bits each for the baths, lessen you want to use the one down at the barber shop. Only costs two bits there. I guess my missus could press your dress for you, if you give it to her when she comes up."

Ned slapped the required money down on the counter before Jessica could open her coin purse; then he withdrew two quarters.

"I can use a haircut," he said when Jessica looked up at him. "I'll be back later and meet you before we go to the bank. What about you, Jedidiah?"

"Ned, I'm not going to let you pay for my room," Jessica said, frowning.

"Too late," he returned. "I already did. Jedidiah?"

"Well, now," Jedidiah drawled. "Ain't been in a hotel for a long time. Think I'll just go on up an' see if them beds are as soft as I remember." He dug into the pocket of his buckskins and pulled out a small, leather pouch. "But I kin pay for my own room."

Ned accepted the coins Jedidiah held out to him without protest and settled his hat more firmly on his head.

"See you later," he said with a nod to Jessica.

Before she could register another objection, Ned turned and left the desk. He ignored her calling after him and let the door slam behind him.

The clerk scrunched up his shoulders, expecting a crack

to appear in the door's window at any moment. When it failed to materialize, he let his breath out in a sigh. At least he wouldn't have that deduction from his small salary this month. Reaching behind him, he handed Jessica and Jedidiah each a key from one of the hooks on the wall behind the desk.

"Your room's 'bout halfway down the hall on your left, miss. Number eight. Number ten, for your friend. I'll send my missus right up."

The hotel door opened again and Jessica turned to see Ned toss two packs inside. "Figured you might need these," he said before he quickly disappeared.

Jessica recognized her own pack, but a strange one was beside it. She glanced questioningly at Jedidiah.

"Yep, it's mine. Left it out there by your horses. I'll get 'em for us."

Jessica didn't wait for Jedidiah. She quickly began climbing the stairs, but a second later, she heard the whisper of Jedidiah's moccasins behind her. Determinedly ignoring him, she went directly to the door of her room.

Jessica felt her pack nudge her in the side and she took it without looking at Jedidiah. Her eyes slid sideways, though, when she sensed him move away and she watched him walk down the hall to the door adjacent to hers. Darn it, she should have insisted the clerk give him a room on another floor. She firmly turned away to fit the key into her lock, but as she opened the door she heard Jedidiah call out to her.

"'Preciate the job offer, miss. I got a couple of things to do, so don't worry if you don't see me 'round this evenin'. I'll be there when you need me."

"Jedidiah, that job offer . . ." But his door closed behind him, cutting off Jessica's words. " . . . is no longer open," she said to the closed door. She shook her head and for a moment considered knocking on his door to demand his attention. The thought of a hot bath to soothe her travel-worn muscles won out. She would tell him later.

Chapter 5

A few minutes later, Jessica opened her door in response
to a knock, and saw a small, gray-haired woman holding
a pail of steaming water. She quickly reached to take the
pail and received a grateful look from the woman's tired
eyes as she rubbed her back.

Glancing over the woman's shoulder, Jessica saw a
much younger, blonde-haired woman with two more pails
of water.

A shy smile lit the blonde's face when she met Jessica's
gaze. "Hello, I'm Eloise. We've brought your bath."
Before Jessica could respond, Eloise lowered her head
and walked into the room.

Jessica followed as Eloise crossed the room, dumping
her pail into an enamel tub behind a dressing screen. As
soon as they put their pails down, the gray-haired woman
reached across the tub and turned on a water tap.

"Don't know why Mr. Baker don't get running hot

58

water in here, too," she said as she stood and again placed her hands in the small of her back. "Heard they've got it practically everywhere now."

"Why, yes, they do," Jessica agreed. "When I asked the clerk for baths, I didn't dream water would have to be carried up here. I just thought the extra charge would be for a room with my own bath. Heavens, we've had hot running water in my ranch house back home for ages."

The older woman studied Jessica. "Knew you weren't from around here," she said with an emphatic nod. "Wouldn't't've been a man in town not talking 'bout you if you'd been here long."

Jessica laughed and ducked her head to hide her blush. She saw the other woman's hand extended in greeting and quickly raised her face as she accepted it.

"I'm Jessica Callaghan," she said as the woman clasped her hand in a firm grip. "From Wyoming. This is the first time I've been to Baker's Valley."

"Veronica Smith," the woman returned. "Most folks call me Ronnie. Quite a tomboy I was in my younger days. And it's good to see another young person around here, though you ain't missed much by not coming to Baker's Valley before. Even Eloise is leaving, soon as she and her young man tie the knot."

"Oh, you're engaged?" Jessica asked, looking at Eloise, who was fingering the blue dress laid on Jessica's bed. "How wonderful."

Eloise looked up from the dress with a smile that transformed her features. Her blue eyes sparkled as she replied, "It took me long enough to get him to ask me. We courted for over three years."

"Men," Jessica said with a conspiratorial wink. "Why is it we have such a time getting them to see what's best in their lives?"

The three women shook their heads and giggled.

"You're not planning to live in town?" Jessica asked Eloise.

"No," she returned in a somewhat hard voice. "I don't fancy raising my children here. But I hope to come back to visit Ronnie now and then."

"You know, I really don't blame you. Ned and I were discussing what an unhappy atmosphere we found in this town," Jessica stated.

"It's an unhappy town, Mrs. Callaghan," Ronnie replied. "But there's not much any of us can do about it."

"It's Miss Callaghan," Jessica said. "But I wish you'd call me Jessica. Or Jes. Seems like I got a tomboy nickname tacked onto me, too."

"Didn't figure either of those men could've been the husband of a young thing like you," Ronnie said. "And Buster did say you rented separate rooms. But you never know these days. A woman needs a man around to look after her, and many's the young one who's hooked up with an older man for protection."

"Ned's the foreman of my ranch," Jessica admitted. "But he's also like a second father to me and he's a very dear friend. Jedidiah's . . . uh . . . our guide."

Jessica noticed a flick of pain cross Ronnie's face when she started to bend down and reach across the tub for the water tap.

"Here. I'll do that."

"Thank you, Jes," Ronnie said. "And we'll be back in a few minutes with two more pails of water to heat this up a little more."

"Oh, please don't bother. I've been bathing in cold streams since we left Wyoming, and even a warm bath will be a treat."

"No such thing," Eloise denied. "We women appreciate

little things like a steaming bath. You should have seen Tobias's face when I told him that since there was absolutely no way we could have hot running water, I needed a new stove. One with a huge water reservoir on the side." She laughed softly. "He almost had a stroke, trying to figure out how to get that monstrosity out to the cabin. Said he had to put stronger springs on the wagon and use a double team."

When the women's laughter abated, Eloise continued, "But, if you don't mind, I'll just knock and leave the water outside your door this time. Ronnie has to make sure the cook's getting the evening meal ready and I've got to set the tables. Mr. Baker won't be any too happy if he comes to supper tonight and finds something out of place."

"Mr. Baker pretty much runs this town, doesn't he?" Jessica asked.

"That he does, miss," Ronnie agreed as a tight look came over her face. "That he does."

Before Jessica could question her further, Ronnie hastily picked up the empty pails and Eloise draped the dress over her arm. Nodding briefly to Jessica, they crossed the room and closed the door behind them.

Jessica pondered Ronnie's words while she waited for the knock on the door telling her more hot water waited for her. *I wonder what Ronnie meant by no one being able to change the town's atmosphere,* she asked herself. But she never got the chance to ask Eloise. By the time she crossed the room and opened the door after hearing two taps, she only saw Eloise hurrying down the hallway.

Jessica stood outside the bank door that afternoon and watched Ned walk away from her. She had to be satisfied with the teller's assurance that he would pass the needed information on to the illustrious Mr. Baker, since he didn't seem to be available. She would, indeed, have to check back tomorrow morning to conclude her transaction.

Ned could have at least asked her if she wanted to accompany him while he toured the town, instead of leaving her at loose ends until supper that evening. Then she noticed his steps quicken as he neared a set of batwing doors at the edge of the saloon district of town, and smiled to herself. He didn't indulge his secret passion for a nip or two very often, and he definitely wouldn't have been comfortable with her witnessing it—even if she would have been allowed into the saloon.

What could she do to kill the time until Ned met her for their evening meal? She had absolutely no desire to spend that long cooped up in the small, but clean, room at the hotel. The thin walls didn't keep out much sound, and she had listened to Jedidiah's snores the entire time she bathed. Glancing across the street, her eyes fell on the general store.

Her hand crept into her skirt pocket and she hefted the small coin purse nestled there, mentally counting the contents. She had been pretty hard on her men, even if they did deserve it. They probably had managed to shoot a couple of the abundant jack rabbits to go along with their beans and biscuits for supper, but a small treat for them might be in order.

She had noticed some canned peaches on the shelf at the store. Two or three cans shouldn't deplete her resources that much, especially when she thought of her men's scant fare while she and Ned would dine in the hotel that evening.

Less than ten minutes later, Jessica hung up her blue gown and changed into a clean set of riding clothes. Jedidiah's snores no longer penetrated the solitude of her room, and she smiled grimly to herself. Perhaps he had gone about the business he insisted he had to do. It was just as well. She didn't want to tell him he hadn't really been hired when her anger still flared freshly each time she thought of him.

When she picked up the sack on the bed, the cans clinked together, reminding her of her mission. She shoved the note she would leave at the desk for Ned into her pocket as she crossed the room.

As she rode by the large house on the fringe of the town a few moments later, Jessica gazed at it curiously. It surely could house several people, but no activity met her eyes. Drawn shutters even hid the windows.

Jessica noticed a small, wooden sign hung on chains over the porch, swaying in the afternoon breeze. She squinted her eyes in an attempt to read the ornately carved letters— Idalee's. The storekeeper had said something about a place with that name. Perhaps it was a boarding house and they could have gotten rooms cheaper there. No matter now. They would be on their way again tomorrow, with or without Cinnabar. She reined her horse left just past the house.

At least she had allowed Ned to put the bundle carrying her clothes on the second packhorse at the beginning of their journey. Nothing in the saddlebags Cinnabar carried couldn't be replaced. She had to believe the stallion would find his way back to her again. She couldn't lose him, too, so soon after her father's and Uncle Pete's deaths.

A picture of her gentle father swam in Jessica's mind, quickly replaced by the vision of her hours' long vigil by the ice-covered window over two years ago.

The storm had broken that afternoon with no warning, catching many of the hands on the range who were trying to drive the cattle to safer ground. Again and again she had rubbed away the ice on the window to watch one or two men ride into the yard, but not one of them had been her father. Ned found him the next morning, barely a half mile from the ranch.

And Uncle Pete. Funny how close to the forefront of her mind he had been ever since Ned called that old man, Jedidiah, a mountain man. Her memories of Pete's death were fresher—only a few months old.

The old doctor glanced worriedly at the young woman he had brought into the world on a cold winter night much like this one, almost twenty years ago. Having watched her grow up pampered and spoiled by her father after her mother died in the horrible accident the summer following Jessica's birth, the doctor would be the first to admit Jessica hadn't turned into the simpering ninny she could have become.

She had a stubborn streak a mile wide, but also an amazing capacity for loyalty and love for those close to her. Perhaps that capacity would be her undoing this time. He had feared for her very sanity the previous winter after her father's death, and now he could see no way to shield her from this latest blow.

And he knew only one way to tell her—straight out, without giving her any false hope.

"I'm sorry, Miss Callaghan. There's just nothing else I can do. The pneumonia's being complicated by heart failure."

Somewhere in the back of her mind, Jessica had anticipated the doctor's prognosis, but it didn't lessen the thunderbolt of pain that shot through her. Her trembling legs wilted under her and she sank down on the bed beside Uncle Pete.

"Oh God, no! Please, Doctor!" Jessica made no attempt

to disguise the agony in her voice. "I lost Daddy only a year ago. I can't lose my uncle, too."

The doctor patted her awkwardly on the shoulder, avoiding Jessica's ravaged gaze. Instead, he turned away and busied himself returning his supplies to his tattered, black medical bag. It didn't matter how many times he faced the death of one of his patients it never came any easier. Nor did he find it any easier to relieve the pain of those death left behind.

"These old mountain men are tough, Miss Callaghan," he said as he worked. "But they live an awfully hard life, and it eventually takes its toll on them."

The doctor picked up his bag, pausing to take in the young woman huddled on the bed with the now pitifully shrunken figure of a man who couldn't possibly live until morning. He watched Jessica tenderly run her hand across her uncle's fevered brow, then stroke the full beard covering his face. Loud, labored breathing filled the room.

"I have to go now, Jessica," he said in a softer voice.

Jessica choked on a sob. "I understand. Will you c–come back?"

Depends. It's Mrs. Rogers's first baby, you know. First ones can take their time, but you can't tell Mr. Rogers that. He's still waiting down in your living room, probably pacing a hole in your rug by now."

"I know. You go on."

"I've left a bottle of laudanum on the bedside table, Jessica. If his pain gets much worse, you may need it."

"No," Jessica denied emphatically. "Uncle Pete wouldn't want to be drugged."

"Nevertheless, I'll leave it. He's faded quite a bit since I first started tending him, but he's still large enough for you to have trouble handling him if he—"

"I'll manage, Doctor," Jessica broke in. "Thank you for all you've done."

She picked up Uncle Pete's gnarled hand and sat silently until the doctor's footsteps faded. The click of the bedroom door telling her she was alone released her pent-up anguish, and sobs racked her body.

Only Uncle Pete's arrival last spring had finally broken through the grief Jessica couldn't seem to shake after her father Foster Callaghan's death. She suspected that Ned had found a way of getting word to the crusty old mountain man after his and Mattie's alternating pleas failed to halt her fading weight and deep, abiding depression.

Pete stirred slightly and Jessica's head rose in hope. But he only began muttering and tossing his head—the delirium the doctor had warned about. Jessica glanced at the laudanum bottle, then resolutely away as she concentrated on soothing her uncle.

She sat alone with Pete in her father's old bedroom throughout the long night, holding his hand and listening to the wild ravings of stories she had heard in her childhood. Over the years, she had come to think of his tales as just that—tales to entertain a small child. Now she realized Pete had indeed lived through many of his adventures: Indian attacks, grizzly bears, and one tale she hadn't heard before. He must have loved the dark-haired woman he called Caroline deeply. Why had Jessica never heard of her before?

But there were probably a lot of things she didn't know about Pete's life, Jessica realized. Though she had always lovingly called him uncle, he was not her blood relation. Pete Russell and her father had been closer than any brothers, though. Some of her first memories were of crawling onto Pete's knee for a horsy ride, while Foster and Pete spent a lazy evening discussing ranch plans.

And her father had once explained in answer to her questions that he and Pete had started the ranch together. After a few years, though, Daddy said, Pete couldn't resist the pull of the mountains any longer. A time or two she had wondered what catastrophe in Pete's life had ever made him think he could stand being tied to ranching. Especially in the fall, when Pete loaded up his pack mule and set out once again.

He always returned, however. Once in a while at Christmas time and most assuredly every summer, when he exchanged his buckskins for denims and helped around the ranch. When he rolled his bedroll out beside Jessica's during roundup, they talked far into the star-sprinkled night. Jessica poured out her childhood and teen dreams into Pete's willingly listening ears—things she would have hesitated telling even her father or Mattie.

Jessica had always thought of Pete as a very precious part of her family. And now, soon, Uncle Pete's stone would rise among the lonely sentinels in the ranch's ever-expanding graveyard.

Jessica grabbed yet another handkerchief from the drawer in the bedside table. Already several were scattered like soggy snowflakes on the carpet beside the bed, and her red-rimmed eyes were swollen almost shut. Even the soft linen rasped painfully on her tender nose.

"Jessica. Darlin', don't cry."

"Uncle Pete!" The clarity of the brown eyes gazing at her sent a measure of relief winging through Jessica. It was almost morning. Surely if he had lived through the dark night. . . .

"Jessica, honey, I want you to do something for me." A violent coughing spell wracked Pete's body, shaking the entire bed.

"Uncle Pete! Please don't talk. Save your strength."

Pete shook his head against the pillow and took a deep breath. "Can't, darlin'. Don't have much time."

"No! I won't let you die! I can't stand to lose you and Daddy both!"

Pete lifted a gnarled hand and stroked her sable hair. "I've lived my life the way I wanted it, honey. There's only one thing I regret now, and it's too late. Please. Just go to the dresser and pull out that bottom drawer."

Jessica found she couldn't turn away from the plea in his eyes and the anguished voice urging her to grant him this one last request. Slowly rising to her feet, she did as he asked. As Pete continued murmuring instructions, she dug among the scant possessions he had collected over the years until her fingers encountered a piece of rolled-up hide. She carried it back to the bed and watched Pete open it with trembling hands, covered with brown age spots.

"Thought I might find him someday, Jessica. Thought it might be something I could leave him. But I guess he's dead, and I don't reckon I'll see him where I'm going. The innocent go straight to the good side when they leave this earth."

"Who, Uncle Pete?"

Another frenzied coughing spell shook Pete, drowning out Jessica's question. The piece of hide dropped from his fingers onto his stomach, and a thin piece of foolscap fluttered beside it. When the spell at last abated, Pete took a tortured breath.

"W–water, Jessica," he whispered.

Jessica hurriedly poured from the pitcher by the bed and lifted his head. When he managed only a few sips, she urged him to drink again, but he shook his head slightly and turned aside. Trying to steady her own violently trembling fingers, Jessica quickly set the glass down and turned back to see Pete's eyes again open.

When Pete held out his arm, Jessica clasped his hand between hers and curled up beside him on the bed. She carried his hand to her face and rubbed her cheek against the callused roughness of Pete's palm, struggling with everything in her to give him a measure of comfort. Instead, she felt the strength of her uncle's love flowing into her as the old, knotty fingers stroked her.

"You'll be fine, Jessica," Pete said in a firmer voice. "You're strong and you've grown into a beautiful woman. Think of you almost as my own, I do, and I'm proud of you. I love you, girl."

"Uncle Pete! Oh, Uncle Pete, I love you, too. Please don't leave me."

"Shhhh, Jes. I have to tell you."

And while Jessica sat with tears streaming down her face, Pete told her the tale of the map drawn on the hide. How he had been on the supply boat that waited on the Big Horn River, miles north of where Captain Marsh should have met Custer's commanding officer, General Terry. And Gil Longworth, the man in charge of the freight wagon carrying the load of miners' gold, who had arrived scared to death of the throng of Indians in the area.

"We didn't realize until later that Custer's men had already been massacred the day before," Pete murmured. "But Marsh knew he had to get the hell out of there after Longworth told him how hostile the Indians they had spotted were. And Captain Marsh also had an army payroll of gold coins on that boat."

The captain and two of Marsh's trusted officers left on a midnight excursion. They buried the miners' gold somewhere on the west bank of the Big Horn, but Pete had no idea where.

"Just me and the captain buried the payroll, though,

Jessica, after the rest of the men were asleep. We took it to the other bank and up a canyon."

Pete had drawn the map after finding the payroll still in its hiding place a couple years later, figuring someday the captain might want it.

"But the captain's dead now, Jessica," Pete said, his voice now gasping. "We . . . we left the key in the strongbox, but far's I know, no one e–ever went back for that gold. And I never needed it. Never wanted to live the life that money would give me. Never wanted to be burdened by all them possessions."

He drew in a ragged breath. "But you might need it, darlin'. I know how bad off the ranch is gettin'. And that gold will belong to whoever finds it by now. You find it, darlin', and let it be my legacy to you. It and the other I left f–for . . ." His brown eyes closed.

"Uncle Pete!"

For a second Jessica thought he had responded to her; then she saw his eyes staring over her shoulder. His face took on a look of wonder.

"Caroline," he breathed. "Oh, Caroline, my love. Did you . . . did you come alone?"

Jessica glanced over her shoulder, but could see no one. Pete's voice drew her back.

"I see," he murmured. "Then at least we can wait together. You're so beautiful, my darlin' . . ." His last breath left his chest on the final word.

No matter how hard Jessica shook him or raged at the injustice of it, his eyes remained closed and his presence left her. Long moments later, she felt the coldness in the room and pulled herself together long enough to hide the map again in the drawer. She had to go for Ned and Mattie. With their help, she would give Uncle Pete her final gift—a decent and fitting burial.

But she would never touch that gold. It had already cost too many lives. It had to be cursed.

She had decided to touch the gold, Jessica thought as her mind returned to the present and she urged the gelding over a rocky, washed-out portion of the trail she followed. She didn't have any choice after the spring blizzard wiped out her calves. Her only other option, after the banker refused her request for an extension on her mortgage, was to accept Ned's offer of a loan. She wouldn't jeopardize his and Mattie's retirement money.

Halfway across the area, the horse stumbled, then stopped with its foreleg raised. Not noticing, Jessica kneed the horse forward again, then pulled back on the reins when she felt him limp.

"Oh, no," she said aloud as she slid from the horse's back. "You've picked up a stone. I hope it's not embedded too deeply."

She looped the reins over her arms and reached for the horse's foreleg. Before she could get it securely into her grasp, she heard the warning rattle behind her and froze.

The horse heard the snake, too. He neighed shrilly and tossed his head, entangling the reins for a second around Jessica's arm, then sending her sprawling as he pulled free and leaped across the rocky ground out of danger.

She didn't see the snake strike, but she felt its head graze the sleeve of her blouse. When she could focus again after her hard contact with the ground, she saw it recoiling its huge length, and a second later a pair of cold eyes transfixed her. The snake's tongue flicked in and out between its deadly fangs, still dripping venom from the missed strike.

A snake that huge would have plenty of venom left for

another strike, though. And Jessica's eyes widened in horror as she realized it would launch this one at her face—the same place a snake had struck her mother nineteen years ago!

Chapter 6

"Don't move. For God's sake, don't move," a voice whispered clearly.

She gulped, but couldn't force a word from her terror-clogged throat. She couldn't have moved if she wanted to, despite knowing that in a split second the snake would launch itself again.

Flat eyes pinned her in place as the snake drew back its head. A soft whoosh whispered past her and the snake's head fell harmlessly to the ground, leaving the severed coils of the body twisting frantically before her eyes. A knife quivered in the dirt behind the thrashing coils.

She found her voice. Her scream echoed for only an instant after she scrambled to her feet. A large hand covered her mouth, and an arm captured her around the waist. Still terrified, she dug at the fingers covering her mouth, her chest heaving furiously with repressed screams.

"You're safe now," the voice behind her soothed. The

arm around her waist snugged her closer. "I'll let you go, if think you can get yourself under control."

The stern words, spoken close to her ear, were accompanied by a wisp of breath across her cheek. Jessica gulped once again and her fear eased somewhat. Slowly, she nodded compliance against the restraining hand and it fell from her mouth, lingering near in case her hysterics burst free again.

The arm around her waist loosened and Jessica willed her legs to stop trembling. But when her eyes fell on the still writhing body of the snake, she felt a violent urge to shut it out of sight. Instinctively, she turned and buried her face against the male chest behind her, flinging her arms around his waist and holding on for all she was worth.

The muscular arms tightened comfortingly about her and a cheek nestled against her head. She took another gulping breath in an attempt to calm herself, and breathed in a vaguely familiar scent. She couldn't quite place it as she struggled to chase the last lingering vestiges of fear from her mind.

"M–my mother," she said, sobbing. "A snake killed her. It . . . it bit her in the f–face."

"Oh Lord," the voice said. A hand came up and stroked her hair. "You didn't see it happen?"

"N–no." Jessica shook her head against his chest. "I . . . was only a baby. I don't even remember her—just pictures. But I asked Daddy. We used to talk about her, and now he's gone, too."

The stroking hand in her hair stilled for a second, then continued its soothing motion. Her words explained a lot to him. She evidently didn't have anyone to protect her, to tell her how foolish some of her actions were. How she had no business wandering around by herself, putting herself in danger. Even that old man with her back in town hadn't been able to keep her from flying into that drunk from the Lazy B.

"Oh, pretty lady, what am I going to do with you?"

Recognition coursed through Jessica. Only one person had ever called her that. She withdrew her arms and pushed against the firm chest, but the man cupped the back of her head and kept her face firmly in place.

"Don't, pretty lady," the man growled. "You'll be better off if you don't see my face."

"Let me go," Jessica said in a muffled voice. "You won't be able to leave here without my seeing you, and I want to thank you. Besides, I know you're the same person I saw last night."

The fingers tightened in her hair for a second before the large chest under her cheek heaved with a sigh. He couldn't believe how much he really did want her to see him. His hold on her loosened, and she turned her face up to him when he stepped back.

The sunlight fell clearly on his face this time, and Jessica studied his features. She had been right. The eyes were ebony and the hair almost the same color, only darker still, if that were possible. He could have used a haircut, but for some reason the length of the raven locks didn't offend her. Her eyes lingered for a moment on the full lips; then she blushed and dropped her gaze as she recalled the pleasure they had sent through her.

"It . . . it is you," she whispered.

"Uh-huh."

Though he still felt a stir of pity for the somewhat bedraggled figure in front of him, he had to knock some sense into her stubborn head. He wouldn't always be around to pull her cute little behind out of danger. Steeling himself, he managed to put a measure of exasperation into his voice. "And you're the little fool who hasn't got enough sense to know it's dangerous for a woman to wander around alone. I've got better things to do with my time than rescue you from your foolishness. What the hell are you doing out here by yourself again?"

Jessica's eyes flew back to his face and the flush on her face darkened as her temper flared. "I can ride and shoot as well as any damned man!" she spat at him. "And it's none of your blasted business what I do. You've got no right to call me names or question my actions!"

"Well, someone should," he fired back. "Where the hell's your gun, if you're so blasted good with it?"

"It's on the horse," Jessica had to admit to him. "And you know what happened to my derringer. But my men are within shouting distance."

"It would have to be a loud shout," the man growled. "I saw them camped by the stream and it's a good mile from here. If that snake had gotten you in the face like it tried to, you'd have been dead long before you got to them. Even if you had been able to catch that horse in time."

Jessica glanced behind her and the snake's still slightly trembling body sent another pang of fear through her. She hated snakes. She had tried for years to overcome her fear, since she encountered them almost everywhere in the summer. She had learned to be cautious whenever she rode around the sun-warmed rocks where they liked to lie, but every once in a while one would surprise her. Like today.

"I'm sorry," she found herself apologizing. "If I'd had Cinnabar, he wouldn't have bolted. He would have trampled that snake to death."

"Cinnabar? That roan you were riding last night?"

Jessica gasped. "You! You must have Cinnabar! Or one of the men with you last night." She laid her hand on his chest. "Please. I'll . . . I'll find some way to pay you if you give him back. He's . . . I've had him since shortly after he was born. He's one of the few things left in my life that's dear to me."

Her words stirred his sympathy again. She was much too beautiful to have to beg such a favor from him—a favor so easily granted. Guilt filled him, and he found himself unable to tear his black eyes away from her pleading brown ones, the small hand on his chest sending tingles throughout his upper body. His mind ordered his arms up to remove the hand so he could think straight, but, instead, he found his arms curving around her to pull her even closer.

"Pay me, huh?" he said without thinking. "There are other ways to pay a person than with money."

Jessica tried without success to still her hands as they crept up his chest toward his neck. "I . . . I won't . . ."

"No, pretty lady," he said as he lowered his head. "You can set the boundaries of your payment. I won't take more than you offer."

The remembered dreams of the previous night didn't even begin to compare with the reality of once again having his lips on hers. His mouth covered hers softly and tenderly at first, then more firmly as her hands rested on his neck and tugged against him.

She clung greedily to him, her breasts at first only brushing, then flattening against his firm chest as she snuggled against him. It felt so good to be in his arms. All her worries flew away and she found herself yearning never to leave the peace and contentment of his embrace.

But she found something else there, too. The sweet fire stirred sluggishly in her blood at first, then overtook her senses in a rush. When he reluctantly drew his lips away, she threw her head back, offering her slender neck to his ministrations.

He groaned and lowered his head again. She tasted and smelled almost the same as he remembered, except for a faint hint of roses today. And holding her again chased the pain from his mind and made him crave four walls around them, giving them privacy to savor each other for hours. If his senses didn't lie to him, she would enjoy it as much as he would.

Somewhere in the corner of his mind, he heard a tiny voice trying to break through the turmoil of his thoughts. He was taking advantage of her muddled senses. She wasn't completely recovered from the snake's attack or the memories it brought back to her. A moment ago, he'd wanted to comfort her. Now he found himself drinking deeply of the surcease so freely flowing into his mind as he held her.

Angrily, he raised his head and shook it to force the thread of reason back into a dark corner. Though he could never share a future with someone like her, he could have a few minutes more with her right now. He watched her eyes open halfway and the long lashes sweep downward once to flutter against her pink cheeks before she opened them fully again.

Jessica had only a glimpse of the ebony eyes softened now in passion, the pain she had sensed in them earlier pushed aside. She gladly opened her mouth under his again and closed her eyes in pleasure when his hand cupped her breast. She felt him lean back against the rock beside them and grasp her hip with his free hand to pull her against his body.

Far from frightening her, the hardness Jessica nestled against as he spread his legs and lifted her feet from the ground elicited a moan of greedy passion. Her arms tightened around his neck and she clung frantically when a new flame raced through her. Finding herself in no danger of wilting to the ground in his firm grasp, her hand unconsciously flitted across his chest and toward the source of the pleasure cascading over her.

Heated flesh met her exploring fingers as they slid into a hole in the faded denim encasing his legs. She felt him jerk, heard him gasp. She immediately staggered to regain her balance and rubbed at the reddened marks his fingers left on her arms when he thrust her away from him.

He almost lost himself again as he stared into her puzzled brown eyes. Tears misted the question he saw there, and her full lips trembled as she misinterpreted his frowning countenance as anger at her, not the passion it truly spoke of.

"God, pretty lady," he said with a groan. "Don't you know what you do to a man?"

Jessica shook her head silently, sable curls tossing around her dejected face.

"But I know what you do to me," she almost whispered.

All at once a violent blush stole over her cheeks and she whirled from him. She jerked away a step when his hands cupped her shoulders, and rigidly stared into the distance.

"Please," she gulped. "Just leave now. Leave me alone."

"All right," he said quietly. "But I'll be watching you until you get back into town. You won't see me, but I'll be there."

"Just go!" Jessica pleaded.

"I'll make sure both your horses get back to you, pretty lady."

Jessica almost stumbled when she abruptly turned around, but she gasped and quickly pulled her hand from his steadying grasp.

"Cinnabar!" she demanded. "Where is he? You promised!"

"I keep my promises, pretty lady," he assured her. "I wouldn't dream of reneging on this one, especially when I've already received such a delightful payment for it. I can't give him to you right now, but you'll have your horse back by tomorrow."

Jessica found herself believing him as she met the sincere gaze in his black eyes. She nodded her head slightly, unable to tear her own eyes away. Her pink tongue came out to moisten her suddenly dry lips, and she heard the man grunt as though struck in the stomach as he broke the contact.

Jessica watched him move away, then shrank back a step in fear as he made a swipe and picked up the snake by its tail.

"What . . . what are you going to do with that?" she gasped.

"Supper," he threw over his shoulder without breaking stride.

She shuddered and closed her eyes for a second. When she looked again, only empty space met her gaze.

Her words tumbled out without thought. "I don't even know your name!" she called to the emptiness. Only the snort of the gelding standing several yards away answered her.

But she could feel his presence for a long time afterward. She thought she would almost have known he was watching her, even if he hadn't told her. She felt his eyes on her when she picked up her hat before she caught the gelding and deftly removed the small stone from its hoof. She could feel him nod in satisfaction, along with herself, when the horse moved off without a limp toward where her men were camped.

And for some crazy reason she found herself holding back one of the cans of peaches from the men. After she headed back to town and rode out of sight of the camp, she pulled the gelding up beside a convenient rock. Leaning over, she set the last can out in plain sight.

"Dessert," she called out in a shaky voice, then nudged the horse into motion again.

And she felt the moment his eyes left her, when the town came into sight. Her shoulders jerked reflexively, as though from a wrench of loss of contact.

Chapter 7

Though Buster assured Jessica a few moments later that Ned had already gone up to his room, only silence greeted her when she tapped on his door. She knocked a little harder, and heard the bedsprings protest as someone rolled across them.

Ned's strangely muffled voice came through the door. "C–comin'. Just a sec."

The Ned who opened the door wasn't in any condition for Jessica to discuss the tale of her ride with. He swayed as he stepped back, and Jessica caught a whiff of cheap whiskey on his breath.

"Oh, Ned," she said softly. "What would Mattie say?"

"Well, we don't really have ta tell her, do we, Jes?" He winked sloppily at her and twisted his lips into a sly grin.

Jessica found herself laughing at him. "No, I guess we

don't. But I've never seen you take more than a drink or two in my life."

"Haven't too often, Jes. But there's at least one friendly feller in this town. Got to talkin' we did, and time just got away from me."

"And I'd guess the number of drinks you had got away from you, too."

"Must have, Jes," he agreed with another wink.

"Who was he, Ned?"

Ned reached up and scratched his head. "Well, now, come to think of it, I never did get his name. He sure was likable, though."

"He must have been, for you to sit drinking for over two hours with a stranger whose name you didn't even know," Jessica said in a dry voice. "Do you think you can be ready to go down to supper by the time I change? Or should I have Eloise bring you up some coffee first?"

"I'll be ready, Jes. You go on. I'll just wash up and be right there."

Jessica sniffed and turned to the door, where she paused for a moment.

"You might put on a different shirt, too, if you have another clean one. That one smells like tobacco smoke."

She closed the door, then shook her head and smiled to herself as she walked across the hall to her own room. She cared too much about Ned to chastise him for a couple of hours' enjoyment after their long days on the trail.

In her room Jessica walked to the wash basin sitting in the late-afternoon sun shining through the window to warm it slightly. She pulled the shade down, unbuttoned her blouse, and reached for the washcloth to wet it and clean the dust from her face.

The cloth wasn't really as soft as she would have liked. In fact, it rasped against her face slightly, feeling almost like a man's whiskers. She drew it down over her neck and across the tops of her breasts under her chemise.

The coldness of the cloth she unconsciously drew back and forth over her breasts finally brought her to her senses a while later. She gave a start and dunked it back into the water to warm it. After wringing it out again, she stood over the basin and watched the ripples of water calm once more. She stared into the water, now somewhat murky with dust.

She had a face now to put with the voice and body that had kept her tossing and turning all the night before. She could almost see it peering back at her from the water. Those eyes at times so hard with shadowed pain they were as flat as the eyes of the snake on the trail. Other times they softened to almost brown when he looked at her.

She found herself longing for Mattie and the frank talks they shared. How many times had she come home from a barn dance or church social starry-eyed over some young cowboy's attention? There were plenty of stolen kisses in the shadows when couples could escape the sharp eyes of the dance chaperons. None of the kisses she received ever stirred her as much as the stranger's did, though, she admitted.

She had also received her share of rides home from church and of evenings spent on the front-porch swing at the ranch house with one or another of her latest suitors. And, true to Mattie's explicit warnings, none of the young men she allowed to kiss her at the dances or on the porch were satisfied for long with only kisses. Each time the familiar groping would start—whether in the darkness of the front porch or maybe on a picnic she allowed herself to be talked into—she would feel a repugnance crawl through her veins. The suitor would be cut dead by

Jessica's cold eyes the next time he dared approach her.

Not once had she ever even slightly experienced the feelings that Mattie hinted she would find with a man someday.

Maybe that's been the trouble all along, she mused to herself. *All those others were just boys. The person I met out there is definitely a man.*

A man who's seen lots of pain in his probably at least twenty odd years, her mind continued. *Maybe even closer to thirty. A man who has something to hide.*

Instead of the thought scaring her, Jessica felt her heart tug inside her breast.

And how could she ever have imagined how she would feel in those strong arms? Was it the lust Mattie had also frankly told her some people mistook for love? Was there a sensuous part of her that could be stirred to the point where she lost control? To the point where she would have lain down in the stones on the trail with him if he hadn't pushed her away?

Oh, she had no delusions about lust. Who could watch the stallions cover the mares on the ranch, then see them walk away to graze without a backward glance and not know about lust? Quickly satisfied, lust was.

But what about the winter mornings she knocked on Mattie's door to find her still ensconced in bed with Ned, lingering for a moment longer before she rose to face another busy day? And what about the times she came into the kitchen to find Ned sneaking a quick kiss from Mattie before he put his hat on his head and left?

Mattie would only get a dreamy expression on her face when Jessica questioned her. She would know someday, Mattie would tell her.

A sharp rap on the door jerked Jessica around.

"Ready, Jes?" Ned called through the thin structure.

"You . . . you go on down, Ned," Jessica called back. "I'll be there in a minute."

Jessica heard him grumble something about how long it took women to dress as he moved away.

"My God, Storm! I wish you wouldn't do that!" Idalee's hand flew up to cover the low decolletage of her dress as the big man stepped out from behind a sheltering curtain.

She raced across the room when he smiled and held his arms open, straight into his warm embrace. She pressed against him, then threw her arms around his neck to draw his face down for a brief kiss. Her hands caressed his cheeks as she pulled back to look up at him.

"One of these days you're going to give me a stroke."

Storm chuckled softly and released her without answering. Stepping away from her, he settled in a comfortable, stuffed chair beside the curtains. He stretched his long legs out, crossing them at the ankles, before he sighed and smiled at her.

"Wouldn't be any fun if I didn't surprise you once in a while, Idy."

"And how many times have I asked you not to call me that? Huh, Storm?" Idalee said grumpily. "And where the hell have you been all this time?"

"Around," Storm replied vaguely. "I see your language hasn't improved. You got anything here to drink besides that rotgut you serve your customers?"

Storm watched Idalee purse her lips into a disapproving pout at his insult and walk to the velvet bellpull beside the speaking tube in the corner of the room. She hadn't changed at all in the months he had been gone. Still the same proud tilt to the small, pointed chin and the same luster to the red-gold curls tumbling down her back.

Her emerald gown, a bit too much for this early in the afternoon, encased her tiny figure to perfection. Only a spattering of freckles on a pert nose set under cat-green eyes remained to remind him of the pigtailed creature who had followed him around years ago.

Funny. Once he had thought Idalee had grown into the most beautiful woman he had ever seen, though he enjoyed teasing her about the freckles way too much to tell her they only added to her elfish beauty. But today the silky softness of sable curls and the gold flecks in a pair of brown eyes tugged at his senses—and lips just full enough to be meant for kissing.

Idalee had never sat a horse as though born to the saddle, yet still exuded the essence of femininity. And the fuller figure of the pretty lady fit the space in his arms just exactly right.

Storm relaxed a little and allowed his lids to droop over his dark eyes. He would probably never see her again, unless he stumbled across her yet another time when her own foolish actions placed her in danger. Beauty the pretty lady might have, but she obviously had been hiding under a cabbage leaf when the Good Lord passed out brains. She needed a guardian angel!

It damned sure wasn't going to be him, Storm told himself as he tried to fight the drowsiness overcoming him. He needed to talk to Idalee about . . . What? Of course. He really should apologize for not coming to see her as soon as he had escaped, if only to thank her for the comfortable hiding place she'd fixed up for him. He could almost feel safe there. And here. Almost. And damn it felt good after so long on edge day in and night out.

Idalee turned and stilled the terse words on her lips about the lemonade he enjoyed being on the way. Her mouth softened and her green eyes took on a look of love for the large man stretched out before her.

His body almost overpowered the chair, his shoulders touching each side of the curved back. She would have to talk him into staying long enough to give him a haircut. Though the shiny black locks shone with health, they almost brushed his shoulders.

Idalee's eyes traveled down the arms encased by the blue plaid shirt to where his thumbs hooked into his denim jeans on each side of the top button. Plenty of room in the overstuffed chair for his narrow hips, but she knew from the times she teasingly patted him on the backside that the seat of his jeans would be pulled tight.

The front, too, she laughed silently to herself. Maybe she could figure out some way to get him men's clothing from the general store without arousing suspicion. Elias's clothes wouldn't fit him, and that jagged tear on the frayed jeans loomed dangerously close to his crotch—though how anything embarrassing to him might escape the tight material she couldn't imagine.

She would definitely have to find a way to at least get him a pair of jeans, she thought, letting her eyes wander down the thin material covering his long legs. Why, the denim was so worn as to be almost transparent and it clung tightly to his muscular thighs. At least his moccasins looked in fairly good shape, but she guessed he had made them himself.

He was truly a magnificent male specimen. Why, she had even had a short infatuation with him herself in their teens, when both of them were trying to get a handle on their emerging sexuality. Recalling the puzzled look on Storm's face the couple of times they had shared an experimental kiss, Idalee giggled quietly. She had probably had that same look on her own face.

All the books said that flaming passion started with

kisses, passion that swept away reason and ended with a girl getting in "trouble." Or, at least that was what her mother had insisted, though she and her girls knew better now.

But there hadn't even been a tiny spark to begin a flame when she and Storm had kissed. Probably the most mature decision they had made in their teens had been to accept the deep friendship between them, to agree to be there always for one another, while realizing that the love they had for each other wasn't the kind that led to marriage.

With Elias, though. . . .

A soft snore met her ears and Idalee glanced up to see Storm's head cushioned against the side of the high-backed chair. She smiled tenderly, then turned quickly when she heard high heels tapping down the hallway. Before the person approaching could knock on the door and wake Storm, Idalee slipped outside and reached for the tray of lemonade.

"I'll take it, Sassy," she said to the sleepy-eyed woman wearing only a chemise and pantelets above her dangerously high-heeled shoes. "Where's Elias?"

"Oh, he's fixing one of his concoctions in the kitchen, mum," the woman replied in a decidedly British accent. "I went in to get a drink of water and he asked me to bring this to you."

"You're up awfully early, Sassy."

"Not up, mum. Just thirsty. I'm going on back to bed now. I do so enjoy it when I have my bed all to myself."

"Why, Sassy," Idalee said with a smile, "I thought you enjoyed it when you shared your bed, also."

Sassy's lips curved up and her blue eyes took on a small sparkle. "That I do, mum," she said, but almost immediately she frowned slightly. "Well, most of the time, anyway."

"Sassy, you know you have the right to refuse anyone you want to here."

"I know, mum. But needs my tips, I do."

"I've offered to loan you the money to bring your son from England."

"To what, mum? No, not yet. When he comes, it's going to be to a place far away from here, where nobody knows me."

"I understand, Sassy." Idalee shifted the tray in her hand and reached for the doorknob behind her. "For now, you better go on back to bed and get your beauty sleep. You've only got a couple hours left, and men don't tip a girl with circles under her eyes very well."

"Right you are, mum."

Idalee watched for a second as Sassy walked away, waiting until she rounded the corner in the hallway before opening the door. Sassy liked to talk a lot, and she wouldn't put it past the woman to remember something she wanted to discuss and turn back to do just that. Today Sassy's sleepiness overcame her desire to talk though, because the woman didn't hesitate as she made her way down the stairwell leading to her second-floor room.

Closing the door softly behind her, Idalee walked silently to a table to set the tray down. An ice cube in the crystal glass beside the pitcher shifted, tinkling loudly in the quiet room. She felt as much as heard Storm come to immediate alertness, and when she turned back, his black eyes met hers without a sign of drowsiness.

"Storm, you know you don't have to be afraid here. No one saw you come in, did they?"

"'Course not, Idy. But some things just become ingrained in a man."

"I don't need to ask what you mean by that," Idalee said with a sigh. "But you're so tired. Why don't you have your lemonade and then lie down on my bed for a nap? I've got some things to do below and everyone here has strict orders not to enter my quarters uninvited."

"Even Elias, Idy?"

Idalee ducked her head to hide her flushed cheeks and turned back to the pitcher of lemonade. A little sloshed over the side of the glass when she poured it with a slightly shaky hand, but she wiped it on a linen napkin and turned to hand it to Storm.

Storm took a long swallow and sighed contentedly as he leaned back in the chair again.

"You know, Idy," he continued as though unaware of the embarrassment his words caused the petite woman, "I just don't understand it. Why, Elias cooks well enough to have a fine restaurant somewhere. And I've never seen two people who are meant for each other more than you two. Seems a shame you're both buried out here in the wilderness. You always did have a yen for the finer side of life. I remember more than once when I had to pull you away from the fashion magazines each time a new one arrived in the dress shop."

Idalee abruptly turned away from him and flounced over to her bed. She grabbed the newel post holding up the canopy and kept her back to Storm when she spoke. "No, you don't understand, Storm," she threw over her shoulder. "These girls need me. Why, there's not a one of them who isn't working toward getting a better life for herself. They don't stay here long. I know Sassy's got almost enough money saved to bring her son from England and to start a little business of her own somewhere. And I'll bet my corset that Catarina's going to end up leaving with Eddie when he finally gets up nerve enough to break away from that arrogant uncle of his and buy his own spread. Besides . . ." Her voice fell to a whisper, but Storm caught her words. " . . . he hasn't asked me."

Storm rose to his feet and drained his glass before he placed it beside the pitcher. On cat-soft feet, he crossed the room and folded his arms around Idalee. When she turned and buried her face in his chest, he tightened his arms and dropped a kiss on her red-gold curls.

"Maybe you ought to do the asking, Idy," he said in a gentle voice. "Seems to me it shouldn't always have to be the man's responsibility to ask. We're just as afraid of getting turned down as we can be."

Idalee shook her head against his chest. "Oh, I couldn't," she breathed. She drew her head back and stared into his dark eyes. "I couldn't, could I?"

Storm raised a hand and caressed her cheek with his index finger. "Just think on it, Idy," he said. "Time doesn't stand still for anyone. Days pass and turn into years, and neither one of us is getting any younger. You have to decide if this is the way you want to spend the rest of your life, just because you want to rub their noses in the embarrassment you're causing them. Or if you want to reach for the things we dreamed about when we were kids."

Storm dropped his arms and turned to look out the window. "And speaking of time passing, I better get going. You might be surprised, but it's a whole lot easier slipping in and out of town in a crowd than it is after dark. Guess people just aren't as much on guard."

"Storm, don't go," Idalee said as she reached out to grasp his arm. "You need to rest awhile. And I can cut your hair and get you some decent clothes before you go."

"Can't, Idy," he said with a negative shake of his head. "No matter what you think, it's not safe for me here. I just stopped by to let you know I was around and thank you for all you've done."

Idalee sighed hopelessly as she watched him walk to the rear wall and push gently on one of the sections of paneled wood. The doorway to the hidden passageway opened on silent hinges.

"Storm," she said, trying to hold him a moment longer. "Isn't there anything else I can do?"

Storm paused, his hand still on the doorway. "Well, there might be one thing."

"What?" she said eagerly. "There's got to be a way we can clear your name."

"That's not what I meant, Idy. There's only one way to do that, and I'm not sure I have the right to ask that of her." His soft voice took on a thread of steel. "But one way or the other, I'm gonna break the hold those bastards have on this valley. If it means seeing them dead to do it, then so be it. They've already made me an outlaw. Might as well have the satisfaction of at least earning that reputation myself."

"Storm," Idalee said with a gasp, "that's not you talking!"

Storm caught himself abruptly and smiled across the room at Idalee. "Don't worry, honey. I haven't totally given up yet. Anyway, what I was talking about a moment ago. Do you think you might talk Elias into taking you for a ride tomorrow afternoon?"

Idalee tried to sort out her thoughts at his abrupt change of subject. "A ride? Why . . . why, I guess so. We do that sometimes."

"Have you seen anyone new ride into town today?" he questioned her.

"New? Whatever are you talking about, Storm? Well," she admitted when he continued to stare at her in silence. "Well, I did see a man and woman ride in today. The man was older, but the woman was awfully pretty. In fact, they stopped right here under my window for a moment and seemed to be looking at my flowers. Then they went on into town."

Storm again, to Idalee's mind, abruptly changed the subject. "You remember that waterhole where we used to swim when we were kids? Think you could ride out that way?"

"Of course I remember it, Storm. Why wouldn't I? And, yes, it's a pretty ride, and I'm sure Elias wouldn't mind. But whatever for?"

"I spotted a good-looking roan stallion and another horse grazing out that way when I came by. The stallion's bred too well to be a mustang and my guess is he belongs to someone. You might ask that woman who rode in with her friend if she knows anything about those horses when you get them back to town."

"You come back here and explain yourself!" Idalee said with a stamp of her foot as he ducked inside the door. "Storm B—"

His head reappeared, cutting off her words. "I've asked you not to call me that, Idy," he said quietly just before he disappeared again.

Idalee ran across the room, but she already knew he wouldn't be there when she pushed the door open again. She stared down the receding passageway into the dimness, her mind filled with questions. But one thought came to the forefront.

"What about you, Storm?" she whispered into the silence. "When will you be able to reach for the dreams we shared with each other years ago?"

Then, "I love you, Storm," she called quietly into the darkness. Somehow it didn't matter that she didn't dare speak loudly enough for him to hear. Somehow he would know.

Chapter 8

Jessica walked into the bank the next morning, a determined step to her stride. She couldn't wait to get out of this town. The only happy person she had met was Eloise, who caught every eye in the dining room last evening as she served the meals. She hadn't thought to ask Eloise how close her wedding day was, but it must be soon. The blonde had bubbled and smiled at every diner, though once in a while she stared off into space, a dreamy expression on her face.

And today the man had promised her Cinnabar. He hadn't said how, though. Would he deliver the stallion to town? If so, she probably should delay their departure for a while, to give him a chance. Or maybe she would find Cinnabar on the trail. Would the man be with him?

A rancher in worn clothing stepped away from the teller window in front of Jessica, his shoulders slumped and a shattered expression on his face. Immediately, a similarly dressed man moved out of line at the other window and threw an arm across the rancher's shoulders.

"Baker wouldn't let you extend, huh, Cam?"

"No," the man replied in a tortured voice. "The hell of it is, I could've paid what I thought it was I owed on the ranch. But he said there were extra charges I agreed to in that paper I signed. I only wanted another month to pay them, but the teller said Baker wouldn't give it to me."

"Miss? Miss, you're next."

Jessica shook her head sadly in response to the overheard conversation as she stepped up to the window. A few seconds later, she stared at the teller behind the barred window, enraged.

"What do you mean you can't let me have my money? I gave you authority yesterday to wire my bank and have the funds transferred. I wish to make a withdrawal immediately!"

"I'm sorry, miss," the teller explained again in a patient voice. "There are no funds. Mr. Baker always handles that sort of thing and he'd have been the one to wire your bank. He hasn't notified me of any money to be released to you."

"Then I want to see this Mr. Baker immediately," Jessica fumed. "In fact, I asked to see him yesterday, but he apparently wasn't available. I insist on seeing him now!"

"Mr. Baker didn't come in until after you left yesterday, Miss Callaghan," the teller replied. "But he is in now and I'll ask him if he can see you."

"You will not *ask*," Jessica informed him. "You will tell him that I *demand* to see him!"

A man slouched against the door of the office located in the rear of the bank, then straightened, and his lips curved into a smile under his blond mustache. This might be interesting. Things were running so smoothly these days, he could use a little excitement in his life.

He frowned slightly. Well, almost everything, but he could handle that later. Right now, a sable-haired vixen with a body that made his hands itch stood in front of the teller's cage, patting her foot in anger. Wonder what it would take to turn that temper into the fiery passion he could sense under that lushly feminine exterior? It had been too long since any woman challenged his sense of masculinity.

"I'll take over now, Parkins," he called as he crossed the room. "Harlin Baker, at your service, miss," he said when Jessica swung around to fix him with a furious glare from eyes he found a delightful shade of warm brown. Though he could make out the gold flecks in them caused by her anger, they only highlighted a face that was a perfect match for that beautiful body.

"And who might you be, miss?" he questioned with raised eyebrows.

"As if you couldn't hear the teller call me by name perfectly well," Jessica informed him with a haughty look. "Your office is close enough to this teller window for that."

"I apologize, Miss Callaghan." Baker cupped his hand across his stomach and bowed. "It's a delight to see someone as lovely as you in our town. It's been much too dreary here lately."

"I'm not interested in what you think of my looks, Mr. Baker. I'm only interested in withdrawing the funds I had transferred here from my bank in Wyoming and getting some supplies so I can be on my way. But you are right about one thing. This *is* a dreary little town."

Though he normally wouldn't have, Baker ignored the slur on the town—his town. Instead, he made his position in the town clear by allowing his pale blue eyes to wander over her and drink their fill.

Jessica drew in her breath with a gasp of indignation when his eyes lingered on her breasts, encased in the tight bodice of her dark blue dress. Her palms itched with the desire to slap the smug sneer from the full lips partially hidden by the blond mustache. Only Ned's muttered warning of "Jes" stilled her right arm when it came up to do just that.

Satisfied with Jessica's reaction, Baker's eyes went cold and he turned abruptly. "If you'll follow me, Miss Callaghan, we'll continue our discussion in the privacy of my office. There seems to be a slight problem concerning the transfer of funds you requested."

"Problem?" Jessica furiously stomped after him. She heard Ned following behind her, his limping steps hurrying to catch her.

At the door of his office, Baker paused and turned. "You might wish to have this discussion alone, Miss Callaghan," he said when he saw Ned beside Jessica. "After all, cowhands aren't usually invited into business discussions."

Jessica's head rose proudly and she cupped her hand into Ned's arm. "Ned is my foreman and my friend," she informed Baker in a steady voice. "There's nothing I keep private from him."

Jessica heard Ned give an almost silent snort and turned to meet his bemused gaze. The words of their conversation the previous day crept into her mind and, for just a second, she found the face before her fading. In its place she saw a dark, much younger countenance and felt a whisper of air tinted with a vaguely comforting masculine scent feather around her face.

Jessica quickly shook her head to clear it and looked back at Baker. "Ned will be joining us, Mr. Baker."

"As you wish," he said with a shrug. He led the way into his office and motioned for Jessica and Ned to take the chairs in front of his desk.

"No, thank you," Jessica said. "This won't take but a moment. I just need to know how soon my funds will be available."

Baker lowered himself into the padded chair behind the desk before he faced her with eyes faintly hooded.

"I guess that will depend upon how soon you can arrange for your mortgage payment on your ranch in Wyoming to be paid, Miss Callaghan."

"What's that got to do with it?" Jessica asked. "That payment's not due for almost another month yet."

"Oh, yes," he mused. "I do seem to recall Mr. Olson's telegram stating that. But it also stated that he seems to have some doubt of your being able to make that payment. Therefore, he's put a hold on the funds you have deposited with him to assure he's not left totally without at least a portion of his money. You see, my dear, banks have to be careful about losing money. After all, the money we loan out does, in truth, belong to our depositors."

"He can't do that!" Jessica gasped. "He has no right!"

"Oh, probably not legally," Baker admitted. "But ethically, he has to protect his other depositors. I imagine he'd lose a court case over this matter, but you'll have to return to Wyoming and get an attorney to fight it for you."

"But that might take months! And by then I'll have the mortgage payment made. I need funds now to get supplies for my men."

"I'm sorry, Miss Callaghan," Baker said in a voice that belied just that. "There's nothing I can do. By the way, what is it that brings you to Baker's Valley? Surely it's not business that can't be taken care of later."

"It . . . it's not really business," Jessica said in a distracted voice. The worry in her mind crowded out the thought that Baker had no right to question her presence in the valley.

"It's . . . it's land," she said, giving him the story she and Ned had decided to use while they searched for the gold. "I thought maybe to sell out in Wyoming and start again here."

"There's no land available here, Miss Callaghan," he told her in a flat voice. "You might as well look elsewhere—perhaps far south of here."

"Why, of course there is," Jessica said in astonishment. "We rode over a lot of land on the way here with no one on it. We passed a few scattered, smaller ranches, but there's thousands of acres of vacant land."

"Some of that land belongs to the Indians," Baker informed her. "Though I have no idea why our government gave anything at all to those damned redskins instead of just completely annihilating them. And some of the land's free range, which the the government has no intention of selling. The smaller ranches holding on around here don't have enough acreage even to be profitable."

"Then why don't they use the free range?"

Baker rose to his feet. "I'm really very sorry I can't be of any help to you, Miss Callaghan. I—"

The office door opened with a bang as it hit the wall behind it. Jessica gave a start and turned quickly around to see a slightly smaller version of the man behind the desk framed in the doorway. But where Harlin Baker just missed being handsome because of his pale blue eyes set somewhat too close together, this man embodied all the word meant. Jessica couldn't quite quell a stir of feminine appreciation.

His blond hair brought thoughts of sunshine into the room, and a fringed leather riding jacket fit his shoulders snugly. Though, if one went by his manner of dress, he had just come off the trail, the trail dust must not have dared settle on the jacket. Even his boots gleamed smartly and the hat he slapped against his fitted trouser legs kicked up only a minuscule puff.

"Harlin, you old dog," he said in a strangely musical voice for his size. "You don't waste a moment, do you? Why, a beautiful woman rides into town and here you have her corralled already without giving the rest of us a chance even to meet her."

Rather than finding herself piqued at the man's obviously admiring gaze, Jessica felt a flush stain her cheeks. She immediately dropped her gaze when the man's brilliant blue eyes met hers, and studied the toes of her riding boots, sticking out from under the hem of her blue dress. Grasping her skirt, she quickly covered the offending boots she had been forced to don when she realized she had brought a dress with her, but no shoes.

"S–sir," she said in a small voice. "You have no right to say such things about me."

The man crossed the room in two strides and picked up her hand. Before she could stop him, he carried it to his mouth and dropped a kiss on the back of it, his mustache tickling her. He didn't hold her hand any longer than propriety allowed, but Jessica felt his fingertips brush her palm before he released it.

"I apologize if I've stepped out of line, dear lady," he said, smiling. "Oh, not for calling you beautiful. I'm sure your own eyes confirm that to you each morning when you look in your mirror. But you are correct. I don't have any right to say such things to you on such short acquaintance, since we haven't even been introduced yet."

He backed up a step and imitated Harlin Baker's bow of moments ago. However, his bow seemed sincere and his voice echoed his sincerity when he raised his head again.

"David Baker, at your service, my dear. And I already know your name. Why, every man in town knows the name of the sable-haired beauty who rode in yesterday. Is there anything I can do for you, Miss Callaghan? I sensed somewhat of a strain between you and that brother of mine when I entered. I hope he hasn't done anything to upset you. A beautiful woman such as you should be treasured and protected from anything distressing."

Jessica shook her head in denial. "No. It's . . . it's not your brother's fault. There seems to be some problem with my bank in Wyoming. I guess I'll just have to go back there and take care of it."

"What?" David said in astonishment. "And deny us the joy of your presence so soon? Surely there must be something we can do about that. You can't just come into our lives and leave so suddenly."

"Mr. Baker . . ."

"David. Please. And I hope soon you will allow me to address you as Jessica."

"Mr . . . David, then." Jessica looked around almost wildly for Ned and found him leaning against the office wall. When he gave her an encouraging nod, she drew in a steadying breath.

"David, I hadn't meant to stay in town anyway. I just stopped here to replenish our food supply. Someone stole our food pack, along with two of our horses, while we camped the night before last."

"Stole them? Have you reported it to the sheriff?"

"Of course. Ned stopped there yesterday after we arrived in town, but the sheriff didn't seem to think there was much he could do about it."

"Such things should not go unpunished. Since I'm not without influence in town, I'll go over there with you again and make sure the sheriff gets right on this, my dear," David said as he tucked her arm in his and began to lead her from the office.

Jessica tugged against David's arm and threw a look over her shoulder to where Harlin Baker still stood behind his desk. "But . . . but my funds?"

David stopped and turned back to his brother. "Funds? Harlin, are you keeping Miss Callaghan from her funds?"

"It's not like that," Harlin replied in an exasperated voice. "David, we need to talk for a moment."

"Later, Harlin." David waved a hand at his brother. "Right now I'm going with Miss Callaghan. And then perhaps I can talk her into discussing her problems with me over lunch?"

"Lunch?" Jessica said. "But, Mr. Baker, I hardly know you."

"David, please. And if we have lunch together, it will give us an opportunity to correct that, now won't it?" he told her logically. "Oh, don't worry." He glanced sideways at Ned. "You will join us, won't you, sir?" he asked Ned. "I wouldn't for the world jeopardize Miss Callaghan's reputation."

"Well, I . . ."

"David," Harlin said in a warning voice.

"Harlin, I know we have some things to talk about, but you've got to admit they can wait. I can hardly leave Miss Callaghan in distress if there's some way I can help her, now can I?" Ignoring the sputters from his brother, David steered Jessica out the office door and across the bank lobby.

Ned glanced once from Harlin to Jessica's and David's retreating backs before he firmly placed his hat on his head and started after the couple. No, he wouldn't let Jessica's reputation be tarnished, and just maybe there was some way this chap could help her out. He had definitely seemed likable yesterday afternoon while they drank together.

"There you are," Ned said a while later as they approached the hotel. "Missed you at breakfast."

Jedidiah rose from the bench by the door and pulled his hat a little further down on his brow.

"Tol' Miss Callaghan I'd be 'round when she needed me. I don't cotton to spending too much time cooped up indoors, but I keep my word."

David pulled Jessica to a stop a few feet back from Ned and Jedidiah. "Do you know that old man?" he whispered in her ear.

Hearing the mockery in his voice, Jessica raised her head and glared at him. "What if I do?"

"Nothing," David assured her. "Well," he said when she continued to stare at him, "you just seem to have some unusual friends."

"Ned is *not* unusual," she almost spat at him. "And I've hired Jedidiah as a guide. Do you find some fault with that?"

"Since I don't even know the man, I can hardly answer that," David said with a frown. "I suppose those old mountain men ought to be worth something. I'm sure he's able to find his way around. He looks like he's spent enough time out of polite society."

"Oh!" Jessica said with an indignant snort as she drew her arm from his. "I'll have you know my Uncle Pete was a mountain man, and he was one of the most wonderful men who ever walked this earth!"

"I apologize, Jessica. I couldn't have known. Let's don't let a little thing like this spoil our lunch."

"Of course I won't," Jessica said sweetly.

When he reached for her again, she evaded his grasp and walked up to Ned and Jedidiah.

"Mr. Baker has kindly invited me and my *friends* to lunch," she said as she cocked her head at Jedidiah. "You will join us, won't you?"

The full beard hid the quirk of his lips, but Jedidiah's faintly sardonic chuckle sounded softly in her ears, reminding Jessica of her treatment of him the day before. She had the grace to blush slightly, but she kept her gaze on his face.

"Please," she added.

"Well, now," Jedidiah said so quietly only she could catch his words, "since you put it so pretty, little lady, how can I refuse?"

Jessica studied him for a second longer. Why did his choice of words stir something in her mind? But she shrugged and turned to lead the way into the hotel dining room, refusing again the offer of David's arm.

A half hour later, Jessica rearranged the food on her plate once again and finally shoved it back with a sigh. Inviting Jedidiah to join them hadn't been one of her better ideas. The tension at the table knotted her stomach until she could barely taste the succulent steak she had ordered.

She couldn't really blame David, she admitted to herself honestly. In an attempt to fill the long gaps of silence at the table, she had responded to his urgings to tell him how she had come to, as he said, his and his brother's fair town. David had given her his full attention, his manners impeccable and the admiration on his face a contradiction to the wry looks Jedidiah tossed at her now and then.

Not the true story about the gold did she tell him, though. It would take more than a handsome face and twinkling eyes filled with devilment to get that out of her. But the sympathy shining from those same blue eyes when she explained her desire to leave the sad memories of her life behind and start over almost had her believing the tale herself.

David had even once or twice tried to draw Jedidiah into the conversation, Jessica conceded to herself, his attempts meeting a blank wall. Jedidiah would only grunt a noncommittal answer and smack his lips more loudly around the next bite of food he shoved into his mouth.

Jessica glanced at Jedidiah. Why, he had even refused to remove his battered old hat inside the hotel. She watched him wipe the back of his mouth with his hand, then pull the linen napkin from his neck and sit back with a sigh.

"Mighty good," he said. "Almost forgot what store-bought food tasted like."

"Mr. uh, Jedidiah," David said in a pained voice. "A hotel dining room is hardly a store."

"Same thing," Jedidiah said with a shrug. "Sells food a man don't have to trap or ketch himself. Store-bought food."

Jessica couldn't quite contain her giggle and she had to bite her lip when Jedidiah dropped one eyelid in a wink at her. She heard David give a resigned sigh beside her and she hastily lifted her own napkin to her lips to hide her smile.

David raised his hand and immediately Ronnie appeared again by their table.

"We'll have four orders of your delicious strawberry shortcake, Ronnie," he said in an imperious voice.

"Oh, David, no," Jessica said. "Really, I couldn't eat another bite."

"Speak for yourself, Jes," Ned said. "Bet me and Jedidiah have got enough room left to do justice to a piece of strawberry shortcake."

"Sure do," Jedidiah said with a nod.

"Four pieces, Ronnie," David repeated.

"Yes, sir," the woman said before she hurried away.

"Poor Ronnie," Jessica said as she watched the woman leave. "With all she's got to do, I wonder why she's waiting tables. That's Eloise's job."

"You haven't heard, Jessica?" David questioned. "No, I guess you wouldn't have, being newly arrived in town. You wouldn't be tuned in yet to our town's virulently swift grapevine. Gossip sweeps like wildfire through the town when anything either bad or good happens."

From the corner of her eye, Jessica noticed Jedidiah straighten in his chair.

"What happened to her?" Jedidiah asked before Jessica could speak again.

"Did you know her, too, Jedidiah?" David asked with a raised brow.

Jedidiah quickly dropped his gaze. "Not hardly," he said as he speared a last piece of steak from his plate, though he didn't bring it to his mouth. "'Specially since I ain't been in town for a while. Used to know someone called Eloise, that's all."

"I hope the woman you knew fared better than our poor Eloise," David said sadly. "You see, she was found dead in her room at the boardinghouse this morning."

"Oh, no!" Jessica gasped. "Why, last night she served us dinner. How could she have gotten ill so fast?"

"It wasn't illness, my dear," David said with a slight shake of his head. "I'm afraid someone murdered her."

Though she had barely known Eloise, Jessica's face whitened and her stomach churned in horror. Eloise had been so sparkling and alive with anticipation for her future the previous evening. How could such vibrancy be snuffed out so quickly? Suddenly she realized the cause for the morose unhappiness on Ronnie's face she had noticed but been too busy to question on her way to the bank earlier.

"Do they know who did it?" she asked David.

"Not exactly," he answered. "Though there are, again, rumors." He fell silent when Ronnie returned and set their shortcake in front of them.

Before Ronnie could move away, Jessica reached out and took the older woman's hand in hers. "I'm sorry, Ronnie. David just told me about Eloise."

"She—" Ronnie's voice broke on the word, but she straightened her shoulders. "She was a good girl, Jessica," she continued in a firmer voice. "Been with me for over three years. Almost like a daughter to me, she was."

"Did she have any family?" Jessica questioned.

"None," Ronnie said dejectedly. "Orphan, she was. Her parents were killed in a fire on their ranch just before she came here and applied for the job. She and Tobias would have been married next week, though, and she'd have had a family again."

"Tobias? Oh, her young man."

"Right fine young man he is, too. I don't know if anyone's even told him yet. Him and his mute sister live so far out on that there ranch that it's hard to get to them."

"But someone has to tell him! If they were betrothed, he'll want to see she has a proper burial."

"Now, Jessica," David interjected. "It's not your worry. I'm sure the sheriff has already sent someone out to the Jackson ranch."

"Me and Buster will see that she's buried proper, Jes," Ronnie informed her. "We've already ordered the box and the service will be the day after tomorrow. We'll find some way to get word to Tobias so he can be there."

Jessica shoved her chair back. "Well, I'm going back to the sheriff's office and make sure he sends someone out to that ranch right now. Her Tobias will never forgive everyone if he isn't sent word. And it's the sheriff's duty to inform loved ones at a time like this."

"Really, Jessica," David said as he rose to his feet. "This isn't a matter you need to concern yourself with."

"Death concerns everyone, David," she informed him frostily. "I'm surprised a man who seemed so sympathetic over a perfectly healthy woman's loss of a little bit of food and a couple of horses turns a cold shoulder to this matter."

"I'm sorry, Jessica," David said as he humbly hung his head. "I guess it's just that I resent not having a little more time to spend with you. And I do want to help you out of your predicament."

Two sets of chair legs scraped the floor as Ned and Jedidiah rose. Jessica gave a little start as Jedidiah grabbed his chair to keep it from tumbling to the floor after his abrupt shove.

"My problems can wait, David," she said, turning her attention back to him. "Some things are more important. Maybe we'll meet again and I do thank you for lunch." She held out her hand to him and David clasped it tightly for a second.

"We will see each other again, Miss Jessica Callaghan. You can count on that."

"Well, if you say so, David," she said, and firmly pulled her hand free. "And I also thank you for your efforts to come up with an idea to help me out. But I truly don't see anything else to do except go back to Wyoming and sort things out. Good-bye."

"Good-bye for now, Jessica," he murmured as she turned away.

Outside the hotel, Jessica felt Jedidiah grasp her arm. When she looked up at him, she found herself astonished at the cold blackness in his eyes.

"You don't need me right now, missy," he informed her in answer to her questioning gaze. "If you'll tell me where to meet you, I'll be there when you git ready to go."

Jessica jerked her arm free and rubbed at the goose bumps spreading over the area his fingers had covered. "Uh . . . I . . ."

"We've got some men camped about a mile out of town on a creek that runs down from the hill," Ned put in when Jessica stuttered to a stop. "Guess we'll probably be there in the mornin'."

Jedidiah nodded and abruptly strode away.

For a long moment Ned stared after him, then responded to Jessica's tug on his arm.

"We were on our way to the sheriff's office. Remember, Ned?"

"Yeah. Let's go."

As he walked beside Jessica, Ned shook his head. He hadn't seen her so concerned about anything besides her own problems for months, though she wasn't usually that way. More than one family down on its luck in Wyoming had felt her generosity. And Mattie never knew how many stray children she would find at the supper table—just that she had better have enough food to fill several empty stomachs, with scraps left over for an orphaned puppy or kitten.

Heck, Jessica had carried a picnic basket of food with her to school every day, never once bringing even an apple back home. And how many times had a dress Mattie sewn for Jessica shown up on one of the little girls perched at the heavily laden supper table, with Jessica insisting she had already tired of it?

He should have known her natural tendency to nurture the underdog would eventually surface again. The tragic death of the waitress and the fact the sheriff might not stir himself to notify the woman's betrothed angered him, too.

He couldn't help worrying a little at the inopportune timing of this latest crusade of hers, though. She did have that mortgage payment to make, which he guessed he could take care of with one telegram. She would be furious with him, but he wasn't about to see her ranch added to the list of losses she had so bravely borne the last couple of years.

Meantime, he wasn't in any hurry to leave Baker's Valley. Fate had thrown another loop into their lives— one Jessica wasn't even aware of yet. Suspicion nagged at Ned's mind and the promise he had made to himself years ago still held true. Pete's death didn't relieve Ned of the obligation he felt to repay the old mountain man for his own life.

Ned glanced down the street as they paused at the door to the sheriff's office, but he didn't see any sign of Jedidiah.

Chapter 9

Glaring her displeasure at the lawman, Jessica leaned across his desk. "I may not be a citizen of this town, Sheriff, but I *am* a taxpaying citizen of the United States. And I demand that you send someone out to tell that poor young man his betrothed is dead!"

"Just who do you think I can spare, Miss Callaghan?" The sheriff leaned his chair back against the wall behind him, firing Jessica's temper with his indolent slouch. "One of my deputies is investigating that murder case you're talking about and the other's out looking for your horse thief. At yours and Mr. Baker's insistence, I might add."

"Oh, pshaw," Jessica returned. "I'd have been perfectly willing to let that wait if you'd have explained this morning. Good Lord, who can compare the loss of my horses and a little food to a woman's life?"

"I'm not comparing it, Miss Callaghan. I'm only telling you why there's no one to send out to the Jackson ranch."

"What about yourself, Sheriff?"

The chair legs hit the floor with a thud. "I ain't got no desire to go out to the Jackson ranch," he said angrily. "Hell could freeze over before I'd stir myself to inform Tobias Jackson of anything."

"I find that attitude hard to accept," Jessica fired right back. "Especially since part of the taxes Tobias Jackson pays supports your salary."

"Jackson don't live in my county," the sheriff denied. "He lives just over the boundary."

Almost wishing she had brought David Baker with her to back up her demand, Jessica gave an exasperated sigh. This stubborn jackass obviously only practiced Baker law in Baker's Valley.

"Draw me a map of how to get to the ranch," she ordered. "I'll go myself."

"Ain't no ride for a woman to make. You might run into something you ain't prepared for."

"Ronnie said Mr. Jackson's sister lives out there with him. I imagine she makes the ride from time to time."

"Nope," the sheriff told her. "She ain't been in town for over a year. Ever since she got, uh, ever since she went dumb."

"Ronnie told me she was mute."

"Same thing," the sheriff said.

"It's not at all, and I'm sure the girl's brother wouldn't appreciate your slur on his sister."

"Doesn't matter what he thinks. It's the same thing. And I don't give a damn what Tobias Jackson thinks of me."

Jessica picked up a pencil from the desk and handed it to him. "This isn't getting us anywhere, Sheriff. The map."

"It's a good three-hour ride over rough country," the lawman warned, but he took the pencil and grabbed a wanted poster from the stack on the side of his desk. When Jessica only stared at him, he turned the poster over with a muttered oath and began to draw on the back of it.

The sheriff was wrong. It was a beautiful ride—after they finally got started. Jessica chafed at the delay, but had to admit they needed to stop by the general store for at least enough supplies to last the men for another couple of days. Of course they had to eat until she decided her next move, but Ned's insisting on paying for the supplies galled her pride.

She refused to return to the hotel and ask Buster for the loan of a room so she could change her clothes. He would probably demand that she pay for the short time she used it, though she thought Ronnie might have found a quiet corner for her. Instead, she made Ned stand guard outside the stall, holding his gelding, while she slipped into her riding clothes.

Now she looked out over the wildflower-strewn grass before her, and basked in the saffron sunshine warming her shoulders. That grass would fatten cattle to perfection. Not overgrazed like much of the land in Wyoming, it grew knee-high on the horses and waved gently in the afternoon breeze. The same breeze brought scents of the wildflowers to her and she closed her eyes and breathed in deeply.

Her horse stopped and Jessica opened her eyes. Ned sat with his horse turned sideways, blocking her path as he stared ahead of them. She shifted in her saddle in an attempt to see around him.

"Well, I'll be go to hell," she heard Ned say.

"Ned, what is it? Move so I can see."

When Ned only shook his head, she urged her horse around his. Her mouth fell open and she tugged on the reins, pulling the horse to an abrupt halt.

Just as quickly, Jessica gave a glad cry and lifted the reins, her knees already prodding the horse forward again. The animal shook its head, protesting her rapid change of commands, and Jessica shot Ned an angry glance when he reached out to grab her reins.

"Let go, Ned! That's Cinnabar and our packhorse!"

"These old eyes can see as well as your young ones, Jes, and they see the same thing you do. That stallion of yours is flanked by two riders and he don't look a bit happy about it. Best you wait and see why those two have your horses before you go chargin' over there."

The breeze blew Jessica's scent to Cinnabar and he raised his head to bugle loudly. He reared against his restraint, but the pull of the rope around his neck, fastened securely to one rider's saddle horn, brought him back down. Jessica watched in amazement as the smaller of the two riders leaned over to place a hand on Cinnabar's nose. Cinnabar nuzzled the rider back.

Ned's dropping her horse's reins and pulling his rifle from the scabbard drew Jessica's eyes. With a grim smile, she pulled the rifle free from the saddle she had borrowed from Patches.

The man's promise from yesterday rang in her mind. Someone else must have stolen Cinnabar from him, too. Unlike Ned, who casually laid the rifle across his saddle, Jessica snapped her rifle to her shoulder. Her well-aimed shot sent the hat flying from the larger rider's head.

The two riders immediately pulled their horses up and disappeared from their backs into the tall grass. The larger rider swatted his horse's rump, and the animals scattered, with Cinnabar still tied to the saddlehorn of one horse.

"Lordy, Jes," Ned grumbled beside her. "What'd you do that for?"

"They've got my horse," Jessica said grimly. "And I damned sure want him back."

"You ever think they might be bringin' him back?"

Some of the anger left Jessica's face. "Well, no. I just thought . . ."

Swaying grass indicated the two riders' progress as they crawled toward a large rock protruding from the ground. A second later, Jessica realized they had taken shelter, while she and Ned sat unprotected.

"Don't shoot again or I'll shoot back!" a male voice called across the space separating them. "Throw down your guns! Now!"

Ned shot Jessica a disgruntled look and tossed his rifle into the grass. "Do it, Jes," he ordered when she hesitated.

Jessica lowered her rifle and dropped it off the side of her horse.

"Now that six-shooter you've got, man!"

Ned sighed and gripped his pistol with his fingertips. He didn't even usually wear the six-gun, but he had taken to strapping it on after the fiasco of not having his rifle the night they had been attacked. A lot of good it did him now. He held the gun out so the man could see it clearly before he threw it down beside his rifle.

"Mister!" Ned called. "We didn't mean no harm! It's just that those horses you two have belong to the lady here! We just want them back!"

A small head popped up from the rock, immediately covered by a large hand and shoved back down again.

"Ride forward!" the voice ordered. "With your hands out in plain sight!"

Ned spread his arms out and kneed his gelding forward.

When the packhorse balked, Jessica reached for her reins to control it. The rifle ball kicked up a clump of dirt by her side, sending the horse plunging frantically. She screamed and grabbed for the horse's mane just a second too late as a powerful kick from the animal's hind legs tossed her tumbling over its head.

An answering scream came from behind the rock, but Jessica never heard it. The thick grass cushioned her somewhat, but her contact with the ground forced the wind from her chest. Roaring filled her ears as she fought to regain her breath.

Ned glanced briefly in the direction of the rock as he swung from his gelding. The smaller of the two riders slapped at a restraining arm, breaking free to run toward them. Ned only assured himself that the feminine figure in the riding skirt didn't carry a gun before he turned his attention to Jessica.

Gathering her against his chest, Ned held Jessica gently, his gnarled hand stroking her cheek as he watched her wide-eyed struggle for breath.

"Easy, Jes," he said. "It'll come back in a minute. Easy now."

A look of satisfaction crossed Ned's face when Jessica drew in a gasp of air and blew it out with a whoosh. A second later the alarming redness on her cheeks faded and she breathed freely again.

"Oh, put that thing aside, Elias!" a woman said in an annoyed voice.

Ned glanced up to see the woman shove at the rifle barrel pointed toward him and Jessica, but the man with her held it out of her reach.

"Oh, for pity's sake," the woman said. She tossed the man an irritated look and knelt beside Ned. Her soft hand reached out to stroke Jessica's hair.

"I'm so sorry," the woman said. "We didn't mean for you to get hurt. But, after all, you did fire first."

Brown eyes met green, and despite the ignominy of her position, Jessica felt a stir of liking for the woman gazing down on her. She smiled in embarrassment and pushed herself up into a sitting position.

"I'm fine," she said. "Just got the wind knocked out of me. And I'm sorry for shooting, but I've been looking all over for Cinnabar. I was only firing a warning."

"I can vouch for that," Ned put in. "She can shoot the burr off another horse's rump and never disturb a hair on the horse, even when she's gallopin' hell-bent for leather. Heck, won't nobody enter the county fair matches back home if Jes's name's on the list."

"Your warning ruined a good hat," the man said sternly.

The woman giggled softly. "You're just mad because your masculine pride's pricked over a woman being able to shoot like that." Her own hat hung on her back, held by the strings tied through the brim. Sunlight sparkled on her red-gold curls as she held out a small hand to Jessica.

"I'm Idalee Morgan," she said as Jessica accepted the offer of friendship. Idalee glanced up at the man who stood a few feet away, his rifle still at a half-mast of readiness.

"And that wary fool is Elias Gant. Elias, please. I asked you to put that rifle down. These two aren't going to hurt us."

Ned rose slowly to his feet and held his hand out to Elias Gant. "I apologize, Mr. Gant," he said. "I'm Ned Daniels. And we are unarmed. You saw us toss our guns down."

Elias shifted his rifle to his left hand and pointed the barrel down at the ground. He clasped Ned's hand in a firm grip and his lips twitched when he glanced down at Jessica.

"It's not you I'm worried about, Mr. Daniels."

"You'll have to forgive her, Mr. Gant," Ned said after he dropped Elias's hand. "The impetuousness of youth, you know. And I've been Ned, not Mr. Daniels, to people for more years than I care to remember."

Jessica's eyes widened and her shock at Ned's words overrode the meaning. "Ned," she said without thinking, "I didn't even think you knew the word impetuous."

"Lots of things you might not know 'bout me, Jes," Ned returned, lapsing back into his cowboy drawl. "Elias, that's Miss Jessica . . ."

"Callaghan," Idalee finished for him.

Jessica accepted Ned's extended hand and pulled herself to her feet. "I assume you both must be from Baker's Valley," she said when she could face Idalee again, though she did have to look down a couple of inches into the smaller woman's eyes. "Seems like everyone there knows my name, even if I did just get into town yesterday."

"It's not that large of a town," Idalee said with a shrug. She studied Jessica closely. What in the world was Storm's connection to this beautiful woman? "Things do get around," she continued. "What are you doing out here?"

"We're on our way to see Tobias Jackson," Jessica replied.

Idalee gasped, but it was Elias's flat voice that broke the stunned silence. "Tobias doesn't like visitors. Do you have business with him?"

For the first time, Jessica looked closely at Elias, seeing a man only a little taller than herself. A full shock of nondescript brown hair covered his head. He had a straight nose, full lips now tightened, and a firm chin. But the strange, silver-gray eyes surrounded by lush lashes a woman would die for drew her attention almost magnetically.

"I . . . We . . ." Jessica cleared her throat and willed herself to wrench her gaze away and turn it on Idalee. "We . . . we don't exactly have business with Mr. Jackson," she explained. Her voice steadied now that she didn't have to contend with the draw of that silver stare. "We're just carrying a message to him. If you're from Baker's Valley, surely you've heard about Eloise."

Idalee's hand flew to her throat. "Eloise? No. My . . . my place is at the edge of town and I don't usually see anyone until evening. Elias and I have been out riding this afternoon. Please. Tell me what happened to her."

Facing the obvious distress in Idalee's eyes, Jessica found her words dying in her throat. Helplessly, she looked at Ned in time to see him give Elias a meaningful glance.

Elias immediately moved to put his arms around Idalee and his action heightened the terror in Idalee's eyes. Almost before Ned spoke, she was sobbing against Elias's shirt front. Her small fist pounded against his chest and she drew in a breath as she stared up at Elias, tears streaming down her face.

"Why, Elias? Why Eloise?"

"Don't, darlin'," Elias said, his finger wiping away a coursing tear. "You'll make yourself sick crying like this."

"But Eloise!" Idalee said with a wrenching sob. "She never hurt anyone. And what will become of Prudence now? Oh, Elias, Tobias will never get her any help after this. He'll keep her buried out on that damned ranch!"

Elias covered her mouth gently. "Shhhh. We'll talk later, Idalee. Right now, we have to get word to Tobias."

Jessica surreptitiously wiped at the tears threatening her own vision and stepped closer to touch Idalee's arm. "We'll take him word, Idalee. I made the sheriff draw a map to show me where his place is. Don't worry. We'll get word to him in time for the funeral. Ronnie's handling the arrangements, and she'll wait until the day after tomorrow for the burial."

Idalee stepped out of Elias's arms and pulled a handkerchief from the pocket of her riding skirt. She wiped her face clean and gave one final sniff, which seemed to calm her somewhat.

"I'm going with them, Elias," she said with a catch in her voice.

"No, Idalee," Elias returned in a soft voice. "You'll only make it worse. He won't let you come near."

"He probably won't let them near either." Idalee's toss of her head indicated where Jessica and Ned stood close by.

"I'll go," Elias said. "Maybe it'll be easier for him coming from me. In fact." His silver stare took in both Jessica and Ned. "In fact, I think the three of us better go. It might take us all to get close enough to tell him."

"But, Elias, if Jessica can go—"

"Jessica can handle that rifle, as you pointed out a minute ago," Elias interrupted. "You don't know one end of a gun from the other."

"Now just wait a minute, Elias," Ned said, taking a step forward. "If there's a threat of anyone gettin' hurt out there, you and me will go. I don't want Jes put in any danger."

Suddenly Jessica heard a whinny from a distance and saw Cinnabar standing a few yards away. Somehow he had managed to slip the noose from his neck, and he tossed his head up and down, the red mane and forelock catching

121

the breeze and floating around his head. She gave a glad cry and placed her fingers to her mouth.

Cinnabar responded at once to the shrill whistle, and a moment later, he stood quietly while she rubbed her cheek against his soft nose and stroked the sides of his muzzle.

"Oh, it's good to have you back, boy," she murmured, and Cinnabar nickered his agreement.

Jessica stepped back and faced Ned. "I'm going with you, Ned," she said, holding up a restraining hand when he tried to speak. "Ronnie said Mr. Jackson's sister is mute, and she'll need a woman with her if she cared as much about Eloise as her brother did."

"She did," Idalee confirmed, standing beside her.

"Then I'm going," Jessica repeated.

"Jes . . ." Ned tried again.

"Please, Ned," Idalee put in. "Elias is right. We used to be friends, but Tobias would never let me near Prudence now, though I don't really believe he would ever hurt a woman. Tobias won't be any help to Prudence himself when he finds out what happened, and she'll need Jessica."

"Jessica can ride with us," Ned gave in curtly. "But before we get to the Jackson place, I want some answers as to what exactly's going on here. I'll make the decision when we get there as to whether Jes rides in with us or not."

"Agreed," Elias said with a nod. He reached out to give Idalee a brief hug. "You'll go back to town as soon as we round up the horses."

"I will," Idalee said. "And I think I'll close down tonight. I really don't feel I can handle being open."

"That's a good idea," Elias said as he took the reins of the roan gelding. He glanced at Jessica. "Think you can climb on that horse of yours and help me go after the two we were riding—and my hat?"

Jessica's only answer was to swing up onto Cinnabar's back.

A couple hours later, Jessica pulled Cinnabar to a halt between the other two horses and leaned forward to stare at the small ranch spread out below them. Thank goodness the sun lingered in the summer days. The sheriff's words had finally proven true.

They had ridden through some rugged, though still spectacularly beautiful, countryside to arrive at their destination. Even Cinnabar—usually able to navigate any type of ground on fleet feet—pulled up blowing on top of one especially steep ridge. She couldn't imagine trying to cross such country in darkness, but they still had the ride back to contend with.

She waited for Ned to speak. She could tell he wasn't totally satisfied with Elias's explanation of the situation they found themselves in, and a few questions remained in her own mind.

Elias had said that Tobias Jackson had always been a solitary person, even in his youth. In fact, his parents, immigrants who had stayed behind in Baker's Valley rather than continue with the wagon train to Oregon, had kept pretty much to themselves.

Their ways were somewhat different, Elias admitted. Tobias had attended school off and on, but after Prudence was born, the Jacksons sheltered their daughter, refusing to allow her off the ranch unless her mother accompanied her.

"After the cholera epidemic that killed their parents," Elias had said, "Tobias kept the ranch going himself for a while. Idalee and Prudence got to know each other during that time. They'd both been sort of outcasts themselves, and they were as close as any sisters could be. Her friendship with Idalee was probably the only thing Prudence ever stood up to Tobias about."

"Idalee an outcast?" Jessica had questioned. "And how did they communicate?"

Elias's silver-hued stare had immediately told Jessica she had overstepped the bounds of polite questions.

"Prudence could speak as well as anyone else until a year ago," he had said grudgingly. "But I won't be a party to the gossip-mongering concerning either her or Idalee. Tobias sold the ranch that year, and moved up into the hills, where we're headed now. He came back from time to time for supplies, and to see Eloise, of course. Idalee had been hoping that after Tobias and Eloise got married, Eloise would talk Tobias into getting some help for Prudence."

Then Elias had flatly refused to discuss the reason for the enmity Tobias felt toward him and Idalee. It would have to suffice, he had told them, to know that it had started about the same time Prudence had lost her voice. If she and Ned decided they wanted to go back to town, he had added, he would ride on to the Jackson cabin himself and take his chances.

Jessica reached down to pat Cinnabar's neck. The action made her realize she had been so engrossed in Elias's story during their ride that she had failed to question why he and Idalee had had her stallion. But now thoughts of Prudence, whom she hadn't even met yet, pushed aside her question.

That poor woman, Jessica breathed silently to herself.

She watched that poor woman's gray skirt flutter around her legs as she crossed the ranch yard below them. Her slender figure swayed with the effort of carrying a large, wooden water bucket, and Jessica recalled Elias's calling her a girl, rather than a woman. The small figure could, in fact, perhaps be a young girl.

Way too far away to be able to make out any of the figure's features and ascertain her age, Jessica neverthe-less caught the glint in the dark curls tumbling down her back. The dying sun reflected golden highlights from the dark mass. She watched the woman set the bucket on the top step of the porch, then lean back for a moment with her hand against the small of her back to massage it. Jessica could almost feel the aching muscles the woman attempted to ease.

A second later the woman climbed the steps and dis-appeared into the house. A faint echo sounded when she let the screen door slam behind her.

Elias turned to look across Jessica at Ned, the creak of his saddle breaking the silence.

"Well?" he asked. "It will go easier on us if we ride on down while there's still some light left, if you two have decided to go along."

"I'm not so sure," Ned replied. "Might be easier if we go after dark and surprise them. Make sure this here Jackson fellow doesn't do anythin' to us while we tell him what we came for."

"You mean get the drop on him and tie him up?" Elias said.

"Oh, don't be silly," Jessica said.

The noise of a rifle cocking froze the three of them.

"Best you listen to the lady," a steely voice said behind them. "I'm the one who has the drop on you, and I don't want to hear any words from your lying tongue, Elias Gant. Raise your hands."

When Ned cast a warning glance at Jessica, she fought the urge to stick her tongue out at him and the silly gig-gle the impulse sent winging into her throat. The man had them cold and she definitely wouldn't risk their lives by not obeying his command. She raised her hands high above her head.

"Now," the voice ordered. "Turn your horses and go back where you came from. I've already protected my land from a trespasser once today, and I won't hesitate to do it again."

"Well, Tobias," Elias drawled logically, "I just really don't see how we can obey you. How do you expect us to guide our horses with our hands in the air? They might just stampede right down into your yard if we kick them in the sides now."

A brief silence descended and Jessica again found herself stifling the urge to laugh, though she couldn't imagine why. The man's voice told her he meant business, but she couldn't help imagining his look of consternation as he considered Elias's words. A brief giggle somehow passed her clenched lips.

"Shut up!" the man roared. "There isn't a damned thing funny in this!"

Jessica's slight shoulders shook and she had to struggle to keep her hands in the air. She wanted to cup them over her offending mouth and still the laughter, but she knew better than to lower her hands.

"I apologize, Mr. Jackson," she finally managed to gasp. "I guess it's just a woman's hysterics at finding herself on the verge of being shot. But, please. You have to listen to us. We've come here to tell you about Eloise."

The deadly silence lingered for a long moment before Jessica heard the man breathe out the name of the woman he loved. The click of the rifle hammer falling back into place sounded loudly into the stillness, and she waited quietly as the man ordered them to turn around.

Chapter 10

When she finally faced Tobias Jackson, Jessica wondered if the woman she had seen in the ranch yard could possibly be half as good-looking as her brother. They shared the same color hair, but his curled in ringlets and his lashes, almost as lush as Elias's, surrounded deep brown eyes in his handsome face. And his well-muscled body spoke of the maturity of his years.

Those eyes, though, now held an unfailing wariness and warning. He kept his rifle trained on them, one hand near the trigger and hammer.

"What did you come to tell me about Eloise, Elias?" he said abruptly, though a little of the steel had left his voice.

"Tobias, I—I don't even know how to say it. Oh, my friend . . ."

"I'm not your friend any longer, Elias," Tobias growled. "Tell me what you've come to say and leave my land.

Then I'll go to Eloise and see if you're telling me the truth."

"It's not as easy as that, my friend," Elias said softly. "She's dead. Since this morning."

Jessica felt her heart lurch in sympathy as she watched the agony fill Tobias's eyes. She had no doubt he believed Elias when his shoulders slumped and he dropped his head to hide his pain. The rifle slipped forgotten from his hands.

"How?" he asked in a choked voice.

"Tobias . . . she . . . she . . ."

Tobias raised his head, fixing eyes swimming with tears on Elias. "Tell me!" he demanded.

"She was murdered. They found her in her room this morning."

"No! It can't be true! Elias, please. Tell me you're just playing a cruel joke on me."

Elias shook his head and watched his gesture send Tobias wilting to the ground, where he buried his head on his knees. Elias stepped forward, then stopped. But when the sounds of wrenching agony erupted from Tobias's throat, he shook off his hesitation and knelt to put his arm around the other man's shoulders.

For an instant Tobias allowed himself to sag in Elias's arms. Then, with a lurch, he shook off Elias and rose to his feet, wiping ineffectively at his eyes.

"We . . . have to tell Prudence."

"That's why I brought Miss Callaghan with me, Tobias." Elias turned and introduced Jessica and Ned. "I thought Prudence might want a woman with her. Idalee wanted to come, but—"

"I won't have her here!" Tobias bellowed. "I won't have her near Prudence—or let her witness my grief and gloat at me. It's enough that you're here."

"Idalee wouldn't gloat, Tobias," Elias denied. "But I don't guess you'll ever believe that."

"Never!" Tobias spat. "Besides, she'll have her own grief to contend with."

"What do you mean?" Elias grabbed the other man's arm.

Tobias shook him off again and turned furious eyes on Elias. "The bastard came here. I'd heard he escaped prison, and I thought maybe God was smiling on me. But now I see He took His payment for my revenge on my sister's honor by taking Eloise. There's always a price to pay, isn't there? But if I'd only known, I'd have whipped the bastard before I killed him!"

"Storm. Oh, God, Tobias. You don't mean Storm was here?"

"I should've ridden in closer, to make sure of my shot," Tobias said in a deadly voice. "But I couldn't hold back from firing when I saw him below in the yard with Prudence. He had his hands on her—those damned hands that had held her in submission before. I couldn't chance his ravaging her again."

"Tobias, Storm didn't—"

"Yeah! So you and Idalee have said!" Tobias shouted with an angry toss of his head. "Over and over. But the court proved you both lied!"

"Where's Storm now? Tell me, or so help me God, I'll beat it out of you!" Elias demanded.

"Your *friend*," Tobias spat, "is lying dead somewhere near here. He couldn't have gone far, even if he did manage to get on that damned horse and outride me. I was looking for his body when I saw you three coming."

Jessica's eyes were burning with the effort of staring at the two men and trying to make sense of their words.

When Elias raised his clenched fists, she stepped forward, ignoring Ned's hand, which fell an inch short of restraining her.

"Both of you, shut up!" she said. "There's a dead woman back in town who deserves a little reverence from the people who knew her."

"You don't understand, Jessica," Elias said as he dropped his hands. "But . . . I don't guess you should."

Turning, he faced Ned. "Ned, I've got to go find Storm while there's still some light left. Will you and Jessica be able to find your way back alone?"

"I'm going down there with Tobias to break the news to his sister," Jessica informed them both.

"Please, Miss Callaghan," Tobias said, his voice again filled with grief, "I'd appreciate it if you'd do that for me."

"Don't worry, Tobias. That's what I came for."

"Then I'll be going," Elias said as he reached for his horse's reins. "If you aren't in town when I arrive, I'll come back looking for you."

"Elias." Jessica's voice stopped him before he could swing into the saddle. "I'll be all right. Ned could help you. Two people can search more area than one."

"I'm not leaving you alone, Jes," Ned insisted.

"She'll be well cared for," Tobias promised. "I give you my word on that. And with two of you searching, maybe I'll get word sooner that the earth is rid of that bastard for good."

Elias ignored him and looked at Ned. "I could really use your help, Ned. I can assure you, Jessica will be in no danger here with Tobias and Prudence. She can ride back into town with them tomorrow when they come in for Eloise's funeral."

"When?" Tobias choked out.

"It won't be until the day after tomorrow, Tobias," Jessica informed him. "Ronnie has arranged it. I'm sure she can find room for you and your sister at the hotel, if you want to spend tomorrow night in town."

"We'll probably do that," Tobias said, hunching his shoulders and turning away.

"I'm still not sure, Jes," Ned said as he took her arm and moved her off to the side. "Are you sure you want to do this? We don't really know these people. And I ain't so sure about this Jackson feller. He acts damned dangerous to me."

"It's the right thing to do, Ned." She patted his arm comfortingly. "Elias appears to feel that I'll be all right. I don't think he'd put me in a position where I'd be in danger. Even Idalee assured us that Tobias respects women. Prudence will need me, and right now Elias needs your help."

"All right, Jes. But if you aren't in town tomorrow with them, there'll be a whole band of mighty angry cowboys scourin' the countryside."

"I'm counting on that, Ned."

Her words told Ned she wasn't as totally sure as she appeared to be, but he nodded reluctantly and reached for his reins.

Jessica stirred up the fire and threw a dry log on it. She didn't think Tobias would mind her using the wood, but then she realized she really didn't know the man well enough to read his mind.

Oh, well. She shrugged her shoulders inside the cotton night rail Prudence had loaned her. Though she had thought she would fall quickly into a deep, untroubled sleep after her long ride today, she soon found the questions crowding her mind keeping her awake. And rather than spend hours tossing and turning in the small bed she shared with Prudence, she slipped out and sat in the rocking chair in front of the fireplace.

The flames crackled cheerfully, and Jessica sat down with one bare foot tucked under her. Her other foot rocked the chair gently when she touched it now and then on the cold floor. She almost rose to pull the braided rug nearer to cushion her foot, then sighed and settled against the chair back.

The flames blurred a little as Jessica recalled holding Prudence in her arms earlier while the young woman sobbed out her heartbreak at the news of Eloise. And, yes, Jessica told herself, she had definitely held a woman, though a slight-figured one. The breasts Jessica had felt under Prudence's gown confirmed Prudence's maturity. She must be at least almost out of her teens.

But one of the questions demanding an answer in Jessica's churning mind was why Prudence's eyes had already been red from crying when they had come into the cabin. Jessica shrugged. She must have been upset about the man Tobias told them had attacked her.

Idalee had been right. Tobias wasn't worth much at all. He had awkwardly patted his sister's shoulder, but had given up any attempt to comfort her almost immediately. Instead, he had slammed out of the cabin, not returning until after dark.

As soon as Tobias had informed Jessica they would leave at daybreak for Baker's Valley, he had disappeared into one of the small rooms at the back of the cabin and had closed the door. Once, though, while insisting Prudence eat at least a small bowl of the stew the other woman had previously prepared for the evening meal, Jessica had heard Tobias's agonized sobs through the door.

The telltale squeak of the door of the bedroom she shared with Prudence drew Jessica's attention, and she turned her head to see Prudence approaching her.

"Oh, Prudence," she said quietly. "I didn't mean to wake you."

Her short time with the other woman had already shown Jessica that Prudence understood everything she said. They had even been able to communicate a little in sign language, along with Jessica's spoken words. Now she watched Prudence shake her head negatively and pull the braided rug over to sit at Jessica's feet.

"I guess I didn't wake you, huh?" Jessica questioned. "You couldn't sleep either."

Prudence shook her head again and looked up at Jessica.

In the glow of the firelight, Jessica could swear she saw the muscles of Prudence's throat working as though she were trying to speak. Only a soft grunt emerged, though, and Prudence's face took on an almost furious glare. Jessica watched her jump to her feet and pull open the drawer of a small chest beside the fireplace.

Prudence rummaged in the drawer and finally turned with a piece of charcoal and a drawing pad in her hand. With a smile of satisfaction, she knelt down on the rug and motioned for Jessica to join her on the floor.

As soon as Jessica complied, her puzzlement clear on her face, Prudence laid a hand on her arm. She pointed a finger from her other hand at Jessica, then placed that hand over her heart.

Jessica nodded in understanding. "I like you, too, Prudence. Even though we've just met, I think we could become fast friends."

Prudence nodded emphatically before she dropped Jessica's arm and picked up the paper and charcoal. She drew with swift strokes for a moment, then held the paper out for Jessica to peruse.

Jessica tilted the paper so the firelight illuminated it, studying the picture Prudence had drawn. Mountains. The jagged peaks could be mountains or high hills. Clouds shot through with angry bolts of lightning obscured their tops.

"Yes, I see," Jessica said as she glanced at Prudence. "It's the land around you here."

Prudence shook her head and grabbed the paper from Jessica. She took the charcoal and quickly shaded in the clouds on the mountain tops. She pointed at them as her eyes implored Jessica to understand.

"It's not the mountains, is it, Prudence?" Jessica questioned. "The clouds. The clouds mean something."

A fringe of curls fell over Prudence's face as she shook her head up and down. She blew them from her face and tossed her head to throw them back into place. Again she pointed the charcoal at the clouds.

Jessica could feel the other woman's determination to make her understand, and her heart went out to her. What would she do if she ever lost her power of speech? She struggled to comprehend the drawing and found herself playing a word game with Prudence.

"All right, Prudence. They're clouds, but there's something else you want me to see in them. There are all types of clouds. You've colored them in. Black clouds?" she asked.

Prudence nodded.

"All right. Black clouds. There are different types of black clouds. Snow clouds?"

Prudence's negative shake of her head told Jessica she hadn't figured it out.

"Then rain clouds."

Nodding her head, Prudence looked at Jessica with hope in her eyes.

"Rain clouds. Rain clouds bring rain. Rain comes in . . . storms?

Prudence's throat began working again and she nodded furiously.

"Storm clouds," Jessica mused. "Prudence, are you trying to tell me something about this man named Storm whom your brother and Elias were talking about earlier?"

"Sss . . . Sss . . ."

The hiss issuing from Prudence's lips left Jessica no doubt of the other woman's attempt to speak. But Jessica assumed the long-unused throat muscles wouldn't cooperate.

"Prudence, don't," she said as she put a comforting hand on Prudence's arm. "It will come soon, if you relax and keep trying."

Prudence nodded compliance, then touched the clouds on the paper again.

"Storm. Yes, Prudence. I understand. You want to tell me something about Storm."

Prudence drew another stroke on the paper and Jessica recognized the outline of a rifle. The rifle pointed at the clouds, and Prudence added a puff of smoke beside the barrel.

"Yes, I know," Jessica said. "Storm was shot. Your brother shot him."

Slowly, Prudence nodded agreement before she turned her face up to Jessica. Leaving one hand on the clouds, she placed her other hand on her heart.

"You *like* Storm?" Jessica said in amazement. "But I gathered from your brother's conversation that this Storm rav . . ." Jessica couldn't bring herself to say the word.

"But Tobias said Storm hurt you."

The violent shake of Prudence's head told Jessica emphatically that the young woman didn't agree with her brother.

"Storm didn't hurt you? Is that what you mean?"

An affirmative bounce of the tousled brown curls indicated that Jessica had at last gleaned the message Prudence meant to send her.

"Have you told your brother?"

Prudence hung her head and pointed her finger at her ears, then at her lips.

"I see. He won't listen to you when you try to explain."

A hopeless look filled Prudence's brown eyes when she looked back up. She pointed at Jessica, then touched Jessica's heart and pointed back to herself. The despairing look gave way a little to the question in her eyes.

"I see. And, yes, I do like you and I am your friend. If there's any way possible, I'll try to make your brother understand. I'll speak for you."

Prudence leaned over and gave Jessica a hug before she rose to her feet. She pointed to the bedroom door.

"Yes. You go on back to bed now," Jessica said. "I'll be there in a while."

Prudence pointed to her head and widened her eyes.

"No, I won't forget, Prudence," Jessica said quietly. "I promise you."

After Prudence went into the bedroom, Jessica stared at the closed door for a moment. "I sure as heck don't see how I'm going to get anything through the mind of that pigheaded brother of yours, though," she whispered. "But I've promised you I'll try, and try I will."

Jessica turned back to stare into the fire. Just what had she gotten herself into? She had a ranch in Wyoming, demanding her attention—a ranch her father had carved out from the prairie with his own hands—a ranch Mr. Olson would claim in less than three weeks from now.

She and Ned had only come into this beautiful territory to search for the gold Uncle Pete assured her lay buried at the end of his map. She needed that gold, needed it to get her own life back in order.

Prudence's brown eyes, deep with trust before she went back to bed, rose up in front of her. How could she walk out on this small child-woman now? Obviously, Prudence had placed all the trust she held at bay from the rest of the world after her ravagement at Jessica's feet. She had to find some way to help Prudence.

And what damage had been done to the man named Storm? Tobias had mentioned a court hearing—and an escape from prison. Storm had evidently been wrongfully convicted of the rape. What was Storm, whoever he was, doing in the territory again, where the entire population was probably on the lookout for him?

Had she walked into a star-crossed lovers situation where Storm and Prudence were trying to overcome the odds against their love? If that was the case, why didn't they just run away together? Had it been a man she loved, Jessica told herself, a man like. . . .

Suddenly the frown on Jessica's face as she stared into the fire deepened and she slowly turned her head. Something scratched at the door. Up here in the high country, it could be a wild animal. When she glanced at the uncurtained window beside the door, she could swear she saw a head duck back down below the pane of glass.

Jessica rose slowly from the rug and stilled the rocking motion behind her when she bumped the chair. No sense looking around for her rifle. She clearly recalled leaving it in the scabbard of her saddle. Before taking a step, she picked up the fireplace poker. Her bare feet flinching at the coldness of the wooden floor, she gripped the poker firmly and forced her legs forward.

She paused a moment at the door, then lifted the latch as she raised the poker over her head. The door swung back on silent hinges and she gasped in surprise.

Chapter 11

"Shhhh, Jes. For God's sake, don't scream."

"Ned." Jessica lowered the poker and stared at the small man standing in the full light of the moon. "What in the world are you doing sneaking around out there? Why didn't you just knock?"

"Lower your voice, Jes," Ned whispered. "Don't wake up Tobias."

"He's dead to the world," she whispered in return. "But Prudence is sleeping restlessly."

"Too restlessly for you to get your things and slip out?"

"I don't know. What's going on?"

"We need your help, Jes. I'm afraid that man out there's goin' to bleed to death if you don't come. I had a medicine kit in my saddlebags, but nothing Elias or I did seemed to help. I know Mattie taught you somethin' about nursin' bullet wounds."

"You found the man Tobias shot? You found Storm."

"That's his name, all right. At least that's what Elias says."

"Where are the horses?"

"Cinnabar's still in the corral, Jes. You'll have to catch and saddle him. You know he won't stand still for me."

"Wait for me there, Ned. I'll find some way to slip into the room and get my clothes."

Prudence's eyes opened the moment Jessica slipped inside the bedroom door.

"Shhhh," Jessica said unnecessarily before catching the incongruity of the sound. She shook her head, then sat down on the side of the bed to take Prudence's hand in her own.

"Ned's back, Prudence. Oh, I forgot, you haven't met him. He's my friend, and he went with Elias a while ago. You do know Elias Gant, don't you?"

The glow of the moon coming in the window showed Prudence's eyes lighting up and a smile curving her lips.

"They came here with me to tell you and Tobias about Eloise," Jessica continued in a whisper. "And when Tobias told us he had shot Storm, Ned and Elias went out to look for him. Ned says they've found him and he's hurt. I know a little about nursing the injured and Ned wants me to come help them."

Prudence sat up and grabbed Jessica by the shoulders. Her throat muscles worked. "Huh . . . huh . . ."

"Shush. I will, Prudence. I'll help your Storm. At least, I'll do everything I can. But right now, you have to let me get my clothes and go. I'll leave a note for your brother on the table and tell him Ned and Elias couldn't find Storm. I'll . . . Oh, he probably won't believe that Ned just came back for me and we left in the dark to go back to town, but I don't have time to think of a better excuse. I'll see you in town tomorrow. All right?"

Prudence pulled Jessica close and hugged her briefly before she dropped her arms and rose from the bed. Taking Jessica's riding skirt from the nail where it hung, she held it out to her.

Once Jessica was dressed, Prudence held her arms out again. Jessica pulled the girl into her embrace and pressed her cheek against Prudence's. A second later, she slipped out the bedroom door, holding her boots in her hand. The door even cooperated, she found herself thinking with a smile. It didn't even squeak.

"Think you can find it now, Jes?" Ned asked as he pulled his horse up near the crest of a ridge.

"Of course. Why, we're almost halfway back to town and I always was good at remembering the country we crossed."

"Good. Then I'll get goin'. Hope there's enough darkness left for us to do this."

"It's only about midnight, Ned. But you'll have to ride hard. I don't see how you're going to get a wagon out here without someone from town seeing you, though."

"I ain't worried about that. I'm worried 'bout gettin' it back into town."

Ned nudged his gelding and left her sitting in the darkness.

Not waiting until Ned's hoofbeats faded, Jessica urged Cinnabar down the hillside, trusting his surefootedness in the darkness. At least they had crossed most of the rugged country to get there, and she didn't have to worry about Cinnabar's stumbling in the grassy valley she rode across. She glanced up gratefully at the full moon.

Soon the light of a small fire glowed in the distance. As Jessica approached the fire, her horse cocked his ears upright and stopped. The stallion turned his head to one side and Jessica heard a whisper.

"Jessica? Is that you?"

"It's me," she called back in answer to Elias's voice.

Elias stepped out from behind a sheltering rock. "Thought it was, but I wanted to be sure. Come on. He's over here."

A moment later, Jessica knelt by the blanket-wrapped figure beside the fire and gave a start of recognition at the same time as her heart twisted in agony. The night sounds receded around her, enclosing her and the man in a cocoon of silence.

Storm. She could finally put a name to the face that had haunted her dreams. Storm. Elias's friend, Storm, was the man who had made her senses blaze the night before they came into Baker's Valley. Storm had been the man who kept her from dying in agony from a rattlesnake bite.

The deathly pale face belonged to the man she had tried without success to push from her mind. Unconsciously, her hand caressed his wan cheek. Her fingers encountered a frightening coldness and she stifled a gasp of alarm.

Oh, God, she prayed silently, *please don't let this wonderful man be dying.*

Jessica drew her hand back guiltily. Storm. Prudence's Storm. The man Prudence loved, despite her brother's hatred of the man. How could she let herself remember the wonder she felt in this man's arms when he belonged to the poor mute girl she had left back at the little cabin?

Her face narrowed in a frown. And how could he hold her and kiss her that way when he had another woman in his life?

Elias's voice broke into her thoughts. "We've got to do something fast, Jessica."

The world crashed around Jessica, shattering the mixture of wonder and concern holding her in its grip. But she couldn't quite stop herself from just once more touching that cold cheek. She brought her fingers up through the silky hair, pushing it back from his face. Drawing her hand back, she gazed down at it in puzzlement as she rubbed a small ball of something sticky between her thumb and forefinger.

"Jessica," Elias said insistently, finally galvanizing her into action.

She hurriedly wiped her fingers on her skirt and looked up at Elias. "The bullet. Where did it hit?" she demanded.

"It's high on his shoulder. Here. I'll show you."

When Elias pulled back the blanket, Jessica caught her breath at the sight of the blood-soaked bandage. She forced her fingers to begin to unwrap it.

"A shot like this shouldn't kill a man," Elias said. "It's the bleeding. He's bleeding to death."

"The bullet's still in there. That's why," Jessica told him in a shaky voice. "It's going to have to come out before the bleeding will stop."

"Have you ever taken out a bullet?"

"Not by myself," she said tightly. "I helped Mattie once when one of our hands shot himself by accident while cleaning a supposedly empty gun. God, I hope I can remember what she did. Do you have a knife, Elias?"

"Yes, but . . ."

"Put it in the fire to heat the blade. We may have to cauterize this when we get the bullet out."

"Oh Lord," Elias breathed.

Jessica ignored him and stared down at the angry, black-fringed hole on Storm's shoulder. The blood only seeped out now, but it would probably be pouring again by the time she dug out the bullet. Her stomach lurched. She hoped he hadn't lost too much blood already.

"Do you have water, Elias? And a pail?"

"Yes. Ned and I cleaned him up before, but the blood just came back."

Jessica turned and dug in the medicine kit. "Here." She handed Elias the bullet probe. "Put this in the water and boil it."

Without waiting to see if he complied, Jessica removed a bottle of antiseptic from the kit. She snorted in disgust at the lightness of the bottle and, holding it up to the firelight, found it empty. She dropped it and bent her head over the pack again, her fingers groping until they encountered another bottle. Smiling in satisfaction, she pulled out a brown jug.

"Whiskey," she said to no one in particular. "It'll do just as well. It's a good thing he's unconscious, though."

But the moment she poured a measure of whiskey over the wound, Storm lurched and gasped. Black, pain-filled eyes stared up into Jessica's face. He clamped white, even teeth over his lower lip to stifle his groan of agony, but it rumbled in his chest anyway.

"Storm, I'm sorry," Jessica said as she laid a comforting hand against his cheek. "The bullet's still in there, and we have to sanitize the wound so I can get it out."

Storm covered her hand with his own and held it tightly when she would have pulled away.

"Pretty lady," he whispered. "Is it you? Or are you a ghost?"

Jessica laughed softly, though it took every bit of effort she could manage to rearrange her jumbled thoughts. The pleasure racing up her arm from his touch shook her to the core. How could she feel this way about a man lying wounded—perhaps dying—beside her?

"You were supposed to be the ghost, Storm. Remember?"

"I remember, pretty lady. And I guess you must be alive. I sure as hell wouldn't have ended up in heaven if I were dead."

"Don't say that."

Elias knelt beside Jessica. "Do you two know each other?" he asked in astonishment.

"Do we, pretty lady?" Storm's black eyes remained caught in the web flowing between the two of them. "You seem to have found out my name. Shouldn't I know yours?" he asked, though he full well knew the answer.

"It . . . it's Jessica. Jessica Callaghan."

"Jessica."

Never had she heard her name said so tenderly before. She nodded.

"I hope they don't call you Jes," Storm said. "It doesn't suit my pretty lady at all."

Jessica laughed shakily and pulled her hand free. "Well, they do," she said. "And sometimes Jes suits me just fine. Now, you stay quiet and save your strength. This isn't going to be easy for either of us."

"I'll save what strength I can, Jessica. But I can't promise to stay quiet when you start digging for that bullet. Hand me a piece of wood to bite on."

Elias reached behind him and picked up a piece of wood suitable for Storm to hold between his teeth. He glanced at the fire as he handed it to Storm.

"The water's boiling," he told her.

Jessica stilled Storm's hand when he started to put the wood in his mouth. "Here." Picking up the whisky bottle, she held it out. "You better drink some of this first."

When Storm tried to raise his head, Jessica quickly slipped an arm behind his neck to assist him. She smiled down at him as his eyes thanked her for a second, but his head wobbled weakly and she shifted so she could pull his head against her breast. Lifting the bottle, she placed it against his lips.

"Do you need some help, Jessica?" Elias asked.

"No. I can manage."

Lord, she wished she could hold him like this for the rest of the night. She didn't want anyone intruding on the sweet wonder filling her as she held him close. Shaking her head to clear it, Jessica forced herself to remember Storm's wounded condition. She held the bottle up again and urged him to take another swallow.

As soon as Storm complied, he went limp in her arms. She immediately set the whiskey bottle down, then gently lowered him to the blanket. After she brushed back a raven tress, she looked at Elias.

"He's passed out again. It will be easier on him this way."

"No," Storm whispered. "I'm not out, just weak. But go ahead."

Jessica nodded and forced her strangely reluctant fingers to dig into the medicine pack again. She pulled out some clean bandages and a pair of tongs to fish for the bullet probe when Elias held the pail out to her. Laying the probe down on a piece of clean cloth, she allowed it to cool for a moment.

"Do you want some more whiskey?" she asked Storm.

He only shook his head, gritting his teeth at the pain the movement caused.

Jessica steeled herself and picked up the probe. It was still too warm, and she quickly dropped it onto the stack of bandages. She wrapped the top one around the handle

146

and caught her lower lip between her teeth as she reached for the broad shoulder.

What seemed like an hour later, but could only have been five or ten minutes, Jessica stared down unbelievingly at Storm. His eyes, though half shuttered in pain, still remained open. The firelight reflecting in the ebony depths left no doubt as to that. She watched him take the stick from his mouth and hold it instead of tossing it aside.

"Are you going to have to cauterize it?" he asked in a surprisingly steady voice.

"I . . . I don't think so," she replied with a shake of her sable curls. "It doesn't seem to be bleeding that much. I think I can stop it now with a pressure bandage."

"Good." He flung the stick aside. "Then do it. I've got to get out of here."

"You can't ride!" Jessica said with a gasp.

"I have to," he returned flatly.

"He's right about that, Jessica," Elias confirmed. "If he can't ride at least a ways, we'll never get him back to town before daylight. I told Ned we'd meet the wagon partway."

"I'm not going into town!" Storm said emphatically.

"You're not going to have much choice, friend," Elias informed him sternly. "If you think I'm going to leave you out here injured and alone, you've got another think coming. Idalee would have my hide."

"I can't. Elias . . ."

"You know as well as I do that no one will see us bring you in, Storm. But we've got to get moving. Jessica, can I help you hold him while you bandage that wound?"

"Please, Elias. But I'm still not sure the ride won't kill him."

"He's tougher than you think," Elias said enigmatically. "He's had to be."

147

Storm proved the truth of Elias's words. It took both of them to get him to his feet, though, and Jessica believed they never could have gotten him on the horse if not for the well-trained paint. At Storm's command, the horse knelt on his front legs and allowed Storm to lean on his neck while Elias helped lift Storm into the saddle.

"Better tie my legs under me, Elias," Storm said as the pain shot through him. "I'm not promising not to pass out."

As Elias complied, Jessica scattered the ashes of the small fire and poured the remaining water over the embers. Moments later, the trio made their way through the darkness in the direction of Baker's Valley.

Twice over the next hour and a half, Jessica had to call Elias back to Storm's side from where he rode ahead of them. When Storm would sway dangerously in the saddle, she would unthinkingly urge Cinnabar close to help him regain his balance. Storm's stallion would lay his ears back and shy away from what it considered a challenge by the roan stud. However, the paint allowed Elias's mare near.

The third time she asked Elias if perhaps she should ride behind Storm to steady him.

"Can't," Storm answered her through teeth gritted in agony. "Won't . . . won't carry double."

"Is there any whiskey left, Jessica?" Elias asked.

Jessica turned in her saddle and pulled the whiskey bottle out of the medicine pack to hand it to Elias. She watched Storm remove one hand from its death grip on his saddle horn and take a long swallow from the bottle. Then another.

"Better go easy with that, my friend," Elias said dryly. "You'll be swaying in something other than pain."

Storm's paint threw its head up and Elias barely managed to catch the whiskey bottle when Storm dropped it to grab the saddle horn again.

"Someone's coming," Jessica said, her heart in her throat. Both men had made it extremely clear they wanted to encounter no one as they tried to get back to town before daybreak.

"Shhhh," Elias said. "Listen."

Jessica looked over Cinnabar's head, between the ears pointed alertly in the direction ahead of them. A faint jingle met her ears, then a creak of what could have been a wagon wheel in need of grease.

"Ned. Elias, it has to be Ned."

"Probably is," Elias agreed. "But you two stay here while I check."

As soon as Elias disappeared, Jessica saw Storm slump over the paint's neck. She gasped, then slid from Cinnabar's back and dropped his reins to ground tie him.

The paint had no qualms about the woman, standing patiently when she approached. Storm's head lay against the paint's black mane, his silky hairs intermingling with the coarser ones. She gently pushed back the locks hanging down over his face.

"Storm. Storm, it won't be long now. I'm sure that's Ned."

Storm opened his eyes and brought his arm up slowly to capture the back of her head. Whiskey fumes blew around Jessica's face when he spoke.

"Pretty lady. You know, I like that name for you almost as much as Jessica."

He hiccuped loudly and Jessica abruptly cut off her laugh.

"Shhhh. We have to stay quiet, just in case that isn't Ned."

Her hand caressed the silky locks under her palm. How

could a man have such wondrously soft, thick hair? How would it feel under her fingers, thick with lather while she washed it?

Another loud hiccup gave Jessica a start.

"Storm. Shhhh. You've got to quit that."

"S'know how to do it," he said as he nodded his head against the paint's mane. "G—gotta hold s'your breath."

"Then hold it, Storm."

"Need some help." He pulled her head closer to him. "Help me, pretty lady."

Jessica had no doubt as to what he meant. Well, she did have to get him quiet, didn't she? She tilted her head back slightly and allowed his lips to cover hers.

He kissed her softly, gently, yearningly. Oh, so yearningly. She could sense the violent longing in him and it found an answer in her own mind. His hand caressed her sable curls and their lips clung, loosened slightly, then clung fiercely once more.

No fiery passion sparked between them this time, only that tender longing. Jessica wanted to ease not just the pain from his wound, but also the deep shadows that sometimes turned his eyes ebony. At the same time, she surrendered to the persistent desire to touch him, stroking the stubble-covered cheek.

The sound of the approaching wagon broke into their drugged senses, but Storm pulled her back once more when she broke contact with him. He kissed her deeply again for a second; then his head fell limp against the paint's mane.

Jessica's eyes filled with worry and she shook his shoulder gently. "Storm. Storm!" She stepped back from the paint and called toward the wagon, "Hurry. Please hurry, Ned. He's passed out again."

They managed to settle Storm in the wagon bed finally, and Jessica hitched Cinnabar to the back before she climbed in herself.

"Good idea, Jes," Ned said, nodding. "He might come to and need you. It's gonna be a joltin' ride, 'cause the springs under this old thing ain't the best. I didn't have time to check ahythin' out. I just grabbed the furthest one from the livery and snuck a couple of horses out."

"Oh, Ned. What if they arrest you for horse theft when you bring them back?"

"I left a note and a five-dollar gold piece on the desk, Jes, but I figure on gettin' back and retrievin' it before they open. I don't want to have to explain why I needed this wagon in the dark. But somethin' could break down and I left the money so they won't think I stole it or the horses. I'll think of somethin', if we don't get back in time."

"Well, we better get moving." Jessica settled herself by Storm's head and drew it into her lap. "It's still a couple of hours before daybreak, but you're right about the fact that something could still happen."

It didn't. The ride went as smoothly as possible. In the light from the full moon, Ned made his way around most of the holes in the trail. Elias rode ahead and pointed out the easiest route.

Both their eyes missed one hole, though, and Storm groaned and opened his eyes when the wagon jolted over it.

Jessica quickly felt the bandage on his shoulder, detecting no warmth from new blood seeping through it. She picked up the whiskey bottle Elias had placed by her side, and held Storm's head up so he could swallow more of the pain-dulling medicine.

Then she wished she hadn't. He began singing to her, muttering almost unintelligibly, but with a musical lilt.

She made out something about heaven, a pretty lady, a fireplace. Kids? Did he sing something about kids?

The wagon jerked to a stop and Jessica's head came up. She frowned as she looked around her. They were beside the rocky place in the trail where she had encountered the snake. Why had Ned stopped so far from town?

Chapter 12

Staggering under the weight of her corner of the makeshift litter, Jessica finally stumbled onto the last landing. Even though she and Idalee carried the lighter end, they had been forced to stop several times as they negotiated the three flights of stairs. Behind her, she could hear labored breathing as Elias and Ned struggled with the weight of Storm's much heavier upper body. A blank wall stood in front of them now, and Jessica's eyes questioned Idalee when she looked across the litter.

"Elias, please raise the lantern a little higher," Idalee murmured, gasping.

The light illuminated the wall, and Idalee removed one hand from the litter to push against a panel. With a small click, the wall slid back quietly to reveal a large, candlelit room, filled with feminine furniture. Dark shades shuttered the windows to keep any light from penetrating to the outside.

Jessica moved forward with Idalee into the room. They carried Storm to the canopied bed and managed to roll him off the litter onto the rumpled sheets without waking him from his again unconscious state. Jessica breathed a sigh of relief and massaged her aching arm for a second, then turned at Ned's touch.

"I gotta go, Jes. It's almost daylight. I'll leave our horses in the tunnel for now and just get the wagon back."

"Hurry, Ned." She watched him take the lantern from Elias and reenter the opening in the wall, shaking her head in wonder. What a convenient way to slip in and out of town.

They had had to leave the wagon outside the hidden entrance to the tunnel and heave Storm again onto the paint's back. The horses had made their way single file down the length of the tunnel, Elias showing them the way and Ned leading the paint. Jessica had followed on foot with Cinnabar. It had only taken Elias a moment to climb the stairway and come back with a sleepy-eyed Idalee and a makeshift litter, but the trip back up the shadowed stairwell with Storm's unconscious body had seemed to stretch on forever.

Jessica's instinctive sense of direction served her well as she stared at the now-closed panel on the wall. Even if the presence of the woman behind her hadn't confirmed it, she would have known they were in Idalee's house. Set off by itself at the edge of town, it would be the only place in close proximity to the tunnel.

Storm groaned in pain behind her, and Jessica hurriedly turned to see Idalee and Elias removing the plaid shirt from his shoulders.

"Can I help?" she offered.

"Please, Jessica," Idalee said over her shoulder. "Elias

needs to get Storm something to drink and maybe some warm soup from the kitchen. We have to get liquids into him to replace all the blood he's lost."

Elias stepped aside, and Jessica automatically reached out to assist Idalee when she began unbuttoning Storm's denim jeans. She pulled her hand back as though the metal buttons had grown teeth when her knuckles brushed the warm skin on Storm's taut stomach, and drew in a startled breath.

"Oh! I . . . I . . ."

Idalee tossed her an impatient glance. "Come on, Jessica. He's too heavy for me to do it alone and Elias is already gone."

The click of the door latch behind Jessica as Idalee spoke confirmed her words.

"Haven't you ever seen a naked man?" Idalee asked in exasperation when Jessica still hesitated.

"N–no."

But she found herself longing to see this one. She unconsciously clenched and unclenched the hand that had touched him, then resolutely straightened her shoulders and reached for the jeans again.

"Magnificent," Jessica muttered a moment later as Idalee left her to go into a small room set off from the bedroom. She heard Idalée toss a couple pieces of wood into the fireplace as she passed by and realized Storm should be covered against the slight chill in the room. After she reached across him to pick up the comforter, Jessica hesitated, loath to drape it over him. She really should see if he had any more bruises they needed to attend to, shouldn't she?

Tight wrinkles of pain lined the face against the pillow even in his unconscious state, and his suffering tugged at her. She smoothed his brow once and a satisfied smile quirked her lips as his full mouth softened. The white bandage stood out starkly against the dark tan of his shoulder. At least the bleeding was still holding off, despite all the far from tender handling he had undergone.

Her eyes traveled down the fading path of chest hair, to where it bushed out once more just below his trim waist. The evidence of his manhood lay curled in its kinky nest, slumbering now, but she imagined how quickly it could spring to alertness and send waves of pleasure through her.

The muscular thighs, somewhat of a lighter shade than the rest of his body, could cradle her smaller ones firmly. The soft, dark hair continued down his legs, ending at his ankles.

Jessica almost laughed aloud. Though his feet tapered nicely, their stark whiteness stood out incongruously against the rest of his body. She heard Idalee walking back across the room and draped the comforter across his body, snugging it around his neck, as though to hide his body from any eyes other than her own.

"Beautiful, isn't he?"

Jessica pinkened slightly when she realized Idalee had seen her studying Storm's body, but she nodded her agreement.

"I thought only women were referred to as beautiful," she said quietly. "But he's . . . he's magnificent."

"Always has been. My mother put a stop to us sneaking off to swim together on hot days when Storm was barely in his teens." Idalee chuckled as she put a basin of water on the small bedside table, her words sending a stab of jealousy through Jessica. "And you might as well pull that comforter back again. He'll rest easier if we get him cleaned up. Here."

Jessica's eyes widened as Idalee drew two washcloths

from the basin and wrung them out before she handed one to Jessica.

"But I—I couldn't . . ."

Idalee ignored her protest and thrust the washcloth into Jessica's hand. She reached and tossed the comforter away, then glanced at the fire.

"It's warm enough in here now," Idalee said. "Since you're on that end anyway, you take the bottom half. And don't linger too long. I don't want him to chill and it will go faster with both of us washing him."

She handed Jessica a cake of soap and reached to pick up another one.

Jessica stared wide-eyed at Idalee for a second, but the other woman showed her intolerance of Jessica's modesty by ignoring her and bending to her own task. Jessica sighed and tentatively ran the bar of soap over the cloth, then reached to rub it across his trim waist.

"Why, you've got warm water," she said as she realized the cloth in her hand held a measure of heat.

"Of course. Everybody civilized today has it."

"Not the hotel," Jessica said as she moved the cloth lower. She only swiped it quickly around the nest of black curls, then down one thigh and across to the other one.

She turned around and dipped the cloth in the water again before she soaped it again. Lifting one corded thigh, she washed under it, then the other one, scrubbing harder for a second on a dark blemish, until she realized it was a heart-shaped birthmark, not dirt. After she did the same to the remaining length of his legs, even spending a few seconds making sure the spaces between each tapered toe were clean, she rinsed the soap from the cloth and prepared to start again.

"Make sure you get all of him, Jessica," Idalee said, giggling beside her.

When Jessica's eyes flew to the other woman, Idalee busied herself removing the bandage from Storm's shoulder.

"This probably needs changing," Idalee said to herself.

Jessica sighed and picked up the soap again. She forced her hand back toward the springy curls and rubbed a lather of soap over them. Immediately, she felt him stiffen under her fingers and gasped as she drew back her hand.

"Don't worry," Idalee said over her shoulder. "He's still unconscious. It's just a natural male reaction that happens to them sometimes even when they're asleep."

Her words barely penetrated Jessica's mind. She couldn't tear her eyes away from that part of him, now half hard and lying almost on his stomach. How could this send such waves of delight through her? What would it feel like if she could truly feel him inside her? What greater pleasure would she feel?

But, supposedly, he had ravaged a woman. Prudence's face wavered before her eyes. Prudence. Prudence who denied that it had been Storm who hurt her. Prudence who loved this man. He belonged to Prudence and that part of him would be only for her.

Resolutely, Jessica finished her task and wiped the soap from the lower portion of his body. She blanked her mind out while she worked, not wanting to experience again the pain she felt as she thought of Prudence in Storm's arms.

"Jessica, I need your help up here now," Idalee said. "Get some fresh water from the washroom and help me take care of his wound."

When Idalee straightened up from leaning across Storm, Jessica looked at his face in time to see one fully lashed eyelid drop down in a wink when he caught her gaze on him. Blushing furiously, she grabbed the washbasin.

"Well, I'm glad you're awake again, Storm," Idalee informed him lovingly. "Elias will be here with something for you to eat in a minute and I'd have had to wake you anyway."

"Thanks, Idy," Jessica heard Storm say as she hurried to the adjoining washroom.

After dumping the dirty water out and refilling the basin from the hot water tap, she stood gathering her senses for a moment. How long had he been awake?

Long enough, her mind told her.

"Jessica, are you coming?" she heard Idalee call.

Sighing, Jessica picked up the washbasin and turned back into the room.

By the time they had the bandage changed—with Jessica determinedly keeping her eyes fixed anywhere except on Storm's face—Elias had returned with a tray for Storm. Jessica picked up the basin of reddish-colored water so he could set the tray in its place. She couldn't quite hold back a tired sigh.

"Jessica, you've been up all night," Idalee said. "You must be exhausted. I'll feed him if you want to take a bath, and Elias can bring a cot in here so you can catch a nap."

"Oh, but you have several rooms here, don't you?" Jessica asked. "Isn't there another one where I can—"

"No," Idalee firmly interrupted her. "At least, not right now. And one of us needs to stay with him, because there's still the danger of fever from the wound. Go on and draw your bath. I'll get you a gown to wear when you're done and see that your other things are washed and ironed before you need them again."

Idalee walked to a closet door on the other side of the room and Elias followed her. They spoke in murmurs as

Idalee opened the door, their voices too low to carry to Jessica.

Jessica stifled a huge yawn, then glanced down when she felt Storm take her other hand. The dark pools of his eyes beckoned her and she complied when he gently tugged at her hand to pull her down onto the bed. She tried to read his face while he carried her hand to his lips.

Could that be a little admiration there for her? Or maybe . . . something else lingered in the shadowed expression before he shuttered his eyes and kissed her hand. When he opened them again, the expression was gone.

"Thanks, pretty lady," he said as he released her hand.

Jessica cradled her hand against her stomach, her other thumb unconsciously stroking the spot his lips had caressed.

"I . . . I just did what anyone would have done to help," she said softly. "Like you did when you thought I needed help the other night. And the snake. I owe you my life for that."

"Consider any debt between us paid, Jessica," he said as he laid his head back on the pillow. "When your friend Ned gets back, I want you both to rejoin your men and leave, like I asked you to before. Forget you ever saw me."

Jessica shook her head slightly and a sable curl bounced dejectedly across her shoulder.

"You're not a very forgettable person, Storm," she said before she thought.

"Jessica . . ."

"Here you go, Jessica," Idalee said, standing beside the bed. "There's plenty of hot water, so fill the tub as high as you want. And feel free to be lavish with the bath salts and soap. I always am."

Jessica quickly jumped to her feet and took the gown and robe Idalee held out to her. The gossamer feel of it scarcely registered with her as she murmured her thanks and hurried across the room. She closed the door of the washroom firmly behind her.

She failed miserably, though, when she tried to empty her mind as she ran steaming water into the porcelain tub and sprinkled bath salts under the spigot. Forget him? She hadn't lied when she spoke unthinkingly, but she could have bitten her tongue off as soon as the words were out.

His image burned in her mind as she slowly unbuttoned her blouse and draped it on a straight-backed chair near the end of the tub. She sat down and pulled off her boots. Rose-scented steam drifted up from the tub and Jessica tried to concentrate on her anticipation of a luxurious bath to refocus her mind. Instead, the steam reminded her of the mist climbing down into the valley when she first met the man lying just outside the door.

No, that wasn't their first meeting, she realized as she stood up and removed her skirt. The picture of him astride the beautiful paint stallion as he waved his rifle overhead and laughed his disparagement at their ineffective attempts to kill him swam before her. She gulped and her hand tightened on the rim of the tub. What would she have done if they had killed him?

What would I have done if I'd never known him? "Oh, hush!" Jessica ordered her errant mind aloud.

She picked up the riding skirt from the floor to toss it over the chair. Something rustled in the pocket and her brow furrowed, but a glance at the tub had her hastily bending over it to twist the faucet handles closed before the rising cascade of bubbles could spill onto the floor.

That steaming water would feel so good on her trail-worn muscles. She took her underthings off and left them on the floor in her haste. Raising one trim leg, she tested the water, then climbed in and lay back, luxuriating in the soothing warmth. Her hair floated around her in the bubbles, reminding her she had forgotten to pin it up. No matter. With plenty of water, she could refill the tub and wash it.

She closed her eyes, but they immediately flew open. Lordy, she hated it when something tugged at her mind just out of reach. What *was* that in the pocket of her skirt? She didn't recall having anything there except her small coin purse.

She glanced sideways at the chair, then reached out a bubble-covered hand to draw the skirt to her. Her fingers felt in the pocket and she pulled out a folded piece of paper. Now she remembered—the map the sheriff had drawn to show them how to find Tobias's ranch.

Jessica pulled her other hand from the water and unfolded the paper. Well, she wouldn't need this anymore. She could find Tobias's place blindfolded, even after having only been there once. She started to crumple the paper and a word on the other side caught her eye. "WANTED!"

Guess the sheriff had used an old wanted poster for the map. Her curiosity aroused, Jessica turned the paper over. She sat up in the tub with a shot, splashing water over the sides.

"Jessica? Jessica, are you all right? You didn't fall in the tub, did you?"

"I . . ." Jessica forced herself to clear the croak from her throat. She didn't want Idalee coming in here now! "I'm fine," she managed to call out.

"Do you want me to come in and help you wash your hair?" Idalee called back.

"No! No, I can do it."

"You and your modesty." Idalee laughed.

Her voice lowered and Jessica could hear her talking to Storm.

Storm. Storm, whose picture stared up at her from the wrinkled, slightly damp paper in her hand. There was no doubt in her mind: the likeness matched exactly—and the description.

Words jumped out at her. "Rape." "Escape." "Twenty-year prison term." And finally, the large words at the bottom of the paper. "FIVE THOUSAND DOLLAR REWARD!"

Awareness crashed over her. My God! Idalee was sitting out there with an escaped convict! And she herself had been helping that convict, nursing him, knowing full well in the back of her mind who he was ever since she rode into the firelit campsite.

Confusion crowded into her thoughts. The paper fluttered to the floor, and Jessica grabbed the sides of the tub to push herself up. Almost at once she realized the foolishness of her actions and leaned back. For one thing, she didn't even have a weapon with her. And for another—her heart flip-flopped in her breast—for another, she couldn't bring herself to turn the man out there in for arrest even if she did have a gun.

Idalee's words rang in her mind. "He's always been magnificent." Idalee had known him for a long time. She knew Storm had escaped prison. Elias, too. That's why he had been so anxious to get Storm to Idalee's before daybreak and slip him in through the tunnel.

Ned? Did he realize they were helping an escaped convict? Of course he did. He'd heard every word Tobias said on the ridge above the cabin. Why was Ned being so cooperative? Did Elias convince Ned that Storm was innocent, as Prudence had insisted to Jessica?

Jessica glanced down at the paper. Would Ned's basic

honesty force him to turn Storm over to the authorities soon? Would he think the five thousand dollars—money that could help put Jessica's ranch back on its feet—sufficient justification to turn Storm in? She had to talk to Ned as soon as possible!

Jessica grabbed the paper from the floor and ripped it into tiny bits. She dipped her hand under the water and crumbled the pieces into a soggy mass, then tossed them into a basket in the corner of the room.

There! With a grim smile of satisfaction curving her lips, Jessica picked up her washcloth and reached for a cake of rose-smelling soap. The soap slipped from suddenly numb fingers as her eyes flew back to the basket.

What in the world was she doing? Her actions continued to align her with an escaped convict! Storm's face filled her mind—the eyes shadowed with thanks and also that little something else she had caught before he shuttered them. Trust in her?

It had to be trust, she told herself as she searched in the water for the slippery soap. And she couldn't bring herself to betray that trust. Or betray her newly formed friendship with Prudence, her thoughts continued.

Prudence. Yes, she had to let Prudence know Storm was safe. And she would never be able to bring herself to look into the mute young woman's face if she had to tell Prudence the man she loved languished again behind jail bars, when Prudence herself had insisted the charges against Storm were false.

Blocking out the arrow of pain that shot through her mind, Jessica captured the soap and rubbed it vigorously across the washcloth into lather.

Chapter 13

A dying ember popped in the fireplace and Jessica's eyes flew open. For a moment, she snuggled down under the blanket covering her, then realized how warm she was. When she tossed back the blanket, her hands encountered the silken gown.

She let her fingers linger where the gown covered her stomach, luxuriating in the feel of it as she recalled Uncle Pete's gift one Christmas. She never knew how the old mountain man had read her thoughts, since she always told herself she never yearned for the silken underthings and dressing gowns displayed inside one fine shop in town. Somehow each trip would find her with an excuse to stroll by the shop and scan the window display of fashionable gowns, though.

Once in a while she would go in and spend a spare coin on a ribbon or scarf, and each Christmas she would splurge on some nonessential from the shop for Mattie, which Mattie would wear proudly for a day, then tuck away. No sense ruining her finery by wearing it while she did housework, Mattie would say. She would urge the fine shawl or silk gloves on Jessica when they attended church or a dance.

Somehow Uncle Pete had known. She had gasped in awe when she pulled the lilac peignoir and matching dressing gown from the box. The one she wore now was the same color as the one from Uncle Pete.

Uncle Pete. And the gold. Where was she? It had to be daylight, but the room remained shadowed, and the dying fire made it much too hot.

Her gaze fell on the canopied bed and the covered figure on it. Oh, yes. Idalee's bedroom—and Storm. She should check him and make sure his wound hadn't festered. She should be on her own way, too. Time marched resolutely on and the days left for her to find the gold and return to Wyoming were dwindling fast.

Jessica slipped her legs over the side of the cot and rose. Lord, the room was stifling. She crossed to the shade and pulled at it. It slipped from her fingers and clattered loudly as it wound around the wooden spool at the top.

Jessica glanced back at the bed, but the figure on it only stirred and resettled under the covers. She turned back and tugged at the window, finally managing to open it a few inches. Sunlight streamed through the clear panes, and a cool breeze flowed through the opening, drying the slight sweatiness of her body. She lifted the front of the gown a little to allow the breeze to feather across her legs.

Storm tried to shake the lethargy still lingering in his mind from the laudanum Idalee had insisted he swallow. His eyes remained fixed on the window, where an ethereal figure stood. He blinked, but the traces of the drug blurred his vision, outlining the figure in a hazy purple glow.

He squinted his eyes a little and the outline firmed somewhat. Still a purple haze lingered, but a darker shape filled in the center of the violet shadow—a shapely center. The sunlight outlined Jessica's trim figure to his eyes and he found himself unable to tear them away.

Sable curls floated down her back to a tiny waist, and perfectly rounded hips flared out beneath the fall of silky tresses. And legs—legs more defined, since she held the front of her gown up. Legs that tapered down to trim ankles. Legs definitely long and luscious.

He tried to stifle a groan when he felt his organ spring to alertness between his own legs. Damn, he hadn't had this problem since his teen years!

Jessica turned at the sound behind her, unaware that the sun now outlined her uptilted breasts beneath the gown's bodice. She blushed slightly when she realized she still held the hem of the gown in her hands and dropped it quickly. Her embarrassment immobilized her as she tried to determine if Storm's eyes were open.

"Storm," she called quietly across the room. "Storm, are you in pain?"

Pain? God, he felt like he would burst from the pain, though not from his shoulder. His eyes struggled to travel up to Jessica's face, but remained glued on the dark shapes of her nipples. When they crinkled into points clearly outlined by the lilac silk—as though they felt his eyes on them—his voice left his throat in a snarl.

"Get the hell away from that window and put some clothes on! Do you want the whole damned town to see you standing in a whorehouse window!"

Jessica gasped and flew across the room to grab the dressing gown from the end of her cot. Keeping her back to the man in the bed, she threw it around her and cinched the belt tightly. She took a deep breath before she turned to face Storm.

"What do you mean, a wh . . . brothel window?" she demanded.

Damn! The snug belt of the dressing gown only accentuated her body. What the hell had Idalee had in mind by giving her something like that to wear? Why, any man who saw her would want to. . . .

Jessica stamped her bare foot, wincing at the absurd sound it made on the carpeted floor, then crossed the room to the bed. She placed her hands on her hips as she glared down at him.

"I asked you a question, Storm. Does Idalee run a brothel here?"

Storm managed to fix his gaze on her face and a small smile tipped his lips. The gold flecks in Jessica's brown eyes flashed at him, and for some reason he found himself wanting to antagonize her further.

"Why, I thought anyone who came to Baker's Valley knew about Idalee's place five minutes after they got into town. In fact, lots of people ride miles and miles just to get here."

"Harumph. Lots of *men,* I suppose."

"Well, the women get here, too. You're here, aren't you?"

Jessica choked on her rage, her face taking on a hue a shade darker than her gown.

"You—you don't think I work . . . Why you stupid son of a . . . son of a bang-tailed cayuse! I should've left you out there to bleed to death!"

Storm's snort of laughter sent Jessica's anger surging higher. She clenched a fist and barely kept herself from slamming it down on his chest when she remembered his wound. When he grasped her wrist, his weakened state allowed her to jerk her hand free. Or was his weak state caused by the guffaws now erupting unchecked from his chest?

Her anger left her slowly as she gazed down at him, and she raised her hand to smother her own giggles. The laugh crinkles around his eyes told her he was teasing her—and something else told her that he needed this laughter. She hiccuped with the effort of not joining him, then gave the gales of laughter free rein.

Storm reached up and pulled her down onto the bed with him. He quieted for a second, then made the mistake of looking into her face. When she tried to pout, her effort sent another snicker building in his chest. He snaked an arm around her waist and drew her down near the uninjured side of his chest, while they both erupted into more peals of laughter.

Several long moments later, Storm released his hold on Jessica's waist to wipe at his eye. He drew his finger back in surprise and stared at the moisture on it. When Jessica sat up to look down at him, he reached out and wiped his finger on the belt of her dressing gown.

"God, I needed that," he said.

Jessica ran her thumb through the crease around his other eye. She had to fight the urge to lick the moisture from her thumb with her tongue, but she succeeded in wiping it beside the other damp spot on her belt.

"You haven't laughed in a long while, have you?" she asked softly.

His head sagged back tiredly into the pillow. "No," he agreed. "There hasn't been anything to laugh about in years."

"Well," Jessica said with a mischievous twinkle in her eyes. "I guess we'll just have to find someone else for you to mistake for a brothel lady."

Storm's eyes centered on her face. "Why did you call them that, Jessica?"

"What?"

"Brothel ladies," Storm explained. "Most people just call them tarts."

"Most *men*," Jessica returned.

"No," Storm denied, "the women, too."

"I guess so," Jessica said as she shifted to a more comfortable position slightly closer to him, with her hip touching his. Her face puckered into a frown and she unconsciously laid a hand on his chest, one fingernail entwining around a black curl of hair.

"I don't know if I can really explain it," she said. "It's just that . . . Well, I've always felt that there must be a reason for a woman to lead such a life. There aren't a lot of options open for a woman, you know. We're expected to get married and raise children. If that fails, we can run a dress shop. Take in washing. Maybe be a waitress at a cafe or hotel or someone's maid."

"It's not fair, huh?" Storm shifted slightly to raise his leg. Lord, don't let her eyes fall below his waist!

"No, it's not really." Her fingernail curled the ball of hair to her satisfaction and she started on another strand. "A few of us are somewhat lucky. My father left the ranch to me when he died, but then I ran into other problems. After a spring blizzard almost wiped me out this year, the bank wouldn't loan me any money to keep the place going because I'm a woman."

"So that's what you're doing here? Looking for another piece of land to start over?"

Jessica found herself strangely loath to let him believe the story she and Ned had decided on.

"Not exactly. Uncle Pete . . . I . . . ." Her nail scraped a nubbin hidden in the hair under her finger, and it immediately sprang free from the curl. Jessica gasped and pulled her hand back.

"Oh! Oh, I . . ."

Storm chuckled softly and grabbed her hand. He laid it back on his chest and kept it covered so she couldn't remove it.

"You were saying?"

Jessica smiled at him and felt him relax his grip. Jerking her hand away, she quickly rose to her feet and glared down at him.

"I was *saying,*" she said, "we better see how your wound is. Idalee will skin me alive if I let you catch fever from not changing your bandage often enough. For some silly reason, she seems to care for you, although I have a problem understanding her feelings. You're just a typical man, with a marred judgment about women."

"And what's that supposed to mean?" Storm asked with a chuckle as he caught the teasing lilt in her voice.

"Oh, you know," Jessica replied with an airy wave of her hand. "That arrogant male attitude that says a woman should swoon into your arms at just a touch from you."

Storm's quirked eyebrow reminded Jessica she had done exactly that, and she hastily decided to find a different focus for her teasing jibes.

"And . . . well, like a typical man, you have trouble distinguishing what type of women the females you meet are," she continued with a saucy tilt of her head. "You don't seem to be able to tell a lady from a tart. Or a woman from a lady. Or—"

"But I can, pretty lady," Storm interrupted tenderly. "You're definitely a lady." He held out his hand to beckon her. "Come back here and I'll show you how a typical man treats a definite lady."

The twinkle faded from Jessica's brown eyes as she

gazed at him. How silly! She wasn't the swooning type at all, but just then her legs started trembling and the flutter in her stomach had her placing a hand over it, surprised not to feel the skin jumping under her fingers. She took a step forward, her free hand reaching out toward the callused palm waiting for her to grasp it.

The rapping sound of knocking echoed through the room. Jessica's eyes flew to the door, but Storm grabbed her hand when she moved toward it.

"Not there," he said as he nodded behind her. "Over at the tunnel door."

"Who . . ."

"Don't worry. No one knows about it except people we can trust. Go ahead." He gave her hand a reassuring squeeze before he dropped it.

Jessica hesitantly crossed the room and stopped by the panel of wood. Realizing she didn't know how to open it, she glanced back at Storm.

"To your right," he said. "Just above your shoulder. Press the panel fairly hard."

When Jessica complied, the door swung back silently to expose Ned standing there.

"Jes, I'm glad you're finally awake," he said as he hurried past her. "We've got to talk."

"What is it?"

"I ran into that Jackson fellow." Ned glanced at the bed and his voice lowered as he asked, "Are you all right, son?"

"I'm getting there, Ned," Storm answered. "What about Tobias?"

"He didn't believe me when I told him we hadn't found you," Ned replied. "When I left him, he was on his way to the sheriff's office to tell him about you bein' at his place and him shootin' you. I figure the sheriff's gonna start askin' questions real fast."

"And they'll probably search here first," Storm informed Ned. He struggled to raise himself. "I've got to get out of here."

Jessica gasped and hurried to Storm. Sitting down on the edge of the bed, she pushed gently against his chest.

"You're too weak to leave." Her face creased with worry when he groaned and fell back against the pillow.

"I have to," he said in a voice laced with pain. "Idy's the one who'll pay if they find me here. And all the rest of you, too."

"Son," Ned said, "I don't know all of what's goin' on here, but Elias told me a little. Reckon we're in this with you now."

"No!"

Jessica jumped slightly at Storm's loud voice. When he pushed himself upright this time, she glanced helplessly at Ned as her ineffectual hold on Storm failed to push him down again.

"Let him talk for a minute, Jes," Ned said quietly.

Storm steadied himself on one arm and glared at Ned. "I don't want your help. I appreciate all you've done so far, but I can handle it now."

"Been used to ridin' a lonely trail, ain't you, son?" Ned drawled. "Leastways, when you were free to ride."

Jessica's eyes flew to Ned. He knew. He definitely knew and still wanted to help.

"Help me get my clothes on, Ned," Storm almost pleaded. "That's the last thing I'll ask of you."

The pounding on the door two stories below reached even their ears. Jessica gave a start and Ned moved to the bed, a grim smile on his face.

"Don't reckon we've got time for that now. Come on, up with you."

Jessica quickly rose to help Ned. Between the two of them, they managed to swing Storm's legs over the side of the bed.

"Wait, Jes," Ned said. In two quick, limping strides, he crossed the room and grabbed the blanket from the cot Jessica had used. He brought it back to the bed and slipped it around Storm's shoulders. Elbowing Jessica gently aside, he threw the comforter back and pulled the blanket around to cover Storm.

"Now, Jes," he said, "help me get him up and into the tunnel."

Storm swayed alarmingly when they got him to his feet, and Jessica took as much of his weight as she could on her shoulders. Her heart pounding in fear, she staggered beside Storm and Ned across the room. When they finally got Storm onto the landing outside the tunnel door, Ned propped him against the wall.

"The cot, Jes," he gasped. "Hurry. God, he's heavy."

Storm muffled a groan as Jessica slipped out from under his arm. She spent a valuable second glancing at his pain-torn face, then ran to get the cot.

A few seconds later, they had Storm lying on the cot. It barely fit on the small landing and Ned had to move to the first step on the stairs. He leaned across the cot and placed his hands on Jessica's arms.

"Go back in there and get in the bed, Jes. Pretend you've been asleep."

Jessica nodded and reached down to run her hand over Storm's forehead. It came away covered with sweat.

Storm caught her hand, then looked up at Ned. "You're both a couple damned fools, you know that?"

Ned chuckled. "Maybe so."

"Thanks," Storm whispered. He squeezed Jessica's hand and looked up at her. "Thanks, pretty lady. But don't do anything foolish in there to protect me."

"Oh, you know us brothel ladies," she said as she gave his hand an answering contraction. "We're pretty good at thinking on our fe . . . backs," she finished with a giggle and pulled her hand free.

"Jes."

Jessica paused in pulling the tunnel door closed.

"What, Ned?"

"His clothes. They're at the foot of the bed."

"I'll take care of it."

She closed the opening and hurried across the room. Grabbing the denim jeans and blood-soaked shirt, she shoved them under the comforter and climbed into the bed. Footsteps pounded on the stairwell. Loud footsteps, probably made by men wearing boots. She pulled the comforter over her and her eyes fell on the moccasins on the floor. The footsteps came down the hall toward the bedroom and she glanced at the door. They had to be just outside!

Just as a knock sounded on the door, Jessica stuck out one bare foot and kicked the moccasins under the bed. She didn't have time to see if she had managed to hide both of them. The door creaked open a crack as she tugged the comforter over her and laid her head on the pillow.

"Jessica." Thank God, Idalee's voice. "Jessica, are you awake?"

Jessica turned her head on the pillow and raised one hand to knuckle at her eye. She gave a yawn and lowered her hand.

"Well, if I wasn't, I am now. Heavens, Idalee. It sounded like you had a herd of cattle climbing your stairs."

"Not cattle, Jessica," Idalee said as she stepped into the

room. "Just a couple of jackasses."

"Idalee!"

"Miss Morgan!"

Idalee whirled to face the two men behind her. "I'll thank you both to remember that I'm the owner of this place. I've agreed to let you search, but I didn't say I'd keep my mouth shut about my opinion of your tactics!"

"Yeah," Harlin Baker said, standing beside the sheriff. "You always were an opinionated little brat who didn't know when to keep her mouth shut. You just better remember whose town your damned whorehouse is in."

"And maybe you should remember that it's the only house like this for fifty miles, Harlin. And who some of my visitors are."

"You'll go too far one of these days, Idalee. Come on, Sheriff. We came here to search, not to get into a useless discussion with a brothel madam, remember?"

"But I wasn't saying anything, Mr.—"

Idalee threw her hand out behind her. "Search!" she said. "Help yourselves. I'm sure Jessica has nothing to hide."

Harlin Baker stared at the bed as Jessica sat up. "Miss Callaghan? What the hell are you doing here?"

"Obviously, I was trying to get some sleep." Jessica had no trouble putting the proper amount of disgust in her voice. She couldn't abide the men standing in front of her, staring at her silk-clad body. She gave a slight shiver and pulled the comforter over her breasts.

"But—but this is a wh—whore—" Harlin Baker stuttered to a stop.

"A brothel, Mr. Baker?" Jessica asked with raised eyebrows. "Yes, I know what it is." She glanced briefly at Idalee, but saw only a serene smile on the other woman's face.

"And it's a heck of a lot more comfortable than that cheap hotel you own," she continued. "More civilized, too. They've even got running hot water here."

"But Miss Callaghan," the sheriff said. "You shouldn't be in a place like this."

"How do you know, Sheriff?" Jessica said with a wide-eyed stare at the man. "You don't even really know who I am. Why, maybe my ranch in Wyoming is really a place just like this. Maybe Mr. Olson won't loan me any money because he wants to get his lecherous hands on my ladies back there."

"Miss Callaghan!" Harlin Baker's voice thundered through the room. "I insist you get dressed and leave here with us right now. The sheriff's right. This is no place for you. I can't imagine what you're trying to pull, but Olson would have mentioned something of what you claim in his wire to me."

"Mr. Olson. Pooh!" Jessica steeled herself and threw back the comforter. "I'm tired of fighting with Mr. Olson over my ranch. There's no way I can get the money to save it in time and there's not really that much back there to save. Besides, this seems like a much more pleasant way to make a living than dragging cows out of the snow all winter."

She stood up and stretched as though to awaken muscles relaxed in sleep. A smile quirked her lips when both men's mouths fell open as they stared at her. A glance at Idalee showed the small woman biting her lower lip to stifle her laughter and green eyes gazing merrily back at Jessica.

"I thought you said something about searching this room, Sheriff," Jessica said. "Well, hurry up. I want to take a bath. Oh, I guess you'll want to search the washroom before I use it, won't you?"

Jessica glided across the floor toward the washroom. A

quick glance showed her the toe of one moccasin barely peeking from under the bed. She stopped to arch her back and place her hand in the small of it, turning slightly so the profile of her body was outlined to the sheriff and Harlin Baker.

"Oh, my. I seem to have gotten a kink in my back." Assured of the men's eyes on her, she slipped her foot out and nudged the moccasin under the comforter hanging down over the side of the bed.

"Will you two please hurry up and search?" she said grumpily when both men continued to gape at her. "I find myself having to use the other facilities in the washroom, too."

Both men gave a start and Harlin Baker walked across the bedroom. "You check the closet, Sheriff," he said over his shoulder.

"What in the world are they looking for, Idalee?" Jessica asked in a puzzled voice.

"An escaped convict," Idalee said, her lips pursed. "For some reason, they think I might have him hidden here."

"A convict? Why, Idalee, a convict wouldn't have any money. And didn't you tell me earlier that the first thing you did when a man came here was make him show you the color of his money?"

"Shut up, both of you!" Harlin Baker growled. He shoved open the washroom door and took a quick glance inside before he faced Idalee.

"You know damned well why we came here. And I'm not leaving until we've searched every one of these rooms!"

Idalee sighed and walked to the door. "In that case, I guess I better accompany you," she said. "I don't think my girls would like you waking them up and poking around their rooms by yourselves."

The sheriff slammed the closet door, making Jessica jump.

"He's not in there, Mr. Baker."

Harlin strode across the room, his face dark with anger. Grabbing Idalee's arm, he shoved her through the door ahead of him.

"Oh, Sheriff," Jessica called sweetly as the sheriff moved to follow them.

"What, Miss Callaghan?" he asked. "Have you come to your senses about leaving here with us?"

"Why, no, Sheriff. I'm perfectly content here. It's just that . . ." Jessica bent down to lift the comforter from the side of the bed, though not high enough to expose the moccasins hidden behind it. She allowed the dressing gown to fall free and her breasts swung loosely against the front of the gown.

"I just thought I'd remind you to look under the bed, Sheriff," she said with a saucy smirk over her shoulder. "Don't bad guys always hide under the bed?"

The sheriff snorted loudly and strode through the door.

Jessica quickly straightened and ran lightly across the room. Closing the door, she turned the key in the lock before she collapsed against it.

Chapter 14

Jessica tightened her arms around Prudence as the first clods of earth fell onto the wooden pine box, and she pulled her cloak around them both when the rain fell still harder. Even the heavens were weeping, she thought as Prudence buried her face in Jessica's neck and sobbed silently.

Ronnie lifted her bowed head and moved a step closer to Jessica. "Why don't you two come on back to the hotel with Buster and me now?" she murmured quietly.

Prudence clung firmly to Jessica and shook her head against Jessica's shoulder.

"We'll be along in a while, Ronnie," Jessica told the older woman. "I'll stay with Prudence until she's ready to go."

"Don't be too long," Ronnie said. "There's nothing else you can do here now and there's no sense in you both catching a cold." She took Buster's arm and the two black-clad figures moved away.

Jessica's eyes fell on Tobias on the other side of the grave. The only other mourner left, he stood with his head bowed, his hat in his hand and the rain cascading down his face to mix with his tears.

Suddenly Prudence pulled away from Jessica and removed the bouquet of flowers she shielded under her own cloak. She turned and stared down into the gaping hole. Even the grave digger paused in his attempts to fill in the hole hurriedly and get out of the pouring rain when Prudence stepped to the side of the grave.

Prudence dropped the flowers onto the pine box, then resolutely straightened her shoulders. She glanced at Tobias and held out her hand across the opening in the ground.

Tobias met her eyes, shaking his head. "Go on, sis," he said. "Go back to the hotel. I'll be there shortly."

Prudence stared at her brother for a moment before she turned and took Jessica's hand. Side by side, they walked away from the grave, leaving Tobias to say his last farewell to Eloise alone.

When Jessica stopped at the hotel door, Prudence took a firmer grip on her hand and tugged her onward. Reluctantly, Jessica followed her.

"Prudence," she said as Prudence began to hasten her steps. "Your brother said to wait at the hotel."

Prudence shook her covered head. Dropping Jessica's hand, she strode on ahead.

Jessica hurried after the young woman as Prudence neared the door of a saloon. She caught up to her at the door, but Prudence only shot her a glance and hurried onward. A moment later, Jessica stifled a horrified gasp when Prudence left the walkway and started across the space separating Idalee's house from the rest of the town.

"Prudence, no!" she called, and began to run. She slipped in the mud and when she regained her balance, she looked up to see Prudence climbing the steps to Idalee's house.

"Oh, my God," she breathed. "Tobias will kill her."

She had to admire the plucky young woman, she told herself seconds later as she climbed the steps. She heard the door open and Idalee give a glad cry as she gathered Prudence into her arms.

Idalee quickly drew Prudence into the house and held the door for Jessica. As Jessica paused to remove her cloak and shake out the rain, both women turned at the sound of heels tapping on the stairway. Jessica's cloak fell unnoticed to the floor as she and Idalee made a bee-line for the stairwell.

"Prudence, stop!" Idalee called frantically as she lifted her skirts and ran up the stairs.

Prudence paused on the landing and waited for them. When Idalee took her hand, Prudence pulled away and faced her determinedly.

"Sss . . . Sss . . ."

Jessica met Idalee's puzzled look. "Somehow she knows he's here, Idalee. And I don't think she's going to leave without seeing him."

"Who?" Idalee questioned.

"Storm," Jessica replied. She faced Prudence and confirmed the young woman's suspicions in a hushed voice. "Yes, he's here, Prudence. But no one else knows and, if your brother finds out, he'll have the sheriff back out here."

Prudence covered her mouth with her hand and shook her head. Her brown eyes pleaded with Jessica.

Jessica nodded slowly. "All right, Prudence, though we'll have to be quiet. We don't want to wake Idalee's other, uh, guests."

Prudence shot Jessica a look that told Jessica she knew exactly what type of guests resided in Idalee's house before she gazed questioningly at a bedroom door over Jessica's shoulder.

"He's on another floor, Prudence. Come on, Idalee," Jessica said as she moved toward the stairwell at the far end of the hall. "We can always tell Tobias she came here to see you if he shows up."

"Oh, he'll show up," Idalee grumbled as she followed the other two women. "He'll know where to look when he can't find her and then all hell will break loose."

"Maybe not if we hurry," Jessica said as they quietly made their way up the final flight of stairs. She stopped outside Idalee's bedroom door and turned to Prudence.

"You can only stay a moment, you know that, don't you? It will be too dangerous for Storm if you're caught here."

As soon as Prudence nodded, Jessica pushed open the door. They found Storm sitting up on the side of the bed, struggling to pull the newly washed plaid shirt over the bandage on his arm.

"What are you doing?" Jessica gasped, but Prudence shoved her aside and ran across the room, into Storm's welcoming embrace.

Storm hugged her tightly to him. He grimaced in pain when she threw her arms around his neck and buried her face on his shoulder, but his hand came up to stroke her hair.

"Shhh, sweetheart," Jessica heard him murmur. "It's all right. I'm going to be fine."

Prudence clung tightly to him for a moment, then

straightened in his arms. While Jessica and Idalee watched in amazement, she began twisting her fingers strangely as she stared at Storm's face.

Storm reached up and covered her hands with his own, stilling them.

"Good. Good, darlin'," he said. "You're learning fast."

Prudence freed her hands and made a few more nonsensical—to Idalee and Jessica—motions. Storm answered her with a nod, and Prudence placed her hand over her heart. Then she leaned down and kissed Storm on the cheek.

"I love you, too, darlin'," Storm said. He gently turned her around to face Idalee and Jessica. "But you've got to go now."

Prudence pointed to the bedroom door and nodded.

"She's ready to leave now, Idy," Storm informed them as both women stared at Prudence in wonder. "Go on," he urged them as they hesitated. "Get her out of here."

Prudence gave an exasperated shrug of her shoulders and reached for Jessica's hand. She tugged her through the door and, without a backward glance at Storm, started down the hallway.

Seconds later, Jessica tossed her wet cloak around her and hurried out the door after Prudence. A light rain still fell and they both pulled their hoods up. Though Jessica glanced at Prudence now and then as they made their way across the treacherous footing of the soggy ground, she couldn't determine the expression on the other woman's face inside the shadowed confines of her hood. But the words of the one-sided conversation in Idalee's bedroom burned in her mind.

Ned met them at the hotel door and held it open for them. "You're both soaked. Let's go in and get somethin' hot to drink."

Prudence pulled away from Jessica inside the lobby and shook her head, eyeing Ned warily.

"Prudence, this is my friend, Ned," Jessica said. "I told you about him, remember? You don't have to be afraid of him."

Prudence nodded reluctantly, but shook her head again when Jessica reached for her arm. She took a step toward the stairway, then pointed upward.

"All right," Jessica agreed. "Go on to your room. I'll try to see you before you leave town."

Jessica stared after Prudence as the young woman crossed the room and disappeared up the stairwell, her head filled with questions. The door opened again behind them and she turned to see Tobias enter. He nodded at Jessica, but completely ignored Ned.

"I thank you for coming, Miss Callaghan," he said politely. "For Prudence, too."

"She's waiting in her room, Tobias."

"As she should be," Tobias agreed. "And the skies are clearing up. We shall start back to the ranch within the half hour."

"Ned and I are going to get something warm to drink, Tobias. I'd like to say good-bye to Prudence before you leave."

"If you're still here, we'll stop on our way out." Tobias turned and crossed the hotel lobby, his head bowed under the weight of his sorrow.

"That poor man," Jessica murmured.

"Hell, Jes," Ned said as he took her arm and steered her into the restaurant portion of the hotel. "That poor man's not going to be happy until he sees Storm's neck stretched by a rope."

Jessica settled in the chair Ned held for her and shrugged out of her cloak, leaving it to hang on the chair back. She watched Ned take the chair across from her and his hand unconsciously massage his leg after he sat down.

"This rain's not good for your leg, is it, Ned?"

"Nope," he admitted. "I'll get by, though."

Jessica leaned across the table. "When are you going to tell me what the hell's going on around here?" she asked in a tight voice.

Ned leaned back in his chair and met her eyes firmly. "Just as soon as I figger it out myself, I guess," he said with no attempt to evade her gaze. "I'm gonna send the men on home this afternoon. I've already got some more supplies waitin' over at the store for them and we don't really need them with us to look for that gold. Thought about tryin' to make you go with them, but I gave that idea up right quick. Figgered your belly would be mighty sore from being tied across that saddle by the time you got home. 'Sides, most of the men would probably have quit by the time they got you back, lessen we gagged you, too."

Jessica couldn't quite hold back a peal of laughter. She really should chastise him for even thinking of subjecting her to such an indignity, but at least he didn't follow through on it. And he was right. She probably would have driven off all her hands with her sharp tongue.

"There's one other thing you might as well know, Jes," Ned said quietly.

Jessica immediately stilled and stared across the table at Ned's hooded blue eyes. "What have you done?" she asked, her warning clear in her voice.

"It was probably already done. I just stopped by to wire Mattie and tell her to go ahead, but she'd probably already been to the bank. 'Magine she stopped by and took that fancy-pants lawyer with her, too, 'long with that there power of attorney thing you signed. Just in case, you know."

"Ned, I can't let you and Mattie spend your life savings to make my mortgage payment! I won't let you do that! I only signed that in case something came up while I was gone that couldn't wait."

"Oh, I don't guess Mattie really needed that, Jes. Why, she'd've told the whole town that Olson refused a payment on your mortgage if he'd've had the gall to try. Now you've got another three months to come up with your next payment and I guess we'll have enough money left to help you out then, too. We've got quite a bit socked away. Your daddy took care of us right well."

"Ned, that's your retirement money! You can't keep on working forever. Your leg . . . And I won't take money from you!"

"Got your daddy's Callaghan pride, you do," Ned said with a nod. "And once in a while you even do somethin' that reminds me of old Pete Russell. Guess it was all them talks you and he used to have that put some of that spunk in you."

"Ned . . ."

He continued as though she hadn't spoken, "Ever tell you how I hurt my leg? You was pretty young, just barely walkin', so I don't guess you remember. I was a lot younger, too, and still had enough sap in me to want to show off now and then. Had an old range bull that escaped roundup every fall. Your daddy really wanted that bull caught or shot, 'cause the calves he got on the cows weren't worth much."

Ned glanced up as Ronnie set a coffeepot and two cups on the table.

"Is Prudence all right?" Ronnie asked Jessica.

Jessica blinked as she focused on Ronnie's face. "Uh, oh, yes, Ronnie. She's fine. She and Tobias are going home in a while."

"Will you be wanting something to go with your coffee?" Ronnie said after she nodded.

"No, thanks," Ned answered. "Leastways, not just this minute."

Ronnie moved away and Jessica turned her bewildered expression back on the old man. "I don't see where this is going, Ned."

Ned picked up his story where he had left off. "Your Uncle Pete was there that fall. He stayed awhile longer than he usually did before he went up into the mountains to trap. Sometimes he even came back down for Christmas, remember?"

"I remember."

He filled their cups and took a swallow of the hot brew.

"Decided I was gonna get that range bull that year," he said after he put his cup down. "Pete, he thought he might go with me. Said it sounded about as much fun as grizzly ropin'. So we headed up into the hills while the rest of the fellers branded calves.

"Range bulls are tough, Jes," he said as he pushed her cup across the table at her. "Here, drink up. It's gettin' cold.

"Yeah, they're tough," he said after she picked up her cup. "And smart. Lordy, they have to be smart to live through a lot of years on that range back there. But I thought I was smart and tough, too. We picked up the bull's trail and I sent Pete off in one direction, while I followed what I thought were fresher tracks.

"They were fresh, all right," Ned said, nodding. "Guess Pete knew just how fresh, 'cause when that bull plowed out of the thicket into my horse, Pete was right behind me. My horse shied sideways, so Pete couldn't get off a shot at first. Then that there bull's horn caught me in the

188

leg and threw me right out of the saddle. I could feel his breath on my face just before Pete shot and that old son of a gun let out a grunt. He crumbled to his knees and fell with his head right on my chest. A second later, he would have gored my heart out."

"Oh Lord, Ned!"

"Owe Pete my life, I do, Jes. Still do. Never did get a chance to repay him."

"Is that why you came with me to find the gold?"

"Yeah, at first. But now . . ."

"Miss Callaghan! Well, isn't this my lucky day? I knew the sun coming out meant good luck for me."

Jessica frowned as she looked up. Not Harlin Baker! The creases left her face when she saw David Baker standing by her chair. How similar the brothers were, both in looks and voice.

"Hello, David," she said with a smile.

"I'm so glad you haven't left town yet, Jessica."

"Pull up a chair, David," Ned said.

"Thanks." David sat down and inched his chair a little closer to Jessica's. "Tell me," he said as he leaned close to her. "My heart can't stand the suspense. Have you decided to stay in our fair town?"

"No," Jessica said with a laugh. "We can't stay. We . . ."

David picked up her hand and stared into her eyes. "Sweet Jessica, tell me that what my brother said this morning was a lie. Tell me you aren't staying out at that dreadful place."

Jessica stiffened and pulled her hand away. "Idalee is a friend of mine, David. I won't have you talking about her like that."

"I apologize, Jessica, but I want to be your friend, too. And surely that's not a place for you."

"It doesn't matter, David," Jessica said with a shrug. "We only stayed for Eloise's funeral. As soon as Tobias and Prudence stop by to say farewell, we'll be back on the trail."

David rose to his feet. "Oh, yes, the funeral. Such a sad thing. But please stay another day, Jessica. At least let me take you to dinner this evening. After all, it may be my last chance to see you."

"I'm sorry, David, but I really don't think I'll be here this evening."

David glanced at the door, then shrugged his shoulders. "Well, I guess I'll just have to check later and see if you've changed your mind. Harlin sent word he wanted to see me right away. Good-bye for now."

"Good-bye, David," she said, then turned back to Ned, forgetting David at once. "What else were you going to say Ned?"

"Later, Jes," Ned said. "Here come Tobias and Prudence."

Jessica walked down the board walkway with Ned by her side as they headed for Idalee's house. She glanced in front of her once at the retreating backs of Tobias and Prudence as their horses disappeared around the last saloon at the edge of town.

A matronly woman caught Jessica's eye as she passed the general store. Jessica wasn't surprised when the woman sniffed and pulled her shawl tighter around her shoulders instead of returning Jessica's greeting. She raised her head higher and sniffed back at the woman, hearing Ned's snorting chuckle beside her.

"You know what they say, Jes," Ned said, laughing. "Proper women don't associate with brothel or saloon women."

"Well, I'm a proper woman," Jessica said with a decisive nod of her head. "And I'll damn well associate with whomever I please!"

"Hang onto that there spunk, Jessica Callaghan," Ned said. "I've got a feelin' we might need it soon."

Jessica pulled Ned to a stop at the bottom of the steps to Idalee's house. "We need to finish our talk."

"Come on, Jes." He took her arm and gently forced her up the steps. "I've got a few questions I want to ask before I go stickin' my head into somethin' that might just not be my business. And we've gotta get Storm out of here before that sheriff decides to come back and look a little closer under that bed."

"Oh." Jessica dropped her head to hide her flushed cheeks. "I didn't know you could hear me."

"Heard every word. Every word."

Jessica whirled around as soon as she stepped through the door. "Ned! What did you just say? You're going to help Storm hide out?"

Ned shrugged his shoulders and stared over Jessica's head. "Just an idea I've got," he said nonchalantly. "Guess Jedidiah must've got itchy feet and lit out, 'cause I ain't seen him around. Soon's he's able, maybe we can ask Storm to help us. Since he comes from around here, he can probably take us to the gold just as quick as Jedidiah could've."

"Why, of course," Jessica mused. "And if we find it, we can pay him for his trouble. But, Ned, do you think he'll do it? After all, he's on the run from the law. And . . . and if we're caught with him . . ."

"Does that bother you, Jes? If so, you can still catch the train back to Wyoming."

"I'll do no such thing!" Jessica's mind filled with a vision of the man lying upstairs on Idalee's canopied bed.

His pain-shadowed eyes had lingered in her thoughts all day. She blushed and looked away from Ned to hide it. Why, she'd had to clench her fists to keep from tearing Prudence out of Storm's arms earlier.

Ned watched the emotions play across Jessica's face for a moment, then took her arm and gave her a push toward the stairs.

"Well, why don't you go up and check on our future guide, Jes? And wait for me here. I've got some arrangements to make if we're goin' to get this plan in motion. I'll be back either late tonight or just before dawn to get you both. I'm just gonna talk to Elias for a minute, then I'll be goin'."

"Ned, please be careful."

"I will, Jes. I will."

Hours later Jessica paced away her frustration as she walked back and forth on the carpeted floor in Idalee's room. She had already been down the hidden stairs twice to check on the horses. They both stood ready, though they shifted restlessly at their forced inactivity. She had even checked her leather saddlebag to make sure the map still remained hidden in the lining. Her fingers had lingered on the faded hide for a moment before she tucked it down securely again and refastened the snap on the saddlebag.

She glanced at the bed, where Storm's dim outline lay fully clothed. The only light in the room came from the fireplace.

Idalee hadn't told her until after she fed Storm and watched him slip into sleep that she had placed a sleeping potion in his food. Storm had refused to rest all afternoon, alternately pacing the room and threatening to leave on his own. Jessica was amazed at how fast his strength had returned, yet he had stumbled more than once. Idalee told her she had finally decided Storm needed to rest in order to be able to ride with them later that night.

Jessica moved to the door and opened it. She heard a woman's laugh float up the stairwell, then the sound of a door closing, cutting it off. She smiled to herself. Idalee's was in full swing. If she had stayed closed any longer, the town might have become suspicious.

Jessica's face creased into a frown when she thought she heard a footstep on the stairwell leading to the third floor. She had to be mistaken, since Idalee had assured her no one came up there without her permission. She gently closed the door and turned around to stare into the fire.

How long would it take Ned to get back? He must have had this planned all along, she realized. It would have been an easy matter to get the supplies they needed without arousing suspicion. He would just let the store-keeper think they were for their cowhands. But how long did it take, anyway, to ride out to the camp and dismiss the men? What else was he up to?

She shrugged and crossed to throw another log into the fireplace. They might have hot days, but the nights cooled off quickly in the higher altitudes. Idalee had shown her earlier how to open the vent on the register in the room, but she preferred the fireplace heat.

And Ned and Storm. Jessica had never seen Ned take so quickly to another man. Even the new hands he hired now and then on the ranch had to gain his respect—gain it or be on their way. She looked over at the bed. She hadn't even had time to sort out her own feelings about Storm, though she knew in her heart that he hadn't raped Prudence or ever committed a crime in his life. Whatever his story was, he couldn't have good friends like Idalee and Elias—friends who would risk all they had for him—if he were truly guilty.

And Prudence loved him, despite her brother's hatred of Storm. Prudence. Always Prudence. She bowed her head a little. He was Prudence's man. No matter that she found herself longing to be the woman he held close in his arms. No matter that she wanted to be the one to chase away the pain in his eyes.

No matter that for the first time in her life she knew what it was to love a man without reservation. How quickly it had happened. The feelings had begun before she even knew his name. Not just lust, though the fiery passion she felt when he held her seemed a natural part of her love. The pull she felt the first night they met should have told her she had found the man Mattie assured her would come into her life someday.

A light tap on the door drew her attention. Ned. Ned had to be back. She hurried to the door and flung it open without thinking about why Ned had come to the bedroom door instead of the door to the tunnel.

Chapter 15

"S'knew you'd be here." A malodorous whiff of whiskey-tinged breath hit Jessica full in the face and the man pushed into the room. "Lesh see if you're as good's the rest of the whores in this place."

Jessica stumbled and caught herself on the little table beside the bed. Before the scream building in her throat could erupt, the man jerked her against him, one hand closing around her neck. Frantically, she pulled at the bruising fingers cutting off her breath while he pushed her ahead of him toward the fireplace. Her booted feet dug at the carpeted floor, sliding ineffectually forward.

"That's it. Fight me, bitch!" he snarled close to her ear. "I like it rough, too, and I'll give you back as good as you want in just a minute. But first I want to look my fill of you."

He hurled her down onto the carpet. Jessica drew in a breath that eased the threatening blackness in her mind, but her paralyzed throat muscles refused to respond to her effort to scream. He ripped her blouse and chemise down the front, tearing the fabric as easily as brushing aside a spiderweb.

"Ah, that's what I wanted to see."

Jessica arched her fingers and reached for his face. He caught her hands an inch short of their goal, and wrenched her arms cruelly as he shoved them behind her back. Pushing the blouse from her shoulders, he entangled her arms in the restricting material and threw a leg over her to settle himself on her stomach.

When Jessica bucked against him, he tightened his thigh muscles around her and backhanded her across the face. Her head hit the raised fireplace hearth and she valiantly fought the pain shooting through it. Her eyelids fluttered open and she tried to focus on the shape of his face over her, but could only make out blond hair glinting in the firelight. He turned his head to the side before she could see his features.

"Nice bed over there," he muttered, "but I don't think we'll need it tonight." He grabbed a fistful of Jessica's hair, yanking her head around to fix her eyes on the fireplace.

Renewed tears of pain blurred her eyes and Jessica struggled frantically to free her arms. His muffled laughter sounded in the room and he pressed his erection into her tender stomach. Nausea boiled up in her throat.

"I'll kill you!" she hissed, her mind too drugged by the sick feeling spreading through her to realize she could scream now.

He struck her full force on the mouth again and Jessica felt her lip split. Warm blood trickled down her chin and she recoiled in horror when he bent and licked at it with his tongue. Vainly, she tried again to make out his features in the dim light, but he rolled to her side, his body shadowing the light from the fire. In some vague corner of her mind, Jessica heard the bedsprings squeak.

The man hovering over her bent down and grabbed the nipple of one breast in his sharp teeth. He growled and bit harder, worrying the nipple like a dog with a bone.

Jessica groaned in agony and suddenly the pain was gone. And the man, too. A thud echoed through the room and she opened her eyes in time to see the man's body slide down the side of the rock fireplace. A stream of darkness stained the rocks in the wake of his bleeding head and she quickly shut her eyes again.

An instant later she was pulled from the floor and gathered into a warm embrace. Storm. Only Storm smelled like that. She wrapped her arms around his waist and buried her head on his chest.

"Oh God, Jessica," he whispered. "Are you all right?"

She nodded her head against his chest, refusing to relinquish her grasp on him. She gulped furiously, but her sobs wouldn't abate. After one final shudder, she cried hysterically against his chest.

Storm tightened his grasp and cradled her in his arms. Bending his head, he laid his cheek on her sable curls and whispered frantically to her. "Jessica. God, Jessica, I'm sorry for what happened. But please, you've got to pull yourself together. I've got to get out of here."

Jessica gulped back her sobs and nodded her head as she reluctantly loosened her hold on him. Though it felt so good having him hold her, he was right. They couldn't wait for Ned now.

"I'm ready," she said as she swiped at a lingering tear on her cheek. "The horses are saddled and waiting."

"No, pretty lady," Storm said with a shake of his head. "You can't go with me."

Jessica's eyes widened in astonishment. "You mean, you're going to let me stay here and hang for killing Mr. Baker? That's who it is, isn't it? I couldn't see him very well, but . . ."

"Jessica, for God's sake. They'll believe you when you tell them—"

"Sure they will! Here I am in Baker's Valley, where Mr. Baker owns the bank, and the store, and the hotel, and the law—"

Storm gently clamped a hand over her lips. "Jessica, I don't think he's dead. And, damn it, you can't—"

"Mr. Baker!" High heels tapped down the hallway and a feminine voice penetrated through the door.

Sassy! Jessica immediately recognized the voice of the one other woman she had met in Idalee's house. Sassy— who Idalee had told her liked to talk so much.

"Mr. Baker?" Sassy called again. "Are you up here? Mr. Baker, you know Idalee doesn't allow her guests upstairs."

By the time the heel taps stopped outside the door, Storm and Jessica were slipping into the tunnel. The click of the tunnel door sliding shut sounded simultaneously with the click of the bedroom door opening. They managed to tiptoe quietly halfway down the top flight of stairs before the first scream split the air. They made the other two flights in record time, their own clattering footsteps covered up by the sounds of slamming doors and feet running through the house.

Scudding clouds covered the light of the waning moon above them, and Jessica shivered in the night breeze. She had to trust Cinnabar's surefootedness, since she could barely make out the rear of the paint in front of her. Only Storm seemed to know where they were headed.

At first, despite the danger of pursuit, he insisted they travel the road, mixing their hoofprints with the multitude of others. At a small bridge crossing the road, he urged the paint down the bank into a stream.

Cinnabar followed the paint willingly enough, as long as Jessica kept him far enough back not to antagonize the other stallion. Once she had let her reins go slack as she adjusted the torn blouse over her bodice and Cinnabar had reached out to nip at the paint. Both horses had reared and plunged as they sought to assert one's dominance over the other, and only Jessica's and Storm's expert riding had brought them under control.

But the effort must have taken its toll on Storm, because when a cloud momentarily cleared the moon, Jessica saw him slumped in the saddle.

"Storm," she called. "Storm, are you all right? How much farther are we going?"

Storm straightened in his saddle with an effort and pulled the paint over to the side of the trail. He motioned with one hand for Jessica to ride up beside him.

Keeping Cinnabar under firm control, Jessica brought him dancing sideways down the trail. When the stallion tried once again to reach his head out, she pulled firmly on the reins and pinned his head against his chest. She spoke sternly to him, and gratefully saw Cinnabar's ears flick up from their flat position on his head as he quieted.

"Storm, do you know where we're going?"

"There's a place," Storm said through grim lips. "It's near where I first saw you and your men."

"Are you going to be able to make it? It's going to rain in a minute and, if that's where we're headed, it must be another half-hour's ride."

"More like fifteen minutes, if we get moving. I'll make

it, Jessica. The shoulder's not that bad."

"Then why are you in such pain? Has the bleeding started again?"

"Damn it, Jessica, it's not the pain in my shoulder! It's what I've been thinking about. Do you have any idea what you've gotten yourself into by coming with me?"

"Not completely," she fired back at him. "But I'll tell you one thing, Mr. Storm whoever you are. When we get in out of this weather, I want some answers from you!"

A fat raindrop hit Jessica squarely on the nose and she sputtered when the water ran down over her lips. She heard Storm give an exasperated sigh and a second later she urged Cinnabar again behind the paint. The deluge broke a few moments later, making her think longingly of the rain cloak in her saddle pack, but when Storm kicked his horse into a gallop, she leaned down on Cinnabar's neck to follow.

Flashes of lightning lit their way when they galloped across the familiar camp site. Though Jessica's hair hung in sodden tresses, the turbulent wind blew it around her face. Rumbling thunder echoed constantly over the hilltops and just as they reached the other side of the campsite, a bolt of lightning split a tree on the hillside above them, filling the air with smells of ozone and smoke.

Both horses reared in terror until the riders pulled them down to earth. Storm slowed his pace as he urged the paint up the hillside trail, past the boulder where he had first held Jessica in his arms. Despite the pouring rain, he allowed his eyes to linger on it for a second.

When Cinnabar stopped, Jessica raised her head to see the blank cliff face in front of her. The rain streamed down over her face and she blinked her eyes to clear them. She still couldn't see Storm anywhere and her heart raced with fear.

"Jessica, come on!"

Cinnabar's ears pricked up again and, with no urging from Jessica, the horse tentatively made his way around the outcropping that had been shadowed by the darkness. An instant later, Jessica found herself in complete blackness and she pulled the stallion to a halt.

"S–Storm?"

"Just a moment," his disembodied voice came back. "I'm getting a torch lit."

The welcome light of a match flaring briefly illuminated the cave and an instant later she saw Storm hold the torch up over his head.

"Come on," he said as he turned to lead the paint forward. "It's just a little ways back here now."

Jessica allowed Cinnabar to pick his own way across a rubble-littered floor and follow Storm around a sharp angle in the cave wall. When Storm placed the torch in a crack in the stone face, Jessica looked around her and gasped in awe.

It could almost be someone's living room. Pine boughs covered the floor instead of a carpet, but a comfortable-looking stuffed chair was beside a hole carved out of the far wall. Dry wood was in the hole, waiting to be lit into a fire. A small, rather rickety table abutted the other side of the fireplace, a lone chair placed beside it.

While Storm lit two lanterns to add to the light of the torch, Jessica slid down from her mount and watched the rest of the small room come into view. In one corner was a mattress, a down-filled comforter over it. Why, there were even pictures on the walls. No matter that they were drawings by men long forgotten, they suited the decor exactly.

"Why, Storm," she said, "this is nice."

"It's not Baker's Hotel," he said with a grunt as he

leaned down to touch a match to the kindling. "But it does all right for now."

He stood up and Jessica saw him frown at Cinnabar.

"I—I'll take Cinnabar back up . . ."

"No, Jessica," Storm said. "I've got a place fixed on the other side of this cave for Spirit."

"Th–there's spirits in here? My men thought you were a ghost when they saw you."

"Not ghost spirits, Jessica." Storm chuckled. "Spirit's my horse."

"Oh. Well, the name suits him."

"I'm afraid we're going to have to tie the horses, though, instead of leaving them loose in the enclosure. Spirit's not long off the range. He was leading a herd of mustang mares when I caught him again."

"You've had him before?"

"Yes," Storm replied, but though Jessica waited, he didn't continue his explanation. "You keep your stallion there until I get Spirit tied. I'll fill the feed troughs for them and maybe they'll settle down when they get their stomachs full."

Jessica watched Storm pick up one of the lanterns and lead Spirit into the darkness on the other side of the cave. As soon as he disappeared, she again stared around her.

A shelf stacked with supplies, held up by pegs stuck into another crack above the table, ran along one wall. Her eyes traveled somewhat fearfully overhead to the ceiling. Bats sometimes lived in caves, but she saw only a smooth blankness over her.

Jessica shivered slightly as a breeze filtered in behind her. Dropping Cinnabar's reins to ground tie him, she crossed to the fire, knowing the stallion wouldn't move until ordered to.

She held her hands out to the fire and shivered again in

her soaked blouse. The leaping flames warmed the front of her quickly, but she would have to change if she wanted to get dry faster. At least she could put some more wood on the fire.

A pile of logs lay beside the fireplace and she knelt to pick up one. Something caught her eye behind the chair and she glanced over to see a familiar object on a small table. After tossing the wood onto the fire, she moved around the chair to investigate.

What looked like the mouth of a horn emerged from the top of the box—the box that held the horn in place. A lever stuck out from the side and Jessica stared at the contraption in mystification. What was it doing here?

"It's a gramophone," Storm said, making Jessica jump.

"I—I didn't hear you come back."

"Obviously," Storm said. "Let me get the horses settled and I'll show you how it works."

"For heaven's sake, I know how it works. Do you think I'm stupid or something?"

When Jessica rose to her feet and glared at him, Storm's mouth suddenly went dry. The wet blouse clung to her shapely shoulders, though the front of it had dried somewhat. She had tied the ends together just under her breasts, since the buttons had been ripped off. Above the knot, the blouse gaped, allowing him a clear view of her collar bone and the rounded mounds of the tops of her breasts. Her pebbled nipples were clearly outlined by the still-damp material.

Her nipples. That bastard had been biting one when Storm's eyes had flown open. Despite their relationship, he hoped he *had* killed the son of a bitch. How much had he hurt her?

Storm's hand came out and he gently traced a path around Jessica's nipple.

"Does it still hurt, pretty lady?" he murmured.

"A–a l–li–little." Suddenly Jessica found her teeth chattering. It couldn't be from the cold, because a swift heat raced over her body.

Storm slowly untied the knot on her blouse to bare her breasts. He growled softly in his throat when he saw an indentation made from a tooth mark beside the rosy aureola. Tenderly, he cupped his hand under her breast and smoothed his thumb over the mark.

"I should have made sure that bastard was dead!"

"No. Oh, Storm, no." Jessica placed her hand on his cheek, her movement thrusting her breast more fully into his hand. She ought to pull away, but it felt so wonderful having his hand on her.

Storm's eyes went to her face as he continued to soothe her breast. Her breath feathered over his face, drawing his gaze to her mouth. Though the rain had washed the blood away, he noticed the dark bruise on her cheek and the inch-long cut at the corner of her mouth.

His other hand caressed Jessica's full lower lip. "He hit you. We need to get some cool cloths on that bruise."

"The rain cooled it enough, Storm," Jessica found herself whispering as she stroked her index finger down his jaw. "I think it needs some warmth now. Won't you kiss it and make it better?"

Storm groaned and licked his dry lips. "I—I don't think I better."

Jessica stood on tiptoe and tilted her head back. "Please, Storm?" she whispered. "Make the pain better for me and I'll do all I can to make it better for you."

Invisible wires tugged Storm's head downward and he found it impossible to resist their pull. He tried. Oh, how he tried. His traitorous heart pounded at the thought of having Jessica finally in a safe place where he could show her how much he was coming to love her. But his mind shouted silently to him that this happiness, too, would be fleeting.

The mind lost when Jessica slipped her hands around his neck and added her urging to the wires. Just one taste. One taste to make her feel better and let his heart have a few seconds surcease from the constant pain.

Considerate of her injuries, he caught her lips gently, clingingly, before he pulled slightly away. Just once more. His mind joined his renegade heart. The kiss lasted longer this time, though he steeled himself to keep from crushing her against him.

Jessica's fingers crawled into his hair and she refused to relinquish her hold when he pulled back again. Her lips only moved far enough away for her to whisper, "Does it make it better, Storm? It makes it better for me."

"It makes it better, pretty lady," Storm breathed back. "You don't know how much better."

"Show me, Storm. Show me how much better it can be."

She covered his mouth with her own and her lips opened willingly when he forgot his caution and plunged his tongue inside her mouth. She felt her breast surge fuller in his hand and his answering massage that spiraled the rapture filling her even higher. She fit herself against his body, her arms clinging and her soft thighs pressed against his perfectly hard ones.

He drew his head back and kissed the split on the side of her mouth. The bruise on her cheek he licked gently. His tongue pushed back the damp hair and dried the rain from her ear, leaving instead the moisture from his mouth.

When Jessica bowed her head, Storm pushed aside the damp hair from the back of her neck. He spent several long seconds kissing and laving the area when he heard her purr with pleasure at his attention to the sensitive spot. Somehow he found her blouse in his hand and he dropped it to the floor before he kissed a path across her shoulder and down to the breast his hand had neglected.

Jessica gasped and arched against him when he sucked her nipple into his mouth. Oh God, it felt good having him holding her, kissing her, stroking her. She ran her hands across his shoulders and moved them to his shirt buttons. Then back up his corded chest, making sure she didn't touch his injury as she slipped the shirt from his shoulders. She knew that skin—almost every inch of it. It felt so much different under her stroking fingers now, almost silky hot. She caressed the ripples his muscles made as he shrugged his arms free of the shirt.

His arms didn't go back around her again. Instead, he bent slightly and placed one behind her knees, the other around her waist.

"Storm, your shoulder!" she gasped when he pulled her feet from the floor.

Storm ignored her protest. In two quick strides he found the mattress and laid her down on the comforter. His lips covered hers again and he stretched out close to her.

Storm cupped her face and drew back slightly. "Pretty lady, you make me forget everything. We have to stop."

"Why, Storm? Why can't we have this one night? It can't hurt anyone."

"You don't know what you're asking."

"No." Jessica shook her head slightly as she gazed into the black pools of his eyes. "I don't. But I want to know."

The lantern light lit the pain again filling his eyes and Jessica felt her heart lurch. She leaned over and kissed each eye shut, then each cheek, each side of his mouth.

Her lips yearned to feel his fully on them again, and she satisfied that yearning. And the yearning of her breasts to nestle against the corded chest muscles and the thick hair that caressed them.

Storm raised his head slightly and ran his hands down her sides. He unbuttoned the riding skirt and drew it down over her legs.

"I want you, pretty lady," he said as he slipped his hand inside the waistband of her pantelets. "I've never wanted anything as much as I want you." His hand moved to her flat stomach and down between her thighs. "I want the pleasure I get when I hold you and the sweetness and peace I feel when you're in my arms."

Jessica gasped and arched against his hand when he slipped a finger inside her.

"Oh, Storm. Storm, I want you, too. I haven't been able to get you out of my mind since I first saw you."

Storm pushed himself up and stared down at her. "Are you sure, Jessica?" But his hands worked to slide her pantelets down and he tossed them aside.

"I'm sure," Jessica said with a slight nod of her head. She lifted one leg and offered it to him to remove her boot.

Storm bent and kissed her knees as he pulled off each boot. Then he sat back on his heels and unbuttoned the top button on his jeans, then the second one, the following ones, though the strain against the front of the material made it a difficult task. Before he pulled the jeans down over his hips, he removed his moccasins and tossed them aside. On his knees again, he caressed her with his eyes and smiled when he saw a flush climb up her chest and fill her cheeks.

"This may be all we ever have, Jessica," he said quietly. "This one night. There are people on earth who have the power to make sure we can never have anything except this one night."

Prudence. Oh God, she knew he meant Prudence. But Prudence would have him the rest of her life. She couldn't begrudge Jessica this one night. If Storm were her man, though, she knew she would do more than begrudge another woman a night in his arms. She would kill anyone who tried.

He was right. They had to stop but she wanted so badly to touch him just one more time. Tentatively, she reached out and ran her nails softly around the side of his trim waist. When she felt him jump slightly, the movement drew her eyes to the bulge straining beside the open buttons of his jeans. Her hand moved of its own volition down to stroke it.

"This one night, Storm," she heard herself saying as though from a distance. "Please, let's just have this one night with no one else between us. If it's all we ever have, then somehow I'll have to live with that."

Though he must have removed the jeans, later Jessica didn't remember him doing it. But when he lay down beside her, there was no impediment to their matching silky inches of soft skin to firmer, muscular inches.

She would remember his words forever, though. "One night of you will never be enough for me, darlin' Jessica, my pretty lady. Somehow, some way, there has to be a future for us."

Then his lips were too busy caressing her to speak. She writhed under an onslaught of kisses that covered her body. Her lips remained puffed and full when his left hers to linger on her soft neck. Trails of fire followed the paths he traced on her body.

Jessica's hands kneaded his shoulders while his mouth suckled her breasts. Her hands fell uselessly to her side when he moved lower and swirled his tongue in the indentation in her stomach.

He kissed down one slender thigh and licked behind her knee. The heated skin on her body quickly dried the moisture his tongue left on its path to her ankle. One soft instep received his attention, then the other. The trail of fire started back up her leg, flared briefly at her knee again. Then she felt his lips gently sucking at the tender skin on her inner thigh. She arched her back, seeking . . . seeking she knew not what.

Storm knew. He tenderly parted the lips covering the core of her femininity and teased her with the tip of his tongue.

"Storm! Oh! Oh God, what are you doing!" Her head thrashed wildly, tangling her hair into knots.

"I'm making you happy, sweet Jessica," he said, his words barely penetrating her wildly fluctuating emotions. "I'm making you happy, the way you make me feel."

And he lowered his head again. Seconds later Jessica felt a shudder begin in her body.

"Stop!" she almost screamed. "Storm, stop. I can't stand . . . Storm. Oh my God, that feels so good. Don't stop. I . . ."

Her body exploded into a million pieces. The feeling went on and on, tearing her apart but she didn't care. The pieces all fell back together when she floated back to consciousness.

Storm's kiss on her soft stomach lingered briefly, moved up to her rib cage, then to her breasts. Awestruck, she felt the fire rise in her again as he kissed the side of her neck.

"Did you like that, pretty lady?" he whispered. "Did I make you feel better?"

"Yes. Oh, yes, Storm."

"And I can make you feel even better, sweet Jessica."

"H–how—"

His mouth cut off her question. He rose over her and nudged her thighs open further. He pushed his hardness into the welcoming wetness he encountered and thrust forward slightly.

My God! He had to be careful. He should have known she was a virgin.

When Jessica moaned and arched toward him, her silken heat surrounded the tip of him. He found himself powerless when she sucked his tongue deep into her mouth and wrapped her legs around his hips. The barrier to his pleasure broke and he buried himself deep inside her, wrenching his mouth away to whisper soothingly in her ear when he felt her stiffen in pain.

"It's all right now, sweet Jessica. Darlin', it won't hurt again. Trust me, sweetheart."

He withdrew from her slightly and plunged inside her again. He watched her eyes fly open and her mouth round in awe.

"Oh, Storm!"

"Yes, darlin'. Yes. There's only the pleasure now. The pleasure that's only there for two special people. Oh God, Jessica. It's never been like this for me before."

And he carried her to blissful heights again before he sought his own release. Even through the tumult in his own body, he felt her join him this time, making their tumble into ecstasy together the most complete satisfaction he had ever known in his life.

Chapter 16

"Shhhh, honey," Storm said when Jessica whimpered and reached for him. "I'm just going to take care of your horse and put some more wood on the fire. I'll be right back."

"Hurry," Jessica murmured. When Storm tucked the comforter around her neck, she dropped a kiss on his fingers and snuggled deeper. The warmth surrounded her and her eyelids slowly closed.

Storm pulled down a dry pair of jeans from a shelf in the cave and slipped into them before he added another log to the fire. The flames leaped higher, but the smoke, helped by the draft in the cave, ascended through the natural chimney shaft in the rocks above the fireplace. He stared into the flames for a long moment, the light illuminating the haggard lines of his face.

What the hell did fate have in store for him now? He didn't think he could stand much more. Barrier after barrier had been put between him and every person on earth he had ever cared about.

And now this marvelous woman he first saw sitting on the huge roan stallion as though born to her saddle lay within touching distance yet far beyond his reach, reminding him just how much he could never have her. She had come to him willingly, givingly, stirring a passion and longing in him that made a mockery of what he had even imagined he missed.

Sure, there had been women before. Something about his dark looks and his brooding sadness drew them to him. All of them had been more interested in their own pleasure than his, though.

Jessica. Even thinking her name filled him with wonder. Jessica gave freely of herself. She hadn't hesitated to help when he was wounded in the hills. She stuck by him, despite his attempts to run her off. She nursed him, even in the brothel, which had surely sullied her own reputation. She made him laugh and laughed with him. She followed where he led.

He didn't have a damn thing to offer her, because his time would soon run out. The newspapers Idalee kept him supplied with informed him of the new Montana governor's campaign to rid the state of its wild and woolly reputation as they headed into a new century. He didn't have much to worry about from the ineffectual sheriff in Baker's Valley, but sooner or later one of the marshals the governor had appointed would focus his attention on their end of the new state.

Storm sighed and rose to tend to Jessica's stallion. The horse shied at first, but Storm spoke soothingly to it as he took the reins. The pine boughs on the floor muffled the horse's feet, but he noticed Jessica stir slightly as he led Cinnabar across the cave floor.

Cinnabar tossed his head, but Storm managed to slip off the rope halter he had fashioned over the stallion's head and his bridle. Catching a whiff of the grain in the feed trough, the horse lowered his head greedily.

"Good boy," Storm said as he ran his hand along the stallion's neck. "You had a hard ride tonight. Now fill your stomach."

He slid the saddle off and laid it in a corner, then picked up the curry comb. Cinnabar's still-damp coat needed care and Storm brushed at the satiny hide. The horse rippled his muscles in pleasure as the currycomb slid over him, reminding Storm of Jessica's silky body sliding under his fingers.

He hurried the combing, finding himself longing to return to the side of the woman who had come to mean the world to him in so short a time. Quickly, he checked Spirit to assure himself the horse was still tied securely, and tossed another armful of dried grass into the feed trough. But when he entered the warmth of the main cave, he stood over Jessica for a moment, then walked to the stuffed chair Idalee and Elias had hauled out there for him and sat down.

He couldn't have her. So much stood in their way. He should have had plenty to offer her, since he had sure as hell worked his ass off for years to earn his own share of the Lazy B. In the end, though, even the man he'd called father for most of his life failed him.

Jessica languidly stretched under the comforter and her feet chilled when they encountered the coldness beyond the spot where she lay. Lordy, she hated her feet being cold. Usually, she wore a pair of woolly socks to bed, but tonight there should have been another pair of feet to snuggle hers between. She opened her eyes and looked around for Storm.

What she saw almost made her heart break. He sat in the stuffed chair beside the fireplace, his arms propped on his knees and his head hanging down. Was he already regretting their lovemaking? Oh, how could he, when it had been so glorious?

"Storm?" she called quietly.

He immediately straightened and tossed back the hair hanging down in his eyes. The firelight outlined his head, shadowing his face.

"Go back to sleep, honey," he told her. His attempt to hold his voice steady couldn't cover up the pain his thoughts had brought.

"I can't." Jessica rose to her feet and wrapped the comforter around her, trailing it behind her as she crossed the floor. "My feet are cold. I can never sleep when my feet are cold."

Storm held out his arms and Jessica climbed into his lap. He settled her against him, wrapping the comforter around them both. Trying to ignore the silky curls under his neck and the satiny mounds against his chest, he reached down to massage her small feet.

"You are cold," he said quietly. "Want a pair of my socks?"

"No, this will be fine."

He tightened his arm around her and groaned under his breath when she fidgeted to a more comfortable position in his lap.

"Storm," Jessica whispered in a tight voice. "Storm, are you sorry?"

"Sorry?" Storm asked in amazement. "Do you mean making love to you?"

When Jessica nodded against his chest, he took hold of her arms and pushed her slightly away from him. She kept her head lowered until he cupped her chin in his large palm and lifted her face to his. He waited a long moment, until she raised her eyes and glanced tremulously at him, before he answered her with questions of his own.

"Sorry that I've just had the most wonderful experience of my life? Sorry that I held more woman in my arms than I could ever have imagined walked this earth? Sorry that, though I tried with all I had, she gave me back so much more than I wanted to give her? No, Jessica, I could never be sorry for that."

Jessica's heart soared at his words, but she could still sense his holding back on her. "You are sorry about something," she said. "I can feel it."

"All right," he admitted gruffly. "I'm sorry I can't give you more than this. I'm sorry that I can't offer you the life you deserve and be there to live it with you. Too many things stand between us."

"Is one of them the fact that you escaped from prison? I knew that while we were still back at Idalee's, Storm."

"And you still came with me?"

"Uh-huh. Because I knew even then I was falling in love with you."

Though Jessica leaned toward him, her lips begging for his kiss, Storm kept a firm hold on her arms and pushed her even further away.

"Don't, Jessica," he said grimly. "You don't know what you're saying. There's no future with me."

"Then I'll take what I can get now, Storm," she said sadly. "I'll take now and whatever crumbs I can have. I love you, Storm. I'll love you forever, whether I'm with you or not."

Storm pulled her tightly against him and cradled her head against his neck. He dropped a kiss on her head, holding her firmly when she tried to turn her face up.

"You don't even know me, Jessica. There's so many things you don't know."

"I know you're a good man, Storm," she said quietly as she relaxed against him. "I know there are people I've met and learned to respect who care for you. I know you couldn't have done what you're accused of."

She felt his grip on her loosen and managed to push herself free with a swift movement and face him. "I know there's another woman out there you're committed to, Storm. And I won't come between that." She felt her heart wrench in her chest, but she forced herself to continue. "P—Prudence needs you. I realize that."

"She's living in her own hell right now," Storm agreed, sending Jessica's heart plummeting even further. "And that damned brother of hers isn't helping matters any. If he'd just let me be with her for a while, we could get this whole mess out in the open."

"Who—who did ravish her, Storm?"

"She won't tell me," Storm said as he shook his head. "I think she could now. Once when I slipped into the ranch while Tobias was gone, I taught her a little sign language from a book Elias gave me. I left it with her to study. You saw her back in town. She's learning the signs from the pictures in the book, even if she can't read. But the couple of times I asked her what really happened, she froze up on me, and if I pushed her, she'd get almost hysterical. She's not ready yet to tell anyone. Something's holding her back."

"H—have you known her long, Storm?"

"Almost all my life."

"Then I guess you grew up around here."

"Yes." Then he groaned and pulled the comforter around her. "Jessica, darlin', you're going to have to get some clothes on. I can't stand this any longer."

Suddenly Jessica recognized the shape of the hardness she had been trying to shift against to a more comfortable position. She blushed and jumped off his lap.

"I—I'm sorry."

"Don't be, pretty lady," Storm said with a laugh. "I enjoy holding you, and if I didn't think you were too sore right now, I'd carry you right back over to that bed and show you how much I enjoy it."

Rising to his feet, he walked to the shelf holding his spare clothes. He grabbed the first shirt he found, along with a pair of wool socks, and started to turn. His arm brushed against a bundle on the edge of the shelf and it landed at his feet.

When her eyes fell on the bundle, Jessica surged forward. She laughingly swiped at Storm's hand and managed to snag the objects he tried to hide from her.

"You!" she crowed triumphantly as she waved the gray beard and wig just out of his reach. "No wonder Jedidiah disappeared. He couldn't be in the same place as you! That's what I found in your hair the other night when you were wounded—glue."

Storm sheepishly dropped his eyes. "Well, it was my fault you went into Baker's Valley. I had to make sure you didn't get into any trouble there."

"Storm, I had a whole cluster of cowboys with me, not even counting Ned. I'll admit, it's not the most friendly town I've ever been in, but what possible trouble could I have . . ." Jessica's voice trailed off as a humble look replaced the twinkle in her eyes. "I . . . Well, you didn't have to worry," she continued, her voice again hinting at laughter. "I had a friendly ghost protecting me."

Storm briefly joined her chuckles before he thrust the shirt and socks into her hand. "Here, honey. Put these on while I start some coffee. It doesn't look like either one of us will get any sleep tonight."

Jessica accepted the clothing and watched him turn back to the fireplace to scoop coffee grounds from a can, then walk away from her.

"Where are you going?"

"Just to get some water from the canteens."

Jessica kept her eyes on him until he entered the portion of the cave where the horses were stabled before she sat down in the chair and pulled the socks on. Standing, she slowly rubbed the shirt against her cheek before slipping it on. Even though the shirt had been washed, she thought she could detect his smell on it.

She heard a sound behind her and turned. The shirt fluttered around her slender calves and she saw Storm standing quietly looking at her. She laughed gaily.

"I know I look silly, but at least my feet are warm now."

"You look beautiful, pretty lady," Storm said. He walked over and poured the water into the coffeepot, then handed her a brush he had brought with him from his saddlebag. "If you'll wait a minute, I'll help you with your hair."

"That sounds wonderful," Jessica said with a sigh.

A second later Storm settled in the chair and Jessica curled herself on the comforter at his feet before handing the brush to him over her shoulder.

Storm worked the brush through her hair, following each stroke with his fingers. The silky mass took on a life of its own under his palms and he heard the now-familiar purr begin in Jessica's throat.

"Your hair's beautiful, Jessica," he said finally into the lengthening silence. "I've wanted to touch it like this since I first saw you."

"Thank you. Storm?"

"What, pretty lady?"

"Can I ask you a couple questions?"

The brush froze for an instant in her hair, making Jessica regret her words. She sighed in relief when Storm began pulling it through her hair again and spoke.

"You can ask anything you want, Jessica. I'll answer any question you have, I promise."

Jessica stared into the firelight for a moment before she said, "I—I'd at least like to know your last name," she finally forced out.

The brush hesitated slightly again and she heard him sigh behind her then softly chuckle.

"Why, Jessica Callaghan," he said, "you mean to tell me you've just made wild, passionate love with a man whose last name you don't even know?"

Jessica gave a snort and jumped to her feet. "Why . . . why, you . . ."

Storm let out a loud guffaw and held his arms out. "Come here, pretty lady," he said, immediately defusing her embarrassment. "I like you better in my arms."

"Well, I just don't know about that," Jessica said saucily, placing her fists on her hips. "I think maybe we should get to know each other a lot better before I crawl onto your lap again, don't you?"

Storm gave a growl and reached for her. She managed to dance a step away before her foot tangled in the comforter at her feet and she started to fall. A pair of arms caught her and the next thing she knew he held her close to his side, the firelight warming her back.

"Storm, you're going to hurt your shoulder if you keep this up."

"It's healing fine, pretty lady. Exercise will help me work the twinges out of it. Besides, we have to see what we can do about getting to know each other better, right?"

Jessica wrapped her arms around his neck as he kissed her deeply. When his lips left hers and started down her neck, she pulled herself back with a gasp and shook her head. "You—you promised to answer me."

Storm buried his face against her neck for a second, then gave a regretful sigh and raised his head. Brushing the hair from the side of her face as he gazed down at her, he steeled himself for the disgust he would soon see in her gold-flecked eyes.

"My last name's Baker, Jessica," he said quietly.

"Baker?" Jessica asked in astonishment. To Storm's relief, he saw puzzlement rather than revulsion on her face as she continued, "You don't look like your brothers."

"I don't look like Idalee either," he agreed, "and she's Harlin and David's half sister."

Jessica pulled herself up and curled her legs under her. Crossing her arms under her breasts, she waited silently for Storm to continue.

"Oh, hell," he grumbled. He sat up beside Jessica and pulled her around between his legs, facing the fireplace.

"I can't think when I look at you sitting there like that, pretty lady," he explained when she tried to turn around in his arms. "Maybe this will be better." When Jessica sighed in compliance and nestled against him, he stifled a groan.

Jessica laughed softly and scrambled to her feet. She sat down in the chair and urged him to lay his head on her knee. "Is this better?" she asked as she stroked his hair.

"Guess it'll have to do," Storm said with a grunt.

"Now, tell me the rest," she insisted. "Why, Idalee doesn't look any more like Harlin and David than you do. What's the reason everyone looks so different, except for David and Harlin?"

Storm settled his head more comfortably against her

thigh and absentmindedly stroked her slender calf as he stared in the fire, sorting through the memories tumbling into his mind.

"There's a reason, Jessica," he finally said. "You've probably already figured it out. Charles Baker adopted me."

"Who were your real parents?"

Storm drew in a tortured breath and forced the words past his lips. "I don't know, Jessica. Oh, I knew at a young age that the people I was living with weren't my parents. The old man, Jack Wilson, got drunk enough times and told me so, even though he made me use his last name. Mary tried to protect me, but he wasn't much easier on her when he was on the bottle. I don't know how he ever held on to his job at the Lazy B, unless it was because Charles felt sorry for Mary and me."

"Storm, he didn't beat you?"

He nodded against her knee. "Jack said he had to make sure he followed the Bible's teaching. You know, spare the rod and spoil the child."

"Oh, no," Jessica breathed.

"I thought about killing him, do you know that, Jessica? Even at five years old, I'd lie in my bed at night and think up ways I could kill him."

"Oh God, Storm. What—what happened?"

Storm stiffened under her fingers and his hand gripped her calf almost painfully before he realized what he was doing and released his hold.

"Mary died with the fever," he finally said. "She hadn't ever been very strong, and I think I remember her losing a couple babies. At least, she was in bed a long while at different times. Charles sent Fiona to help out during those times and Jack didn't dare interfere."

"Fiona?"

"She was Charles's housekeeper. Or at least, that's the story they gave out. After I went to live in the house, it didn't take me long to realize that Charles visited Fiona's place a lot of times late in the evenings. She lived about a mile away. Never stayed at the ranch past dark."

"But his wife . . ."

"Harlin and David's mother died shortly after David was born. David's about the same age as me. I asked Charles about his wife once, but all he would tell me was that we all make mistakes in our younger days. He loved Fiona, though. You could tell it when they were together."

"And your father . . . I mean . . ." Jessica shook her head in confusion. Which one would Storm call father—Jack Wilson or Charles Baker? Or maybe the mysterious man who had physically fathered him? "Uh, I mean, Jack, the man you lived with before Charles adopted you. What happened to him?"

"I never knew for certain, but I think Charles bought Jack off. The adoption was legal, anyway. I remember us going to court, and Jack rode out of town afterwards. I never saw him again."

"Were you happy with Charles Baker, Storm?"

The silence dragged out as Storm thought about the years he had lived on the Lazy B. His pride would never allow him to tell his adopted father why accidents seemed to follow him around. No sooner would one bruise heal on his body than another one would form. There were even a couple broken bones over the years.

Until the day he finally realized he outweighed his adopted brothers and left them both lying bleeding on the floor of the line shack they had followed him to.

But despite the fact that Charles at times shook his head over Storm's clumsiness, he had treated Storm as his own. He couldn't even seem to hide his preference at spending time with a growing boy who didn't carry his blood, instead of his own sons.

"Yes, Jessica," he said at last. "At times I was happy. I cared deeply for Charles and I even dreamed of running the spread with him someday. Harlin never had an interest in the land at all, and he went back East to school as soon as he was old enough. David made a pretense of learning how to run the ranch, and it must have worked. When Charles was killed, his will left the ranch to David. The other holdings he had built up, including the bank, went to Harlin, and Harlin's expanded them until he owns most of the town."

"Oh, Storm. How could he have cut you out completely, after going to the trouble of making the adoption legal? And you still haven't told me how Idalee fits in."

The coffee bubbled over into the fire, sending hissing steam up from the coals. Storm jumped up and grabbed a towel to pull the hook holding the pot aside and set the pot on the table before he faced Jessica again.

Chapter 17

"Haven't you guessed that, too, Jessica?" he asked. "Idalee is Fiona and Charles's daughter. I'll admit, I was as surprised as Idy when we found out Charles had cut us both completely out. But the will was dated only a couple of years before Charles died."

"Now wait a minute. Idalee's name is Morgan. She told me so herself."

Storm picked up two cups from the shelf and filled them. After Jessica took her cup, he sat down at her feet again.

"She uses her mother's maiden name," he said as he waited for his coffee to cool enough to drink. "Charles made the doctor list him as the father on Idy's birth certificate, though, and I guess Harlin was afraid Idy might use that birth certificate to try to break the will. Anyway, he made a deal with her. He paid her, gave her money he thought she was going to use to leave town, in return for her written agreement not to make any claim against Charles's estate."

"But Idalee didn't leave town."

"No," Storm said with a hard laugh. "Idy's got spunk, she has. She had Elias buy the house at the edge of town for her under the pretense of turning it into a restaurant. She and Elias had always been close, ever since Elias came to work at the Lazy B as a cook for a while and they got to know each other. But Idalee had other plans for the house. You know what she did with it. She's never said why exactly, but I think she wants to rub David and Harlin's noses in what she does, daring them to run her off."

"But what about you? Good Lord, you must have worked with Charles at the Lazy B for at least twenty years."

"Twenty-two," Storm admitted. "Since I was five, like I said. I'm twenty-eight now, but this last year I haven't been near the Lazy B. Oh, Harlin offered me almost the same deal he made Idy, except that I had to legally change my name back to Wilson. I turned him down flat. And, for a while, I thought about fighting Harlin and David for what was mine, but I couldn't get over the hurt of what Charles had done."

Jessica set her coffee down and slipped out of the chair. Placing one arm around Storm's waist, she took his cup in her other hand and put it beside her own.

"Storm, that's enough for one night. This is hurting you too much to talk about." She pressed her head against his shoulder, momentarily forgetting his wound. Feeling him wince under her cheek, she quickly straightened.

"Oh. We better change . . ."

Storm dropped a kiss on her lips, stilling her words. "I told you, the wound's not bothering me. At least, not that much. And neither is talking to you. In fact, it's making me feel a whole lot better. I haven't talked to anyone about this in years. Idalee knows the story, of course, but it's not something we discuss."

Jessica scooted around and laid her head down in his lap. Despite what he said, his shoulder had to be hurting and at least this way she could be close to him. She pulled his hand onto her stomach and covered it with her own.

"Then tell me what happened to Charles and Fiona, Storm. How did they die? I assume Fiona's dead, too, from what you've been saying."

"They died together," he said after a moment. "I guess they would have wanted it that way, but it was such a damned waste. We never found out who shot them."

"Shot them? Oh, Storm."

He continued as though he hadn't heard her, "I don't know why Charles decided to get involved in the bank, either, but he bought it when he heard it was having some problems. People in town were afraid they might lose their savings and started a run on it. Someone rode out to the ranch to tell him, and when he got back from town he told us he now owned the bank. He seemed to enjoy running it, too, because he went into town almost every day.

"David and I were running the ranch jointly by then, but it wasn't going smoothly. We had different ideas about how things should be done, and Charles always seemed to take my side. He and David argued violently about it at times in the evenings. I tried to stay out of it, but I knew what was going on. Harlin came back from school about that time, but he moved into town when Charles asked him if he wanted to learn the banking business."

When he fell silent, Jessica looked up to see him staring into the fire. "You said they were shot," she reminded him, somehow sensing he needed to purge himself of the rest of the tale.

"They were going to be married the next day," Storm said quietly. "Charles never told me why Fiona had refused to legalize their relationship all those years, but she was a pretty independent woman. Idy's a lot like her. Anyway, Fiona finally gave in."

Storm glanced at Jessica. "He was so damned happy, Jessica. I'd never seen him so elated. Fiona didn't go into town much, since I imagine you can guess how the women treated her. Charles insisted she have a new dress made for the wedding, though, and she went in with Charles that afternoon for a final fitting and to pick it up. They never got home that evening and we found them when we went out to search. He had covered her with his own body, but someone had stood over them and made sure they were both dead."

Jessica's eyes filled with tears and she gulped back a sob. "He must have loved her so very much," she said despite the lump in her throat.

Storm straightened his legs and lay down beside her, gathering her against him. "He did. The way I love you. I do, you know, my darlin' pretty lady. I would lay down my life for you in a minute if anyone tried to hurt you. You don't know how much I wish things could be different."

Jessica sobbed aloud, this time for a different reason. The tears spilled from her eyes and she tried to bury her face against his chest to hide them.

Storm cupped her face and his callused thumb wiped the corner of her eye. "Jessica? I'm sorry. If I'd thought my telling you how I feel would make you cry, I'd have . . ."

"Oh, hush, Storm Baker," she said as she placed her index finger on his lips. "Can't you tell the difference between a woman crying from sadness and one crying from happiness? I love you, too. I've already told you that. But I thought . . . Pr—"

"Don't think, Jessica darling," he said as he lowered his head. "Just let me love you again. Please. I love you and need you so much."

He stopped with his lips a bare inch from hers. "Unless . . . Jessica, I don't want to hurt you."

"The only way you could hurt me would be not to love me again, Storm," she said as she closed the distance separating them.

Storm glanced at Jessica the next morning while he led Spirit toward the cave's entrance. She still sat curled up in the middle of the comforter, dressed only in his shirt and socks.

When she sensed his eyes on her, Jessica glared briefly at him. After an instant, she tilted her chin up in stubborn defiance and turned her head aside.

He busied himself for a few minutes, removing supplies from the shelf by the table and storing them in his saddlebags. After he dumped the coffee beans into a cloth sack and pulled the drawstring, he looked down at the table. Jessica's breakfast of biscuits and bacon remained untouched on her plate. He really should have waited until after she ate before he told her his plans, he guessed, but who would have thought such stubbornness lay under that pretty exterior?

Storm picked up the plate and crossed the room. Kneeling in front of her, he offered it to her.

"You're going to have to eat something before we leave, Jessica. It's a long ride to the next town with a train stop, and you'll get mighty hungry before we get there."

Jessica grabbed the plate and put it down by her side. She recrossed her arms under her breasts and stared over his shoulder, refusing to speak.

The go-to-hell look on Jessica's face flared Storm's

temper and he rose over her.

"You're going to eat before we leave, damn it! And then you're going to get dressed or I'll put your clothes on you myself."

"I'm not going anywhere near a train stop!"

"You're going if I have to tie you on that horse," Storm said through gritted teeth. "It's too dangerous for you to stay with me."

"I'm not leaving until I find what I came here for. Maybe you can hog-tie me and carry me out of here, but I don't think you'll have the guts to show your face in town."

"I can always go in as Jedidiah," Storm reminded her.

Jessica's mind searched frantically for another argument. "You—you'd have to ride right up to the station with me. Someone might recognize your horse."

"I guess I'll just have to take that chance then, won't I? You obviously won't go on your own."

"Don't you dare try to make me feel guilty, Storm! Besides, by the time we get to the nearest town, my face will probably be on those wanted posters right along with yours. Even if Mr. Baker isn't dead, you don't think he's going to let an attack on him go unavenged, do you?"

"All the more reason for you to get out of here until we can get this mess straightened out, Jessica. You don't have a chance in hell of finding any land around here right now. Or any time in the near future either. Harlin and David are determined to own this entire county. They've even tried to make Tobias sell out to them, just because his ranch borders on the edge of the Lazy B."

The mutinous pout returned to Jessica's lips and her chin rose an inch higher. "What if I'm not looking for land?"

"I don't give a damn *what* you're looking for, Jessica. Don't you see what a mess you've gotten yourself into by helping me? Once you get back to Wyoming, you'll be safe for a while."

Safe, but in debt to Ned for her ranch, Jessica thought. Maybe she should tell Storm about the gold. She *had* to find it. Part of Ned and Mattie's life savings were at risk now, too.

"I'm sure you've got friends there," Storm said, breaking into her thoughts. "Maybe even a smart lawyer, who can clear you of this mess."

A contemplative look filled Jessica's face. "As a matter of fact," she mused, "I do." She scrambled up and rested her hand on Storm's arm, tilting her face up to him. "Come with me, Storm. I do know someone. He's the attorney I use and he also handles criminal cases. He'll help you, too."

And maybe Frederick could find a way to forestall Olson's foreclosure, if her delay in finding the gold made her miss her next payment. She probably should have gone to see Frederick before she left Wyoming, instead of allowing her pride to keep her from admitting to her friends how desperate her financial situation was. Right now, though, Storm's plight seemed more important than her holding on to her ranch.

"I can't leave Idy here alone right now, Jessica. Lord knows what happened after we left there last night."

"Just how in hell do you think you're going to help her when you have to hide out here? Damn it, it makes more sense to get some help to clear your name!"

"I fight my own battles, Jessica. I always have and I always will."

"Ned was right. You ride a lonely trail, don't you, Storm?"

"I've had to. Come on. Eat your breakfast and get dressed."

"All right," Jessica agreed, startling him with her compliance. She sat down and picked up a biscuit and piece of bacon. "Maybe you're right. I'll go back and get Frederick to help me. He's always done anything I've asked him to do."

"Who the hell's Frederick?"

Jessica munched some of the biscuit in an attempt to still the twitch at the side of her mouth. She swallowed, then bent her head so her hair would slide down to hide her face while she tore the rest of the biscuit open and placed a piece of bacon inside it.

"He's the attorney I mentioned," she said before she took another bite.

"Oh," Storm muttered. "And he'll do anything you ask, huh?"

"Umph," Jessica said, her mouth full. She swallowed again and busied herself making another sandwich. "Like I said, he always has before."

Storm stared down at the shining curls hiding Jessica's face for a moment. "Just how well do you know this Frederick?" he asked before he could stop himself.

"Oh, I've known him for years," she said, waving a hand vaguely in the air. "He's a marvelous dancer."

Storm tightened his hands into fists, then turned abruptly away from her. "I'll get your horse ready while you dress."

The twitch in her cheek stilled with no problem as she tossed her hair back and watched him cross the cave floor. She hadn't really lied to him, she told herself. Frederick really was a wonderful dancer, even if he was three times her age. And he did do everything she asked him to, as long as she paid his fee.

She swallowed the last bite of the sandwich, though it tasted like dry leaves in her mouth. Taking the second one with her, she rose and went to the fireplace, where her riding skirt lay over the chair back, now dry. She stuffed the sandwich in the pocket before she shrugged into the skirt and picked up her blouse.

It really was almost beyond repair, and she had another one in her saddlebags. But her lips quirked and she slid her arms into the torn blouse, tying it tightly under her breasts just as Storm led Cinnabar into the cave.

"I'm ready," she said when he glanced at her. "Maybe we should wait for Ned to find us, though. I don't think I have enough money for train fare to Wyoming."

Storm's eyes lingered on the open neck of her blouse before he determinedly looked away and handed Cinnabar's reins to her. He reached up to pull back a rock beside the supply shelf and drew out a bag of coins, which jingled when he held them out to her.

"Idy brings this out now and then. For some damned reason she thinks I deserve part of her profits from the brothel, just because she started it with Baker money. I've been keeping it for her and Elias, when they finally make up their minds to get married, but she won't mind if you use it."

Jessica nodded and took the bag, only removing a couple of coins from it before she handed it back.

"You may need more than that," he said, frowning.

"No." She placed the bag again on the shelf and hid it behind the rock. "This will be plenty."

"You and your pride, Jessica Callaghan."

"Yep," she said saucily. "Ned calls it the Callaghan pride. You seem to have your share of that wicked vice yourself."

"Sometimes it's all a man has to keep him going," he said quietly.

"I understand," Jessica agreed. Then her eyes fell on the

gramophone. "You promised to play the gramophone for me. I really enjoy listening to music. Ned even said something about getting Mattie one for Christmas this year. He said she'd seen it in a catalogue."

"There's no time now, Jessica. Maybe another time." He muttered under his breath as he turned away, "That is, if there ever is another time for us."

Jessica didn't bother answering as she led Cinnabar after him. There would be another time for them. And lots more times after that, she vowed silently to herself.

Outside the cave entrance, she mounted Cinnabar and urged him after Spirit. She barely noticed the brilliant sunrise as she trusted Cinnabar to pick his own way down the narrow trail. She glanced down at her rifle, riding securely in the scabbard, and her hand went behind her to assure herself the saddlebags were fastened tightly to her saddle.

Storm kicked Spirit into a canter across the small valley floor and Jessica followed willingly until they nearly reached the top of the hill on the other side. There she pulled her horse to a halt.

"Storm," she called before he could ride out of hearing. "Storm, I think Cinnabar's picked up a stone."

As Storm turned Spirit to ride back to her, Jessica reached down and touched Cinnabar on his shoulder, clicking softly under her breath. The stallion immediately lifted his front leg. She watched Storm pull Spirit up a few feet away and slide off to ground tie him. When he had taken a couple of steps toward her, she jerked her hat from her head and kneed Cinnabar forward.

"Hie! Hie, Spirit!"

Cinnabar nimbly jumped around the startled Storm and flattened his ears as he lunged at the other stallion. Spirit reared his defiance, but Cinnabar's shoulder hit him in the side, knocking him out of the way of his plunging path.

Jessica quickly tightened her reins and brought Cinnabar under control, urging him across the hilltop and down the other side. She heard Spirit's hoofbeats behind her as the stallion sought to avenge himself on Cinnabar, and smiled in satisfaction.

Spirit wouldn't follow her far. Even above the pounding hoofbeats of the two stallions, she heard a loud whistle from Storm split the air. The sounds behind her immediately stilled and she leaned down on Cinnabar's neck, urging him faster.

"Come on, boy," she called, and saw Cinnabar's ears flick back at her words. "Spirit's probably just as fast as you, and the only hope we have is to get a good start on him."

As though understanding her, Cinnabar stretched his legs even farther apart, until Jessica could swear they were floating over the ground. The pounding hooves and bunching muscles under her told her differently. She brushed at the flying mane stinging her eyes as she sought to make her body smaller, and her mind worked frantically. Never had she been so glad that once-traveled country became firmly embedded in her mind.

There. Over that next hill. She pulled slightly on Cinnabar's reins, urging him into a wide sweep toward the top of the hill. Seconds later, she pounded down the other side, with only Cinnabar's sure gait keeping him from sliding down on his haunches.

The mares in the herd of mustangs threw up their heads when they heard the huge stallion rushing at them. Nearby, a bugle of defiance sounded and Jessica glanced to the side to see a black stallion pounding toward them. Cinnabar hesitated slightly, but Jessica slapped her reins on his rump and called sternly to him. Reluctantly, Cinnabar answered the pressure of the reins as she guided him a far distance around the mares before she slowed to turn her head over her shoulder.

The black stallion slid to a stop and quickly turned around. He reared again and Jessica heard an answer to the bugle he sounded come from far behind her. Now, if only she was right and this was Spirit's former herd. She trotted Cinnabar to the top of the next ridge and held her breath as she watched the scene below her.

Storm frantically sawed on Spirit's reins, but the stallion only tossed his head and continued his headlong plunge toward the black horse. For a moment Storm seemed to lose control of Spirit and only a few yards separated the two furious stallions. Spirit stopped to rear and Storm jerked his head around to turn him back the way they had come.

Jessica gave a sigh of relief as she saw the black stallion go in pursuit, then stop to look back at his mares. She sent Cinnabar down the side of the hill, which would hide her progress from Storm.

The stream rushed angrily past her, swollen from the rains of the past two days, as she urged Cinnabar into the water. When he tried to head downstream, she firmly guided him into the onrushing current. The sounds of a waterfall grew louder the further upstream Cinnabar plodded.

The waterfall barely topped Jessica's head when she guided Cinnabar out of the stream and over beside it, but it would do just fine. As she suspected, she found enough space behind it to hide both her and the horse. Mist from the falls drifted over them, and she reached back for the cloak in her saddlebag. After wrapping it around her, she slid down from the horse's back and gingerly made her way to the edge of the shelf behind the pouring water. A convenient rock allowed her to hide and peek now and then over its top.

Though she watched for over half an hour, she saw no sign of Storm, and relaxed somewhat. He would have had no trouble following her tracks to the stream once he managed to get Spirit past the mustang herd, and the black stallion surely would have quickly led his mares away when he realized Spirit wouldn't challenge him further. With any luck, though, Storm would think she had taken the easier path downstream, when he didn't find her tracks on the other side.

She shivered once inside her cloak as the mist penetrated even the thick lining, and determinedly glanced at the sun to mark the time. She would wait at least another half hour.

From time to time, she looked at Cinnabar. The stallion's ears were much sharper than her own, and even through the pouring water he would hear anyone approach. The horse remained standing quietly, waiting for Jessica's next instructions.

She finally mounted again and slowly urged Cinnabar out of their hiding place. Her eyes scanned the area around them, seeing no sign of another horse. She thought briefly about stopping long enough to build a fire and dry out, but the sun already shone hot overhead. Instead, she tied her cloak over Cinnabar's rump to dry and let the sun warm her shoulders.

She didn't need the map. She knew exactly in which direction the next landmark was. Ned had made himself familiar with the map, too, and sooner or later he would know where she had headed.

First the gold. Besides the threat of losing her freedom if she was arrested for assault, Ned's paying her mortgage note still galled her pride. She damned sure wasn't going to ask him to pay for a lawyer for her. With the gold, she could hire the finest lawyers in the country to fight any charges the Bakers would fling at her and Storm.

Storm. Her eyes continued to scan the hills around her and she snorted softly to herself when she realized she was actually hoping to see him. Once she frowned slightly as she recalled her vow never to touch the gold, which might be cursed.

The curse seemed all too real to her for a moment, even reaching out to touch the people who only searched for it. She had never been in such a mess in her life. Lordy, Uncle Pete and her father would turn over in their graves if they knew she was worried about her face appearing on a wanted poster. The prospect of spending time in prison sent a chill up her spine, and she found herself wondering how long Storm had been in jail.

Maybe the curse could be broken. After all, she never would have met Storm if she hadn't come to search for the gold. She never would have seen the pain leave his eyes or notice them turn into black pools filled with love for her.

She kicked Cinnabar into a canter across another valley. Some way, she would see those eyes fill with love for her again and the pain erased forever from the shadows hidden in them—even if he could never be hers totally. She had promised him she would take only the crumbs of his life. She had to be content knowing they were both putting aside their love for Prudence's happiness.

It hurt, though. Oh, how much it hurt, especially since Storm had admitted his own love for her.

Chapter 18

Something tugged at Jessica's mind as she pulled Cinnabar to a stop, and stared out over the vast valley before her. Scattered groups of brown, white-faced cattle checkered the rolling green grass as far as she could see. This must be part of the free range Harlin Baker had mentioned.

She had ridden warily all day, chafing at the delay her detour around Baker's Valley made necessary. Now this. Where there were cattle, there could be men tending them. Keeping Cinnabar on the edge of the timber line, she urged him forward to make another wide sweep around the valley. Crossing it directly would have saved her several hours, but not if someone discovered her.

A crackling in the brush drew her attention and Jessica reined her horse in as a cow, followed by a spindly legged calf, emerged from the underbrush. The cow stared at Jessica for a second, then dropped its nose to nudge the calf ahead of it. Jessica had plenty of time to study the tilted *B* on the cow's flank.

"That's the Lazy B brand," she said softly to herself. "Oh, Cinnabar, I hope we don't run into any of those cowhands. I doubt if they'll even stop to ask questions if they recognize me. They'll shoot first."

How had Storm ever stood it? she asked herself. After only a day of hiding—being on the run, she guessed it was called—she didn't think she could take much more. Every slight sound sent her head turning toward it until she could determine the cause.

A deer bounding through the brush made her heart pound wildly, and before crossing each hilltop, she dismounted to crawl warily to the crest and study the land before her. But she guessed riding alone, and being free had to be better than staring out from cell bars.

A while later she again snaked her way up a hill and peered anxiously over it. The low-hanging afternoon sun was close to the horizon, and in the distance she could see new rain clouds gathering. She thought she could already hear the thunder, before realizing it was her stomach growling with hunger.

She had eaten the biscuit sandwich at noon, but it hadn't even begun to fill the empty space inside her, and she didn't dare try to shoot any of the abundant jackrabbits. The noise from her rifle would surely bring the entire countryside down on her.

She gazed at the whitewashed buildings below her. A large ranch house nestled against the foot of the hill, surrounded by scattered outbuildings. The largest barn she had ever seen was set off by itself, and what seemed like miles of white plank fence bisected different portions of the land. The fence even bordered a drive leading up to the house, and it stretched several hundred yards to the intersecting dirt road.

Jessica lifted her field glasses to her eyes to read the letters cut into the sign at the end of the drive. Though she had to read them backward, Lazy B stood out clearly.

So this was the ranch where Storm had grown up. She trained the glasses on the house, surprised to see weeds almost up to the porch. On closer examination, she could see faded patches of paint on the house and a broken window covered by a haphazard board. Funny. Given David Baker's immaculate appearance whenever she saw him, she wouldn't have thought he would let his house go to seed.

The back door slammed and Jessica turned the field glasses toward the sound. A slovenly dressed woman walked across the yard, throwing what looked like potato peelings out from the dirty apron she held turned up in her hand.

"Here chickie, chickies." The gruff voice floated across the still air and reached Jessica's ears. "Come on, you damned varmints!"

Across the yard, Jessica watched white chickens emerge from different hiding places. Instead of converging in a flock toward the proffered food, they hesitantly made their way forward. Once the woman moved a fair distance away, a chicken ran up, grabbed a potato peeling, and raced across the yard, squawking and flapping its wings in an attempt to protect its food.

The next chicken wasn't as lucky. The woman stopped for a moment, then threw a large handful of peelings close beside her. An instant later, the chicken dangled from her hand. She carried it, squawking loudly in distress, to a chopping block, which had a hatchet embedded in it.

Jessica shivered and lowered the glasses. For some reason she found herself thinking the woman was going to enjoy killing that chicken. She cautiously began making her way back down the hill, her stomach rumbling louder as she thought of the delicious chicken and dumplings Mattie made.

Hours later, Jessica sat huddled under a rock outcropping which she had carefully searched for snakes, staring down at Tobias's ranch. Welcoming lights shone through the clear window panes, but she didn't dare try to see if the welcome would extend to her. The lone piece of beef jerky she had found in her saddlebags settled like a lump in her stomach, nothing like the stew she had eaten at the little cabin during her first visit there.

A streak of lightning split the air and the rain pounded harder. She pulled Cinnabar's saddle a little further under the rock and watched him turn his rump into the wind. Bowing his head, the horse stood resolutely, accepting the fury of the storm.

Maybe the storm would prove to be a blessing, Jessica told herself. It would give her some cover to slip down to Tobias's barn and at least get Cinnabar some grain. In a few minutes, she would go. She leaned back against the rock while she waited for the rain to slacken again.

Bright sunlight woke her, and Jessica gasped as she sat up. She bumped her head on the rock above her and bit back a moan of pain. Gingerly, she rubbed the spot on her head and uncurled her legs from under her. No way would she be able to steal a portion of grain for Cinnabar in broad daylight. She sighed and crept out from the overhanging rock.

Her eyes searched for Cinnabar until she saw him cropping grass a ways off. Well, at least he would have that to eat. Her own stomach rumbled alarmingly.

Maybe Tobias was out somewhere on his range. As soon as the thought entered her mind, Jessica heard the barn door creak open loudly below her. Tobias crossed the yard, heading for the house.

So much for that idea. Prudence would never turn her away, but how could she know what Tobias had heard about the incident in town? Probably nothing, her mind insisted, since it was fairly clear no one came out to his ranch very often, but she couldn't take that chance. If he had heard, Tobias wouldn't want an accused murderess around Prudence.

Jessica wearily saddled Cinnabar and rode him around the edge of the hilltop. An hour later, she looked back from the bank of the Little Big Horn River to the cliff face beyond Tobias's cabin. There. That had to be what she remembered.

Though it had been shadowed somewhat, since she had first seen it close to sundown, now full daylight shown on the cliff face. And a face it definitely was. She had studied that landmark on the map for hours, trying to decipher it. The moment she had glanced at the cliff from Tobias's porch, something had clicked in her mind.

The craggy cliff had the look of a man's face. Shaggy eyebrows hovered over two holes in the hillside and an outcropping between them was the nose. The stratums of rock beneath the nose curved up into a mouth, covered by a line of trees—the mustache.

The nose on that face pointed directly to where the gold was buried. She could see the dotted line in her mind, though the map was still in her saddlebag. She and Cinnabar splashed across the Little Big Horn, and headed toward where the smaller river intersected with the Big Horn River, somewhere in the distance. It couldn't be too far, if she was still able to see the cliff face from the bank.

Scarcely two hours later, Jessica pulled her gloves on and turned over a rock on the riverbank. Swallowing the gorge rising in her throat, she forced her fingers to pick up one of the leeches clinging to the underside of the rock. It wriggled and squirmed in her fingers, and she quickly threaded it on her hook, then turned to toss her fishing line into the river.

Almost at once she felt a tug on her line and had a fat trout flopping in the sand at her feet. That darn gold could just wait awhile longer. First, she desperately needed to fill her stomach. She cleaned the fish with sure strokes of the knife she removed from her saddlebag and spit it on a green stick over her fire. One fish might not be enough. While the first one browned over the flames, she caught several more, enough for her supper, too.

Jessica finally leaned back and patted her full stomach. That had to be the best trout she had ever eaten even without the benefit of any salt or pepper. The rain seemed to be holding off, too, so maybe her luck was changing.

She scanned the area around her. The river was at a much lower elevation than the hills she had ridden through, the peaks of the hills catching the storm clouds behind them. She squinted her eyes, but no stretch of the imagination showed her the cliff face she searched for. Sighing, she rose to her feet and whistled for Cinnabar. Several canyons intersected the river and their sides were higher than where she made camp. She would just have to search until she found the one shown on the map.

To Jessica's delight, the first canyon ridge she rode along just had to be the right one. The clouds in the hills dissipated and she could make out the cliff face in the far distance. She stopped Cinnabar when she thought her own nose was pointed directly at the nose of the cliff man and turned to look behind her.

There. She marked the place in her mind. A bubbling creek ran across the rocks in the canyon bottom and the spot she stared at was just on the other side. She wouldn't know for sure until she climbed down and checked the distance to the river, but it just had to be it. No way, though, could even the surefooted Cinnabar manage the steep canyon sides. She would have to leave him on top.

Jessica slid to the ground and opened her saddlebags. She pulled the map out, along with a small hand spade she had brought with her. Then she patted Cinnabar on the nose.

"You stay here, boy," she said. "I have a feeling that, in just a few minutes, you're going to have a very rich mistress."

Cinnabar tossed his head at her and gazed up the canyon. When Jessica left him and started down the steep canyon sides, he whickered after her. A second later, he neighed shrilly and moved to the edge of the canyon. His front hoof pawed at the ground, knocking a shower of stones down on Jessica.

"Cinnabar, quit it!" Jessica called up at him. "Settle down!"

The horse reared and neighed loudly again. Jessica thought she heard someone call her name, but it couldn't be. She was alone. She determinedly began making her way down the canyon bank.

"Jessica! Don't, Jessica!"

No mistake this time. And if she didn't know better, she would swear she recognized Storm's voice. How had he found her? If he thought he could keep her from the gold, he would have to think again, she told herself as she continued her descent.

No way in hell was she going to allow Storm to hogtie her and carry her to the train, not when she was only a few feet from her goal. Uncle Pete had meant for her to have that gold, though Pete couldn't have imagined at the time that she would also desperately need the gold to clear her lover's name—and hers.

Jessica heard her stomach rumble again. She paused a few feet from the bottom of the canyon and shook her head. She couldn't still be hungry. It must be thunder. She would have to hurry before the rain started again.

But the thunder didn't go on and on. Suddenly she realized what that noise had to be. She glanced down at the creek at her feet and saw it already beginning to swell with new water—dirty water. Dirty water rumbling down on her with the speed of a freight train from a flash flood begun up in the hills.

Jessica's throat constricted with terror as she tried to scramble back up the side of the canyon. Her fingers grabbed at bushes on the bank, more than one of them pulling loose, causing her to slide back down each time she gained a few feet. The easy downhill path proved dangerously treacherous as she tried to ascend it.

The thunder of the water rose until it drowned out even the sound of Cinnabar neighing shrilly above her. With a final surge of effort, Jessica managed to grasp a rock and pull herself up. She glanced to the side in horror to see the wall of water only a few yards away. She threw herself down and tried to work her way on hands and knees up the side of the canyon. The rocks bit into her knees and palms, splitting them open and leaving behind spots of blood as she crawled.

"Jessica! Jessica, I'm coming! Hang on, darlin'!"

Storm appeared on the top of the canyon wall. He scrambled over the side, but the wall of water hit Jessica full force, tearing her violently away from her hold on the rock and sending her tumbling through the surging current.

She surfaced briefly once, gasping for air. The floodwater carried with it everything it found in its path and buffeted her from every side with small rocks and even trees. She went under again and fought her way back to the surface.

A huge tree trunk bore down on her just as her head split the surface again. She gasped in terror and tried to dive under the tree, but it hit her squarely on the head. A peaceful blackness descended as she went limp.

Never had Storm been so glad of Spirit's speed. The stallion hit the riverbank running full out just as the floodwaters entered the river. Storm headed Spirit into the current, his eyes frantically searching the violently roiling flotsam around him.

She had to be there. He couldn't let himself think about her lying battered and broken under all this. Spirit dodged around a tree and Storm felt a rock hit his leg, sending a shooting pain up his thigh. He gritted his teeth and pulled Spirit's head back around when the horse tired of fighting the current.

Oh God, maybe he should have waited to see what happened to her after the wall of water hit. But all he could think about was getting to the river in time to pull her out. He would have wasted valuable time scrambling down the bank and into the water himself.

A huge tree trunk swirled toward him, and Storm felt Spirit swerve under him to miss it. A branch protruded from the side and Storm instinctively reined the horse further aside to miss it. A flash of white caught his eye. Jessica had worn a white blouse!

He frantically pulled Spirit back into line with the tree trunk. The limb swept by him and he reached out. His fingers closed around the scrap of white cloth and he curled them into the fabric and pulled with all his might.

Jessica's head surfaced and lolled back into the water. Storm gripped Spirit with his knees and reached out with his other hand. He caught her arm and managed to bring her onto the saddle in front of him. Spirit willingly turned back to ride with the rushing current and swam with sure strokes toward the bank as soon as the current slackened somewhat.

Keeping a firm grip on the cold body in his arms, Storm slid down from his horse. He knelt and cradled her close, his hand stroking the side of her icy cheek. Her lips were so blue, she was so still. She couldn't be dead. She couldn't be!

"Jessica! Oh God, darlin', what have you done to yourself? Nothing's worth your life."

When she didn't respond, Storm forced himself to loosen his hold on her and turn her onto her stomach. He knelt over her and pushed against her ribs. Once. Again. Jessica did not move under him.

Storm sobbed once, then raised his head. "Damn you!" His voice echoed throughout the river valley. "Damn you!" he screamed again. "Let her live! Let me at least know she's alive somewhere and I'll never touch her again!"

His head fell down onto his chest and he pushed again on Jessica's ribs. Suddenly a gush of river water erupted from her mouth.

"Yes! Oh, yes, baby," Storm said, forcing himself not to push too hard on her as a surge of hope rushed through him. "Come on, pretty lady. You can do it!"

Jessica coughed and more water flowed out onto the sand under her mouth, mixed with the contents of her stomach. She stirred under Storm. He leapt off her and pulled her into his arms again.

"Jessica. Come on, pretty lady, open your eyes."

Though her chest rose and fell rhythmically with her breathing, Jessica remained unmoving in his arms. Storm laid her back down and quickly ran his hands over her body. He couldn't detect any major injuries, though her arms were scraped and bruised, her fingernails broken. Finally he cupped her head and tenderly his fingertips massaged her head.

Jessica moaned in pain when his fingers encountered the huge knot, but her eyes remained closed. Noticing her blue-tinged lips, Storm gently lowered her to the ground. He had to build the fire up quickly, or she might die.

A sense of *deja vu* stole over Jessica when she opened her eyes. Storm sat beside her, bent over, with his arms propped on his knees and his head hanging down. A fire flickering on the other side of her cast some light into the darkness, but Storm's hair hid his face from her.

She turned her head slightly to try to see him better and pain shot through her temple. A moan escaped her lips.

Storm immediately raised his head and scrambled to her side. "Jessica! Jessica, are you awake?"

"Uh-huh," she said softly. "It hurts when I move, though."

"Don't move, darlin'. Stay quiet and I'll get a cool cloth for your head."

Jessica opened her eyes to see Storm's face hovering over her. "Well, I'm damned sure going to move," she said with determination. "I'm hungry. I've been hungry for two days and I finally managed to get something to eat. Now I feel like I didn't even eat at all."

"Honey, I've already got a pot of soup on the fire. You don't have to move. I'll get you some." He started to stand up, but his legs felt like the water in the river behind him. He took a steadying breath and touched her cheek.

"Oh, pretty lady," he said quietly. "I thought I'd lost you. No amount of damned gold could be worth your life."

Jessica gasped and winced in pain as she tried to sit up. She pulled against Storm's hand for a moment when he held her down on the blanket, unable to overcome the weakness in her body. The pain pounded in her temple, but she forced out her question. "How did you know about the gold?"

"I wasn't sure just what it was," Storm admitted. "Now I know."

"The map. You found the map while you had Cinnabar and you knew where I'd be going."

"Right. And I'm damned sure glad I did."

Jessica placed her palm over Storm's hand on her shoulder. "I am, too, Storm. I am, too."

Storm turned his hand over and squeezed Jessica's before he rose to his feet. "I'll get you something to eat, honey. You just lie quiet."

A moment later, Storm sat beside her and tenderly lifted her into his arms. When Jessica reached for the spoon in the bowl, he shook his head and laid her hand back on her stomach.

"I'll feed you, honey. I don't want you to exert yourself right now. That blow on your head could still be mighty dangerous if you try to move around too much."

Jessica sighed complacently and reclined against his arm. She opened her mouth after Storm picked up a spoonful of soup and blew on it gently before holding it out to her.

"Ummmm. Oh, that tastes good."

"Well, enjoy it. It'll probably be fish again tomorrow."

"Again! You saw me catch those fish?"

"Uh-huh. I've been waiting here for you."

"F . . . umph!" The spoon cut off Jessica's words and she had to swallow before she could speak again.

"For how long?"

"Only a couple hours before you showed up. I staked Spirit back a ways and went to get him after I saw you ride toward the canyon. Just as I got my saddle cinched up, I heard Cinnabar neigh and saw you disappear over the edge of that damned bank."

Storm dropped the spoon into the bowl and pulled her tight against him. "Oh, Jessica. When I heard that water rushing down that canyon, all I could think about was how I had only thought my life was empty before. I knew that if you died, there'd be no reason for me to go on living."

"Storm, I didn't die," she soothed as she raised a hand to slide her fingers into his hair. "I'm here, and you're going to play hell getting rid of me the next time."

Storm chuckled and loosened his hold. Picking up the bowl of soup, he settled it on her stomach and offered her another spoonful.

"Seems like you wanted to get rid of me, too," he said. "How the hell did you know that mustang herd would be there?"

"I didn't for sure, but it worked. And as soon as these floodwaters go down, we can get what I came after and both go to Wyoming."

Storm's hand stilled for a moment; then he tilted the spoon into Jessica's mouth. He silently reached for another spoonful.

Jessica reached out and stayed his hand. "Storm? You will help me get the gold, won't you?"

Storm nodded slightly. "If that's what you want. But I'm not going to Wyoming with you."

"Why not?" Jessica demanded.

"I made a vow while you were in the river. Look, you wouldn't be in this mess if you hadn't gotten mixed up with me, so I promised I'd get out of your life and leave you alone. I'm going to keep that vow."

She bit back the laugh that tried to bubble up in her throat. How many times had he already said those same words to her in one manner or another? When he continued to gaze down on her, waiting, she guessed, for her to say something else, she laid her head back against his arm and sighed deeply.

"You didn't have a thing to do with me climbing down into that canyon when I knew it had been raining up in the hills. Heavens, Storm, I've ridden the outdoors enough to know how flash floods happen. I just didn't think. Thank God you were here.

"Now," she said after she lingeringly caressed his cheek, "I'm still hungry. And I'm getting awfully cold." She reached for the soup bowl and tilted it up to take a swallow. After she put the bowl down beside her, she sat up, shaking her head when Storm tried to pull her back into his arms.

"I can finish now," she said. "Won't you put some more wood on the fire? Brrrr. I feel like I've got river water running through my veins."

She watched Storm shrug and stand. While he added more wood to the fire, she quickly scooped the remaining soup into her mouth, then lay down and pulled the blanket over her. When Storm looked at her again, she shivered and clutched the blanket around her neck.

"I'm freezing," she said. She pulled the blanket slightly away and peeked down inside it. "Why, I don't have any clothes on. Don't we have another blanket?"

"No, we don't. My bedroll got wet when Spirit swam in the river after you. I'll get you some dry clothes from your saddlebags."

"If all the other blankets are wet, where will you sleep? If you think I'm going to hog all the warmth while you sit up in the cold, you're wrong. You can share the blankets with me. That way we'll both be warm."

"I can stay warm by the fire, Jessica." Storm knew immediately he had lost the argument when Jessica pursed her lips into the familiar pout. She started to throw the blanket back and he reached out to stop her hand.

"All right. I told you I didn't want you exerting yourself, and I guess you will if you're shivering. Wait until I get my moccasins off."

"Ummmm, good," Jessica said. "You can snuggle your feet up to mine and keep them warm."

Chapter 19

Jessica ran as fast as she could, but the thunder of hoofbeats behind her grew louder. Where was Cinnabar? She couldn't even whistle for him. She needed all her breath to try to outrun her pursuers. Her heart pounded madly, the sound echoing in her mind. She just couldn't go any further.

Suddenly she didn't need to run. The hoofbeats rose to a crescendo, and a hand grabbed her from behind, tossing her over the saddle of the rider's horse. She screamed wildly and pounded her fists against the rider's leg.

"No! Let me go! I didn't mean to kill him!"

In the next heartbeat she found herself staring out from behind jail bars. Prudence stood looking in at her, her brown eyes fixing Jessica with a glare and her mouth set in stern lines.

"You! You killed Mr. Baker, but it is not that you'll

hang for! You took Storm from me. For that, you'll never be forgiven!"

Jessica grabbed the jail bars and shook them. "You can speak now! You don't need him! Please, I love him!"

"He wasn't yours to love. He's mine. He's always been mine and you had no right to him."

"No! Oh, please . . ."

"Jessica, wake up. You're having a bad dream. Wake up, honey."

Jessica's eyes flew open and she stared wildly up into Storm's face. "Storm? I thought . . ."

"It's all right, honey," he soothed. "It was just a dream."

Just a dream, Jessica's mind echoed, but threads of truth spun through the dream. She shut her eyes and turned her head aside.

"I'm all right now. You . . . you can let go of me."

Storm stared down at her for a moment, a frown on his face. Why did he suddenly feel a change in her this morning? She had stayed in his arms all night, resting peacefully as long as he held her close.

He sure as hell didn't get much sleep. Each time he tried to shift and put at least an inch or so between him and her nakedness, she whimpered and edged close again. He finally slipped from the blankets as the false light of a predawn lit the sky, plunging immediately into the river's cold water.

The river ran by them placidly again this morning, having carried away the debris of the flash flood the day before. His emotions darned sure weren't placid. The cold swim hadn't assuaged the ache in him at all. It had only reminded him of how much he had promised to give up.

"I'll get some breakfast going," he said abruptly as he stood.

Jessica nodded slightly, expecting the pain in her head

to come crashing in at her movement. It came, though not nearly as hard as she anticipated. Opening her eyes, she raised her hand to probe tenderly the knot on her head. It took her a second even to find it, since the swelling had receded during the night, but she winced a little when her fingertips found the center of the wound.

That pain couldn't begin to compare to the twisting in her heart, however, as she watched Storm prepare their meal.

He wore a shirt against the chill in the morning air; it hung unbuttoned over his chest. The old, faded denim jeans—the tattered and torn ones he had worn when he killed the snake—encased his lower body.

When he stood for a moment with the coffeepot in his hand, Jessica found her gaze centered on the spot where the material was missing on his thigh. She thought she heard him groan, but when her eyes went back to his face, they met the back of his head.

Noticing his damp hair, Jessica glanced at the river. He must have already bathed this morning. She shivered a little as she gazed at the now gentle river current and recalled the violent turbulence of the previous day. If Storm hadn't been there, it could so easily have snatched her life.

Before they searched for the gold today, she would somehow conquer her trepidation of the water. The dunking the day before couldn't by any stretch of the imagination be called a bath and she could still feel grains of sand clinging to her body.

She looked at Storm as he walked to their saddles and picked up a canteen of water. He kept his back to her and filled the coffeepot.

Jessica closed her eyes before he turned around. The dream—the dream was true. She had even gone to sleep the night before thinking about her Wyoming ranch and Storm by her side as they worked to bring it back to its former grandeur. She hadn't even once given a thought to Prudence and her love for Storm.

Storm hung the coffeepot over the fire and glanced at Jessica.

"Jessica, are you in much pain this morning? I think I've got some medication in my saddlebag."

Pain? Her lashes fluttered open and she stared at him for a long second. Medication wouldn't help the pain she felt. It was just something she would have to learn to bear.

"No," she said at last. "My head hardly hurts at all this morning."

"What about the rest of you? That water really knocked you around."

Jessica tentatively stretched out her legs and flexed her arms. She felt a twinge here and there, but everything worked all right. She gathered the blanket around her and sat up. "I think I'm going to be fine. At least, as soon as I get a bath."

Storm nodded. "I'll help you after we eat," he said before he turned back to turn over the pieces of fish frying in the skillet.

Like hell you will, Jessica thought. Her newly formed resolve wouldn't hold up if he even touched her once. It needed time to firm and set if she expected it to carry her through the next few days. And—her heart wrenched—for, the rest of her life.

She held her tongue while they ate. Only once did she murmur anything to Storm, and then only to tell him how delicious the fish tasted. He remained strangely silent, also, only nodding his acknowledgment of her words. She held her empty plate out to him when he reached for it, surprised to see her hand shaking.

The plate almost slipped from Jessica's numb fingers and Storm quickly covered her hand with his to keep it from falling.

"You're still weak this morning."

Her eyes filled with tears at the tenderness in his voice.

He took the plate in his other hand and set it down beside him. He continued to hold her hand, though she tugged it gently. When he looked back at her, he saw her head bowed, the sable curls falling around her face to hide it. But she couldn't quite hide the sound of the muffled sniff from him.

"Jessica." He cupped her chin and tilted her face up. Her brown eyes refused to meet his gaze and he watched her blink her lashes rapidly, trying to stem her tears.

"Jessica, what's wrong? Where do you hurt?"

"Let go of me," she managed to say in a strangled voice. "Please."

Reluctantly, Storm dropped his hands to his sides and leaned back on his heels. He didn't understand it. For some reason she had raised a barrier against him today, making it clear she didn't even want him to touch her. He watched her curl her arms around her stomach, as though fighting some agony building in her.

"Darlin', please don't cry," Storm pleaded. He reached out a hand to her again, but pulled it back. "Tell me where it hurts, my pretty lady. I'll try to make it better."

His words undid her. Oh, why did he have to call her his pretty lady? She lifted her tear-streaked face and stared longingly at him.

"It hurts all over. I don't know how I'm going to stand it for the rest of my life. I love you so much, Storm."

He could no more have stopped himself from gathering her into his arms than he could have single-handedly stopped the floodwaters the day before. He carried her with him as he stretched out on the blanket and held her tightly to him. He kissed the tears from her face and scattered kisses on her cheeks, her chin, the sides of her mouth. When she gave a glad cry and curled her fingers in his hair, he claimed her mouth fully.

A long, tender moment later, he pulled his lips gently free and nudged aside the hair by her ear.

"We've still got today, darlin'," he whispered. "And tomorrow's never a firm promise for anyone. Let me love you just once more. Let me fill myself with you, with your sweetness and your love for me. Let me give you all the love I have for you while I can."

"Today. Yes, today," she whispered in agreement. Tomorrow would come eventually. Even the power of her love for him couldn't hold back the relentless march of the sun across the sky. But they had today. Today they had their love.

Jessica willingly arched against him when his hands stroked down her back and around to her breasts. She tightened her fingers in his hair and pulled his face down to her. Her lips sought his greedily, as greedily as her tongue sought to slip inside his mouth when he opened it slightly. She strove for dominance for only a second when his tongue swirled around hers, then she moaned in surrender.

Surging sensations swept over her as Storm kneaded her breasts and ran his thumbs over the stiffening nipples. An aching void spread through her. She wanted him so badly. Her fingers left the silky nest of his hair and pulled the shirt from his shoulders. She gasped when his lips left hers and his hands left her breasts, purring contentedly when his mouth found one breast while he freed his arms from the shirt.

When he pulled her close again, she ran her hands over the muscles on his back. His hand on her hips snuggled her against him and she eagerly complied with his insistent pressure. She heard him groan in displeasure when the denim material kept him from the heat he sought.

Storm's hands worked at the buttons of his jeans, but Jessica reached down and covered them with her own. Exerting a will she didn't know she possessed, she pulled herself away from him and sat up.

"Let me," she breathed shakily. "I want to do this."

Storm drew in a deep breath and nodded his compliance, his smoky black eyes held by the passion in her gold-flecked ones. When he could tear his gaze away, he ran his eyes over her, immediately focusing on one rosy breast tip peeking through the sable hair falling over her shoulder.

"You better hurry, pretty lady," he growled. "I won't be responsible for what I do if you take too long."

Jessica laughed softly and held her hands a scant inch from the front of his jeans.

"You have to promise," she said in a languid voice. "You have to promise that you'll let me take as long as I want."

When he remained silent, she ran one fingernail above the band on his jeans and smiled in satisfaction when he closed his eyes and groaned.

"All right, pretty lady," he finally managed with a soft laugh of his own. "Have your way with me."

"I mean to," Jessica replied. "Put your arms behind your head."

Storm clenched his fists for a second, then did as she asked. He watched her from beneath his passion-heavy eyelids as she reached again for his jeans.

Jessica pursed her lips into a mock frown as she worked

on the top button. "Oh, dear," she said quietly. "It seems to be stuck."

"Jessica," Storm growled, the warning clear in his voice.

"Oh, here it comes."

She looked up and met his gaze as she slowly worked the button free and reached for the next one. But she stopped and ran her fingertips over the bulge near the buttons, where the fragile threads threatened to burst when she touched them.

Her fingers slid down and into the hole in his jeans. She could barely touch him at this angle, but even the slight pressure of her fingertips when they brushed him elicited another moan from Storm. When his eyes closed as he tried to keep his body still, she finally, slowly, freed the remaining buttons.

Jessica widened the opening, then slid her hands around his waist and under the jeans. She tugged on the jeans and smiled when Storm raised his hips so she could pull them down.

Her fingers lingered awhile on his back side. How many times had she been stirred by how snugly he fit the denim material there? Bending her head, she kissed a path down his thigh, her half-opened eyes noticing again the dark spot. After giving one tender flick of her tongue over the heart-shaped birthmark, she pulled the jeans from his body.

Her hair brushing against his stomach and the tender caresses on his legs sent a wave of fire over Storm's entire body. He opened his eyes to see Jessica's small head bent over him, her lips and hands working a magic on him that couldn't be denied.

Even the magic of their shared passion couldn't begin to compare to the other emotions surging through him. She gave so much to him, wanting his pleasure to be as great as hers. And he had no doubt she, too, was filled with the wonder of their need for each other when she threw his jeans aside and tossed her hair back to look up at him. Her heavy eyelids almost completely shadowed her brown eyes, now a dreamy, paler color. Her lips were swollen from his kisses.

"Do you like it when I touch you, Storm?" she asked in a husky voice.

"You shouldn't even have to ask, pretty lady," he replied in a voice aching with need. "But I'll tell you if you want me to. I love it when you touch me. I love you, my Jessica."

A satisfied smile curved her lips. "I thought so, but it's nice to have you tell me that I'm pleasing you. Do you like it when I touch you here?"

He gave a deep growl, and in one swift movement, he captured her and swept her under him. Gazing down into her twinkling eyes, he said gruffly, "You know I do, but all promises are off when you touch me there. Remember that in the future."

Immediately, the mischievous glint faded from her eyes. "The f–future?"

"Oh, God. I'm sorry, Jessica. Don't."

His lips covered hers and his hands began tracing her body. For a moment, he felt her stiffen in his arms, but a second later, she sighed in surrender and wrapped her legs around his.

His own words nagged at his mind for an instant before he resolutely shoved them into a corner. The future was tomorrow. Today he had his pretty lady in his arms and could drink his fill of the love and contentment and the passion he found there. He gave himself up to the sweet fire that consumed them both.

*　　*　　*

"It's my turn now," Jessica said an hour later as Storm washed the last traces of soap from her hair.

"What do you mean?"

"You helped me bathe. Now I'll help you."

"Darlin', this river water's cold."

"Funny." Jessica stood up and splayed her hands on his chest, as she tilted her head back to gaze merrily at him. "I'm not a bit cold."

Storm laughed and bent his head to kiss her. He had a glimpse of her lips pursing into a sly grin before he found himself on his rear in the river, staring up at her giggling above him.

"There. Now sit still while I get the soap."

"I've already had one bath today," he said grumpily as he propped his hands on his bent knees. "And I took it for a different reason than to get clean. Do you know what you did to me each time you snuggled against me last night?"

She laughed gaily down at him. "Mattie never mentioned that way of cooling off an over-ardent swain. I'm surprised every woman doesn't carry a jug of cold water with her wherever she goes."

Storm lunged for her, but Jessica danced away and splashed through the water to the shore, where they had left their soap and towels. She picked up a jar containing the soap for her hair and turned back to face Storm.

"Come on," she said. "Sit back down. You're too tall for me to wash your hair when you stand."

He lowered himself into the water, keeping his eyes on her when she approached him. When she opened the lid on the soap, the scent of roses filled his nose. Immediately, he recognized the sweet-smelling soap he had used on her hair moments before.

"You're not going to use that on me. That's a woman's soap."

"Oh, pooh! You men use stuff that smells. Lordy, some of the men at the barn dances outsmell the women with that pomade they put on their hair and the lotion they use on their faces after they shave. Now, just shut up and turn around."

"I can't stand bossy women," Storm grumbled, but he complied.

He relaxed when she dumped a portion of the soap on his head and handed him the jar over his shoulder. Her fingers worked the soap through his hair, and when her hands left him, he turned around to see her bent over, cupping water into her hands. The water landed on his face when she sluiced it over him without noticing his altered posture.

Storm sputtered and glared at her, but he couldn't control his own merriment when she clasped a hand over her mouth to try to still her laughter.

"If you'd only do what I tell you to," she said when she could control her laughter, "you wouldn't get yourself into so much trouble."

"But I like the trouble I get into with you, pretty lady," he breathed softly.

Jessica felt her legs threaten her with a dunking again in the river. She stiffened them determinedly and pointed a finger at him. "Turn around."

"I like the view this way much better."

"Storm!"

He tossed the soap jar at the bank, where it landed in the soft sand. Shifting in the water, he opened his arms to her. "You can reach my head just as well this way. You're getting water in my face anyway."

Jessica sighed in surrender and stepped between his legs

into his embrace. She pushed his arms slightly away when he tried to hold her close.

"I need more water. You hair's not wet enough to lather real well yet."

Her pert rear rose right in front of his eyes when she bent down and Storm stifled a groan. And one cupped handful of water didn't suffice. She had to have another, then another. Satisfied at last, she began working the soap into a lather in his hair.

But this sure as hell hadn't been one of his better ideas. Now her flat stomach lingered a bare inch from his lips and the sensuous feel of her fingers in his hair overcame any thought that the cold water in which he sat would cool him. Already he had been wanting her again and now that part of him that he had kept under rigid control while he bathed her sprang into full command of his body.

"Jessica, I can't stand much more of this!"

"Shhhh, I'm almost done. I just have to rinse you off."

Oh, no. He wasn't going to watch that shapely rear end tantalize him again.

"I've got a better idea."

Jessica squealed when he grabbed her and carried her into deeper water. She managed to swallow a breath before he pulled her under with him and opened her eyes to see him shaking his head from side to side to rid his hair of the soap. An instant later she drifted with him to the water's surface. Finding the depth too much for her shorter legs, she wrapped them around his waist and placed her hands on his shoulders.

"I just don't know what I'm going to do with you," she said with a false sigh. "You break promises and won't do a thing I tell you to do."

Storm nuzzled her throat, then raised his lips to whisper

in her ear. "I'm sorry I broke my promise to you earlier. Maybe I can make it up to you."

"How?"

Storm planted his feet a little firmer in the sandy soil beneath them and shifted her slightly against him.

"Ohhhh," Jessica breathed. "But . . . here?"

"Um-hum."

Chapter 20

On the edge of the canyon wall, Jessica straightened in indignation, her hands on her trim hips as she glared at Storm.

"I'm going down there with you! I've come this far, and you're not going to keep me from being in on the end of it!"

"You don't have your full strength back, Jessica. You should have stayed back in camp and rested, like I asked you to."

"Your shoulder isn't completely healed either. And you damned sure didn't worry about my health all morning," she fired back at him. Her heart softened when she saw the look of abashment on his face and she reached out a hand to him.

"Storm, I'm perfectly capable of going down there with you. Believe me. And it hasn't been raining up in the hills today. There's no chance of another flash flood."

He studied her, then nodded his head as he took her hand and squeezed it. "All right, pretty lady, but let me hitch a rope to Spirit before we climb down. That way we can get back up faster if we need to."

Though she knew his idea made sense, Jessica waited impatiently while Storm looped his rope over the saddle-horn and tossed it down the side of the canyon. The delay chafed at her. She was so close now.

You weren't in such a hurry this morning, she heard her mind say. She blushed and dropped her head, willing herself to submissiveness as Storm tested the knot on the rope and ordered Spirit to stand firm until he returned.

"Jessica?"

She looked up to see Storm standing on the edge of the canyon wall, motioning for her to join him. Together they made their way down the rock-strewn course, climbing around the debris that littered the path from the flood. When they reached the bottom where the creek flowed, she turned to Storm.

"I lost my spade yesterday," she said worriedly. "What are we going to dig with?"

"I've got a knife," he replied. "But I don't think we're going to have to worry about that. Look."

Jessica followed his pointing finger to the spot she had marked in her mind the day before as to where the gold would probably be buried. She gasped and splashed across the creek, her mind trying desperately to deny the evidence before her eyes.

After climbing a few feet up the far bank, she knelt beside the piece of wood sticking up from the rocky ground. Her hand went out and she brushed a few grains of sand from the letters staring up at her—U. S. Cal. . . .

"I'm sorry, honey. I guess that gold you were looking for must have been a lost army payroll, huh?"

Jessica couldn't seem to force herself either to stand up or to answer him. All her hopes, all her dreams, everything Uncle Pete had wanted for her. The flash flood had swept everything beyond her reach.

She glanced to the side and reached her hand out to pry loose an object wedged tightly against a rock. If she'd had any doubt, the lock now in her hand, still attached to the clasp that had secured the wooden box, dispelled it. The key was missing, of course, snatched away by the violent waters. She shook her head sadly and dropped the lock.

"Well," she said as she stood up at last, "it just wasn't meant to be. I shouldn't feel so bad, I guess. I've been chasing rainbows, with greed in mind, and Daddy always told me only hard work ever paid off, not dreaming of getting something for nothing."

"Wait a minute, honey," Storm said as he knelt in her place. He dug in the soil for a moment with his knife, nodding his head when he felt the blade hit something below the sand. He loosened the soil around it before brushing the dirt from the remaining half of the strong box.

Storm pulled the wood free and dumped the dirt from it. A large, leather pouch hit the ground amid a shower of small pebbles and sand.

"Here. The water didn't get this." He held the pouch out triumphantly to Jessica. "And here." He dug into the sand and brushed the gold coin against the side of his denim-clad leg before handing it to her. "You can keep this as a souvenir."

Jessica gazed at the twenty-dollar gold piece for a moment before she slipped it into her pocket. But when Storm rose to his feet beside her, she thrust the leather pouch into his hands.

"You open it," she said. "I—I can't."

268

"Uh-uh." He picked up her hand and dropped the pouch in it. "Somehow, I think this was meant for you. Otherwise, why didn't it go with the rest of the gold? And it's not part of the payroll. I think I know what's in it."

"What?"

"Open it and see."

Jessica reluctantly plucked at the rawhide thong holding the pouch shut, but it had swelled and tightened. She accepted Storm's knife when he held it out to her and the sharp blade quickly sliced through the knot. She glanced up at Storm, who nodded encouragement at her. With trembling fingers, she pulled the pouch open.

A frown of disappointment shadowed Jessica's face. She reached in and picked out a few pebbles, then spread them out in her hand.

"They're just rocks, Storm," she said forlornly. "They're kind of pretty, but they probably aren't worth anything. There's a million rocks around here."

"Not like these. Those aren't just rocks, honey." He picked one up and pointed to a yellow vein running through it. He took the knife from her and pricked the vein with its tip. A small flake fell free.

"Haven't you ever seen raw gold before, Jessica?"

"Gold! You mean, these are gold nuggets?"

"Yep. And look at this one. It's almost pure gold, like most of the rest of them in your hand. Wherever these came from, it's a rich enough lode to make a man's eyes bug out and send the gold fever racing through this state again."

"I thought this area had all been mined out."

"So did everyone else, Jessica. But some of those old prospectors were cagey fellows, and they were mighty leery of claim jumpers. Whoever found this might have been waiting until things settled down and we had a little more law in the country before he filed his claim. Or . . ." Storm's voice dropped. "Maybe it's not from around here."

Jessica's fingers tightened around the pouch, but she opened her hand almost immediately. "Storm, there's something else in the bottom here. Hold out your hands."

Storm cupped his hands for Jessica to pour the contents of the pouch into. The nuggets heaped in a pile, almost overflowing his cupped palms. He caught his breath at their value as he watched her slip her fingers into the pouch and draw out a piece of waterproof material, bound together with what looked like catgut.

Jessica reached for the pocket knife again, which Storm had laid on a nearby rock, and slit the catgut. After unfolding the piece of hide, she gasped and her face filled with wonder.

"It's smaller, but it looks like the same type of map Uncle Pete drew to show where the payroll was buried. Look, Storm. Oh, it is. Here's his name at the bottom!"

"Here, honey," Storm said, wanting to get a look at the map. "Let's put these back in the bag."

Jessica tucked the map under her arm and held the pouch open. The nuggets tumbled down the funnel of Storm's fingers into the leather pouch, and she shook her head in amazement. There must be dozens of them, their dull yellow color brushed by the sunlight streaming down on them. She had no earthly idea how much they were worth.

"Well, honey," Storm said as he brushed a clinging piece of gold flake from his palm, "looks like your uncle may have found one of the mother lodes. Didn't he mention this to you, too?"

"He . . . he died before he could finish his story. He was trying to tell me about something else I would find when he—he . . ."

"Honey, don't," Storm said as he cupped her head and dropped a soothing kiss on her lips. "He obviously loved you and now you've found what he wanted you to have. I just wonder why he never worked the mine these came from himself."

"I'll tell you all about Uncle Pete later, Storm. He wasn't the type of man who would have found happiness in being rich. He valued his freedom to roam the mountains he loved so much. Look at the map now. Can you tell where this mine might be? Is it around here?"

Storm accepted the map and studied it for a few moments. Suddenly his face darkened into a fierce scowl. "Damn them. So that's why they want Tobias's land!" he snarled.

"Storm? What are you saying? Is the mine on Tobias's property?"

"Part of it could be," he admitted. "But it's not really a mine. It's just a vein of gold right now."

"Oh. Then I guess I should tell Tobias about it." Her spirits fell again. Within the last few minutes, she had lost not one, but two fortunes. At least she still had the nuggets.

"You don't understand," Storm said. "Gold veins don't follow any predictable pattern. As far as I can tell, this spot on the map is right on the corner of Tobias's property. The vein could run right down onto Tobias's land, or it could go the other way, into free land where you can still file a claim. The government's allowing people to file claims for mineral development. But," he added in a warning voice, "it might run onto the Lazy B, too."

"Lazy B? Baker property? You think the Bakers somehow know about this gold and they've been trying to buy Tobias's land?"

"They've been trying to buy it up until now, Jessica. But Harlin and David won't let Tobias's ownership of this land stand in their way. They'll get it one way or another."

"You mean they might kill him?"

"People have killed for less. And gold does funny things to men."

"Not to Uncle Pete," Jessica defended stoutly. "He wouldn't have given up his freedom for any amount of gold."

"He sounds like my kind of person, Jessica."

"You would have liked him. But right now, we have to decide what to do next. I can't see us just riding in and asking Tobias to let us search his land for a vein of gold."

"You're sure as hell right about that."

"Hello! Jessica! Storm!"

They glanced up to the canyon rim, where Ned stood with his hands cupped around his mouth. Jessica smiled and waved at him, motioning for him to join them.

"No," Ned called back. "My old bones won't stand a trip down there. Did you find anythin'?"

"We'll be right up, Ned!" Storm yelled back. He took Jessica's hand and helped her down to the canyon floor.

Ten minutes later Ned shook his head and handed the map back to Jessica. "Why, that old rascal. All that time he could have been as rich as a king, but he wandered around in those old buckskins and moccasins. He only wanted to trap enough for his food and essentials and find his . . ."

"Ned," Jessica demanded impatiently, "how much do you think the nuggets are worth? Storm says most of them are pure gold."

"I'd say there's enough there to pay off your mortgage and buy you the finest herd of cattle you've ever seen, Jes. Gold prices climbed after a lot of the mines started peterin' out. You've got a small fortune in your hand."

Jessica thrust the pouch at Ned. "Here. You keep it for me. I'd feel funny carrying all that around. And I want you to take enough of it to pay you and Mattie back, with interest."

"I've got a better idea," Ned said. "I think we should put this in a safe place until we can come back and claim it. We've still got to get Storm out of this mess, and no tellin' what we'll run into the next few days."

"No!" Storm said flatly. "You take that gold and get yourselves back to Wyoming. I can take care of myself."

Ned spat a wad of tobacco juice to the side, then winked at Jessica. "Well, son," he drawled when he looked back at Storm, "I just don't see how you think you're gonna make us do that. 'Sides, thanks to Jessica's tender heart and nursin' you, we've gotta clear her name, too."

"Oh, Ned," Jessica interjected when Storm scowled and opened his mouth to speak. "What happened back in town? Did Mr. Baker die?"

"He was alive and kickin' the last time I seen him, Jes. Him and his brother, too. More's the pity after what happened to you. 'Course, I was keepin' myself out of sight and peekin' around the stairwell. Idalee told me what had happened after I came in through that tunnel again, and I didn't think it was a good idea to go snoopin' around in town. Turned out I didn't need to. They brought a whole committee of men with them when they came out to Idalee's. Don't know how I could have misjudged a man so."

"What do you mean, Ned?" Jessica questioned.

"Why, they was gonna take Miss Idalee to jail," Ned snorted.

Storm took a step toward Ned, his face filled with fury.

"Now, now, son," Ned said as he raised a hand to stop Storm. "They didn't take her. But they had it all figured out in what they thought was a legal manner. Said she contributed to the injury of one of the town's outstandin' citizens and her place was a blight on their precious town's image."

Ned laughed, then choked when his cud of tobacco caught in his throat. He hawked it loose and spit it out before he continued. "Well, Miss Idalee, she asked them just what they thought all them saloons in town did to the town's image. And she asked the men if they'd ever caught any of those unmentionable diseases from her girls. When that didn't seem to be workin', she kind of looked at each man and mused what their wives would do if they knew just where they had been *playing poker* from time to time."

Jessica joined Ned's laughter when he cackled loudly and slapped his knee. Even Storm found a smile crawling over his face.

"I tell you, it didn't take them men long to start slippin' out the door," Ned said when he could speak again. "Them Bakers looked around and saw all their supposed witnesses settin' their hats on their heads and hightailin' it out of there. I think they still might have tried to get the sheriff to take Miss Idalee with him, but she said something about some woman who Harlin is courtin'. Well, that finally took the wind from their sails and the Bakers stomped out."

Jessica breathed a sigh of relief. "At least Mr. Baker's not dead. I don't think I could have lived with that."

Ned shot a flat look at Storm before he reached in his pocket for his tobacco chaw. "Might of been better if he was."

"Ned, don't say that," Jessica demanded. "We can't just go around killing people we don't like. This country will never become civilized that way."

"Yeah," Storm snorted. "We should let trials and the law take care of it!"

Jessica shivered slightly. "Oh. I—I don't think I'd like to go to trial in Baker's Valley."

"Believe me," Storm returned grimly, "you wouldn't."

"He's right," Ned said. "Elias told me how Storm got railroaded. Them Bakers brought in a drunken judge, who kept his bottle right up there on the bench with him. And if all them witnesses actually saw what happened, it must of been like one of them peep shows."

"Ned!"

"Sorry, Jes. It didn't matter anyway. Elias said the judge slept through most of the testimony."

"But where was Prudence? Surely she could have found some way . . ."

"She wasn't in any shape to testify, even if Tobias would have let her," Storm informed her quietly. "You don't want to know what that bastard did to her."

"She is now, Storm. She still can't speak, but she's trying awfully hard. And she's learning to communicate in other ways. You said yourself she's getting good with sign language and I know she's even learned to draw pictures and get her thoughts across. That's how I learned it wasn't you who ra–ravaged her."

"And just who will she tell, Jessica? The sheriff? He's controlled by Harlin. An old drunken judge?"

"Well, now," Ned put in, "there might just be someone who'll listen to her. I heard there's a federal marshal on the way here. He's lookin' for some escaped convict."

"We have to contact him!" Jessica said excitedly. "We have to make him listen to us."

"He won't be here for a few days yet, Jes. And even then, we're goin' to have to be mighty careful how we do it. We're all three wanted. Baker filed assault charges against you and me."

"Oh, how stupid," Jessica said without thinking. "How could he have thought it was you who pulled him off me and—"

The hurt look on Ned's face stopped Jessica cold. "Ned. Ned, I'm sorry."

"I could've done it, Jes," Ned said. "Man gets riled, he can do things people don't think he can. Woman, too."

"I just meant . . . Well, I mean it was dark in the room. He couldn't possibly have seen who attacked him."

Jessica's voice lacked conviction and Ned nodded wryly at her. "One of these days, Jes, you just might run into a situation where you have to do somethin' you think you can't do. Then you'll see what I mean."

"Ned's right, Jessica," Storm said. "Or you might have to endure something you never thought you could take."

"How long were you in jail?" Jessica asked quietly.

"Six months."

"Oh, Storm."

Storm rolled his shoulders to ease the tension before he took the hand she held out to him. "It's over now," he said. "And I don't intend to go back—not alive, anyway."

"Don't say that! Please!"

"Reckon I know he means it, Jes," Ned said. "So we're just gonna have to lie low until we can get out of this mess."

"I know a place we can stay," Storm told Ned. "I'll get things packed and the horses ready while Jessica tells you where it is."

After Storm moved off, Jessica sighed and moved closer to Ned. "There's a cave where he's staying, but it's awfully close to town—where we camped the night before we went into Baker's Valley."

"Been there with him, huh?" Ned said with a soft laugh. "And I'll bet I know why you let us worry about you so long that night you wandered off. And where that food came from the next morning."

"Yes," Jessica admitted distractedly. "But, Ned, I want to talk to you about something else. I'm not so sure it's a good idea to stay here. I tried to talk Storm into going to Wyoming with us so we can get Frederick to defend him."

"Old Hickory Nuts himself, huh? Might be a good idea, Jes."

"What—what did you call him?"

At the astonished look on Jessica's face, Ned broke out into loud guffaws. "N–never mind, Jes," he said as he swiped at a tear leaking from his eye. "You better ask Mattie what that means."

Jessica watched Ned as he walked over to help Storm with the horses, his shoulders still shaking as he snickered under his breath. What in the world could Mattie tell her about nuts, other than that they tasted wonderful in her cookies and cakes? Jessica shrugged her shoulders as she saw Ned murmur to Storm for a moment, then saw Storm throw back his head in laughter.

When Storm glanced at her, Jessica crossed her arms under her breasts and whirled away from them. Men!

Chapter 21

Jessica's pique didn't last long after they broke camp. Her mind quickly turned to cataloging the various repairs and improvements the gold would allow her to make on the ranch. After, that is, she paid Ned back every single penny he had expended on her behalf.

The leather pouch rode securely in Ned's saddlebag, since Jessica adamantly insisted she didn't feel comfortable carrying it. They could leave it safely hidden in the cave, she informed Ned, while they planned their next move.

The flatter land in the river valleys quickly rose into hills as they neared Tobias's ranch. The tall grass muffled the sound of the horses' hooves, and the three riders kept a leisurely pace, each lost in their own thoughts. Storm finally decided to alter their course in order to bypass Tobias's place at the same moment the first faint echo of shots rang out.

Storm pulled Spirit to a halt. "That's coming from over by Tobias's place!"

"Oh my God," Jessica breathed. "Do you think it's—"

"I'd bet my life on it."

"Then, let's go. We have to help him!"

Ned's hand shot out and grabbed Cinnabar's bridle. "Now you just hold on there, Jes. You ain't ridin' into any shootin' match!"

"Ned, let go. We're wasting time. Prudence and Tobias need our help!"

"And you're the one keepin' us from doing just that," Ned informed her grimly. "I want your promise that you'll go straight to that there cave and wait for us. We can't help them if we gotta worry about you."

"Storm?" Jessica met the same flat stare in Storm's eyes when she turned to him.

"You're holdin' us up," Ned reminded her.

Jessica pulled her reins from Ned's hand. "Go then, damn it."

"Your promise, Jes," Ned insisted.

Jessica could almost feel Ned's eyes center on the corner of her mouth. With a determined effort, she thinned her lips and nodded her head, while her hand slipped down behind her leg to hide her crossed fingers.

Both men stared worriedly at her for an instant longer.

"I said yes," Jessica finally spat at them. "What more do you want?"

"Hold Cinnabar, Ned," Storm said quietly.

Storm eased Spirit's head close to the horse's chest and reached out his arm. He pulled Jessica close to him and kissed her firmly.

"Please, pretty lady," he said when he released her, "I can't take another chance on losing you."

Jessica shyly glanced at Ned, but he winked solemnly

at her and nodded his head. When Storm placed his finger under her chin and raised her face to his, she gave a resigned sigh. How could she lie to him when Storm looked at her with so much love? She lifted her hand from its hiding place and uncrossed her fingers.

"I promise," she said.

"Thanks, pretty lady."

Jessica kept a tight rein on her horse as the two men galloped away. Waiting until after they disappeared from sight, she kneed Cinnabar in a slightly different direction, which would take her unobserved past Tobias's ranch.

The closer she cantered to the ranch, the more clearly she could hear the shots, even over the hilltop cutting off her view. At last she could stand it no longer, and pulled the stallion back into a slow walk as she glanced up at the top of the hill. She could at least see how things were going. The firing had increased dramatically in the last few seconds. Ned and Storm must have arrived.

Jessica turned Cinnabar up the hill, pulling him to a stop a few feet from the crest. After removing her rifle from the scabbard, she dismounted and moved in a running crouch the final short distance.

Good Lord! How long had they been fighting down there? Not one window remained unbroken in Tobias's cabin, and bullet holes pockmarked the logs on the entire front of the structure. Splinters of wood littered the front porch.

The clear view she had of the destruction almost made Jessica reach for the field glasses at her eyes before she realized she hadn't even brought them with her from her saddlebag. She was close, too close. She started to duck her head and scramble below the crest, but froze when she saw a man behind a rock near the cabin.

The man's arm came back and a torch arched through

280

the air to land on the cabin roof. Immediately, the dry wooden shingles caught, and within a few seconds smoke billowed over the scene.

Frantically, Jessica's eyes scanned the hillside behind the cabin for a sign of Storm or Ned. She caught the flash of a rifle and saw Storm run from behind a rock to another one, a little further down the hill. But two rifle shots, one from the direction of the rear of the barn and one from behind the horse trough, pinned him into place. He would never make it close enough in time to fight the fire!

Her heart beating rapidly, Jessica stared back at the little cabin. The door flew open and horror stole over her when Prudence appeared, her back bent as she pulled on something just inside the door. Jessica peered through the smoke until Prudence tugged Tobias's shoulders through the doorway, then remembered the man behind the rock.

Jessica instinctively snapped her rifle to her shoulder and fired. The man jerked and the shot he had aimed at Prudence went wild. He dropped the rifle and clasped his hands over a billowing dark spot on his chest as he slowly collapsed on the ground.

Jessica aimed her rifle at the horse trough. The shot spattered water into the air, but the man behind it scrambled away unscathed and ran toward the back of the barn. A moment later she heard horses' hooves, and two men disappeared over the hill behind the barn. She sent another shot winging after them, just to assure herself they wouldn't return.

A whiff of smoke brought Jessica's attention back to the cabin as Storm and Ned ran into the yard. Ned grabbed Prudence and carried her wildly struggling body away from the burning cabin while Storm pulled Tobias a safe distance from the shooting embers carried on the breeze.

They would need all the help they could get to put out the fire, though.

Jessica whistled for Cinnabar and swung onto his back even before the horse could stop beside her. Grasping his mane to keep herself in the saddle, she sent him plunging and sliding down the hillside.

Though she expected a tongue-lashing for her disobedience, Storm hardly glanced at her when Jessica slid from Cinnabar's back to where he knelt over Tobias.

"Help Ned with Prudence," he ordered her, then stood and raced back toward the cabin.

Jessica ran to Ned and managed to grab one of Prudence's flailing arms. "Prudence!" Jessica shook her arm, then reached to pull Prudence's face around to meet her eyes. "Prudence, it's me. Jessica. You're going to be all right!"

Prudence wrenched herself free from Ned's hold to bury her face in Jessica's neck. The silence of the heart-wrenching sobs wracking Prudence's body only served to make them more wretched, and Jessica felt her heart go out to the young woman. It must have been horrible for her and Tobias inside the now-desecrated cabin.

"For God's sake, Jes," Ned said. "Get her under control and see what you can do for Tobias."

"Ned? Where are you going? The fire . . ."

"We'll never get that fire out with just us," Ned said grimly. "Only thing we can do is try to save what we can from the cabin."

"You and Storm be careful. Please!"

Ned nodded and determinedly turned away to join Storm, leaving Jessica to deal with the hysterical Prudence. Jessica comforted Prudence for only a second longer before she pushed her away and gripped her by the shoulders.

"Stop it now, Prudence! Stop it! Your brother's lying over there hurt and we have to help him!"

Immediately, Prudence quieted and wiped at her eyes. When Jessica hesitantly released her, Prudence hurried over to kneel by Tobias and Jessica followed her somewhat reluctantly. She'd had a glimpse of Tobias's white, drawn face before Storm sent her to help Ned with Prudence.

Jessica knelt beside the young woman and forced herself to tear open Tobias's blood-soaked shirt. Swallowing her nausea, she stared at the gaping wound just under Tobias's rib cage, near his lung. The man couldn't possibly still be alive. Storm had probably realized that when he sent Jessica away.

Tobias drew in a gurgling breath and Jessica's astonished gaze flew to his face.

Prudence scrambled to Tobias's head and pulled it into her lap. Her eyes implored Jessica to help her brother.

"I'll get the medicine kit," Jessica told Prudence. She stood and called Cinnabar. With her canteen and the medicine kit in her hands, she knelt back down, knowing there would be nothing in the kit that could help Tobias. She had to try, though, for Prudence's sake.

The sun slipped behind the hills while Jessica worked, the flames from the burning cabin lighting the area around them. She cleaned the wound as best she could. The blood-drenched ground around Tobias stained the knees of her riding skirt with a sickening wetness that made her stomach roil.

Jessica's red-tinged fingers smeared the wad of white bandages she finally pressed against Tobias's side and grimly held in place until she could tape it tightly. When blood still oozed around the bandage, she sat back on her heels and glanced worriedly at Prudence's face.

Reading the message Jessica couldn't hide in her eyes, Prudence shook her head wildly. She gathered Tobias's head even closer and bent her face down to his as Storm joined them.

"P–Prudence."

Jessica gasped aloud when Tobias's eyes fluttered open, willing herself to silence instead of insisting he not talk. He had the right to use his remaining strength in his own way—the same as Uncle Pete had done in his last few minutes. When Storm reached down to her, she allowed him to pull her up against him, leaving Tobias and Prudence some privacy for their final moments together.

"Prudence." Tobias managed to lift his hand and weakly stroke Prudence's cheek. "You know how much I love you, sis."

Prudence nodded her head as the tears streamed down her cheeks. She took his hand and brought it to her lips to kiss it.

"Yeah, and I know you love me. But who . . . who'll take care of you now?" He tore his eyes away from Prudence's face and fixed them on Jessica. "Miss . . . Miss Callaghan?"

Jessica pulled herself from Storm's arms and knelt again on the ground. "I'll see to her, Tobias. Don't worry. You have my promise."

Tobias nodded slightly, then looked past Jessica. "You. You saved my sister's life, Storm."

Storm shook his head. "Jessica's the one who shot the man aiming at Prudence."

"Then I . . . I've got more to thank you for, Miss Callaghan."

"Tobias, don't worry about it," Jessica insisted. "I already love Prudence like a sister. I'll do everything I can to see that she's happy."

284

Tobias centered his eyes on Storm. "Storm," he said. "I have to tell you. . . ." A wracking coughing spell shook Tobias's body, cutting off his words.

Feeling sure this spell would cause Tobias's final breath, Jessica shifted slightly to reach a comforting arm out to Prudence. She pulled back when Tobias spoke again.

"S–Storm. I have to say it."

Storm joined the group on the ground and placed a hand on Tobias's shoulder. "Don't, man," he said softly. "It's not necessary."

"It is!" Tobias said insistently. His indrawn breath sent another coughing spell through him, and a stream of blood ran down the side of his mouth. He let Jessica wipe it away before he again fixed his gaze on Storm.

"P–Prudence told me. Sh–she made me listen while . . . while she drew those pictures. She . . . she showed me the sign book you . . . you left her and wrote them down. I found them in the book and read the meanings. I . . . I'm sorry I misjudged you. Damned sorry."

"It's over now, Tobias."

"No," Tobias denied. "You're still charged."

"Did she tell you who actually did it, Tobias?" Storm asked.

Tobias shook his head and turned his face up to Prudence. "You have to tell, sis. Promise me you'll tell, so our f–friend's name can be cleared and the right man can be punished. I . . . I can't do it for you."

Prudence nodded her head as her shoulders shook with grief.

Tobias sighed in relief and closed his eyes. Though the group around him waited, his chest didn't rise again.

Prudence flashed a terrified look at Jessica, then bent her head and pulled Tobias's head to her chest. She tightened her arms around him and rocked him, her shoulders shaking in agonized silence.

Jessica reached out, but Prudence shook her hand off. Reluctantly, Jessica allowed Storm to lift her to her feet again.

"Leave her a moment, Jessica," Storm said softly. "She needs this to know how final it is."

"It is, Storm," Jessica said in agreement. "Death is so final. How can anyone kill another . . . Oh my God!"

"Jessica. What's wrong, darlin'?"

Jessica tore herself from his arms and ran for the horse trough. She gripped the corner of it with one hand, the other clutching at her stomach. Bending her body almost double, she heaved violently. Even long after she emptied her stomach, the painful gagging tore through her body, bringing up sour bile until even that faded. Still, she heaved.

Storm stood silently behind her, the medicine pack in his hands. When she continued to heave, he dug into the pack and brought out the bottle of whiskey. Dropping the pack to the ground, he pulled his bandanna from his neck and dipped it in the horse trough.

Storm set the whiskey bottle on the edge of the trough and firmly took hold of Jessica to pull her upright. Thrusting the wet bandanna into her hand when she batted at him, he held her tightly until she ran the cloth across her face.

"That'll help, honey." Keeping one arm firmly around her waist, he reached down for the bottle. "And this will help more. Here."

When Jessica dropped the bandanna from her face, Storm lifted the whisky bottle to her lips and quickly tipped it up. He managed to get her to take a swallow, but pulled the bottle away when she gasped as the fiery liquid hit her empty stomach. He only waited a second, though, until she caught her breath. Then he shifted his hold to the back of her head and forced several more swallows down her throat.

Jessica finally tore the bottle away from her lips and swiped at it. "You . . . you're trying to drown me!"

"No, honey," Storm denied. "Just trying to keep you from getting hysterical."

Jessica buried her face in the wet bandanna. "S–Storm," she gulped, keeping her head bowed. "Storm, I k–killed that man."

"I know, darlin'," Storm said soothingly. "But he would have killed Prudence. I was trying to work my way around to him after he threw the torch, because I knew he probably had it in his mind to shoot Tobias and Prudence when they ran out. I never would have made it in time. You had to do it, honey."

She dropped the bandanna and looked up at him as she tried to quell her shaking shoulders. "That's what you and Ned meant, isn't it?" she said forlornly. "When you s–said sometimes people have to do things they don't think th–they can."

"I'm just sorry you had to find out the truth of that so soon. It's something a person should never have to face."

"Who . . . who . . ."

Storm remained silent, but Jessica straightened her shoulders and turned away. "I'll ask Ned, then. Or go see for myself."

Storm refused to release her. "He was one of the Lazy B hands," he said reluctantly.

"Not . . . not one of the men we saw in town! What was his name?"

"Don't, Jessica. It won't help any—"

"Which one?" She demanded again. "Waco or . . . or Red?"

"It was Red, honey," Storm admitted.

She wished she hadn't asked. It only made it worse, if that were possible, now that she could put a face to the man who had crumpled under her bullet. Her stomach roiled again, and Jessica grabbed the whiskey bottle from Storm's hand. Tipping it up, she took two more long swallows.

"Whoa, honey," he said as he gently took the bottle from her. "You might have to help us with Prudence. She doesn't seem to take too kindly to Ned."

"Yesh, Prudence," Jessica slurred. "I'll . . . I'll help you, Shtorm. Wheresh Ned?"

"Oh, honey, I think I already let you have too much," he said with a small chuckle. "Ned's up on the hill, making sure those men don't sneak up on us. But I don't think there's much chance of that. In fact, I doubt if they'll ever come back to this territory. They won't want to face the Bakers' wrath when they find out their men failed to kill both Tobias and Prudence. I've got a feeling the Bakers won't have any more success in getting this land from Prudence than they did Tobias."

"P—Prudensh. We have ta go to her, Shtorm." Jessica wobbled away from him.

Storm sighed and pushed the cork into the whiskey bottle. Hearing a footfall close behind him, he turned to see Ned approaching.

"They're gone, son." Ned nodded toward where Jessica knelt beside Prudence and Tobias. "How . . ."

"Tobias is dead," Storm said quietly.

Ned bowed his head for a second, his lips moving soundlessly. When he looked back at Storm, he said, "Think you can handle things around here alone for a while? Someone ought to tell Elias. Man's friends should know when he passes."

"I'll handle it, Ned. We'll stay here tonight. Move things into the barn for shelter. Keeping busy will be the best thing for Jessica, though only time will help Prudence."

"How's Jes takin' it?"

Storm immediately knew Ned wasn't referring to Tobias's death. "About like we did the first time we had to kill someone, Ned," he said wryly. He held the whiskey bottle up.

"Yeah, I remember. Look, I'll try to get back before mornin'. If not, I'll go to the place where we camped that Jes told me about."

"Watch your back trail, Ned. I don't think they'll hang around, but you can never tell for sure about skunks like that."

"Don't worry, son. I've dealt with my share of varmints over the years. Their smell usually gives them away."

Chapter 22

Ned dismounted at the horse trough, and let his gelding's reins trail on the ground. He was getting too old for these nighttime forays. He probably should have taken the bed Idalee offered and waited to ride out with her and Elias later, but, hell, he couldn't have slept anyway. And he darned sure wouldn't have been able to send his own messages from the telegraph office.

No, better to let Elias handle that and follow later with Idalee to pay their last respects to their friend. He hoped Elias didn't get caught sneaking into the telegraph office, but Ned had to agree with him that they couldn't trust the operator not to pass the messages on to the Bakers.

A multi-talented man, that Elias. Who would have thought Elias had such an interest in newfangled gadgets? Learned that code they used to send words across the wires from a book, he told Ned.

Oh, even Ned had heard of that there Mr. Bell, who Elias

said he corresponded with. Ned had already ordered one of them gramophones for Mattie's birthday next month, and he even talked on one of them tellyphones one time at the fair in Cheyenne. Prudence would do well to listen to Elias's insistence that she travel to that Boston school Mr. Bell set up years ago, if her speech continued to elude her.

But Ned shook his head as he walked toward the barn, recalling one of his other conversations with Elias. If the Good Lord had meant men to fly, he would have given them wings. Mr. Bell didn't have a snowball's chance in the hot place of figuring out a way to get men up there with the birds!

Ned entered the barn and paused, his eyes adjusting to the dimmer light. The smell of smoke lingered in here, too. He guessed it had already penetrated the bedclothes he and Storm managed to pull from the burning cabin. They wouldn't be able to save anything else from the charred logs now littering the cabin site. Only the stark outline of a large, cast-iron stove stood out amid the rubble, the lone object that had withstood the white-hot heat.

Ned peered at the three figures on the pile of hay. Jessica sat with her blanket around her shoulders, her own gaze on Prudence and Storm. Prudence's head was on Storm's shoulder, her small hand clasped in Storm's larger one.

Sensing Ned's presence, Jessica glanced up. "She wouldn't stop crying," she said softly. "And her hysterics were making her sick. Storm has been holding her all night."

"She needed to cry it out, Jes. Sometimes that helps a bit, even for us men. And Idalee will be here in a while to help with her. She and Elias are both ridin' out."

Storm opened his eyes and slowly tried to draw his

arm from beneath Prudence. A frown crossed Prudence's tear-ravaged face, but she settled back into the hay when Storm tenderly brushed her hair back and dropped a kiss on her forehead. He pulled the blanket around her neck and rose to his feet, silently motioning for Jessica and Ned to follow him out of the barn.

"I didn't get the graves dug last night, Ned," Storm said as he stretched a few kinks from his muscle in the sunlight. "I'll start on them now. How soon will Elias be here?"

"Said they'd leave at dawn," Ned informed him. "They're probably only a couple of hours or so behind me. Idalee sent some food with me. It's in the pack on my horse, Jes. Think you can fix it for us while I help Storm?"

"I'll take care of it, Ned. But don't you think you should rest for a while? You've been up all night."

"I'll rest in a while."

Storm moved toward Jessica and reached an arm toward her waist. "Are you all right this morning, honey?"

Evading his arm, Jessica nodded her head and moved out of his reach. "I'm fine. You need to worry about Prudence now. If she wakes . . ."

"I'll be close by. Call if you need me."

Jessica walked away from them to Ned's horse. She stood for a moment until she heard their receding footsteps behind her before she allowed herself to bow her head. Yes, she would call him, but not for her own needs. Only Prudence mattered now. She had to remember that. She had to.

"Those sons of bitches! If I ever get my hands on them again, they'll damned sure wish they'd never double-crossed me!"

"For God's sake, David, shut up! Do you want everyone outside this office to hear you?" Harlin leaned across his desk and glared at David. "What do you expect out of the scum you hire out on that ranch? They sure as hell didn't help you keep your herd of cattle together."

"Don't tell me my business, big brother," David growled warningly.

"Someone should, David. I've been telling you for over a year that this town won't continue to support us the way you spend money on your trips to San Francisco and all the other places you go."

"There's sure as hell nothing around here to do. Besides, we won't have to worry about money once we get that gold mine going."

"You'll never get Tobias to sell. Hell, for all you know, he killed your men rather than them just hightailing it for parts unknown."

"Something's going on out there," David said. "I saw that illegitimate spawn of our old man heading out that way with Gant a while ago. And if Red's dead, it's no big loss. I'd have had to get rid of him anyway sooner or later, after he told me exactly where that vein he stumbled across was. I'll find it on my own as soon as we get that land."

"You better do something pretty quick. I knew someone would come after Storm. We should've concentrated on getting rid of him before that federal marshal got wind of where he'd been seen. We don't need a marshal nosing into our business. I wish I knew who sent that wire."

"You can bet your ass it didn't come from here. Old Fred's got orders to give you copies of every wire that goes out or comes in. Someone must've ridden to Hardin to send it. Besides, he's after Storm, not us."

"For God's sake, David! Use your damned head! If even one person talks to that marshal while he's here and files a complaint, the marshal can call in bank examiners. And those examiners can look at every scrap of paper connected to the bank, even how I ended up owning the bank. You sure as hell better hope that will you had forged in San Francisco can stand up to a handwriting analysis."

"That forger was the best money could buy, brother. You ought to know. You paid for it."

"I'd feel a hell of a lot better if I knew you'd destroyed that other will."

"That's my collateral, Harlin, old boy. How'd you like to split all you own with Storm and Idalee? Isn't it better just to give me a little money now and then?"

"A little?"

"Look," David said, "we're going out there right now and see what's going on. I want to know what happened to those men."

"Out where?"

"To Tobias's ranch."

Jessica eased her aching body down beside Idalee and Prudence and, for the first time that day, allowed herself to relax somewhat. She had spent the entire afternoon scrubbing blankets and clothing to remove the smell of smoke from them, shrugging off the other two women's attempts to help her. Finally she had dumped out the last kettle of murky water, and rinsed the remaining few items in cold water drawn from the well.

Flames from the fire curled around the new log Idalee had tossed on it, crackling and spitting in the still evening air. The aroma from the pot hanging over the fire stirred hunger pangs in Jessica's stomach.

"It's going to be a beautiful sunset," Idalee mused.

Jessica nodded. For the rest of her life, sunsets would remind her of the first glimpse she'd ever had of Storm. So would just about everything else in her life bring thoughts of the man she loved, she realized. The warmth of the fire reminded her of their time together in the cave. Even the people beside her had come into her life after she had met the man the law labeled an outlaw.

She would never again hear a coyote howl without recalling that first night, or see a wild mustang herd without the ghost of a paint stallion rising up in front of her eyes. And how would she ever be able to enjoy slipping off on a hot day to bathe and wash her hair in the little stream running through her ranch? Maybe her cowhands had been right that first night about ghosts. She would definitely carry Storm's ghost with her always.

Idalee shifted slightly and closed the book she held in her lap. "That's enough for now, Prudence," she said. "You can't learn it all in one day."

Jessica glanced curiously over at Prudence to see her nod her head and rub her hand across the child's slate on her knees.

"You two have been working together for over two hours," Jessica said. "What on earth's kept you so busy?"

"Prudence wants to learn to read and write," Idalee said with a smile. "It was Elias's idea for us to bring these things out with us. He figured they'd . . ." She slipped a comforting arm around Prudence's waist. "They'd help her to have a new focus for her mind right now."

Prudence looked over her shoulder toward the new grave on the hillside behind her, only allowing her gaze to linger on it for a second. She turned back to Idalee and lifted her hands in front of her.

"Whoa, Prudence," Idalee said with a small laugh. "It's

going to take me some time, too, to learn your new language. Go slower."

Prudence slowed her motions with her fingers and after a moment, Idalee nodded in understanding.

"While I've been teaching Prudence," she explained to Jessica, "she's been teaching me. But I'm afraid it's taking me a lot longer to learn than her. Prudence already had a basic grasp of her letters from the sign language book Storm gave her."

Prudence moved her fingers again, but Idalee frowned at her.

"I'm sorry, Prudence. What . . ."

Prudence picked up the slate and drew a few quick lines on it before she held it out to Idalee.

"You know, Prudence," Idalee said, "you could be a pretty good artist if you put your mind to it."

When Prudence nudged Idalee on the arm and nodded in Jessica's direction, Idalee blushed prettily.

"Of course I want Jessica to know," she said. She held the slate out so Jessica could see the ring Prudence had drawn on it. "Elias and I . . . Well, we're going to be married. Can you believe it? That crazy fool was afraid to ask me. He thought I wouldn't say yes."

Jessica gave the smaller woman a quick hug. "I'm so happy for you, Idalee. I can't think of two people meant for each other more than you and Elias."

"Aha!" Elias said from behind them. He reached down and pulled Idalee to her feet, the slate falling unnoticed from her hands. "I've got witnesses now. If you try to back out, I'll sue you for breach of promise."

"You'll sue *me?*" Idalee said saucily. "If I remember right, I'm the one who did the asking and you're the one who said yes. If anyone breaches a promise, it'll be you."

"Never," Elias said with a shake of his head. "I've got you now and you'll never get rid of me. Come on. Let's go watch the sunset."

Jessica watched them walk away, then turned to Prudence when she felt her hand on her arm. She accepted the slate Prudence held out to her and glanced down at the ring. When Prudence lifted her hand and pointed to the side, Jessica saw Storm standing at the corral, his back to them as he watched the horses inside the fence.

Jessica dropped the slate and scrambled to her feet. She didn't need Prudence to remind her that Prudence and Storm had plans for their own impending marriage. But when she caught the puzzled look on Prudence's face, Jessica rigidly controlled herself. Her promise to Tobias rang in her mind.

"You'll be happy, too, Prudence," she said sternly. "I promised your brother and I meant what I said."

Prudence continued to stare at her with bewilderment, and Jessica turned her back to stir the pot. She had to live with her decision, but she couldn't bring herself to discuss it openly with Prudence. Prudence need never know how much her own happiness would cost Jessica.

Or what had happened between Jessica and Storm. Try as she might, though, Jessica couldn't bring herself to feel guilty about their glorious lovemaking. She guessed it must be some terrible character flaw in herself.

At least, that was the decision she had come to during the long, dark hours of the night, after the whiskey fumes cleared from her mind. Lord knew, she had discussed the exact same thing with Mattie often enough, when one of her friends had sobbed out a broken heart on Jessica's shoulder after learning of a boyfriend's unfaithfulness. Though Mattie always insisted there was two sides to each story, Jessica knew she could never bring herself to add that kind of pain to Prudence's recent losses.

She couldn't completely blame Storm; she had been a very willing participant in the rapture they found with each other. In fact, she had begged him for the time they had together, promising to be happy with only that and make no demands for the future.

Was it possible for a man to love two women at the same time? It must be, because Jessica had no doubt in her mind that Storm loved her. The tone of his words had been too sincere, the dark eyes too filled with love for her to be reflecting a lie. She had come to know him so well. He was too honorable to walk out on his commitment to Prudence.

At least he and Prudence hadn't been already married, Jessica had tried in vain to rationalize during the night. At least she and Storm hadn't broken the commandment against adultery, though they had given in to their passion without the sanctity of marriage vows.

She had scrubbed harder on the smoke-saturated blankets that afternoon each time the word "adultery" crept into her mind. Hers and Storm's love had to end now. She had to get far away from him before he married Prudence. It would be horrible if she found herself tempted after Storm was married—much more horrible than what had already happened, which was bad enough.

"Is that food ready yet? I'm starving to death."

Jessica gripped the ladle tighter and concentrated on stirring the contents of the pot to keep herself from whirling around at the sound of Storm's voice.

"I think it's probably ready," she said as she heard him settle himself down beside Prudence. "I'll go wake Ned up."

Without glancing at the couple on the blanket, she hung the ladle on the side of the pot and walked away. Just inside the barn door, she turned back. The firelight out-lined the profile of Prudence's face as she stared up at Storm, who sat close by her side. As Jessica watched, Storm nodded his head and slipped an arm around Prudence's small shoulders to give her a hug. Jessica determinedly blinked her eyes to stop the tears trying to creep down her cheeks, and forced herself to turn away.

An hour later, Ned pushed his plate aside and fixed Jessica with a penetrating look. "You're just pushin' that stew around on your plate. How 'bout puttin' some of it in your stomach, where it belongs?"

Jessica gave a guilty start and speared a piece of meat with her fork. She slowly raised it to her mouth and took a small nibble.

"Huh," Elias said with a laugh. "I told you it needed a little more salt, Idalee."

Idalee swatted his arm. "I was cooking long before you decided you wanted to learn, Elias Gant! And I didn't learn my cooking skills from any book. I'll have you know, my mother was the finest cook in the territory."

"I give up," Elias said as he held his hands up to ward off another swat from Idalee. "I promise, I'll never try to tell you how to cook again."

Idalee dropped her hand and turned a worried gaze on Jessica. "Are you feeling all right? You've been awfully quiet this evening."

"I . . . I'm just tired," Jessica replied with a small sigh.

"You should have let us help you this afternoon. There was no need for you to wash all those bedclothes by yourself."

Jessica looked up to see the faces around the fire turned toward her, and shrugged irritably. She forced herself to take another bite of the stew and to maintain her silence until the conversation began to flow again. Then she surreptitiously set the plate down and edged her leg a few more inches away from Storm's thigh beside her.

"Well," Jessica heard Ned say when she again began paying attention to the conversation, "I think we might as well, since we're here anyway. How about you, Jes?"

"Uh, I'm sorry, Ned. What did you say?"

"Just that we might as well follow that map Pete drew, since we're so close anyway. It's up to you, Jes. Pete left that map to you."

"But the land belongs to Prudence," Jessica insisted. "Whatever gold is on it will belong to her."

Prudence leaned forward past Storm and shook her head at Jessica. She moved her fingers rapidly, then looked up at Storm.

"She wants me to tell you what she and I discussed this afternoon, Jessica," Storm said. "She won't touch a penny of the gold from that mine unless you agree to take your share. After all, your uncle found it first and she wouldn't even have known about it without the map Pete left you. She wants the two of you to share it equally."

"No!" Jessica gasped as she rose to her feet. The last thing she wanted was to be tied in any way to Prudence once she left Montana. She dug into her riding-skirt pocket and pulled out the map.

"Here." Jessica tossed the map into Prudence's lap. "It's yours now. I don't want anything to do with it."

Prudence picked up the map and looked at the fire. Quirking an eyebrow at Jessica, she casually flicked her wrist toward the fire. When Jessica couldn't quite stifle a cry of dismay, Prudence stood and handed the map back to her. She held her other hand out to Elias and took the piece of paper he handed to her, then motioned for Storm to stand.

Storm watched Prudence for a moment before he turned to Jessica. "She says you called her your sister last night and she wants to know why you dislike her today."

"Oh, Prudence, I'm sorry you think that," Jessica quickly replied. "It's just that . . . I'm going back to Wyoming in a few days." Jessica blurted out the first excuse that came into her mind, failing to notice Storm stiffen beside her. "I've got my ranch to take care of and I don't want any ties here in Montana to distract me."

Prudence had to tug on Storm's arm for a second to get his attention. When Storm translated Prudence's hand movements for Jessica, his voice remained flat. "She says that she realizes you have friends in Wyoming, but you've also made new friends here. She wants to know if your experiences here have upset you so much you can't accept your new friendships. And she says she's sorry you had to kill that man to protect her."

"It's not that, Prudence." Jessica couldn't meet the other woman's eyes and stared over her shoulder. "I'm sorry I had to kill that man, but I would do it again to save your life." Suddenly she turned away. "I don't want to talk about it right now. Please."

Prudence stepped around Jessica and held out the paper she had taken from Elias, urging Jessica to accept it. When Jessica stared questioningly at her, Prudence looked at Elias and nodded her head.

"It's a deed giving you half interest in that mine, Jessica," Elias said. "I don't know how legal it is, but Prudence asked me to draw it up this afternoon."

Jessica sighed resignedly but refused to accept the deed Prudence held out. "Let me think about it, Prudence," she said finally. "We haven't even found the mine yet. I'll . . . I'll let you know my decision after we do."

Prudence shook her head and looked to where Storm

had stood to see him walking away from the group around the fire. She frowned at his retreating back for a second, then thrust the paper into Jessica's hands and hurried after him.

"I think you've got yourself half of a gold mine, whether you want it or not, Jessica," Elias said with a soft chuckle. "You didn't know Prudence before she . . . Well, before anything happened to her. She was a stubborn brat at times when we were growing up. And I think she's getting some of her old spunk back."

"I'm glad," Idalee said. "I thought Tobias's death might just send her over the edge, but it seems to have made her stronger."

"She's going to have to be strong," Elias said. "It's not going to be easy for her to make it on her own."

"She'll always have us, Elias. And Storm." Idalee rose to her feet to stand by Jessica. "Don't worry about Prudence, Jessica. Storm told us that you promised Tobias you'd take care of her, but you don't have to feel guilty because you have your own responsibilities."

"The best thing I can do for Prudence I've already decided to do," Jessica said tightly. She handed Idalee the map and deed and turned away with a sob, heading in the opposite direction from the barn.

Ned's voice stopped Idalee when she started to go after Jessica. "Don't, Idalee. Let me talk to her. I think there's somethin' she needs to know."

A moment later, Ned leaned on the corral fence beside Jessica. "Pretty night," he said after glancing up at the stars overhead. "The moon's already wanin', but a man could almost reach out and grab a handful of those stars."

"Y—yes, it's beautiful, Ned. If you don't mind, I'd like to be alone for a while."

Ned ignored her and propped his hat on the post beside

him. Reaching up, he scratched his gray head and mused, "How long we been here, Jes? Over a week, I guess. Goin' on three weeks since we left the ranch. Lordy, seems like a lots happened in such a short time."

"What are you trying to get at?"

"Just thinkin' out loud. Did I ever tell you how I met Mattie?"

"Ned, I don't want to hurt your feelings, but I'm not in the mood for one of your stories tonight. And, yes, I know how you met Mattie. She told me. It was at a barn dance."

"Bet she didn't tell you we eloped two days after that dance, did she?"

"No," Jessica admitted. "She didn't tell me that part. That seems like an awfully short time to know someone before you get married."

"Happens like that sometimes, Jes. 'Course, sometimes it takes a couple of people years to get together, like Elias and Idalee. But I've never been sorry Mattie and I didn't pussyfoot around each other and waste a lot of years we could have been together."

"You've been happy. I know that. Maybe someday . . ."

"Maybe someday what, Jes?"

She gripped the fence rail under her hands tightly. "Maybe someday I'll find a man I can be happy with like Mattie did, Ned."

"Thought maybe you already had."

"If you mean Storm . . ." Jessica choked on a sob and fell silent.

"Don't mean no one else, Jes. Thought you two loved each other. What happened?"

Jessica stood frozen beside Ned, staring unseeingly before her. She jumped slightly when Cinnabar walked up to her and butted his head against her shoulder. When she turned her head, her cheek met the horse's soft muzzle, and she gripped a handful of Cinnabar's mane as she steeled herself to speak.

"Storm is going to marry Prudence. He told me that soon after I met him. And Prudence confirmed it this afternoon."

"Why, that son of a bitch," Ned said angrily. "Maybe he's not as much like his daddy as I thought he was."

"What do you mean? Storm doesn't even know who his real father was. He told me so in . . . in the cave."

"Guess you might as well know, Jes. I've had my suspicions ever since he came into town dressed as Jedidiah. Didn't you notice how much he looked like your Uncle Pete in them old buckskins? And when I saw him without that disguise, when Elias and I found him shot in the hills, I was pretty damned sure I was right. He was the right age. 'Course you don't remember Pete when he was young, but Storm looks just like him."

"Uncle Pete never had a son, Ned. He and Daddy were such close friends, surely one of them would have told me . . . Wait a minute. Uncle Pete told me about a woman named Caroline the night he died. Is Storm . . ."

"Pete and Caroline Russell's son?" Ned finished for her. "Yep, I'm finally sure he is. Caroline died in childbirth, and Pete left his son with Caroline's sister while he worked off his grief. Only thing is, when he came back for the boy a few months later, he couldn't find them. Spent the rest of his life off and on tryin' to, too. I found out the rest of the story from Idalee."

"Idalee? Why hasn't she told Storm?"

"She will soon. It's not something you just blurt out to a man."

"I did the right thing then."

"What's that supposed to mean?"

304

"You said Uncle Pete searched for his son for years, until the day he died, I'm sure. Some of what Uncle Pete said when he was dying is starting to make sense. I didn't mention it before, but he saw a vision of Caroline at . . . at the end. He asked the vision if she had brought anyone with her. He must have meant his son, because he'd said a few minutes earlier to me that someone he'd been searching for must be dead. So when Storm and Prudence marry, Uncle Pete's son will have the gold he found."

"Yeah, I guess you're right, Jes. But I'll bet old Pete wouldn't be very proud of his son right now."

"It's not our business, Ned," Jessica said as her shoulders slumped and she leaned her head against Cinnabar's neck. "Storm's doing the honorable thing. After all, he was committed to Prudence long before I met him and she needs him m—more than I do. We can't hurt Prudence."

"Now what asinine poppycock are you spouting, Jessica?" Idalee asked as she came up behind them. "I told you Elias and I would see to Prudence. Where in the world did you get the crazy idea your and Storm's love would hurt Prudence?"

Chapter 23

"I'm sorry, Ned," Idalee said. "I know you said you wanted to talk to Jessica yourself, but . . . Well, I care about her, too, and . . ."

When Ned cocked a quizzical eyebrow at Idalee, she clasped her fidgeting hands to quiet them and lifted her chin a little.

"Oh, hell," she admitted with a little puff of breath. "All right, I was curious as to how Jessica reacted when you told her about the diaries. But I do want to see Storm and Jessica as happy as Elias and I are."

"Diaries?" Jessica asked.

"You haven't told her yet?"

Ned shook his head. "Not that part, just who Storm's father was. Go ahead and tell her the rest, Idalee. I was just about to."

"My mother kept diaries all her life, Jessica," Idalee hastened to explain when Jessica frowned at her. "After she died, I put them away. I guess I just didn't feel right prying into her life after she was gone. But when Ned started asking Elias questions about Storm, Elias told him he should talk to me. After all, Storm and I grew up together on the Lazy B."

"So the diaries were what confirmed Ned's suspicions?"

"Yes, Jessica. My mother and Mary, the woman who raised Storm for the first five years, were very close. Mother nursed Mary through a couple miscarriages and she said in one diary that Mary knew she wasn't going to make it after the last one."

Idalee shook her head. "Mary felt guilty about what she'd done, taking her sister's son and keeping him from his father, but she'd lost so many babies and Storm was all she had. Mother wrote it all down, in case Storm wanted to know someday. When Father adopted Storm, he asked her to wait until Storm was older to tell him. It's all there—even the fact that Mary's sister's name was Caroline Russell. We haven't had a chance to tell Storm since I dug out the diaries a few days ago."

"When you tell him," Jessica said quietly, "make sure he knows he had a wonderful father. And make sure he knows that Uncle Pete never gave up looking for him."

"I think you ought to be the one who tells him, Jessica," Idalee said sternly. "After all, you're obviously the one who loves him."

Not wanting Idalee to see the ravagement stealing over her face, Jessica whirled to put her back to the other woman. "And Prudence is the one he's going to marry, Idalee. She can't tell him as easily as you can, can she?"

"Jessica, that can't be true!"

"Maybe I can't communicate the way you're learning to with Prudence, Idalee, but I can understand her. And this evening she only confirmed what Storm had told me

307

earlier about their marriage plans."

"Well, this is the first I've heard of it," Idalee said huffily.

The sound of hoofbeats interrupted their conversation, and the three of them turned to see the paint stallion disappearing around the side of the barn. A second later, Elias joined them.

"Storm says he's going to stand guard tonight," Elias informed them. "I told him I'd take a shift, but he almost bit my head off. Do any of you know what put a burr under his saddle?"

"I want to talk to Prudence," Idalee said, shooting Jessica a perplexed look.

"She's already asleep," Elias said. "She's been holding up pretty well, but she's really exhausted. Storm spent a few minutes with her before he settled her into her bedroll, and I think we ought to turn in, too, Idalee."

Idalee sighed in compliance. "I guess it can wait until morning." She allowed Elias to take her arm and walked away with him.

"Elias is right, Jes," Ned said. "We're all tired. Let's turn in and we'll get an early start in the mornin' to find this mine."

"I'll be along in a minute, Ned."

As soon as she was alone, Jessica gripped the railing again and stared up at the hill behind the ranch. She thought she caught a flash of white from Spirit's rump on the hillside before a cloud scuttled across the dim light of the waning moon. She scanned the crest after a while, hoping to see the outline of a horseman along the ragged ridge, though she knew Storm would be foolish to give away his presence while he stood guard.

After she finally gave a tired shrug and turned away to walk toward the barn, a sensation crawled up her spine, much like when she had taken the peaches out to her cowhands. She resolutely straightened her shoulders and kept walking. His ghost would be with her always, she knew. And she had lied to Ned. There would never be another man in her life after Storm.

"I think your Uncle Pete would have wanted you to be there, Jes."

"I know, and I will be, Ned. But please come with us. I just . . . I don't want to be alone with . . ."

"All right, Jes. I'll get my horse ready."

As Ned moved away, Jessica poured the dregs from her coffee cup into the fire. The flames sputtered and hissed for only a second before the heat evaporated the moisture and they blazed merrily again. If only she could pour out the misery in her heart and get rid of it that easily.

An unpleasant chill stole over Jessica and she whirled to find Storm standing within a few inches of her. The flat stare in his black eyes chased away the morning warmth, intensifying the icy fingers on her spine.

"Ned told me he's going with us," Storm said in a harsh voice. "What's the matter? Did you think I might steal your precious map and keep the mine for myself?"

"Of course not," Jessica denied, confusion at his obvious distrust of her crowding her mind. "Why on earth would I think something like that?"

"I've had a long time to think—all night. I guess some women might enjoy a little adventure with a man they think's an outlaw. But when it comes right down to letting the whole world know they've been consorting with a man who's a convict, that's a different story."

"You know I don't believe that you hurt Prudence!"

"Doesn't matter, does it? A thing like that follows a

man all his life, even after he clears his name. I know how people are."

"Ned says he's ready," Elias said as he walked up to them. "How long do you think you'll be gone, Storm?"

Storm tore his eyes away from Jessica's astonished gaze and shrugged his shoulders. "Probably not more than two or three hours, Elias. By the way, keep your rifle with you. I saw some tracks out there this morning that I don't think came from our horses. They're probably from that horse Red was riding. It's been wandering around here. But keep on your toes."

"Right."

Storm turned and strode away.

"Aren't you going with them, Jessica?" Elias asked.

"You're damned right I am! How dare he act like this whole mess is my fault because I'm some snippety fool who can't see over my turned-up nose?"

Elias took a step back when Jessica turned her furious, gold-flecked eyes on him for a second before she stomped after Storm.

"Whew," Elias breathed after Jessica got out of hearing. "Maybe Storm should marry Prudence instead. I wouldn't want to try to keep a saddle on that filly if she didn't want to be ridden."

"Your saddle's already spoken for, Elias," Idalee said as she placed a hand on his arm. "And don't you forget it."

"Morning, honey," Elias said as he dropped a kiss on her lips. "I thought you were still resting."

"I've been talking to Prudence," Idalee told him. "Well, not talking. Communicating with her, I guess you'd say. I knew I was right. Somehow Jessica's got the wrong idea about Prudence and Storm. And as soon as they get back, I'm going to have a talk with our new friend, Miss Jessica Callaghan."

* * *

Ned pulled his gelding to a halt to give it a breather, and turned to Jessica when she stopped Cinnabar beside him.

"What the hell ails him, Jes? He's gonna kill these horses if he keeps goin' at this pace."

"I guess he just wants to get us out of his hair as soon as he can. The anxious bridegroom, you know."

"Well, I ain't killin' my horse for no man. Storm!" Ned called when Storm drew Spirit to a halt to look back at them. "We need to rest these horses!"

"You can rest them over here," Storm called back. "Come on!"

Ned growled a soft oath under his breath, but lifted his reins to urge the gelding forward. When he and Jessica rode up beside Storm, Ned looked down the hillside and shook his head.

"This is a far as I'm goin'. These horses will never make it down there, and neither will this leg of mine."

Jessica stared down the shale-covered area before them. A rock slide had washed out the trail, and several large boulders blocked their path. The horses couldn't possibly make their way around them.

"Is there another way to where we're going, Storm?" she asked.

"Where we're going is just about a half mile past this slide. If we ride around, it'll take us another hour or two. There're canyons on both sides of us."

Jessica dismounted from Cinnabar and handed her reins to Ned. "Then I guess we better leave the horses here with Ned and get going. I wouldn't want to hold you up any longer than we need to."

Besides, she told herself a moment later as she slipped and slid down the shale-covered slope, as soon as they got to the mine site, she was going to have a private talk with Mr. Storm Baker—or Russell!

She followed Storm down through the slide zone, gritting her teeth each time he held out his hand to help her around a rough spot. Once they had made their way to the bottom of the canyon, Storm led her around a bend and further into the depths of the canyon. A small stream ran by their feet, but left plenty of room for them to walk beside it.

"Wait up, Storm," Jessica finally said. "I'm thirsty."

She leaned down and cupped a handful of water to her lips. As she started to reach down for another swallow, she heard Cinnabar neigh behind her and turned. She couldn't see around the bend to where Ned waited.

"I guess he's having some trouble keeping those two stallions apart. We should have thought of that and tied them instead."

Storm shrugged and moved away without answering her, leading the way down the canyon before he began scaling the side of the wall.

A lot sooner than Jessica would have thought possible, Storm halted and knelt beside a scattering of small, smooth stones. He picked one up and rubbed it between his fingers, then ran his eyes over the other stones around him.

"Someone's been here before us," he told Jessica.

"How do you know?"

"These stones were a claim marker. And right over there's your mother lode. I guess your uncle rolled that big boulder in front of his diggings so no one would notice them. He probably started that rock slide years ago, too, so the stream wouldn't wash the gold down to lower ground."

"Why would he do that?"

"That's usually how men locate a mother lode, Jessica.

312

They find flakes or even nuggets downstream and follow the stream up into the hills to see where the gold came from. Pete made sure no one would find this one until he was ready for them to."

"But that boulder's just up against another bunch of rocks."

"Not there, Jessica. The boulder slipped in a mud slide. That's probably why someone riding by here could see the excavation. It's up there."

Storm climbed a few more feet up the slope and pulled at some dead branches on the hillside. When they fell away, he stepped back so Jessica could see past him into an excavation dug into the ground. He held his hand out, and Jessica allowed him to pull her up beside him.

"Look in there, Jessica. You can see the sun falling on that streak in the rock. It's almost pure gold. No telling how far back into these hills it goes."

Jessica pulled her hand free and moved away from Storm. "It's very pretty. Or at least, I guess it will be when it's turned into coins or jewelry. I assume we're still on Tobias's land?"

When Storm remained silent, Jessica glanced at him to see him studying the hillside around them. A frown marred his face for a moment; then he walked a few paces inside the excavation. Striking a match, he held it over his head as he peered around and traced his hand along the dull yellow vein in the wall of stone. The match burned down and he dropped it to the floor before he reemerged from the excavation.

"If I'm right," he said when he rejoined Jessica, "that's Lazy B property on the other side of this hill. We'll have to study the map at the land office, though, to be sure."

"Then you think the vein runs that way."

"Hell, I'm no mining engineer, but I've been in a few

gold mines in my life. I'd say it's a real possibility."

As Storm turned sideways to scan the stratums of rock on the hillside, Jessica studied his profile. Images of her Uncle Pete swam in her mind and now she could see the resemblance Ned spoke of. She had seen Pete stand like that in the fall when he gazed westward toward his beloved wandering grounds. He always had that same proud tilt to his head.

Suddenly she had an image of Pete sitting by the fireplace one night when she had crept back downstairs after being awakened by a clap of thunder. He had sat in front of the fire with his hands on his knees, his head bent. When he heard her approach, she had caught the pain in his deep brown eyes before he managed to cover it up and hold his arms out to her. She had seen that look of pain before—in Storm's eyes. Storm's eyes—so much like Uncle Pete's.

Jessica felt her heart wrench as she gazed around her. How close had Uncle Pete come to finding Storm in his wanderings? Cross-county, instead of the circuitous route she had taken, it couldn't be more than an hour's ride to the Lazy B.

"I guess I'll never know," Jessica mused.

"No, you won't," Storm agreed, startling Jessica for a second. "You'll be safe and sound back on your ranch in Wyoming if this mine ever gets started. Safe and sound, with no ties to Montana."

"Damn it, Storm!" Jessica flared. "You're the one who kept telling me to go back to Wyoming all along! You've been trying to get rid of me since the first time we met. Well, don't worry. I won't hang around and complicate things for you!"

"Complicate things for me?" Storm fired back at her. "How in hell could my life get more complicated? I've still got a rape charge hanging over my head, and even if I manage to get out of that, there's still the charge for escaping prison. That's against the law, too, even if I'm proven innocent on the other charge."

"You'll be able to work it out," Jessica said as she tore her gaze away from his ravaged face. "Ned and I agreed to get Frederick to help you."

"I don't need any help from your old lover!" Storm spat. "I'll handle things alone—like I always have!"

Tears filled Jessica's eyes, blurring his image. She clasped her hands across her stomach and turned her back to him to hide her face. Alone? No, he wouldn't be alone. She would be, though.

Storm knotted his fists at his side to keep from reaching out to her. But when her small shoulders started to shake, he couldn't keep from moving close to her.

"I'm sorry I yelled," he said quietly. "I want you to be happy, Jessica. Wherever you are, I want you to know that I wish that for you."

She only shook her head and sniffed loudly, her sob-clogged throat making it impossible for her to answer him. She felt something flutter beside her cheek and unclasped one hand to reach for the bandanna Storm held over her shoulder. She wiped at her streaming eyes, then held it close to her nose for a moment, breathing in his scent.

"Can—can I keep the bandanna, Storm?" she asked when she could control her sobs.

"Oh, pretty lady," Storm breathed, "don't you know I'd give you the world if I could? I'm just sorry my love isn't enough, since it's all I have right now."

Slowly, Jessica turned as she felt his arms go around her. She lifted her head to see his face drawing close to hers and pushed gently on his chest. "We . . . we can't, Storm."

"Can't we?"

He gently claimed her lips at first, then more fiercely when he felt her surrender to him. He pulled her close, holding her as though he could never let her go. And how could he? She was his world—his reason for living. She chased the darkness from his life and brought in light and hope again.

Storm cupped the back of her head and tangled his fingers in her sable tresses to hold her face up to his when he wrenched his lips away. He was shaking so hard, he gritted his teeth and clenched his hand in the back of Jessica's blouse, willing his trembling to stop. When she raised a tentative hand to his cheek, Storm buried his face in her neck.

"I can't do it," he groaned. "I can't let you go. I love you so damned much. There has to be some way . . ."

Jessica rubbed her cheek against his dark hair and sighed softly. "I'll always love you, Storm. I want you to know that."

He jerked his head up and stared down at her, his brow creased in puzzlement. "Then why? For God's sake, why are you leaving before we can work this out? How can you just throw away what we could have? Listen, Jessica, I'll accept your Frederick's help, if that's what it takes to clear me. And I'll make you proud of me somehow."

"Storm, you've got it all wrong. I could never be ashamed of loving you. But—but what about Prudence?"

"Prudence? I don't see—"

"Well, isn't this a tender scene? Are you two planning what all you can buy with that gold behind you?"

Jessica stared wildly over Storm's shoulder, meeting David Baker's icy gaze. She felt Storm's fingers tighten reflexively in her hair for a moment before he gently loosened his hold and turned while pushing her behind him.

"What the hell are you doing here, David?" he said in an ominous voice.

David leveled the rifle at Storm's chest and worked the lever to pull a shell into the chamber. "Don't try it, Storm," he said when he saw Storm glance at the rifle he had propped against a rock. "I might just have to shoot your friend there if you lunge for that rifle."

Chapter 24

Storm ignored David's warning. Shoving Jessica at the excavation, he dove for his rifle.

Storm's quick reaction worked, freezing David into uncertainty for a second as he wavered his rifle between the two scrambling figures. When David finally centered the rifle on Storm, his shot echoed a split second after Storm's. Only Storm's shell found its mark. David's bullet buried itself harmlessly in the ground beside Storm's shoulder after the rifle butt shattered in David's hand.

"Damn you!" David shouted as he dropped the useless gun and stared down the barrel of Storm's rifle. "You'll pay for that!"

Storm slowly rose to his feet, keeping his rifle trained on David. "Jessica," he called over his shoulder, "are you all right?"

Jessica scrambled out of the excavation, brushing dirt and dust from her clothing. "I'm fine," she assured him as she hurried to his side. "Just what the hell *do* you think you're doing, David? You've got no right out here!"

"That's where you're wrong, Jessica," David replied calmly. "Any citizen has a right to capture an escaped convict." He carefully kept his hands away from the pistol on his hip while he spoke, but his eyes slid to the hillside just above where they stood. "Isn't that right, Harlin?"

Both Storm and Jessica heard the rifle cock above them, and Storm didn't need the confirmation of Harlin's voice to know David wasn't just trying to trick them. He pulled Jessica close to his side as Harlin spoke.

"Drop that gun, Storm. You don't have a chance in hell of getting me before I can get off a shot. You know I'm a better shot than David. I always have been."

Storm threw his rifle down. "Leave Jessica out of this, Harlin," he called after his gun hit the ground. "She's got nothing to do with what's between us."

David quickly stepped forward and retrieved Storm's rifle. For a tense moment he pointed it at Storm's chest, keeping it trained on him even after Jessica twisted out of Storm's hold and stepped in front of him.

"Hiding behind a woman, Storm?" he asked with a raised brow. "I'll bet Pa wouldn't be so proud of you if he could see you right now."

Storm grasped Jessica firmly by the shoulders and pushed her to the side. When she struggled against his hold, he drew his eyes away from David and spoke curtly to her. "Stay out of it. I don't want you mixed up in this."

"Storm—"

"I mean it, Jessica."

"Better listen to him," David said. He took a few steps forward; then his arm came up swiftly and he brought the rifle butt down on the side of Storm's head. A satisfied smile quirked his lips as Storm crumpled silently to the ground.

"You bastard!" Jessica screamed.

She launched herself at him, catching David off guard. They both tumbled to the ground, Jessica frantically beating her fists against David's chest. When she landed on top of him, she arched her fingers and dug her nails into his face, barely missing his eyes.

"You stupid bitch!"

David brought his knotted fist up and hit Jessica full force on the side of her face. She crumpled against him and he shoved her inert body aside to rise over her. Wiping at the blood streaming down his face, he cocked the rifle and pointed it again, a mad light filling his eyes.

"For God's sake, don't, David!"

Harlin scrambled down the hillside. He stopped a few feet from his brother, and spoke soothingly to him when he saw the familiar glint in David's eyes. "You can't shoot her, David. Remember what we found out about her. You sure as hell don't want that damned Wyoming attorney after us. He used to be one of the fastest gunslingers around and he'll have the whole state of Wyoming down on us if anything happens to her."

"The damned bitch tried to blind me! And that gunslinger's an old man by now. He doesn't scare me!"

Harlin quickly tried another tack with his brother. "Think for a minute, David. For once in your life, think before you act," Harlin pleaded. "What chance will we have of getting this gold if we have to explain a dead woman's body out here?"

Harlin slowly breathed a sigh of relief as some of the insane light left his brother's eyes and David reluctantly lowered the rifle. He pulled a handkerchief from his coat pocket and handed it to David.

"Here. Clean up your face and let's get on with what we planned. I want to have Storm back in town, waiting for that marshal when he arrives. That way, he won't hang around and start nosing into our business. He can just take his prisoner and leave."

David gingerly wiped at his face and turned his flat stare on Storm's prone body a few feet away. He noted the blood streaming from the gash on Storm's head, mixing with the raven hair, and an ugly smirk crossed his face.

"I'm going to make sure that son of a bitch never gives us any more trouble," he said in a cold voice. "I want him dead this time. We should have had that damn judge order him hanged the last time, instead of just sending him to prison."

"That would have been going too far. Elias Gant was stirring up things against us in town even before the trial. He only shut up after he heard Storm escaped, but you can bet your ass he won't stand still for us showing up in town with Storm's dead body."

Jessica fought the receding blackness in her mind, some instinct telling her she was in danger. She stifled a moan of pain and rigidly fought the desire to move her aching neck. Tentatively, she slit her eyelids, but a curtain of hair covered her face. The voice she heard told her the full measure of the danger she sensed.

"We're going to have to get rid of all of them some way, Harlin. At least Gant and that damned half sister of ours. I can handle Prudence. She'll sign her name on the deed giving us this ranch after I get done with her again."

"Yeah, unless you go too far with her, like you did that waitress. You disgust me, David. A man shouldn't have to beat a woman to have satisfying sex with her. Why in hell didn't you keep your sex life out of Baker's Valley and in San Francisco, where it belonged? At least there you paid for the whores you used."

"You don't understand, brother," David said as he looked into Harlin's disgust-filled eyes. "Do you know how many nights I listened outside that bitch's door while the old man screwed her?"

"Oh God, David." Harlin swallowed nausea as he realized the vacant look in David's eyes meant he didn't even see him. He watched a dribble of saliva crawl down David's chin, and turned away to stare at the hillside behind him as David continued talking.

"Every damned one of those women was her, Harlin," David mused in a soft, sickening voice. "Every drive I made into their bodies, every blow I landed on them, paid her back for what she did. She's the one who brought that bastard Storm into our house and gave Pa someone else to love. We should have had that love, Harlin. You and me."

"Stop it, David!"

"There's only one way to stop it, Harlin. They all have to die. Do you know how many times I tried to wipe it out of my mind in San Francisco? Do you have any idea?"

Harlin whirled, glaring at David. "I know you let the Lazy B go to hell while you pursued your sexual needs!" he yelled. "Then when I wouldn't give you any more money from the bank, you came back here to Baker's Valley and continued your decadent adventures."

"We can end it right now," David pleaded. "Let's get rid of all of them. Then I'll be free. Can't you see that? Just knowing Storm and Idalee are alive keeps driving me. Help me, Harlin."

"I've helped you all your life, David," Harlin said through gritted teeth. "And you're forgetting about that marshal. How in hell will we explain a bunch of dead bodies to him and the governor of the state? I keep telling you that you've gone too far, David."

"No, brother," David denied, "not nearly far enough."

"Forget it, David. If that marshal leaves without giving us any trouble, we'll be all right. If not, we can take the money that's left in the bank and ride out of here. Go to Mexico and start over."

"I'm not going anywhere as long as Storm is alive!" David screamed. Clasping a hand to the side of his head, he pulled frantically on his hair. "He's got to die!"

David wrenched a handful of hair from his head and lowered his arm to stare at it for a second before he turned his maddened gaze on Harlin. "He's still in my head, Harlin. You see? I can't get him out of my head as long as he's alive."

When David turned and pointed the rifle again at Storm, Harlin leaped forward. He knocked the rifle aside, but not before David managed to pull the trigger. The sound of the shot echoed along with Jessica's scream as she lurched to her feet and ran toward Storm.

Harlin caught Jessica's arm before she could kneel by Storm and jerked her around to face him. "You stupid bitch. How long have you been awake?" he demanded as he grabbed her other arm and shook her wildly.

"Let me go! Storm. Oh, Storm!"

"Shut up!" Harlin gripped her arms bruisingly and held her still. "He's not dead, but he will be before morning. You've made sure of that, lying there, listening to us. You've left me no choice now. And after it's done, you're going to listen to me describe to David every twitch he made at the end of the hangman's noose!"

"What do you mean, Harlin?" David asked, licking his lips as he stared at Jessica's stark-white face and horrified expression.

"Take your bandanna off and tie this little wildcat up, David," Harlin demanded. "Then you're going to listen to what I've got to say. Thank God one of us keeps his wits about him."

David removed his bandanna and quickly bound Jessica's hands behind her. When David shoved her away from him, Jessica landed in the dirt at Harlin's feet. Harlin stood over her, his fists knotted at his side.

"If you try to move, I swear I'll let David have you," he growled.

"Please," Jessica pleaded. "Storm needs help. He's bleeding."

"That's just too damned bad," Harlin snarled. He remained standing over Jessica, taking no chance she would disobey his order not to move, while he spoke again to David. His words increased the horror spreading through Jessica's mind.

"Listen, David," Harlin said, "I've got a better idea now. I'll take Storm back to town and parade him down the main street before I have the sheriff lock him up. It won't take much to get the men in town fired up about lynching a rapist. Then when the marshal arrives, we'll have a whole town full of witnesses as to what happened."

Harlin watched his brother closely as David took a deep, steadying breath while he stared down at Storm. "Think about it, David," he continued in a comforting voice, the only voice he had ever been able to use to get through to his brother over the years. "Think how he'll look kicking at the end of a rope."

"Yes," David breathed out in a sibilant sigh. "Remember how men look when they hang, Harlin? How black their faces get and how their tongues stick out? Remember how they smell when . . ."

Jessica sobbed and pulled her legs under her to try to stand, but David quickly whirled toward her. The look in his flat, pale eyes pinned her effectively to the ground.

"What about her?" The hoarseness in David's voice sent a new chill down Jessica's spine. "She knows everything now."

"We'll have to take her with us, David. She'll be our safe passage out of the territory."

"But all this gold!" David said with a whine.

"Is that gold worth you hanging from your own rope, David?" Harlin demanded. "If it is, you're on your own. I can arrange Storm's death, but there's not time to make sure Idalee and Gant can't get to that marshal. I'm not staying around to watch you hang, too."

"Don't leave me, Harlin."

"Then for once in your life listen, David. The money left in the bank will allow us to go somewhere else. I'll clean it out after the town takes care of Storm and meet you at the Lazy B. We'll have all night to be on our way. You take this bitch with you. The rest of them back at Tobias's will be out of our hair looking for her. Just make sure you keep her alive. Remember, she's our ticket out of here."

"Idalee will still be alive."

"Good Lord, David! We'll hire someone to come back and take care of her—someone I pick this time, instead of that unreliable scum you always get hooked up with!"

"You'll never get away with this!" Jessica screamed.

"Shut up!" Harlin snarled. "And get on your feet, unless you want me to change my mind and get rid of your lover over there right now. If you give me even one more minute's trouble, I'll forget all my plans and do just that."

"You're going to kill us anyway," Jessica said, sobbing.

"Do you want to watch me kill Storm first?" Harlin said as he stared down into Jessica's frantic eyes. "I saw you in his arms when we came up. Do you want to watch him die, inch by inch?"

Terror clogged Jessica's throat as she caught a glint of the madness she had recognized in David's eyes growing in Harlin's. She shook her head wildly and tried to rise to her feet.

Harlin reached down and jerked Jessica up, keeping a firm grip on her arm as he bent his face close to hers. "Then you better do exactly as I tell you," he said in an icy voice. "You're going to walk ahead of us while David brings Storm. If you make one wrong move, I'm going to help David kill him. Slowly."

"He's hurt. He can't walk."

Harlin ignored the plea in Jessica's sobbing voice. "Tie Storm's hands and go get a hatful of water from the stream, David," he ordered. "We've got to get back to the horses so we can ride out of here."

The frenzied terror clouding Jessica's mind heightened as she watched David tie Storm and head for the creek. Each time Harlin glanced away from her to assure himself David followed his orders, she twisted her bound hands behind her back, trying to free them. But the knots held firm.

There had to be something she could do. Her feeling of helplessness grew with her terror. When David threw the water in Storm's face, waking him from his unconscious state, she took a step forward.

"Don't," Harlin warned.

Jessica froze and watched Storm slowly sit up. He glanced at her, and she gasped softly at the blood running down the side of his face.

"Jessica?"

"I'm all right, Storm."

"And if you want to keep her that way, you'll get on your feet," David said as he backed a few steps away from Storm, the rifle covering him. "Don't give us any trouble while we walk back to the horses."

A moment later the small party made its way back up the canyon floor, with Harlin keeping Jessica a good ten feet in front of David and Storm. When Jessica tried to slow her steps, Harlin grabbed her arm and shoved her forward, reminding her with a mutter what would happen if she caused him any problems. Giving up any thought of further resistance, she plodded along beside him until they reached the rock slide they had climbed down only a half hour before.

"Ned," Jessica gasped as she stared up the rock slide. "What have you done with Ned?"

Halfway up the slope, Jessica saw a booted foot sticking out from behind a rock. Immediately, she recognized one of Ned's old, run-down boots.

Harlin laughed coldly and pulled her after him as he climbed the slope. She had time for only one frantic glimpse of Ned's still face as she passed his prone body, but her ears caught the sound as Ned drew in a tortured breath.

"Stop!" she cried as she tried to free her arm from Harlin's grasp. "He's still alive. You can't just leave him there!"

Harlin almost wrenched her arm from its socket when he ignored Jessica and jerked her forward again.

"You want me to finish him off?" she heard David say from behind her.

"No!" Harlin called over his shoulder. "We're too close to the top of this hill. A shot might carry down to Tobias's and bring the rest of them up here. He didn't see us and

327

we need the extra time it will give us while they search for these three when they don't come back."

At the top of the slope, Jessica stared around her, her eyes searching for Cinnabar. She saw only two strange horses and Ned's gelding, all three tied to some bushes at the side. She heard the sound of someone falling behind her and whirled to see David standing over Storm.

"Get up, you bastard," David growled. "And get on that damned horse!"

Jessica's eyes filled with tears as she watched Storm struggle to his feet and stand swaying beside David. She wanted so badly to go to him, but she didn't dare. She could only stand beside Harlin while Storm stumbled toward the horses.

David untied the gelding's reins and prodded Storm in the back with his gun. "Get on," he ordered.

"I can't mount that horse with my hands tied," Storm said, gasping with pain.

Harlin moved Jessica into Storm's line of vision and pointed his rifle at her head. "You can and you will, Storm. We don't have time for any of your tricks."

Harlin allowed Jessica only an instant to stare into Storm's ravaged face before he gripped her by the hair and turned her back around. The sight of the rifle on the edge of her vision froze her in place, keeping her from giving in to the yearning in her to turn back.

"Help him up, David," Harlin said. "And tie him in place. I don't want him trying anything on our way back to town."

Tears streaked Jessica's face as she frantically searched her mind for any possible way to escape. This just couldn't be happening. Damn that gold! The curse was reaching out to take Storm's life—and hers. While she remained trapped at the Lazy B with a madman, Harlin would take

Storm to Baker's Valley and organize a lynch mob!

"Please . . ." she started to beg. Harlin tightened his grip in her hair, the pain sending more tears coursing down Jessica's face.

"I won't tell you to shut up again!" Harlin snarled.

Jessica listened to the movements behind her, hearing the squeak of saddle leather and Storm's labored breathing. David passed her and grabbed a rope from the saddle of one of the other horses. Though her vision was blurred, she caught the chilling look David threw at her from narrowed eyes as he strode back toward the gelding.

Harlin finally relaxed his hold on Jessica and shoved her toward one of the other horses. After lifting her into the saddle, he untied her hands briefly, then retied them to the saddle horn.

Jessica twisted her head around, trying but unable to catch sight of Storm behind her. The horse shifted under her as David approached and Harlin handed the reins to him.

"Remember what I said, David," Harlin warned. "We need her to make sure we get out of here with no interference."

"I hear you, Harlin," David growled as he swung up into the saddle and settled himself behind Jessica. "But you better not be late. I don't fancy waiting all night out there at the ranch, wondering what's going on. Don't come until after you see Storm swinging at the end of that rope, though. If I can't be there, I want all the details from you."

Chapter 25

Only once on the ride to the Lazy B did Jessica make the mistake of surreptitiously trying to work her hands free from the saddle horn. She heard David's snort of laughter in her ear just before his hand closed over her breast and twisted it cruelly. Her scream of pain only made his fingers clench harder, and his laughter turned into a cackle in her ear. Mercifully, his hand dropped a moment later.

"Do you want me to turn you loose? Huh? Is that what you want, you bitch? Just say the word and we'll stop for a while. Harlin only said I had to keep you alive. He didn't say what shape I had to have you in when he came for us. We can just finish what we started in the whorehouse that night right here, if that's what you want."

"You!" Jessica gasped. "I thought . . ."

"What?" David prodded when she fell silent. "Tell me what you meant or I'll . . ." Swiftly, David tore open her blouse and shifted his reins to his other hand. He arched

330

his fingers into a claw and held them a scant inch from her other breast.

"I'll tell you!" Jessica cried. "I thought it was your brother that night. I didn't know it was you."

"Harlin?" David asked with an astonished laugh. "That brother of mine doesn't have the guts to treat a woman like she deserves." His fingers relaxed somewhat and he flicked his thumb across Jessica's nipple, then cupped his palm under her breast.

Jessica shuddered, but made no move to pull away, even when David rested his hand holding the reins against her crotch and pulled her back against him.

"No," David continued in a musing voice. "Harlin doesn't know how good it can make a man feel to see a woman beg and plead for her life, how much better it can make me feel when Fiona screams out how sorry she is for what she did.

"But you still haven't told me enough times to make me believe you, have you, Fiona?" David breathed softly. "Maybe this time it will happen. Maybe this time I'll finally believe you and I won't have to look for you anymore."

"I'm not Fiona," Jessica managed in a strangled voice.

David laughed wildly. "You always say that, don't you, Fiona? Just like you always tell me how sorry you are every time. Remember? Remember how you begged and said you'd do anything I wanted, if I'd only let Pa live?"

"My God," Jessica whispered.

David caught her words. "God won't help you, Fiona. He knows it's not right for a man to turn from his own blood sons and give his love to a whore's daughter and a boy he adopted. I saw the will, did you know that, Fiona? No one knows I hid it behind that loose stone in the fireplace, not even Harlin. He knows I have it, though. How do you think I got him to do everything I wanted over the years?

"Answer me, damn it!" David screamed when Jessica remained silent.

Jessica couldn't control the shiver of dread crawling over her skin. Her bound hands gripped the saddle horn in front of her and she forced her words from a throat clogged with terror. "Y—you threatened him with the will."

"Yes, I did," David admitted. "You aren't so dumb after all, are you, Fiona?"

Jessica shook her head, the only answer she could give.

"But I'm smarter," David said with another wild chuckle. "I'm smarter and I always get what I want. And now I'll have all the money from the bank, too. I won't have to beg Harlin for money."

"But . . . but you said . . . You promised Harlin . . ."

"You didn't think I'd really leave the ranch, did you, Fiona? Huh? Why, I'll never leave the ranch. You're there. You'll always be there. My brother will bring that money out and then I'll have all I need to live on after I turn him in for robbing his own bank. I'll tell them he must have buried the money, but it will be all mine. I've always been the smart one and I've never let Harlin push me around. He won't this time either. And after that, I'll get that gold. The money from the bank will get the mine started, and I'll never have to beg anyone for money again. See how smart I am, Fiona? I let Harlin do all the talking back there, while I made my own plans."

"But . . . Oh my God," Jessica breathed. "He's your brother."

"He should have remembered that, Fiona," David insisted in a hollow voice that told Jessica he had indeed slipped into the throes of insanity. "He should have remembered that a person doesn't go against his own blood. Pa did that and I had to make him pay for it. I had to. It's just not right."

David finally fell silent, and though he kept his hands busy moving over her body, Jessica swallowed her revulsion. Frantically, she searched her mind for words that might trick David into releasing her. Could she insist she needed to make a nature stop at the side of the trail? She shivered involuntarily at the thought of his eyes watching her while she slipped down her underwear.

Could she spook the horse, hoping it would unseat David and leave her on its back? What if he pulled her with him, despite her hands being bound to the saddle horn? Once on the ground, he would surely follow through with his threat to rape her.

Clearly, any attempt she made to reason with him while he remained in the throes of madness would only endanger her further. Nothing she could think of would break through the insanity clouding his mind. But somehow she had to find a way to escape before Harlin carried out his plan to have Storm hanged.

As David rode his horse through the weed-choked yard of the Lazy B, Jessica stared around her, hoping desperately for a sign of someone to help her. The corral stood empty and broken windows on the bunkhouse met her eyes. She heard an eerie creak and turned her eyes on the barn, only to see a door swinging on one hinge, the other one broken.

Even the chickens went about their business of searching out bugs in the tall grass in a strangely silent manner. A rooster hopped onto a broken railing of the hitching post beside them, flapped his wings, then opened his mouth. Not a sound came out, though, when the rooster glanced at them. He hopped back to the ground and walked away in his stilted gait.

David swung down from the horse and untied Jessica's hands. He pulled her roughly to the ground, then reached for the hem of her blouse to tie the gaping opening shut over her breasts. Seeing her eyes fall to the gun he still carried on his hip, he grabbed her hands again and wound the bandanna around them.

"If you know what's good for you," he said in a low voice, "you'll keep your mouth shut until we get up to the bedroom. You won't look so pretty with half your teeth missing if I have to shut you up myself."

Jessica felt a glimmer of hope. If he was worried about her screaming for help, there had to be someone else in the house. After one look at his face, though, Jessica had no doubt he meant what he said, and she nodded reluctantly. She felt his hand go to the back of her blouse and walked beside him as he guided her up the steps and through the door at the end of the porch. Once inside, she stifled a sneeze as she gazed around her at the dusty room.

"Guess Old Maude's gonna need another lesson on how to keep the house clean," David said as he led Jessica toward a stairwell in the corner of the room. "I can take care of that later. Right now, we've got better things to do."

When David shoved her toward the first step, Jessica glanced into the mirror on the bureau beside the stairwell. Though the glass reflected the dinginess of neglect, she thought she saw the shadow of a face staring back at her— a vaguely familiar face. Where had she seen it before?

Craning her neck around toward an open doorway as David pushed her up the stairwell, she found it empty. If anyone had been there, they thought better of interfering with David.

The bedroom David led her into was a huge room and, surprisingly to Jessica, sparkling with cleanliness. David stopped inside the door and watched her closely as she gazed around her.

Her eyes tried to avoid the huge, four-poster bed in one corner of the room, covered by a deep blue comforter. Instead, she concentrated on the flower-sprigged wallpaper of blue flowers which matched the bedspread. She directed her gaze to the windows.

Clean, snow-white curtains billowed in a breeze flowing through their slightly open frames, and Jessica found herself amazed to see the sun still above the horizon. Surely more time than that had passed since she had ridden out of Tobias's ranch that morning.

David turned the key in the door latch behind him, the sound loud in the quiet room. He held the key up before Jessica's eyes and then slipped it into his pocket while his cruel stare kept her frozen in place.

"I've kept it just like you fixed it up when you thought you'd live here, Fiona. Maude knows I better never find a speck of dust in this room. And look."

He walked over to the bureau against the wall and picked up a cut-glass bottle. Pulling out the stopper, he tipped a drop of the contents onto the carpet.

"See?" he said as the aroma of honeysuckle filled the room. "It's your favorite scent. I've kept it ready for you, too. I want you to put some on now."

When David turned to put the stopper back on the bureau, Jessica lunged wildly for the window. A splinter of wood pierced the palm of one bound hand as she threw the frame further up. Ignoring the pain, she flung her body forward. The roof of the porch below her would break her fall and then she could. . . .

The cruel hand in her hair brought a scream of pain from Jessica as she was jerked back into the room.

"Shut the hell up!"

Though Jessica fully expected David's fist to come crashing into her face again, he held her in front of him and shook her. The sickening scent of honeysuckle surrounded them.

David shoved her to the floor and stepped over her to close the window. He turned back and raised one shaking hand to point at the bottle on the floor. "Pick it up!"

Jessica cringed against the floor until he took a threatening step toward her. Scrambling to her knees, she crawled over to the bottle and reached across the soaked portion of the carpet to clasp it in her still-bound hands and held it out to him.

"No," David said. "Put it on your body, Fiona. I love to smell it on you when we're in bed."

"I'm not Fiona!" Jessica cried.

David shook his head sadly as he stared down at her. "You always say that, don't you, Fiona? Why do you always say that? Does it make it more exciting for you to pretend you're someone else when you're going to bed with another man besides Pa?"

"David, I'm not—"

David took another step and grabbed her shoulders to pull her to her feet. His fingers bit cruelly into her, and his maddened eyes fixed on her face, overwhelming her with horror.

"Put it on, Fiona!"

A spray of spittle covered Jessica's face when he spat the words at her. Slowly, she tipped the bottle up against the side of her neck.

"Not there." David dropped one hand from her shoulders and tore the knot in her blouse open. He pushed it from her shoulders, and his tongue came out to moisten his lips as her breasts came into view.

"There," he said in a strangled voice.

Somehow Jessica managed to pull her arms up far enough in the restricting blouse to tip the bottle between her breasts. Swallowing her nausea, she released her hold on the bottle when David reached to take it from her. He dribbled more scent along the top of her breasts; then the back of his hand rubbed across her as he worked the liquid into her skin.

Her tensing muscles gave away her intent and David easily avoided the knee Jessica brought up viciously toward his groin. His roar of insane laughter filled the room as he hurled her on the bed and pinned her down with his body.

"You never forget, do you, Fiona?" he said while he threw his thigh over her wildly flailing legs. "You remember how I like it. Come on. Fight me some more."

David buried his lips against her neck, his saliva running down across Jessica's bare shoulder. Through her horror, Jessica realized her struggles only inflamed David further, but she couldn't still her frenzied thrashing. She screamed again, and David clapped a hand over her mouth and drew his head back far enough to stare down at her.

"No, no, no, Fiona," he whispered. "Why do I always have to gag you?"

A movement above them caught Jessica's attention and her eyes opened wide in terror as she stared over David's shoulder. She could see an arm—a hatchet—a hatchet descending in a deadly arc, the sharp edge directed at David's head.

At the last split second, the hatchet turned sideways and the flat of it hit the back of David's head with a sickening crunch. He didn't even moan in pain as his dead weight covered Jessica's body. Immediately, someone jerked him off her, throwing David onto his back beside her.

Jessica scrambled away from David, against the wall behind them, her hands up in front of her face to ward off the blows she expected. But a soothing voice cut through the sound of her wildly pounding heart. "He won't bother you no more, missy. He didn't remember I had my own key to this room."

Slowly, Jessica dropped her hands and opened her eyes. The slatternly woman she had seen feeding the chickens several days ago stood beside the bed, the hatchet hanging from one hand and her other hand outstretched toward Jessica. Dried brown splotches covered her dress, and her gray, matted hair surrounded a face wrinkled with age. The brown eyes radiated a sense of sympathy as she motioned for Jessica to come to her.

With a sob, Jessica scooted across the bed and into the woman's arms. She vaguely heard the hatchet drop to the floor before the old woman's arms closed around her and she pulled Jessica's head down to her drooping bosom.

"There, there," the woman comforted as she patted Jessica's shoulder and allowed her to sob out her terror. "Old Maude won't let him hurt you again."

Jessica regained some control of her sobbing and raised her head to glance sideways at the bed.

"Is he d–dead?"

"No," Old Maude said. "I thought I could kill him, but I couldn't. Guess we'll have to leave that up to the law." She dropped her hands from Jessica's shoulders and picked up the hatchet to hand to her. "You watch him now," she said with a nod. "I'll get some rope so we can tie him up."

Jessica shook her head and backed away from the hatchet. "I . . . I'll get his gun. He's still wearing it."

"All right, missy," Maude said. "Let me cut your hands free first."

338

Jessica held her breath as Maude neatly sliced the hatchet through the bandanna. As soon as her hands were free, she massaged the reddened skin on her wrists while Maude stepped to the bed and gingerly drew David's gun from his holster.

"Here," she said as she gave the gun to Jessica. "I don't think he'll come to, but you better not think twice about shooting him if he does. He's an evil man."

"I know," Jessica agreed.

Jessica kept the gun trained on David as Maude left the room. Her skin crawled as she forced herself to stare at him, watching for even a twitch of his fingers indicating a return to consciousness. She glanced briefly at the window to see the sun in almost the same place as before. Thoughts of Storm filled her mind, but she couldn't leave until she made sure David couldn't follow her. She had heard somewhere that madmen somehow found measures of strength sane people didn't have.

Maude's clumping footsteps sounded in the hallway, muffled as soon as she stepped onto the carpet in the room.

"Here." She handed one coil of rope to Jessica. "You better help me. We ought to hurry and get him tied. I don't know how hard I hit him."

As she swung David's legs up onto the bed and jerked his boots off to tie the rope around his ankles, David moaned. Quickly, she wrapped the rope tight and knotted it, securing it to the post at the bottom of the bed. She grabbed the gun from the mattress and stood back to look at Maude.

The old woman already had David's hands tied tightly to the post at the head of the bed and she moved over beside Jessica. Standing silently for a moment, the two women watched David's eyes flutter open.

When David started writing in his bonds, Maude walked to the bed and dangled the hatchet in front of his eyes.

"You remember Bessie?" she said in a deadly voice.

David shrunk back in terror as the hatchet's sharp blade barely missed his neck.

Maude twitched her wrist and the hatchet swung like a pendulum back and forth.

"I know you do," she said as she watched his eyes center on the hatchet. "Couldn't never prove it, but my mind's clearer now than it's been since those men found her frozen that winter, them bruises all over her. Been kind of addlepatted since then. It's clear to me now, though."

"Who . . . who's Bessie?" Jessica gasped, her own gaze centered on the hatchet.

Maude let the hatchet drop a scant inch, and the blade left a thin line of blood on David's neck. He screamed in horror. Maude lifted the hatchet and stepped back from the bed.

"She was my daughter," Maude said. She glanced at Jessica. "You look a lot like her."

"And David . . ."

"Almost lost my mind, I did," Maude continued as though Jessica hadn't spoken. "Fact is, I guess for a while I did. Something kept me here, though. Told myself it was because I was too old to find another job, but when I saw you today, I knew what I had to do. Now maybe Bessie can rest in peace."

For an instant, Jessica found herself thinking perhaps she was in a room with two mad people, until Maude gave a soft laugh beside her. When Jessica looked into the other woman's face, a clear gaze met her own.

"I'm so sorry for you," Jessica said quietly. "Do you think you'll be all right here with him? I know the sheriff in town isn't worth anything, but there's a federal marshal coming. If he's not there yet, I'll send someone else out to help you."

Maude hefted the hatchet in her hand. "I'll be fine, missy. You got something that needs taking care of back there?"

"They're going to hang Storm," Jessica told her. "I have to hurry."

"Storm? I remember him . . ."

"Maude, I don't have much time. Please. I have to go."

As Jessica ran toward the doorway, Maude's voice stopped her. "Better grab one of my old shirts by the back door to cover yourself, missy. And there's hot water on the stove if you want to get some of that smell off you."

Jessica glanced down in amazement at her bare breasts spilling out of the torn blouse. A wave of honeysuckle filled her nose. She tossed a grateful look at Maude and hurried through the door and down the hallway, tucking the pistol into her waistband as her feet flew down the stairs.

Jessica ran through the doorway she thought led into the kitchen and over to the back door. Grabbing an old flannel shirt from a peg, she stood for just a second, staring longingly at the pail of water heating on the stove. A bar of soap sitting on the windowsill by the stove decided her. She picked up a hand towel and dunked it into the water, then wrapped the soap in it and carried it with her as she retraced her steps and headed out the front door of the ranch house.

David's horse neighed shrilly and shied sideways when Jessica clattered down the porch steps and ran toward it, her blouse tail flapping behind her. She spent a precious

341

minute calming it after she grabbed the reins, then flung herself into the saddle.

The horse responded willingly to her urging, galloping out of the yard. As she went under the Lazy B sign at the end of the rutted drive, she secured the flannel shirt under her leg and scrubbed the towel across her breasts. After the soap slipped from her grip inside the towel, she kept working the towel over her.

She couldn't tell if the smell was gone or not as the wind created by her frantic pace flew past her. She finally dropped the towel, also, and shrugged out of the torn blouse, shifting the reins from hand to hand as she discarded it and managed to don the flannel shirt.

A mile from the ranch Jessica forced herself to slow the horse to a ground-eating canter. She would never make it to town in time to save Storm if she rode the horse to death. Oh God, if she only had Cinnabar. It had to be at least a two-hour ride to town and the sun would be down by then.

Over the next hour, her horse slowed from his canter to a bone-jarring trot. Flecks of foam flew from his muzzle and at last he settled into a walk. Jessica couldn't force herself to kick him into a faster pace. She would let him rest and gather his strength for a mile or so first.

She topped a rise in the dirt road leading to Baker's Valley and gave a shout of gladness.

Chapter 26

"Elias!" Jessica screamed.

Steeling her heart against the cruelty to the horse, she kicked it again into a gallop to cover the few hundred yards separating her from the two riders approaching. An answering shout came from Elias as he raced his own horse toward her, Cinnabar trailing behind. The small figure on the paint stallion outdistanced Elias, and Prudence slid to the ground to meet Jessica as Jessica pulled her horse to a plunging halt and bounded from her saddle.

Jessica dropped her reins and returned Prudence's brief hug just as Elias reached them.

"Where's Ned?" Jessica demanded as Elias swung down beside her and handed her Cinnabar's reins.

"He's going to be all right, Jessica," Elias assured her. "Idalee's taking him back into town right now. He got a pretty good knock on his head, but he managed to tell us he'd had a glimpse of David Baker just before he hit him. Where's Storm?"

"He's in Baker's Valley! Harlin has him and he plans to convince the town to lynch Storm. Come on!"

Jessica swung onto Cinnabar, leaving David's horse to find its own way back to its stable.

"What about David?" Elias called to Jessica as they raced down the dirt road.

"He's been taken care of!" Jessica yelled back. "I'll tell you later!"

She bent over Cinnabar's neck and the stallion soon left Elias far behind. Another set of hooves kept pace with the thunder of Cinnabar's, though, and Jessica glanced once briefly to her side to see Prudence sharing her wild ride. The paint stallion matched Cinnabar stride for stride, and Jessica caught the grim set of Prudence's mouth as she leaned close to Spirit's neck.

For once in her life, Jessica realized she had misjudged the distance she must travel. The sun slipped beneath the horizon as the next hour passed and still the road stretched out before her. She and Prudence were finally forced to slow even their powerful horses, lest they break the stallions' willing hearts and kill them.

Jessica glanced over her shoulder, seeing no sign of Elias. She didn't really expect to. His horse couldn't possibly have kept up with the two stallions. The emptiness of the road behind them, dust still settling in the fast fading light, emphasized how alone she and Prudence were.

Her mind swung to the task they would face in Baker's Valley. How would she ever be able to talk any sense into a lynch mob? Her experience with the sheriff had told her that he was bought and paid for by the Bakers—and Harlin owned almost the entire town. She couldn't think of one person there she could turn to for help.

Maybe Ronnie, but what could three women do against a mob of men, especially when one of them was mute?

The stallions blew and snorted, their proud heads remaining bowed. They would have to be walked awhile longer before Jessica could risk trying to get any renewed speed from them. She looked over at Prudence.

"Can you handle a gun?" she asked.

Prudence nodded emphatically, but pointed to the empty scabbard on Spirit's saddle.

Jessica glanced down at her own scabbard, thankful to see the butt of her rifle protruding from it. She pulled the pistol from her waistband and reined Cinnabar close enough to hand it to Prudence. Neither stallion protested their closeness to each other, confirming to Jessica their exhausted state.

"You may have to use that," Jessica flatly informed the other woman. "Do you think you can?"

Prudence's eyes hardened and she nodded slowly at Jessica.

"I don't suppose you have any idea how much farther it is to town."

Prudence shifted the pistol to the hand holding her reins and held up five fingers to Jessica.

"Five minutes?" Jessica questioned.

Prudence shook her head.

"Miles?"

Prudence nodded.

Oh Lord, Jessica thought to herself. They could have covered the distance in a few minutes if the horses had been fresh. At this pace, complete darkness would be on them by the time they reached town.

How long would it take Harlin to rouse the men into a lynch mob? She mentally counted the number of saloons in town as she realized today was Saturday. The town's population would be swelled from the outlying ranches, the men having been drinking in the saloons for most of the day. It wouldn't take much for Harlin to plant the seed of revenge in their drunken minds.

She couldn't even begin to imagine what she would face. She'd had very little experience with men whose minds were clouded with whiskey. Her father had only to get a hint of one of his hands drinking while on the ranch to send the hand packing. And look how she had flown into Red that day, unaware that a man's normal chivalry toward a woman would be absent when he was drunk.

She'd never been afraid of a man in her life until Red and the Bakers. The code even most of the roughest men lived by protected women from mistreatment. If a man did get out of line, there were always other men around to beat some sense into him. But she'd never had to deal with drunks or insane men—or a mob with a whiskey-induced lust for blood.

In Jessica's mind Red's and David's faces multiplied a thousand times and her heart dropped in dread at the thought of trying to reason with a mob made up of such men. Or maybe . . . God, she could only pray Storm wasn't already dead.

Beside her, Prudence kicked Spirit into an easy lope. Jessica realized Cinnabar's breathing had evened out and his head rode proudly again on his arched neck. She urged the stallion after Spirit, covering the remaining distance to town again in a fast canter.

Jessica's fears were confirmed when they rode past the empty saloons on the edge of Baker's Valley a while later. The swelling sound of angry voices further down the street led her and Prudence toward the lynch mob.

At least there still might be some hope, Jessica thought as she grimly pulled her rifle from the scabbard. Surely if Storm were already dead, the men would be back in the saloons, celebrating their shameful deed.

Her mind could never even have begun to imagine the scene they found in front of the sheriff's office. The roar from at least two hundred men swelled when the door of the building flew open and several men Jessica didn't recognize dragged a bound Storm down the steps. She and Prudence pulled their horses up abruptly and stared wildly at each other. What chance did they have against so many?

The growling roar surged higher as one of the men led a horse beneath the sign on the sheriff's office and another man tossed a rope over the sign. Good God! They were going to hang him right there in the middle of town!

Willing hands lifted Storm and shoved him onto the horse, where he sat outlined in the lantern light, with the rope dangling over his head. A man reached up and snagged the rope over Storm's wildly thrashing head as Jessica pulled her rifle to her shoulder.

She didn't even have time to mutter a prayer as the man slapped the horse on the rump. Her bullet severed the rope and the horse surged into the crowd, Storm still on its back and the hangman's noose that should have broken his neck dangling uselessly.

The men in the crowd captured the horse before it could break free. Several turned their heads, searching for the reason for the broken rope, but their voices had drowned out even the sound of Jessica's shot.

"Get another rope! Another rope! Who's got another rope?" The words echoed simultaneously from the mob.

Jessica raised her rifle again and urged Cinnabar forward. The stallion's powerful front shoulders sliced

through the throng as easily as he brushed aside underbrush while chasing cattle. Jessica tightened her finger
twice more on her rifle trigger, shooting over the crowd's
heads.

There were still two bullets left in her rifle when she
drew Cinnabar up sideways in front of the horse Storm
sat on again under the sign. A shouted order from Jessica
sent Cinnabar's rear legs slashing outward and the men
behind the stallion scrambled to safety.

"Put your damned guns away!" a voice of reason yelled.
"That's a woman. We ain't here to hurt no women!"

Jessica smiled grimly and tugged on Cinnabar's
reins to make him rear, scattering the remaining men
facing her. She swept her rifle in a deadly arc as the
roar of the crowd quieted somewhat, though angry
mutterings among the men continued.

"For God's sake, Jessica, get out of here!" Storm cried
from behind her. "You don't stand a chance against this
mob!"

"Shut up!" Jessica threw over her shoulder. "I'm not
going to let them hang you!"

"Jessica . . ."

"Listen to me!" Jessica screamed at the crowd. "Do you
have any idea what you're doing? If you do this, every
one of you will be guilty of murder!"

"And he's guilty of rape!" a man yelled back. "He's
already escaped prison once. We're going to make sure
he pays for his crime this time!"

A roar of agreement surged from the crowd, and Jessica
fired one of the last remaining bullets from her rifle, tem-
porarily silencing them.

"You don't know what you're talking about!" she
screamed. "This is all the Bakers' doing. Where's Harlin?
I'll make him admit—"

"Here I am, Miss Callaghan," Harlin Baker called as he stepped forward on the walkway. He turned his attention immediately to the crowd of men.

"Don't listen to her, men!" he called. "My brother and I found her out in the hills with this man. She's been helping him hide. He's her lover!"

Angry hands reached for Cinnabar, and the flow of men overpowered even the huge stallion. Jessica felt her rifle jerked from her hands as she was pulled from Cinnabar's back. A pair of hard arms circled her and dragged her onto the walkway. Suddenly another rope appeared, and a man tossed it over the sign again.

The angry voices in the crowd drowned out Jessica's screams as a man rode up behind Storm and began to fashion the rope into another hangman's noose. She struggled wildly against the arms restraining her, and a wave of agony sent tears coursing down her cheeks as she realized her attempt to reason with the crowd had failed. Harlin was going to win.

"Oh God! Please listen to me!" she screamed, but the man holding her finally clamped his hand over her mouth.

All at once the tone of the crowd changed again. The men's heads began turning over their shoulders to look behind them. The angry growl died, replaced by a spreading silence, cut only by another woman's shrieking voice.

"You're wrong! Stop this madness! Harlin's lying to you! It wasn't Storm who hurt me! Listen to me!"

As Jessica watched in helpless astonishment, Prudence urged Spirit through the crowd, batting at men with her pistol. When one man stepped in front of her to reach for Spirit's reins, Prudence fired the pistol at his feet, sending the man back to the side of the pathway and clearing the way for her. The man reached for his gun, but a rough-dressed cowboy beside him gripped his wrist in a steely grasp.

"You take a shot at that woman and it'll be the last damned shot you ever make," the cowboy growled in a deadly voice.

Even behind Prudence the pathway remained open as the men stared at her in wonder while she rode through them, her once mute voice echoing over their heads. "I tell you, Storm didn't hurt me!" Prudence yelled. "It was David Baker!"

Prudence finally managed to turn her horse in front of Storm, and her angry eyes flashed in the lantern light as she gazed out over the now-quiet crowd.

"David did it!" She pointed her finger at Harlin. "Your brother. And you knew it. You told me you'd kill my own brother if I told! But I couldn't tell, could I? Your brother took my voice, along with my chastity! But God gave me back my voice in time to make you both pay for all your evil ways!"

While amazed murmurs ran through the men, Harlin surged forward. The man holding Jessica dropped his arms and lunged for him. They hit the walkway in a heap, and several more men sprang forward to secure Harlin. They jerked him to his feet and turned him to face Prudence.

Jessica's voice demanded that the men listen to her now. "David's also the man who killed Eloise," she shouted at them. "I heard them talking after they attacked Storm and me, and Harlin had plans to clean out the bank tonight while you men were busy hanging Storm. He was going to meet David out at the ranch and head for Mexico with your money before the federal marshal who's on his way here arrives. Harlin's been stealing from the bank all along, giving David part of the money. They didn't want the marshal looking into things."

Too late Jessica realized her words had again inflamed the crowd. The men holding Harlin began dragging him toward the horse Storm sat on, while other men pulled Storm to the ground.

"Hang the bastard! We've had all we're going to take from those damned Baker brothers!"

How he ever heard her, Jessica never knew, but Cinnabar responded to her wild whistle and surged toward her. She leapt toward the hitching rail in front of her, one foot making contact with the cross post before she sprang into her saddle. She managed to grab the pistol from Prudence's fingers before the crowd separated the two horses.

Jessica fired the pistol at the men's feet with her first shot. Then she trained it on one of the men holding Harlin.

"Do you want to be the first one wounded?" she yelled. "Because I'm not going to let you make another mistake tonight. Can't you see what you're doing? You're lowering yourselves to the Bakers' level!"

"You're a stranger here!" a man shouted from the crowd. "You don't know how we've been held hostage by Harlin and his brother."

"Harlin and David didn't hold you hostage," Jessica fired back. "You held yourselves hostage by not standing up to them. If you want law and order in this town, you have to be willing to stand up and be proud of yourselves first."

"Take her!" another man yelled. "We can take her."

Storm shouldered his way through the crowd to stand by Cinnabar, his arms still bound behind him. He stood for a moment, his shoulders straight and his dark eyes sweeping over the men. When he spoke, he kept his voice low, and the men quieted to hear his words. "And which one of you is going to be the first to shoot a woman? Because that's what it'll take. I know this woman. She'll fight for what she believes in, and she believes you should let the law handle the Bakers. Have you sunk so low that you can't realize that Jessica's telling the truth when she says you'll be just like the Bakers if you hang Harlin without a trial first?"

Almost half the men hung their heads and reholstered their pistols. A few silently slipped away.

"If anyone has a score to settle with the Bakers, I do," Storm continued in a reasonable voice. "I spent six months in jail because of them, but I agree with Jessica. We can't take the law into our own hands."

Prudence urged Spirit forward. "And I have a score to settle, too," she called to the remaining men. "They took from me what I wanted to give to the man I found to love. Have any of you lost as much as I have? Can any one of you look at me and say it wouldn't matter if the entire territory knew the woman you married had been had by another man first?"

Mutterings of shame ran through the rest of the men and they broke up into twos and threes as they walked away. A sudden spurt of activity on the walkway drew Jessica's gaze and she saw Harlin land a punch on the jaw of the man holding him. Before anyone could react, he ran into the street and threw himself onto a horse tied at a hitching rail.

"Don't!" Jessica screamed as she saw several men draw their pistols again, aiming at Harlin. "I'll get him."

Jessica shoved the pistol into her waistband and jerked the dangling rope from above her as she kneed Cinnabar past Storm. Her hands flew as she refashioned the rope into a loop and twirled it by Cinnabar's side as he galloped after Harlin's horse. The loop flew through the air before Harlin had gone even a hundred yards, settling over his shoulders.

Like the well-trained cow horse he was, Cinnabar threw himself back onto his haunches, jerking Harlin from the saddle. Jessica urged her horse back to his feet. Hand over hand on the rope, keeping it tight, she rode Cinnabar forward.

Several men had already gathered around Harlin. Jessica ignored them as she glared down at the prone man.

"Dying quick is too easy for you," she said in a flat voice. "I want to see you pay for your crimes."

"I didn't do anything," Harlin whined. "I didn't even take the money from the bank yet. You've got nothing on me."

"You knew about everything David did and you covered up for him. Not counting the fact that I'm sure an investigation of the bank will uncover your embezzlement, you're an accomplice to all the crimes David committed. You'll get plenty of prison time for that, even if you don't hang alongside David for the murders of your parents and Eloise."

"What are you talking about, Jessica?" Storm said from beside her.

Jessica glanced down to see Storm untied now, a deadly glint emanating from his cold eyes. She flicked her wrist to loosen the rope holding Harlin, and tossed it to the men surrounding him before she slid to the ground.

"Oh God, Storm," she said quietly. "I'd give anything if I didn't have to be the one to tell you this. But David admitted it while he took me to the Lazy B. He killed your father and Fiona because your father had changed his will. I don't know if Harlin was there or not."

"I wasn't!" Harlin cried. "I mean . . . I didn't fire even a shot. David! David did it!"

Storm took a step forward, his fist clenched at his side.

"Storm, please," Jessica begged as she caught his arm. "Remember what you said to the men back there."

Storm stared at Harlin as he cringed back against the men holding him.

"Don't kill me! Please," Harlin pleaded. He threw his head sideways to fix eyes streaming with tears on one of the men beside him. "Don't let him kill me. Please!"

Jessica turned away sickened when a wetness spread over the front of Harlin's trousers. She felt Storm reach over and take the pistol from her waistband, but she couldn't force herself to look at him. He would do what he had to do. She wouldn't beg him again.

Storm trained the pistol on Harlin and the men holding him stepped back. Harlin fell to his knees, his head bowed over his steepled hands and his sobs echoing through the silent street.

"Where's the sheriff?" Storm asked in a cold voice.

"He's gone," a man standing a few feet from Harlin informed him. "He ran out the back door of the office when we went in to get you."

"Get on your feet, Harlin!"

"No, Storm. No. Please don't shoot me!"

Storm lowered the pistol and his shoulders slumped. "Damn you, Harlin, I'm not going to shoot you. Get on your feet and walk to the jail."

Harlin raised his head as Jessica finally glanced at him again. He sat in the spill of light from a lantern one of the men held, and he turned his ravaged face up to Storm.

"You . . . you mean it? You're not going to shoot me?"

"It would sicken me to kill a yellow belly like you, Harlin," Storm told the cowering man. "But if you don't get on your feet, I'm going to start shooting into parts of you where it won't be easy for the doctor to dig the bullets out."

Harlin scrambled to his feet and stood swaying for a moment before one of the men grabbed him and shoved him in the direction of the jail. Harlin kept glancing over his shoulder as he went, but Storm never moved to follow them.

"You did right, Storm."

Storm threw the pistol into the dirt and turned to Prudence. "I know," he said. "But I wanted that bastard dead with everything in me."

"Not everything, Storm," Prudence denied. "You're too good to have followed through on killing him."

Jessica stared at the two of them for a moment, then turned away. The tears threatened again in her eyes, for the same reason. She was still going to lose Storm, only this time not to death.

"Where are you going, Jessica?"

She stopped, not turning around. "O—over to Idalee's. I want to see if she's there yet with Ned."

"I'll go check for you, Jessica. Don't you want to be with Storm right now?"

Slowly, Jessica turned back to them. "Me? But you . . ."

Prudence laughed low and shook her head. "Idalee told me what you thought, Jessica Callaghan. And to a point, you were right. I do love Storm, but it's the love a sister has for a brother, like I loved Tobias. And that's all Storm feels for me, too. He's only been trying to help me face things and learn to speak again. And I guess you must have that same type of love for me in your heart. You wouldn't have been willing to give up the man you love to me otherwise."

"What's she talking about, Jessica?" Storm asked.

Jessica ignored him and slowly raised a hand to wipe a stray tear on her cheek, keeping her gaze on Prudence. "Do you mean it?"

355

"Of course, Jessica. I wouldn't lie to a friend, who's like my own sister."

Jessica gave a glad cry and flung herself into Storm's arms. They tightened willingly around her, and she clenched her hands around his neck as she babbled wildly to him. "Storm, I'm sorry. Please forget what I said about going back to Wyoming. I love you. I'll stay with you, wherever you want to live."

"Shut up, pretty lady." Storm's lips assured him Jessica would follow his whispered order for once. A long moment later he raised his head to gaze down at her face, finding it filled with the love he had thought he would never see again.

"I love you, pretty lady," he said softly. "I don't know what was going through that lovely head of yours, but just now I don't give a damn."

Jessica cupped the side of his face in her hand and pulled him back for another long kiss.

"I guess the curse is broken now," she murmured when she could speak. "If there really was such a thing."

"Curse?" Storm asked as he caressed her cheek. "What curse?"

"Now, don't you get the idea that I believe in ghosts or really believe in curses. I . . . I'm not really superstitious. It's just . . . for a while it seemed anyone who touched that payroll gold, or even Uncle Pete's gold, had nothing but heartache in their lives."

"It brought us together, darlin'. And it brought David and Harlin to justice. I'd say those are blessings, not curses."

Suddenly Storm swept her up and carried her to the walkway. He settled himself down and pulled her into his lap, cuddling her close as he gazed out over the now-silent street.

"Now," he said, "explain yourself, Jessica Callaghan."

Jessica laughed up into his face. "You said a minute ago that you didn't give a damn."

"I changed my mind," he informed her. "Do you know what you put me through back at Tobias's? Hell, all kinds of things went through my mind while I stood guard that night. Nothing mattered anymore—not even clearing my name or getting my rightful share of the Lazy B. It was all ashes, unless I had you with me to share it."

"Oh, Storm, I'm sorry."

Quickly, Jessica explained to him how she had misinterpreted Prudence's feelings and how she had felt bound not to take the mute woman's love from her.

"It was all a mistake," she concluded. "And . . ." She slipped a sideways look at Storm and giggled softly. "I guess now you just have to figure out whether you want to keep Charles Baker's name or change your name again to Uncle Pete's. I rather prefer Russell, myself, but I'll use whatever name you decide on."

Storm's arms tightened around her and a frozen look came into his eyes.

"Storm?" Jessica questioned. "You are going to ask me to marry you, aren't you?"

When Storm remained silent, Jessica pushed herself out of his arms and stood over him, her hands on her hips. "Well, if you don't, then I'll ask you! Just like Idalee asked Elias!" she said as she planted her feet firmly and glowered at him. "Will you marry me, Storm Baker—or Storm Russell?"

Suddenly Jessica clasped a hand over her mouth. She had forgotten. He didn't know. And the fury invading Storm's eyes as he rose told her he wasn't a bit amused by her words.

"What the hell are you talking about?"

Chapter 27

Jessica backed away, holding her hands up in front of her. "Storm. Listen to me. I forgot you didn't know. Really, I did. So much has happened . . ."

Suddenly Storm's laughter rang out and he sat back down on the steps and held out his arms.

"Yes," he said when Jessica only stared at him in amazement. "Yes, I'll marry you," he continued when she still gaped at him. "I don't know what you're hiding from me, but tonight I've come close to death and watched you place yourself in danger to save me. Come here!"

Tentatively, Jessica approached him, and Storm surged forward to grab her arms and pull her back onto his lap. He held her close against him, his arms tightened into steel bands so she couldn't attempt to escape.

As if she would, Jessica thought to herself as she realized what his hold on her meant. She nestled her head against his neck and sighed contentedly.

"I'm going to hold you to that, Storm. It's not every day I swallow my pride and ask a man to marry me."

Storm's laughter rumbled in his throat, and he dropped a kiss on her nose. "And you better never do it again, pretty lady," he said. "Because from here on out, you're mine alone. Whatever we have to face, we'll do it together. By the way, how did you get away from David? I should have killed that bastard."

Jessica straightened up abruptly. "Oh, that's something else I forgot. We've got to send someone out to the Lazy B immediately. I don't know if Maude will keep her promise or not. She's already nicked David's neck once with her hatchet and I don't think she's really that stable herself."

"Maude? Old Maude? Hatchet? Jessica . . ."

Storm's astonishment allowed his arms to loosen and Jessica jumped to her feet, tugging on his hand. "Come on. Who can we send?"

The sound of hoofbeats drew their attention, and Storm and Jessica turned to see a lone rider coming down the street.

"That's Elias," Storm said unnecessarily. Jessica, too, had recognized the horse.

"Guess I missed all the action," Elias said with a tired sigh as he pulled his horse up to them. "What happened?"

Storm held the reins of Elias's horse as he swung down. He explained the previous events in a few, short sentences.

Too few and too short, Jessica thought. How could so much be condensed into so few words? She held her tongue until Storm finished, then spoke up. "We need to find someone to get David at the Lazy B, Elias. Or maybe we should go ourselves."

"That won't be necessary, Jessica," Elias informed her.

"There's a few men in town we can trust. I'll go round them up and send them on their way. But what's this about some woman out there with a hatchet?"

"Just tell the men to approach with caution," Jessica said with a gay laugh. "Maude's been practicing with that hatchet on the chickens out there, and she's pretty good with it."

Elias shook his head at her and walked away toward the saloons. "Wait a minute," he said as he stopped and looked back at them. "Those men will probably all be drunk as sin and I don't think we want a repeat of tonight's lynching attempt. Anyway, I want to check on Idalee first. What do you think about sending a posse of women out to the Lazy B, Storm? Think a few women might have a better chance of reasoning with the hatchet lady?"

"I think you've got a hell of a good idea, Elias," Storm agreed.

Jessica yawned sleepily the next morning as she stood between Storm and Ned at the train depot. Heavens, they had been up talking most of the night at Idalee's.

Finding Ned not nearly as badly injured as she imagined, she had asked Storm to allow Ned to be the one to tell him what they had uncovered about Pete's life. After all, she informed Storm, if not for Ned's suspicions, the mystery of Storm's background would have remained hidden.

Ned adamantly refused even to talk to the young whippersnapper until Jessica explained her changed attitude toward Storm. She smiled to herself as she recalled the satisfied look that came over Ned's face when Jessica admitted her own part in the misunderstanding between her and Storm.

"Always did have that tender spot in your heart for the

strays, didn't you, Jes?" Ned had said. And Jessica knew he wasn't only referring to Prudence.

Now Storm would no longer be a stray or an outcast. Before the day was out, he would be her husband. Even now the brothel was humming as the women prepared for the double wedding for Jessica and Idalee that afternoon.

Jessica shook her head and smiled to herself as she recalled Sassy's answer when Jessica inquired how on earth they would ever get the lone minister in town to perform a wedding ceremony in a brothel.

"Idalee deeded this place to all of us equally after she and Mr. Elias leave for New Orleans," Sassy had said with an emphatic nod of her head. "If that minister wants to keep coming here until he finds a wife of his own, he'll perform the service all right."

Jessica giggled under her breath and Storm looked down at her with a frown.

"What's so funny?"

"I was just recalling yours and Elias's faces early this morning after the women came back with David Baker. You both acted like you were scared to death they'd truss you up and take you to jail unless you agreed to having the wedding today. I've never seen two men more afraid of a few defenseless women."

"Defenseless? Did you see Maude when Idy asked her to tell her own version of how she rescued you?" Storm gave a mock shiver of horror. "I could just see that hatchet in her hand. I still can't believe you asked her to stand up with you."

"Well, I did," Jessica said sternly. "Idalee has Prudence and I wanted my own matron of honor. Mattie can't be here or it would have been her."

"Don't be too sure of that, Jes," Ned said with an enigmatic smile at he nodded his head to the train coming down the tracks.

The train's whistle cut the air, drowning out Jessica's insistence that Ned explain. It pulled to a screeching halt in front of them while Ned ignored Jessica's tug on his arm and her renewed demands for his attention. She finally stamped her foot and crossed her arms under her breasts when Ned and Storm exchanged a twinkling look over her head.

"Men!" she muttered under her breath.

Her pique gave way to joy an instant later when the conductor assisted a small, round woman down the steps. She started forward, then stopped and glanced at Ned.

"You first," she said. "Tell her I'm waiting to welcome her."

Ned nodded and spat the wad of tobacco from his mouth before he walked quickly over to Mattie.

"Uh-oh," Jessica breathed softly as a tall, elderly man came down the steps behind Mattie, standing quietly until Ned finally released his wife.

"That must be Frederick," Storm said as he looked down at her with a wry quirk to his lips. "Think he'll want to dance with you at our wedding?"

Jessica blushed as Storm slipped his arm around her waist and pulled her to him. "Guess I better keep a close hold on you until after the wedding. I wouldn't want you to change your mind between now and then. I never did get a chance to wind up that gramophone in the cave and show you that I can dance just as well as the next man."

A light dawned in Jessica's face and she turned a mischievous grin up at Storm. "That's how you did it, isn't it? I already figured out you probably did the Indian chief with a picture and lantern light behind a set of your empty buckskins. And a friend of mine in Wyoming has a gramophone and a lot of different platters. They played music, but I'll bet sounds could be recorded on them just as easily. Sounds like rifle shots and hoofbeats."

"I guess you'll just have to buy one with your share of the gold mine Prudence gave you and try it out for yourself," Storm said.

Jessica's lips drooped into a pout, but just as suddenly her eyes widened when the next passenger stepped from the train. A silver badge glinted on the man's chest as he moved toward where they stood.

"S–Storm," she whispered. "It's the marshal. And he doesn't know yet . . ."

"Mornin'," the tall man said as he stopped beside them. "You must be old Pete Russell's son. I met Pete a few times over the years and I can tell just by lookin' at you. But you're probably goin' to have to show that lawyer feller over there your birthmark before he'll turn over your inheritance to you. Right suspicious fellers, them lawyers are."

A puzzled look crossed Storm's face as he held his hand out to accept the marshal's handshake.

"Marshal Jennings," the man introduced himself. "And I'm glad I didn't make this trip for nothin'. I assume my other prisoners are in jail?"

"How . . ." Jessica could only shake her head and stare at the marshal, her words refusing to form coherently in her mind.

"Don't I get a hug?"

Jessica's eyes flew to Mattie, and she flung herself into Mattie's arms. The two women clung tightly for a moment before Mattie pushed her away and ran her eyes up and down Jessica.

"Gone and grown up on me, haven't you?" Mattie said

with a satisfied nod. "'Bout time, too."

"Oh, Mattie, I was grown before I left Wyoming."

"Not completely, honey," Mattie said. "Woman's never completely grown until she has a man of her own to love. Figured you'd find that out someday. Now, let me meet this man who finally made a woman out of my little girl."

Mattie gave Storm the same up-and-down perusal as Jessica introduced him, and Storm found himself holding his breath. Lord, what in heaven had happened to all the women in the world overnight? Why, just yesterday he had lived in a world run by men, and now he found himself wondering if there was a woman left who needed a man's protection.

Storm breathed out a sigh of relief as Mattie nodded and kissed him on the cheek. "You'll do," she said as she stepped back. "And Ned tells me there's a wedding to go to. Best you don't be late now, hear?"

"N–no, ma'am," Storm agreed.

Jessica giggled softly as Storm watched Mattie take Ned's arm and lead him and the marshal away, an astonished look on his face.

"I feel the same way at times, son," a voice said. Both Jessica and Storm turned to look at Frederick.

"We'll talk later," Frederick said after he introduced himself to Storm. "There's a little matter of some paperwork to straighten out on that mine your father found. And, of course, you've got half of Jessica's ranch back in Wyoming. Pete and Foster owned it together, but both their wills stated it would be Jessica's alone unless you were found. I imagine you do have a heart-shaped birthmark on your thigh?"

"He does," Jessica excitedly informed Frederick. When Frederick quirked an eyebrow at her, she dropped her head to hide another blush stealing over her cheeks.

Both men roared with laughter for a second, but it died in their throats when Jessica managed to control her embarrassment and stare at them, her eyes filling with the gold flecks of anger Storm knew so well. He pulled her into his arms and Jessica's eyes immediately softened again.

"It won't matter, honey," Storm said. "The ranch would have been ours together anyway after we were married." He looked at Frederick. "But that mine belongs to Prudence Jackson. Her brother owned the land it's on."

"Don't matter," Frederick denied. "Old Pete's claim was filed all legal and proper, both in Montana and Wyoming. The mine goes to his son, Storm Russell."

"Do me one favor, Frederick," Storm said, "don't tell Prudence. Just draw up a deed giving her half of it. Is that all right with you, honey?" he asked belatedly when he remembered the woman in his arms.

"Of course, Storm. And here, Frederick."

Jessica pulled the ribbon-wrapped piece of paper from her riding-skirt pocket. "I've already shown this to Storm. It's Charles Baker's new will, splitting all his holdings among his own sons and Storm and Idalee. I had Sassy bring it in from the ranch last night. The other will's probably a forgery, and I imagine there will be a big mess now with David and Harlin under arrest."

"Not much, Jessica," Frederick informed her. "Law says no one can profit from their own evil deeds, and from what I hear about these Baker boys, there's plenty of evidence against them."

"How in the world do you, Mattie, and the marshal know everything that's gone on here, Frederick?" Jessica asked.

"Why, telegrams, of course," the lawyer told her. "They

started arriving while we were still in Wyoming and were
signed by someone named Elias Gant. Those wires were
almost as good as one of them serial stories in the newspapers. We found one waiting at almost every stop we
made on the way here. Made pretty good reading, too,
if a person liked to read them romance stories. Now, if
you'll point me in the direction of this wedding, I'll get
going. Want to be one of the first to dance with the two
brides. Always did like to dance."

Storm quickly gave Frederick directions, keeping his
arms firmly around Jessica when she would have followed
Frederick.

"Not yet, pretty lady," he said when she gazed up
at him. "Something tells me we aren't going to have a
moment's privacy the rest of the day, and we sure as
heck didn't get any last night."

"You better get used to it, Storm," Jessica said with
a smile of love. "I think you've ridden your last lonely trail."

"Thank God," Storm breathed before he kissed her.

COMING IN AUGUST 1993
TIMESWEPT ROMANCE
A TIME TO LOVE AGAIN
Flora Speer
Bestselling Author of *Viking Passion*

While updating her computer files, India Baldwin accidentally backdates herself to the time of Charlemagne—and into the arms of a rugged warrior. Although there is no way a modern-day career woman can adjust to life in the barbaric eighth century, a passionate night of Theuderic's masterful caresses leaves India wondering if she'll ever want to return to the twentieth century.

_0-505-51900-3 $4.99 US/$5.99 CAN

FUTURISTIC ROMANCE
HEART OF THE WOLF
Saranne Dawson
Bestselling Author of *The Enchanted Land*

Long has Jocelyn heard of Daken's people and their magical power to assume the shape of wolves. If the legends prove true, the Kassid will be all the help the young princess needs to preserve her empire—unless Daken has designs on her kingdom as well as her love.

_0-505-51901-1 $4.99 US/$5.99 CAN

LEISURE BOOKS
ATTN: Order Department
276 5th Avenue, New York, NY 10001

Please add $1.50 for shipping and handling for the first book and $.35 for each book thereafter. PA., N.Y.S. and N.Y.C. residents, please add appropriate sales tax. No cash, stamps, or C.O.D.s. All orders shipped within 6 weeks via postal service book rate. Canadian orders require $2.00 extra postage and must be paid in U.S. dollars through a U.S. banking facility.

Name _____

Address _____

City _____ State _____ Zip _____

I have enclosed $_____ in payment for the checked book(s).
Payment <u>must</u> accompany all orders.☐ Please send a free catalog.

COMING IN AUGUST 1993
HISTORICAL ROMANCE
WILD SUMMER ROSE
Amy Elizabeth Saunders

Torn from her carefree rustic life to become a proper city lady, Victoria Larkin bristles at the hypocrisy of the arrogant French aristocrat who wants to seduce her. But Phillipe St. Sebastian is determined to have her at any cost—even the loss of his beloved ancestral home. And as the flames of revolution threaten their very lives, Victoria and Phillipe find strength in the healing power of love.

_0-505-51902-X $4.99 US/$5.99 CAN

CONTEMPORARY ROMANCE
TWO OF A KIND
Lori Copeland
Bestselling Author of *Promise Me Today*

When her lively widowed mother starts chasing around town with seventy-year-old motorcycle enthusiast Clyde Merrill, Courtney Spenser is confronted by Clyde's angry son. Sensual and overbearing, Graham Merrill quickly gets under Courtney's skin—and she's not at all displeased.

_0-505-51903-8 $3.99 US/$4.99 CAN

"AN ABSOLUTELY SUPERB ACCOUNT OF WAR AT THE LEVEL OF THE INDIVIDUAL SOLDIER . . .

This is a major contribution to Vietnam War literature, particularly of action at the small-unit level."
—*Military Review*

"Keith Nolan's research, his comprehension of the political as well as the military actions, his careful concern for those who were there, and, most of all, his writing, are superb. I recommend *Ripcord* without stint or reservation."

—STEPHEN AMBROSE

"With *Ripcord*, Keith Nolan has added another significant battle history to his impressive list of works on the Vietnam War."

—JOHN DEL VECCHIO
Author of *The 13th Valley*

"The U.S. Army and Marine Corps have their Boswell in Keith Nolan, whose twenty years of dedicated research have resulted in ten superb books about the Vietnam War. *Ripcord* is his best yet."

—LT. COL. GARY D. SOLIS, USMC (Ret.)
Author of *Son Thang*

*Please turn the page
for more reviews. . . .*

"NOLAN ONCE AGAIN CAPTURES THE STARK REALITY OF COMBAT IN VIETNAM."

—*U.S. Naval Institute Proceedings*

"*Ripcord* is the story of one of the last major engagements between U.S. military forces in the Republic of Vietnam and elements of the North Vietnamese Army (NVA). However, readers should not be surprised if this battle is unknown to them. Astonishingly, it went virtually unreported by the media at the time, largely because of the close wraps imposed by the Military Assistance Command Vietnam headquarters in Saigon, which feared that the heavy U.S. casualty lists might touch off a second 'Hamburger Hill' debate on the floor of the U.S. Senate. Thus, even thirty years after the event, this is not a battle that will be recalled by many, save the participants themselves and the few who may have read of it in an after-action report, or perhaps through the occasional professional journal. That is to say, it was an unknown battle until Keith Nolan rightly decided that this is a story that had to be told.... Military professionals and historians alike will be gratified that Mr. Nolan made that decision."

—*Marine Corps Gazette*